THE JOHNSON JOHNSON MYSTERIES

Johnson Johnson (his first name is the same as his second), portrait painter, yachtsman and unpaid official investigator is the hero of Dorothy Dunnett's ever popular mystery series featuring Johnson's yacht *Dolly* and taking in a whole range of exciting and exotic locations.

Johnson's present way of life dates back to the death of Judith, his wife, in a mysterious crash from which he himself escaped with serious injuries. (The events immediately following the accident are told in the novel *Tropical Issue*, previously entitled *Bird of Paradise*). Since then, as trouble-shooter and government watchdog, he has drifted about the world on his yacht *Dolly*, painting the portraits of the famous, and welcome everywhere as an amiable if dishevelled guest. Despite his self-imposed detachment, he has a ruthless knack of altering the lives of the people he meets, and especially those of the young women who narrate each adventure, very few of whom understand him at all. What other purpose he may have at present is unclear.

The order of publication of the Johnson novels is not the strict chronological order of the story so far, which begins with *Tropical Issue*. The four adventures that follow, which can be read in any order, are *Rum Affair*, *Ibiza Surprise*, *Operation Nassau* and *Roman Nights**. The events in *Split Code* (previously called *Dolly and the Nanny Bird*), which is next, take place a few months before the action of *Moroccan Traffic*, the seventh novel.

*These four novels were previously titled: *Dolly and the Singing Bird*, *Dolly and the Cookie Bird*, *Dolly and the Doctor Bird*, *Dolly and the Starry Bird*.

TROPICAL ISSUE

TROPICAL ISSUE

Dorothy Dunnett

ARROW BOOKS

Arrow Books Limited
20 Vauxhall Bridge Road, London SW1V 2SA

An imprint of the Random Century Group

London Melbourne Sydney Auckland
Johannesburg and agencies throughout
the world

First published in Great Britain by Michael Joseph Ltd in 1983
Arrow edition 1991

3 5 7 9 10 8 6 4 2

Printed and bound in Great Britain by
Cox & Wyman Ltd, Reading, Berkshire

ISBN 0 09 984660 8

To most of my clients, bifocal glasses are asthma. All those words are spelled correctly. I looked them up.

Whether they're in show business or not, most people want to look good, and it's part of my job to help them.

I can make people look terrible, too, if I have to. I am, you might say, in the conversion business.

A few top names don't care what they look like at home, or even in public. Johnson is one of that lot.

Johnson wears bifocal glasses. I'm speaking of Johnson the portrait painter. You wouldn't think Rita Geddes and Johnson had much in common, except that we both paint, in our way, people's faces.

Wait till I tell you.

The day I met him is fairly easy to remember, because I spent the night in his apartment. In his Mayfair apartment, which he had loaned to a photographer pal who wanted the use of his studio.

The photographer pal was Ferdy Braithwaite. He needed the studio for a photo session with a rich American client. And I had to meet Ferdy there, to fix the client's face for the photos.

I worked quite a lot with Ferdy Braithwaite. Between us, we made brides look contented and fiancées and graduates pure. When, instead of retiring, he decided to divorcify into film shorts, I helped him with screen make-up too.

The camera never lies. Ferdy's Leica will end up in Heaven, but it's the bad fire for him and me and Max Factor.

King Ferdy, the photographer with the most subjects. And the most money. And the fastest turnover in crumpet. I called him Ferdy, and he called me Rita.

Behind my back, he called me his Scotch Bird of Paradise. Considering the fees that I charged him, I wasn't bothered.

I have been in Mayfair, London, before, on jobs for photographers. The penthouse flat of Ferdy's pal Johnson was in shopping-trolley distance of Asprey's, Sotheby's, Hermès, and four shops selling Persian carpets whose names I am not going to look up.

To get into this apartment block, you have to pass a pair of round trees, two lots of armoured plate glass, and a doorkeeper three feet higher than I am, who said, 'Now then. You don't want to come in 'ere, do you?'

'I'm not desperate,' I said. 'But business is business. Seventeen B? Mr Johnson's studio flat?'

'Business?' said the doorkeeper. He followed me through the inner glass doors and into a marble foyer full of contract plants, looking hard at this case I was holding.

'Goin' fishing then, are you?'

A security man looked up from behind a counter. The doorkeeper said, 'This little lady's brought a fishing-tackle case to do business with 17B. I think we might just take a look at it.'

'I think,' I said, 'that you might just phone 17B and say Miss Geddes is here to see Mr Braithwaite.'

The security man put his newspaper down, and the doorkeeper leaned on the counter. 'Oh, yes,' he said. He looked at his chum. 'She's goin' fishing with Ferdy.'

Beginning with my hair, the security man's eyeballs were punting all over me. It must have been dead dull that morning. Then he pushed his chair back and got up, which made it official.

He said, 'Have to be Ferdy's date, wouldn't it? She's not givin' Johnson a whirl after that plane crash an' all, unless she gives 'im a ride in 'is wheelchair. Goin' to cheer 'em up, darlin'?'

He held a hand out, and the doorkeeper whipped my case neatly out of my fingers and laid it flat on the desk.

Until he did that, I was quite interested in what he was saying about Ferdy's pal Johnson and some plane crash.

I never read newspapers, but I know what's going on. I never miss a news broadcast or the share prices reports. My mother's two-storey house with double garage has a radio in every room, and three television sets and a video.

As the doorman grabbed my case, I said, 'Hang on. Is the man in 17B the same as Johnson the painter?'

One of the best-known international figures in the field of portrait-painting, the announcer had said. *Sole survivor of a private plane crash on the Continent.*

The security man was dialling 17B. 'Thought you knew Mr Johnson,' he said reproachfully. He spoke into the phone and replaced it. He said, 'All right. Let's see inside this one.'

I stared at him. 'Did you speak to 17B just now?'

'Come on,' he said. He tapped the case. 'Rule of the 'ouse.'

Rule of the house, nothing. I'm all for security, but this was plain bloody nosiness.

I looked at the doorkeeper. 'You've checked me out,' I said. 'I don't have to show you anything.'

The doorkeeper was feeling great. 'Cheer old Johnson up, won't she?' he said. 'Fairly jump out of 'is nightshirt, 'e will. What's in the case, then? Whips and handcuffs?'

'Blood,' I said sourly. 'I've come straight from the mortuary.'

I can cope with aggro. I can cope with most things. You get fed up with it.

I took the case by the handle. I said, 'You open it, you pay for it.'

I am four feet eleven inches high, but I could tell without cricking my neck that they were leering.

The doorkeeper jerked the case forward. The security man banged the catch and flipped the lid back. They peered inside together.

That way the blood got them both. A jet of Dark up the security man's nostrils and all down his collar and uniform front. A jet of Standard circling the doorkeeper's cap and then sprinkling his suit like a crop-sprayer.

A kinky pal fixed up the tubes for me. The release catch is in the case handle. I only flip it if I'm annoyed. The stuff inside is protected by polythene.

I shut the box and whipped it off the desk while the two yobs were still snorting and groaning; dabbing their faces and starting to claw their bloody clothes off.

It looked like a clip from Hammer Films. It had given their day a real buzz. I hoped they were grateful, but I didn't stay to make sure. I just got to the lift before they did.

I wasn't sorry. They were wrong, and I'd warned them. If they complained, Ferdy would fix them. And if he didn't, I could take care of myself.

I pressed the button for flat 17B and, while the lift rose, I checked out my hair and my lashes and my earrings.

The mirrors didn't crack or anything.

Just before the lift stopped, I took out my lipstick and wrote BLOOD on the glass, just to needle the Hit Squad when they found it.

Or, if you want the truth, I wrote BLUD. You can't take a dictionary everywhere.

The door to flat 17B was opened by a pretty woman in a white service coat and fading make-up over an anxious expression.

She changed it to a nice smile, and asked me in, as if she saw me every day. 'Mr Braithwaite won't be a moment. I'm just making you both some fresh coffee.'

She glanced at my case as I walked through, but didn't mention it. She said, 'I'm Mr Johnson's housekeeper. Would you like to take anything off?'

For Ferdy, I'd put on a grey knitted shawl over a grey quilted jacket over a grey Fair Isle Navajo waistcoat over a woollen shirt and gauchos and legwarmers. And gloves.

I was hot.

I took off the shawl and the gloves and the jacket in a double bedroom which was full of new furniture like a hotel room. I checked out the bathroom, and put my case in it. Then the woman took me to the studio.

The apartment was big. The tiled hall was covered with rugs from one or other of the four carpet shops, and had tasteful pillars with sculpture on them. There were more boxes of contract plants. There were gilt wall lights with glass earrings everywhere.

There was also a wheelchair, for God's sake, outside one of the bedrooms. And from inside, the rattle of clinical snoring.

The owner of the flat was still in it.

I hadn't been warned. Good old Ferdy.

Ahead, the owner's housekeeper was opening the door of the studio. A lot of daylight came out. I went in. The studio itself seemed to be empty. Mr Braithwaite was still just coming.

I thought of the complaints coming up from below, and made my number with the housekeeper, quickly.

'I hope,' I said, 'that Mr Johnson is keeping better? It must have been a terrible crash.'

She stood in the doorway, her hands clasped together. 'He's very much improved, thank you,' she said. 'It will be a long business, of course. But he's making great strides now, considering.'

She said it as if she had had to tack it on the gates for a week, and five doctors had signed it. Then a phone rang in three different rooms and she excused herself. A moment later I heard her reeling off the same answer.

Between then and the time she brought coffee, in bone china with bluebirds on it, I counted two more calls and a ring at the doorbell. Whatever he paid her, Johnson's housekeeper was earning her salary.

I also had a good look at the studio.

The crippled pal Johnson was rich. The walls were all done in watered silk wallpaper, and there were fancy tables with marble tops and flower arrangements; and silk lampshades everywhere held up by Chinese ladies selling kippers.

There were a lot of expensive mirrors, a sort of enamelled screen, and a grand piano. The piano was groaning with shiny boxes of tantalized fruit, a stack of new hardcover novels and eight flowering plants, two of them still in their tissue.

In the middle of the polished floor, the rugs had been rolled back to make way for Ferdy's lighting gear, with coils of cable lying everywhere; and the easy chairs and the sofas had all been pushed to the walls except for a fat two-seater meant, I could see, for the client.

The north wall and half the ceiling were made out of glass, providing cut-price light for artists and cameramen. There was no sign of any painting equipment.

A balcony ran along half the back of the apartment, and the view was great. You could see Midas and Selfridge's and the queue outside the American Embassy, and people blowing whistles all round Claridge's.

I wondered what Ferdy was paying Johnson for the use of his studio, and hoped it was less than Mrs Natalie Sheridan was paying Ferdy for photographing her. I was spooning the last of the sugar into my third coffee when a door opened somewhere, and I heard footsteps and a voice, and there on the studio threshold was Ferdy, with his arms stretched out sideways like Jesus.

'Rita! My gorgeous Toucan!' he bellowed.

I just managed to put the bluebirds down and get up, before I was lifted out of my legwarmers, and crushed against all the silk neck-scarf and cashmere.

Ferdy's tongue in your mouth was a bit like a doormat dipped time about in brandy and nicotine. Ferdy was great for kissing.

He'd had enough practice. If you believed all you heard, Europe's leading magazine and society photographer was by now into his third round of crumpet.

Ferdy was the original population explosion. Working with him was great, because he had all this energy left over from the Army. He was big, with suntan all over his head, and a fuzz of sideburns in a sort of speckled fawn.

He looked like a goalie. He would, I knew from experience, take no for an answer, after a struggle.

Now, he put me down just as the housekeeper came in, smiling, with a fresh cup and saucer. In exchange, he gave her the sugar bowl, which she went off to refill. He stood, looking at me over the bluebirds.

'Rita, my sweet sucrose junkie. A great big bikini and little black teeth, darling. It isn't worth it. Let me look at you. There's something different.'

He walked all round me, still hugging the teacup.

'Not the hair: still that boring old magenta and blue. And the Dracula eye-shadow. And the Biro finger-rings. But where are the stripes, darling? The tattoos? The gold balls in the nose?'

'I slept in,' I said. I knew he would notice when I left off the face-painting.

'*And* the clothes,' he went on. He twirled a chair and sat down, while I filled his cup for him.

'All that lovely warm wool, just like Johnson. You should see Johnson's cardies; straight out of the *Personality Knitting Quarterly*, and the same page, too, I shouldn't wonder. You could swap your back numbers.'

The Navajo waistcoat was a Lauren. The rest of the gear cost just under eight hundred pounds in South Molton Street, which he knew and I knew he knew.

I said, 'What about Johnson, then? He's here, and you didn't mention it?'

The sugar came back and I poured myself more coffee and added three spoonfuls before Ferdy drew the bowl slowly away.

He said, 'I told you, my small plain and pearl, my tuppence coloured. My studio's being rewired, and Johnson's lent us this one to photograph the great Mrs Natalie Sheridan, who arrives at any moment. Ask me, What about Natalie, then?'

'You told me,' I said. 'She likes you to do her publicity stills. She flies in this morning, gets made up for the photographs, goes off to the Award Lunch and then flies back to wherever she came from, or maybe some-where else. And I've told you before. I don't like creating one make-up for two different scenes.'

A row of capped teeth appeared between Ferdy's sideburns.

He gave a howl. 'You're spooked!' he said. 'You're nervous of Natalie! You're an ignorant dwarf with a stupid conk and hockey legs and pink hair, who's frightened of Natalie Sheridan! I apologize for taking the bowl away. Have some more energizing, comforting sugar.'

It was true that I have a stupid conk and hockey legs and pink hair. It was even true that I was unstriped because of this engagement. It was not true that I was nervous.

Who is Natalie Sheridan? A syndicated political journalist. A divorcee. An economist. A maker of sharp documentaries with powerful pals in five continents. A rich woman. A woman.

Nothing there, as I see it, to worry Rita Geddes.

'Are you joking?' I said. 'She asked for me, I didn't ask for her. If she isn't nice to me, I'll do her up like Elephant Man, and then where will your bleeding photographs be?'

Ferdy and I stared at one another, a thing he sometimes does, until one of us blinks. It tells you not to take his insults for real. Sometimes it goes on for so long you need eye drops.

The housekeeper broke it by coming to tell us that Mrs Sheridan's maid had arrived, and her secretary, and a fitter with the clothes she was going to wear, and that they were all waiting, installed in the guest suite.

And that Mr Braithwaite's assistant had sent to say he couldn't manage.

The housekeeper, in a quiet way, looked a bit worn. I guessed that the appointment had been for Mrs Sheridan, dressed, not for Mrs Sheridan undressed with her groupies.

Ferdy wasn't upset. He said, 'Poor dear Johnson,' sadly to me, and turning, walked out the studio door, pouring charm all over the housekeeper.

I didn't mean to be charming to Ferdy. As soon as he came back, I put in my tuppenceworth, coloured or not.

'I won't,' I said.

I've doubled as Ferdy's assistant before, and the insults get to be real. Ferdy's assistants are always away at the dentist's, or the police station.

The doorbell rang.

'You will,' said Ferdy. 'There's Natalie.'

There are times when I get fed up, living among giants. Everyone knows what Natalie Sheridan looks like: five foot ten, waving (natural) blonde hair, hollow cheeks and a 36–26–36 figure with no silicone in it, below the neck anyway.

Today she was wearing Halston, and had just had her hair put up in a blonde chignon plait round the corner, as we had cause to know, because her usual hairdressing lady had had a call to Kensington Palace and couldn't fit in a personal visit.

She was also wearing a diamond brooch, a fancy ring, and a scent specially brewed for her.

She gave Ferdy a prim kiss on each cheek while she drew her gloves off; shook hands with me without a flicker of shock; and observed that it had been very good of me to come up specially from Scotland, and she hoped I had had a good journey. Which was more than Ferdy's silicone had thought to produce.

Then she turned away, saying, 'Well: there isn't much time, is there? Miss Geddes and I will be as quick as we can,' and walked out towards the guest bedroom.

I waited until she was out of earshot.

I said, 'Ferdy! You're scared of her! You're a famous photographer with a house in Barbados and a prostate problem and two accountants under the doctor, and you're scared of that plastic think-tank!'

At that moment the plastic think-tank came back to the doorway and said, 'Are you coming, my dear?' Musically.

I found my legwarmers beginning to move towards her quite fast, and I let them.

A lady used to high command, was Natalie Sheridan.

The bathroom had a good chair and make-up lights round the mirror. I took off a couple of things and put on my overall, and then began to lay out my stuff on the vanitory, with the door open a bit so that I could see when my client was ready.

The maid, a hefty American pensioner referred to as Dodo, was in the bedroom stripping Mrs Sheridan down to the waist like a paint job.

The lady from the designer's, who was used to it, sat bolt upright in a corner doing a visual check of Mrs Sheridan's latest known measurements.

Murmuring into the telephone was a smart young secretary-man from an agency, perched on one of the beds among all the laid-out clothes and tissue paper. My shawl and quilted jacket, I noticed, had been shoved in a heap on a pillow.

As well as smart, the secretary was red in the neck due to an eyeful of Mrs Sheridan's two suntanned boobs, plump as onions and alert, each of them, as a breeding budgie.

She was in the middle of dictating cablegrams, which the secretary did his best to receive through the back of his head until she draped a towel round her shoulders.

After that he watched her nervously. There were still six inches of tanned skin to be seen between her skirtband and the edge of the towel, which was white, Turkish and monogrammed JJ in one corner.

Still talking, she lifted and looked at the corner, revealing a budgie.

The man from the agency jack-knifed quickly over the phone. Natalie said, 'Miss Geddes — may I call you Rita? Perhaps, before we begin, I should just go and see Mr Johnson. Across the hall, I suppose?'

I stood in the bathroom doorway, a tube in my hand. Having invaded pal Johnson's flat, she was about to walk into his sickroom. I said, 'Mr Johnson's asleep.'

'Oh, you know his room then,' said Mrs Sheridan. 'This way?'

She was already out in the hall, and would soon hear the musical effects, so I didn't stop her. It did cross my mind that Ferdy would never get the use of this studio ever again. I was annoyed that time was going, and I couldn't get started. I wanted to make a good job of Natalie Sheridan.

In fact, she was back in a trice, with the towel neatly tucked in her waistband. One minute I smelt her scent, and the next she was there at my elbow.

'Well, we really must get on, mustn't we?'

We must. It meant she hadn't seen Johnson. And as the sort of drum-roll went on from the bedroom, that either the housekeeper or Ferdy had stopped her.

And my money, I can tell you, was on the housekeeper.

It had been a struggle. But here at last was the great Mrs Sheridan, sitting in front of the mirror and saying, 'All right. Now Rita, just do what you can.' And we were off.

When I am working with make-up, I'm happy.

Cosmetics are only paint, and paint is only a way of creating an illusion. You can learn all that stuff at art college. I did. Beauty colleges teach it too, and there are company courses of all sorts.

But it's not like painting a jug. In private practice, you have to sort out for yourself what your customer really wants, and get as near to it as you're able.

With Natalie Sheridan, I had an easy job and a hard one.

Her face was good, for pushing forty. She had had her face lifted once, so the chin was firm. Her skin was clear, with a light year-round tan that showed off all that blonde hair.

She didn't need line fillers. Her eyes had large, smooth lids; her lips

13

were thinnish but workable, and her cheekbones were a gift. You could see why the cameras loved her.

I had the kind of false eyelashes she was used to. The permanent work on her eyebrows and her hairline had been done by her own man, Kim-Jim Curtis.

And that, if you like, was the snag.

I had to do this make-up to a standard set by Kim-Jim Curtis, who had been with her for years. And who for years had been her gofer, her make-up artist and her hairdresser in her New York apartment, her Paris nook, and her Madeira hideaway.

What's more, I had to do it if possible better, because Kim-Jim had suggested me for this London job. And if Mrs Sheridan was impressed, more would follow.

I knew about Kim-Jim. I'd met him.

A few make-up specialists develop private clients all over the world and live the rich life, flying from party to party to paint on the faces. Some make a success with one client, and get themselves on to their personal pay-roll for life.

Not many employers can afford a service like that. Natalie Sheridan was one of them.

The best T.V. make-up man she ever came across was this big red-headed Californian, twelve years older than she was; and she bought him as soon as she met him.

Kim-Jim was perfect for her. He had social sense and camera-sense. He could make her look right for any setting she wanted to queen it in.

And that's a great art, and it only happens when the artist really hits it off with his client.

Kim-Jim Curtis, I suppose, fell for Natalie Sheridan from the beginning.

She slept around, according to Ferdy; but with partners so well protected, usually at government cost, that the public never got wind of them. If Kim-Jim knew, and he must have known, he didn't split on her.

When she didn't have anyone else, he maybe went to bed with her; but I don't suppose he tore the sheets getting there. There was a sort of motherly side to him. He can't have had much drive, to stay with her all that time as he did, just working on the odd film if she let him.

It was on one of those that he'd seen me in action. That was why Ferdy had been told to get me for Mrs Sheridan's make-up in London. Bossy Natalie might be, but she wasn't silly. If Kim-Jim said someone was good, she would listen to him.

Ferdy thought I'd wiped off my face-stripes because I wanted Kim-Jim Curtis's job, and not just some chance work in London.

He was wrong, but not all that wrong. It doesn't matter now, anyway.

All the same, I wonder sometimes what would have happened if I hadn't made such a success of her face. If I hadn't changed her colouring very slightly. If I hadn't spent all the time I could spare fixing her weaker profile, so that, keeping his word, Ferdy could give her some photographs of her left side, instead of all the rights she was used to.

But then, if I'd been bad at my job, I'd be dead by now.

Twice, before I had finished, Mrs Sheridan excused herself and, sitting up, called out a few more commands to the secretary.

Both times, I noticed, she had a good look in the mirror. The second time, she said, 'That's coming along very nicely. I like the eye-shadow.'

The eye-shadow was different from Kim-Jim's, and so was what I had done to her nose. She hadn't noticed that yet.

I finished exactly within the time I had set myself, and just before her deadline for dressing.

She took a long, sharp look then, when I'd removed the towels and the headband. She said, 'A very nice job, Rita. I'm sorry there wasn't more time.'

Which you could take either way and would stop me from getting swell-headed.

Her dress was silk, with tapestry flowers on it, and there was a velvet jacket to match, and a lot of Italian suede.

She looked smashing.

In the studio, Ferdy treated her like a duchess, and behind her back, put both his thumbs up.

He had the cameras waiting. He got the lights right, and I bovvered about, holding things and switching things, and standing on chairs, which I am very used to. Mrs Sheridan stood, sat, leaned and smiled, and Ferdy shot film. Rolls and rolls of it.

Then it was over, and she was stretching and smiling, while he told her how great she had been. The fitter had gone, and so had the agency man. There was only the maid Dodo left, packing things in a case in the bedroom.

Mrs Sheridan said, 'I do have some time in hand. Ferdy, I really can't go without seeing your Johnson.' You couldn't call her a quitter.

I waited for Ferdy to talk her out of it. He just smiled at her. Like all session people, he'd gone into photographer's menopause. I don't think he even heard what she said. I could see him wondering if he had put any film in the camera and wanting to throw back a whisky and lay someone.

Mrs Sheridan waited, turned and just left. Since the housekeeper wasn't there either, I followed my afternoon's work out of the studio. Then, in the interests of Ferdy's business arrangements, I hung about while she walked to the invalid's door and rapped on it.

The snoring stopped.

'Mr Johnson!' she said. She looked marvellous. 'It's Natalie Sheridan. Mrs Sheridan. An old friend of Roger van Diemen. May I come in for a moment?'

I didn't hear an answer, but she put her hand on the doorknob and opened it.

She stopped on her way through. I didn't blame her. I could see the bed myself, and it was empty.

I couldn't see much of anything else, because of this very large, very old sheepdog just rousing from sleep. It got up and shook itself blearily. It peered round and saw Mrs Sheridan and liked her right away. It came to her knee, gently slavering on the silk tapestry.

Natalie took three quick steps back and it followed. Then it sat down and thumped its tail carefully.

She looked at it thoughtfully; then, stretching her hand, rubbed its head under the matting.

'Goodness gracious,' she said. 'You're an old gentleman, aren't you, to be going about on your own?'

A new and jaundiced bass voice answered. It wasn't the dog.

It said, 'She's fourteen. Die for Mrs Sheridan, Bessie.'

The dog rolled over, looking like an old hobnailed hearthrug. Across it, Natalie and I both gazed at Ferdy's pal Johnson, in dressing-gown and pyjamas, standing like you or me outside a sort of small sitting-room.

I know polite rage when I see it.

Mrs Sheridan didn't.

I looked at her being beautiful. Then I raised my voice and roared, 'Ferdy!'

When in doubt, attack, is my motto. But I didn't like those few words of Ferdy's pal Johnson, and I didn't think Pal Johnson liked us.

He was years and years younger than Ferdy, and about three inches shorter. He had the sort of nose that looked as if it might have been broken a long time ago, and expensively set. He had the sort of mouth that didn't go in much for lips.

The top half of his face was filled in by a lot of dead-looking black hair, a pair of strong-minded black eyebrows, and his glasses. What was left looked definitely unhealthy.

Behind me, Ferdy came out of the studio, looking vague but willing, and the bifocals, shifting, trained on him.

Ferdy didn't fall to the floor or anything. He just gazed back and said, 'My God. Candles In Shapes You Never Thought Of. Should you be up?'

Nobody rushed to answer him. I kept my mouth shut. Disappointed noises were coming from the dog.

Americans are good in a social crisis.

In a trail of high-class fabric, Mrs Sheridan lowered herself and massaged the sheepdog's billowing stomach. 'We've offended man and dog: how horrible of us,' she said; and rose just as nicely. The dog got up like a dog.

Mrs Sheridan moved forward to the owner of the flat and stood before him, tilting her gorgeous french-pleated head and looking rueful and sympathetic and friendly at the same time. The eyelashes, the lid colour, the high-lighter, the eye-liner and the work on her eyebrows all did a great job.

She said, 'It's Mr Johnson, isn't it? You've been so kind, letting Ferdy use your wonderful home. I wouldn't have disturbed you for worlds, but I just had to say hello and thank you to Roger's friend. He wanted to know how you were, and I swore I wouldn't go back without seeing you. And now I can tell him. You're walking about. That's so splendid. He'll be so pleased and happy to hear that.'

Almost any answer might have come from under the bifocals, you felt,

17

or none at all. The owner of the flat had both hands behind him, and he didn't bring one of them forward. Mrs Sheridan, no fool, hadn't risked holding hers out.

There was another brief silence. Then Ferdy's pal said, 'Of course, you know Roger. Give him my regards. Let me give you a sherry. Ferdy?'

'Do the honours,' said Ferdy. 'Come along in.' And taking big swerves round the dog, he walked Mrs Sheridan quickly through to what seemed to be, right enough, a small sitting-room.

The guy in the dressing-gown didn't shift. I saw he had a stick sunk behind him like a third leg, and that both his hands were actually on it.

The housekeeper showed in a doorway, looked at him, and then went away again. The phone rang, and I could hear her answering it.

Looking at me, the guy in the dressing-gown made an announcement. 'You're Ferdy's assistant. You didn't meet a somewhat blood-boltered couple of porters on your way to the lift?'

Which explained the stony welcome, now I thought of it. Not all the telephone calls had been about potted plants.

I said, 'Maybe you don't mind having your guests body-searched, but there's nothing soft about me. If you don't report them, I will.'

A fight wouldn't have worried me; but he backed down. 'Whatever you say,' Pal Johnson remarked.

I waited, but that was all he said. 'You'll report it?' I said.

'Why not?' He still stood like a road surveyor. He added, 'I can't really go in until you do.'

I could tell from his voice that he wasn't even trying to needle me, which annoyed me a lot. However, there was no point in flogging it.

I walked past him into the sitting-room and took a seat not too near Mrs Sheridan, who looked sort of inquiring. Ferdy poured me a vodka martini which brimmed over as he watched his pal Johnson come in after me and sit down. Questions about the little delay hung like balloons all round his sideburns.

Johnson said, 'We decided to enter in order of zip-codes. Mrs Sheridan.'

A half-drunk glass of whisky was already standing by the high-backed leather chair he had picked to sit in. He raised it to her, and to me, and drank a lot of it.

Natalie took a good American slug of hers and said, 'We were so shocked by it all. I hope you had the best medical care.'

I began to lose interest in the conversation. She knew, and so did I, because I'd heard her ask Ferdy, that Pal Johnson had been two months in the best and dearest clinic in London before his lovely family carted him back to their country mansion. She was making small-talk.

I don't like small-talk. I looked round the room, which was rigged out like the others in brand-new furniture, this time study-type with oak tables and deep-buttoned leather. On one of the tables was a filing-basket of opened letters, and beside it on the floor stood a plastic bin full of new handwritten envelopes with stamps on them.

Mrs Sheridan's chat moved from the guy Johnson's health to this friend of hers, Roger van Diemen, who had also had a bad illness but seemed better now.

I tried to read the names on the envelopes, and couldn't. The curtains were made of silk velvet. In the corner I could see a T.V. but not a video. The word 'bananas' came into the talk.

I looked at Ferdy, who had mentioned it, but couldn't pick up the reason.

No one looked at me, which was all right. Our client had gone on to talk about something she was doing in films, which Ferdy knew about also. She and Ferdy swapped news about cameramen, and she worked the talk round to include painters and some clever compliments about Johnson's work.

Johnson said the odd word, but hardly more than that. I began to wonder why she was bothering. Perhaps because he was well-known. Perhaps because he was snooty, and she felt challenged to try and unbend him.

There was no doubt, either, that she was good at it. Smooth, and funny, and interesting, but letting Ferdy shine too, so that she didn't seem to make all the running. She tried to get a shine on Johnson as well, but he wasn't having any, although he stayed polite as polite.

He didn't signal either, but Ferdy must have come to his senses at last and remembered which of them owned the studio. He stood up, glanced at the clock, and offered, heartily, to top up his famous customer's sherry.

She took the hint and rising, said she really must go.

Ferdy saw her out. I heard her saying, 'I couldn't refuse, but he looks very poorly. Will he paint again, or is it quite hopeless?' She sounded disappointed. Perhaps I was wrong. Perhaps she'd hoped to trap him into painting her portrait.

He must have been good once, if Natalie Sheridan wanted him. I didn't hear what Ferdy answered, but it was bound to be tactful.

Excused from rising, Johnson was sitting nearer the door than I was, and had probably heard the lot. If he did, he paid no attention. When

I looked at him, he was pressing a wall bell. His fingers had ink on them. Ferdy's voice got fainter, as he saw Natalie out to the lift.

The housekeeper came in, looked at her boss and at me, and then went over and collected the envelope bin. As she passed him, Pal Johnson remarked, 'You've met Connie, haven't you? Mrs Margate?'

The housekeeper smiled. She said, 'Miss Geddes has been working ever since she arrived. You give her another drink.'

It struck me as funny that the owner of the flat called Ferdy Ferdy and his housekeeper Connie, and that everyone called Johnson Johnson. Then the housekeeper went out and Ferdy came in and Johnson said, 'Your Bird of Paradise is to have another vodka martini, Ferdy.'

I glared at Ferdy but he didn't notice. He said to Johnson, 'Well, you've run out of vodka. Where do you keep your supplies in this bloody awful apartment? Who in Christ's name did it up?'

'A very rich decorator,' Johnson said. 'Ask Connie where the stuff is.'

'And that's another thing,' Ferdy said. 'That woman Connie's exhausted. You should go back to Surrey. I don't know why you came here. The family didn't want it.'

The guy in the dressing-gown lay back with his feet on the dog. He remarked, apparently to me, 'You'd better choose something else. He isn't going to get you a vodka.'

Ferdy, worrying about Connie Margate, never noticed. He said, 'She can't go on sleeping here every night. She's got her own house to run. She'll get ill, and then where will you be?'

'Back in Surrey. I thought that's what you wanted. I'm going to bed,' said Pal Johnson, and took his feet off the dog.

I wasn't going to help him. He was doing Ferdy the favours. Ferdy said, 'You can go to bed if you like, but I'm going to send that woman home for twenty-four hours. She can have one good night's sleep in her own bed, and a day free of you and your telephone calls. What are you eating?'

'Humble pie,' said Johnson shortly. He had his hands on the arms of his chair, and had stuck there.

I got up to go away. Every girl knows what happens when a man suddenly needs help in the house. I didn't want to be caught there when Ferdy let the housekeeper off as a reward for lifting Johnson out of his chair.

Ferdy suddenly caught sight of me leaving, and leaped up saying, 'Now Rita? Who's Ferdy's best friend? Who got to meet Natalie Sheridan?'

He followed me into the bedroom forbidding me to leave, and would have chummed me into the bathroom too if I hadn't locked the door.

When I came out he had gone, and I put on my shawl and stuff and picked up my case and went to tell Mrs Margate I would let myself out. I didn't want to get within arm's length of the guy Johnson or Ferdy again.

Mrs Margate wasn't there. Instead Ferdy was in the kitchen, surrounded by bowls and packets and pans, with a warm smell coming from the cooker already.

'She's gone,' he said. 'Put your case down, darling, and go and help Johnson to bed while I make us some lunch.'

Ferdy is quite a good cook. My mother, Robina, is the best cook I ever knew, and I learned a lot from her that even Ferdy didn't know. I stood thinking, while he looked up from his pan, his capped teeth like barley in his speckly fawn whiskers.

'Go on, darling,' he said. 'Natalie's decided to give London another two days, and wants you to do her for her parties. Why pay for a hotel? Think how Scotch and saving it will be. You sleep on one side of Johnson's guestbed and I'll sleep on the other.'

'You sleep on both sides,' I said. 'I'm not staying. I lied to you. I know you had your prostate fixed.'

'All right,' he said. 'Don't stay. Just help while I get the meal.'

To tell the truth, he had a point. By afternoon, the security shift in the hall would have changed. I put my case down. 'On one condition. I make the meal and you help your crippled chum. What's his first name?'

'Johnson,' Ferdy said. 'Same as his last. The registrar had a stutter. Call him J.J. if he ever speaks to you again. That's the melted butter, and there's a dish in the oven. Call when you're ready.'

He disappeared. I put my case out of harm's way in the bedroom, took off my shawl and jacket and waistcoat and shirt and put on my overall again. I caught sight of my unpatterned face below the Dracula eye-shadow and if the butter hadn't started to burn, I would have painted my cheeks then and there, in pure protest.

As it was, I went back to the kitchen and made a smashing meal for all of us, which Ferdy and I enjoyed, and which Pal Johnson either forgot, ignored or slept through, according to Ferdy. Then I found something for Bessie, and left Ferdy to wash up while I took her out for her aged business.

The two new men in the foyer gave me some long funny stares but didn't stop me, mainly because Bessie would have stopped too, and that to some purpose.

It took longer than I expected, since Bessie, having held out as far as the middle of the pavement and no further, celebrated her general relief by flopping off through every alley after her favourite smells, of which there are more in Mayfair than you would think.

I hadn't taken a leash, and by the time I got my hand in her collar, she was far from 17B, but in among the dress shops, the ivory shops, the gift shops and the shops making handmade chocolates, so that I rather took my time getting back.

The new doorkeeper stepped in front of me.

He was smaller than the last one: only two feet higher than me. He said, 'Oh yes. You're the jokey lady who bloodied up Ned and Josser?'

'And they deserved it,' I said. The dog, fawning, dripped Standard Dribble on the doorkeeper's trousers, and I waited for the accidental black eye.

The doorkeeper said, 'Good dog, then. Wish I'd seen that: my Gawd, what a picture! Where's the blood come from, then?'

He was cheerful. The new security man left the counter and joined us. He was cheerful too. 'Important make-up lady, isn't she?' he said. 'Ned and Josser weren't to know. You should have told them, Miss. 'E's a real fan of yours, Mr Braithwaite.'

Ferdy? Ferdy explaining and soothing? Ferdy down in the foyer spreading Largs?

The security man said, 'If you're goin' up now, Miss, there's this parcel. The boy took it up to deliver it, but nobody answered the door. Of course, Mr Johnson's not up to walking.'

Bessie was at the lift, waiting.

I didn't join her.

I didn't take the parcel.

I said, 'But Mr Braithwaite's in the flat. Didn't Mr Braithwaite come to the door?'

They looked at me, and I brought my voice down. I said, 'Didn't Mr Braithwaite go up to the flat again after he spoke to you?'

'Oh no, Miss,' the security man said. 'Out on the street like a rocket, he went. A heavy date, he said, and he was late for it. My Gawd, that's a character ... Do you 'ave a key to 17B, Miss? Mr Braithwaite left one for you, in case.'

King Ferdy the Rat.

I turned to make for the street. Bessie joined me, her tail wagging. I halted.

My case was in the flat, too. And my money.

I returned to the desk. I said, 'Do you know Mrs Margate's address or phone number? Mr Johnson's housekeeper?'

They didn't. I thought.

Ferdy's flat was being rewired. It was empty.

Natalie Sheridan wanted me for two days. I had no flat, no hotel room, no money and an Old English Sheepdog.

There were a number of choices.

I could shove Bessie into the flat, lift my gear and walk out.

I could tell the men down below what had happened. They could ring Meals on Wheels or the Salvation Army to rescue the guy upstairs if they felt like it. Ferdy would be mad, but it was Ferdy's fault anyway.

On the other hand, Ferdy could do me down with Natalie Sheridan.

It wasn't likely. He enjoyed life, and it took a good push before he got the knives out. But everyone knew what happened then.

I didn't want Mrs Sheridan put off me. I didn't much want to walk round finding a bed. A free night upstairs had something to it. And sure as eggs, I'd have no come-on from the resident cripple.

I took the key and went up in the lift with Bessie. Someone had wiped off my lipstick from the mirror, and had written TA LOVE on the door. I read it.

Ferdy was a bastard, but I supposed I'd go along with it in the end, as per usual. Twenty-four hours was all he claimed the housekeeper needed.

I could stick it till lunchtime tomorrow. And if I could, the guy Johnson would have to.

I got to his door and nearly changed my mind when I heard the phone ringing behind it. But however feeble, the man could surely take his own calls, if I answered the doorbell and fed him.

I unlocked the door and walked in, shooing Bessie before me. I shouted. 'It's Miss Geddes back, Mr Johnson! You've got another palm for your parlour!'

I don't know whether he heard me, but I could hear his voice on the phone, so I suppose he did. I shut the door and went to choose a bedroom. The one I'd used seemed to be the main guestroom. It smelt of Mrs Sheridan's scent. It had a phone in it.

It struck me that I had some calls to make if I was staying in London. I picked up the phone, and found I was listening to Johnson's caller.

It was a woman, and she was in the middle of reading a lecture.

'Well, you can't stay there, can you? If you don't go back to your people, then you might as well come to us. Daughter Joanna would love it. She's made you some rather drippy jam.'

Johnson's voice said, 'If I don't go home, I'd have to go to the Judge's.'

There was a silence. Then the woman said, 'Yes, I see that. But it's too much for Connie.'

He said, 'I'll get help for her. Really. It's all right.'

'And later?' She still sounded doubtful. 'Don't you want to get away from those phones? Where's *Dolly*?'

'Still refitting.'

The woman said, 'You could be in the Caribbean by the early summer. Why don't we send Lenny down to sail her out? We're not using him. He could take her to Tenerife and wait till you were ready. Or take her across himself with Raymond or somebody. You could fly over.

'You know everyone over there. You could stay anywhere you want, or on board if you didn't want company. I'll tell Bernard.'

'Something to look forward to?' he said. The put-down in his voice was like the one I'd had.

There was another silence. Then she said, 'Believe me, you won't feel as tired as this all the time. All the same, I don't know what you were thinking of, letting these people in. What's she called, this girl Ferdy's wished on you?'

'I don't know. Geddes, I think,' he said.

'And what's she like?'

There was another silence. Then he said, 'Small. Tough. Scottish. She's listening to you.'

The bastard. I whipped the receiver away from my ear without thinking, and so missed the first half of a very smart leave-taking. I heard Johnson say, 'It's too much trouble for you. No, please don't. But of course I'll remember. Give my love to Joanna.'

Then the woman rang off, but he didn't. He just laid the phone off the rest, so no more calls could get in.

It also meant that I couldn't phone out.

As I've probably said, attack first is my motto. I got up and banged on the door of his bedroom. Why not?

I had credit cards and an account. I could go to a hotel. Pal Johnson wasn't going to suffer, with his folks and the Judge and Joanna's mother and all to mollycuddle him. So I walked into his room without waiting too long for a sniffy invitation. He wasn't likely to be taking calls starkers.

Starkers he wasn't, but the Owner of the Apartment he certainly was, sitting straight up in bed as if he'd money rammed into both pillows. On the bed stood the filing basket full of letters, florists' cards and parcel tags, and beside it a tray of pens and paper and stuff he'd been answering with.

The phone was purring beside him on the table. I put the receiver back on its rest and said, 'I have some calls to make. Do you want me here or not?'

'It depends rather,' he said, 'on whether Ferdy comes back.'

A man of few words. What he meant was, he couldn't be bothered to row, but he wasn't going to lease 17B as a knocking shop.

I said, 'There's nothing for him to come back for. How long is your housekeeper taking?'

'Till tomorrow night, I imagine,' he said. 'I should have asked Ferdy.'

The phone rang, and he looked at it. He didn't pick it up. It went on ringing. I said, 'I'll go into the kitchen and whistle,' but got no reaction. Against the ringing, he said, 'Stay or leave as you like. You need a bed?'

The ringing came to an end, and he turned his head and unhooked and laid down the receiver. 'I'm afraid that is essential,' he said.

Behind the table, there was a telephone socket in the skirting. I got down on my knees and, pushing aside Bessie, who wanted to die for me, unplugged the cable. In two other rooms, the telephone started to ring again.

I got to my feet. Johnson pulled the blotter over his knees and picked his pen up, as if in return he'd unplugged me. I stood and looked at him sorting his papers.

I wanted to make calls and receive them from, for example, Ferdy or Natalie Sheridan.

The Owner wasn't going to answer the telephone. Which, if I stayed, made me his personal answering service.

He had started writing again, and I might as well have been a pot with a Zulu in it. I walked out and into the studio. I sat down at the piano and treated it to a yard or two of punchy Scott Joplin, waiting for the ringing to end so that I could start to make my phone calls.

I stopped because my legwarmers had got stamped down to my ankles, and the way I felt about the tantalized fruits told me I was starving.

There was a phone in the kitchen. I had just got a pan out when the ringing stopped and I made a dive to unhook the receiver. The ringing started again as I did it, and a voice spoke before I could get the thing down. 'Connie? Is that you? How is Mr Johnson today?'

This time, it was a man. I had the answer ready on tap. 'Very much improved, thank you,' I said. 'It will be a long business, of course. But he's making great strides now, considering.'

There were three more calls before I got all my outgoing ones. One of them wanted to know who I was, and I told him I'd been sent by the escort agency.

I made an omelette and ate it with a glass of milk while I was talking. Then I made another omelette, plated it, and carried it through the hall, having taken the other two phones off their hooks.

I banged on the Owner's door, and got an immediate answer. 'Come in. You were good enough to answer the phone?'

I put the plate on his blotter and handed him a knife and fork. 'It was an accident. Just folk with good wishes.'

'Did they leave names?' he said. He looked down at the plate and added, 'Have you eaten?' There were a dozen new addressed envelopes on the table.

'I had the one I practised on,' I said. 'Did you want their names? There wasn't a pencil.'

The Owner picked up the fork. 'They'll ring again,' he said. 'If you took their names, I could ring back some time. The only people I'd need to speak to are my own family. They'll say who they are. And people called Ballantyne.'

He looked up and said, 'Of course, I'm deeply obliged. If you have to go, would you be very kind and take Bessie down to the doorman? He doesn't mind walking her.'

'I'll walk her last thing,' I said. 'And post your letters. I've got Ferdy's key. Would you like some tantalized fruit from the box?'

You could see him think about it, but not for long.

'Not very much. You have them,' he said.

He hadn't complained about the Scott Joplin, so I went and played some more, and fed Bessie and watered her, and then switched on the T.V. I'd noticed in the wee sitting-room. I remembered at the same time that, though I'd fed the Owner, I'd forgotten the liquids.

I rooted out a nice selection of bottles, and ice, and some big and small glasses, and carried it all to the bedroom.

The door was ajar, and behind it, Bessie lay on the rug, snoring heavily. Above her on the bed, the Owner was sleeping too, on his face, with his bifocals thrown on the sheets anyhow. I put them where I left the whisky, and took a vodka for myself back to the sitting-room.

I used to be good at cartoons at college. After I finished my drink, I filled in time drawing Ferdy ogling Mrs Sheridan, and Mrs Sheridan dropping towels in front of the bug-eyed agency man.

The block and crayon came from the studio, where I'd found where Johnson kept all his painting things. They hadn't been used for an age. The palette had lost all its stickiness and the rags were all hard.

There were two more calls. One was from Ferdy, roaring tight from a night-club, and bellowing housekeeper's instructions about food, pills and Bessie. I put the phone down on him.

Later, I took Bessie out on the pavement and the security man held the door for me. Back in the flat, I left her to push her own way into the Owner's room, having no mind to get mixed up with bedtime ablutions.

I found a box of chocolates and some grapes, and took them to the big bedroom.

There were no satin nighties or black lace undies in any of the fitted drawers, which was a pity. It made you wonder what Ferdy and Pal Johnson actually had in common, apart from short tempers. However, the beds were made up. They were new, too. The sheets had sticky corners where the price labels had been.

I was tired. I wakened four times: twice with burglar alarms going off in the Persian carpets and once because of some drunks. The last time, I couldn't make out what it was, and then realized that it was Bessie not snoring. There was a light on under my door, and the sound of somebody chatting.

I could just make out that it was the Owner, moving about if not racing, and talking to Bessie. I took it that he had wakened up and was going to bed officially, without bothering to find out if the flat was crowded or not.

I had the feeling that, so far as he was concerned, we were all invisible anyway, with the possible exception of Bessie.

I was just dropping off to sleep again when the funny thing happened.

It began with a ring at the doorbell.

For a moment, I thought it was yet another bloody phone call. Then I came properly awake, and remembered it was two in the morning, and I was in a strange block of flats with a moody bastard, and if the doorbell rang, he wasn't going to do anything about it, but I'd have to.

I got up, draped myself in the quilt, and marching out, put the hall light on. There was, I saw, a light under the Owner's door. The doorbell rang again.

I walked through the hall, and stopping just short of the door, yelled through it, 'What is it?'

A cockney voice said, 'Mr Johnson? Security.'

After all the jokes down below, you'd think Security would damn well know Johnson couldn't come to the door. I said, 'What is it?'

Pause. No quick thinker, this voice. Then it said, 'Are you alone, Miss?'

'No,' I said. 'Mr Johnson's here, but he can't come to the door. What is it?'

It was great news for two in the morning. He wanted to come in, because a man had been seen hanging about. A big fair man in black, lurking outside. By the fire escape leading to 17B's back balcony.

Damn Ferdy.

I wasn't going to open the door at this time of night, whoever this guy said he was.

I would have to go and search through the flat myself. There was an umbrella stand under my nose with various sticks in it, and some pretty sharp knives in the kitchen.

I rather wished I was wearing something handier than a quilt, but if all else failed, I could smother the guy if I caught him.

I explained this through the door. It didn't go down well. There followed a fairly noisy argument, with the security man standing outside demanding to get in.

It was cut short by the well-known crack of the Owner's voice.

Propping up his bedroom doorpost behind me, Pal Johnson said, 'Must we wake the whole building? Ask him his name. If it's Ritchie Tiller, and he had a new grandchild last Tuesday, let him in.'

It was, he had, and I did. I waited, wrapped in my quilt, while Grandfather Tiller came in, properly uniformed, searched the apartment, and found nothing and nobody.

He refused a drink, apologized to the Owner and me for disturbing us, and went away.

Pal Johnson, getting up from the hall chair, was kind enough to thank me as well, before tapping his way to his room and shutting his door with a snap.

I watched him go. I didn't get back into bed, although I put out the hall lights and my own. I sat in my doorway and waited. I was interested.

Johnson's room was the only one the security man hadn't searched.

Naturally. Johnson had been awake ever since the intruder had been glimpsed, and in any case, had checked the curtains and cupboards himself.

So he said.

And since the security man believed him, the security man couldn't know, as I did, that Johnson didn't smoke cigarettes.

And wouldn't therefore have wondered, as I did, about the smell of good cigarettes that had floated very faintly from the open door of Johnson's room.

I waited a long five minutes before I heard the voices from behind the same door.

One was Johnson's. The other man had a lighter voice, and seemed, keeping it low, to be trying to speak at some length, while Johnson kept cutting him off. They were quarrelling.

There was no doubt they knew one another. There was no doubt either that they were good at keeping their voices down. I crouched in my quilt at the door, and I still couldn't make out the words properly. It was maddening.

I tumbled back to my room when the voices stopped. But instead of Johnson's door opening, there was a rattle of curtain rings. His guest was using the window, the balcony and the fire escape.

There was a view of the fire escape from the studio. I didn't switch on any lights. I just stood in my quilt, and watched this broad-shouldered menace in black come out of the Owner's room and whizz silently down.

I saw his face in the mews light, and it was battered and tough, like those guys who get sent to the Sitwells. His hair was curly and yellow.

I slipped back to the hall. In the room of the Owner and host, a window closed and I heard curtains shutting again. No wonder he hadn't wanted the building roused.

Whatever the quarrel had been, no one had slugged him, it seemed, at the end of it.

Pity.

I didn't know what he was up to, but in his state it couldn't be much. You meet all sorts in show business and nothing in the sex line surprises me, which is not to say all of it appeals to me.

I had no doubt, really, that Ferdy's pal hadn't been murdered, but it was a shame to go to bed without checking it.

I tapped on Johnson's door, neatly wrapped in my quilt, and asked him if he would like a wee cup of tea to send him over.

I was ready for most things except absolute silence.

I gave him time to be in the bathroom, get his glasses on, find his stick, put on his dressing-gown, get the other three guys out from under the bed.

I gave him time to die, and then stopped tapping and turned the door handle.

This time the door was locked. No punk with pink and blue hair was going to turn over his bedroom again.

I nearly went to phone for help. He must have realized, then, that if he didn't answer, that's what would happen.

He spoke.

He said, 'Miss Geddes. Will you get the hell back to your room and *leave me alone?*'

That looks almost polite. You didn't hear the voice that he said it in.

I picked up my quilt and got out of it.

3

The next time I woke in 17B it was daylight, and the streets were full of window-cleaning vans and bankers and shop girls, which meant that eight-thirty had not yet clanged everywhere. As I got up, one of the Persian carpets shut off its alarm, and soon the other did.

My hair was a mess. Leaving my lashes lying, I went to the kitchen, and found the Enemy already there with his stick, boiling a kettle.

His hair was combed, and he had his glasses and his dressing-gown on and an unsurprised expression, which meant that he had heard me moving about although I hadn't heard him.

I wasn't sure what he would say, but he'd brought back his manner to neuter. 'Good morning,' he said.

No skin off my nose. (More's the pity, as my Geddes aunt in Troon was happy to say.)

I hadn't expected to see him. My feet were bare, and I hadn't yet pulled on my gauchos, but I wasn't bothered. I had a long shirt on.

I said, 'Oh, hullo. I came through for some eggs. Don't you do something, all of you, about those shop alarms?'

His kettle was singing. Using his stick, he moved about, collecting tea and a teapot and stuff with one hand. 'The eggs are over there,' he said. 'Did the alarms keep you awake as well? I'm sorry about the excursions.'

Excursions wasn't what I would have called them. I took four eggs, cracked and separated them, and put the whites into the mixer. 'It didn't worry me,' I said. 'You'll scald yourself with that kettle.' Ferdy wouldn't like it, and I didn't know where the lint was. I lifted the kettle for him, filled his teapot, and went back to scoop my eggs into a bowl ready to take out.

He didn't ask why I wasn't cooking them. He just said, 'I suppose everyone asks you this. What do you do with the yolks?'

'That's for your diet,' I said. 'If I have to go, I'll leave you some lunch. Just general invalid mush?'

It was pretty rude, the way it came out. Instead of pouring his tea, he put his back against Poggenpohl's best, and apparently settled for entering the contest. In a sort of a way.

He said, 'Do you have a boyfriend?'

None of Ferdy's queer friends are anything to do with me, but I like to know where I am. Now I knew where I was. I said, 'It doesn't bother me, what people do. Don't drag me into it.'

He gave some thought to that. Then he said, 'Last night ... I didn't mean to be short. It was awkward.'

'Pass him to me when you've finished with him,' I said. Stupidly.

I saw him field that. He knew I'd heard something, but not that I'd seen anything. He said, taking it in, 'You were watching.'

It was time to get out of the subject. He was well-known, and loaded, with a reputation to protect. I didn't want him to see me as a danger. An annoyance, O.K., but not a danger. I wanted friends in high places, not enemies.

I said, 'I've got a very short memory. You'll have noticed.' I tried the whipped whites with my finger.

The bifocals remained trained on my face. Then, whatever he saw, his lips almost appeared. He said, 'Yes, I've noticed. Who rang last night?'

'Mr Braithwaite,' I said. 'Just to say he couldn't come back.'

He waited, and I let him. He didn't prompt me. After a bit, I said, 'Well, there were others, but I don't remember them. Just get-well calls. I hadn't a pencil.'

'I see,' he said. That was all. Not the world's greatest talker. He turned round, propped himself up and began pouring tea. I went back to my room and rubbed the eggs into my hair to fix the spikes again.

The doorbell rang twice while I was doing it: once with milk and the papers, and once for the post. The kitchen was empty again, so I put the milk in it, and left the papers and mail on the hall table.

Bessie appeared in the hall, and stood at the door hopefully in a cloud of old dog. I'd forgotten her.

I went to look for my gloves, but couldn't find them. I put on my gauchos and stockings and boots, and lifting my shawl, went to ask Bessie's boss where the leash was.

He was making his bed, I was glad to see. He told me what I wanted to know, thanked me on Bessie's behalf, and asked me to wait while he looked for something.

It was a fresh, sharpened pencil. I didn't give him the papers or the letters. If he was feeling that full of beans, he could get them himself.

This time Bessie didn't make it out to the pavement. It was Ned and Josser on duty and, for a moment, the smiles disappeared, but Ferdy, whatever his faults, must have done them proud before leaving. The doorkeeper took a deep breath, and the last I saw, he'd got a pail out of the cleaning cupboard, and had gone to look for hot water.

I walked beside Bessie past the most interesting shops and then lost my bloody way. I got back, with some trouble, through the Rolls parade.

I had meant to be earlier. Mrs Sheridan, for example, might be trying to phone me.

Outside 17B an elegant, youngish woman in a tweed suit and scarf was raising her hand to the doorbell. She turned at the sound of the lift, clucked to Bessie, and then gave me a doubtful smile. 'Is Mrs Margate still away?' she said. 'I'm an old friend of Mr Johnson's. I just wondered how he was this morning.'

It was the voice of Joanna's mother, from yesterday's overheard phone call. Come, no doubt, to see what was small, tough and Scottish.

I said, opening the door, 'He was sweeping the floor when I left him. What name shall I say?'

She followed me in, gazing at everything. 'Emerson. Lady Emerson,' she said. There was a new pile of letters, stamped and ready for posting on the table, and I saw her glance at them, while she petted Bessie. She was good-looking.

I left her there while I looked for the Owner, who had moved, I found, to the sitting-room. He heard, without comment, that he had a female visitor. His face kept itself to itself, as well, when he heard who it was. He just asked me to show her in.

I heard her say, 'Jay, you look awful. I have an ultimatum.'

I didn't hear his reply, but I heard the tone of it, before the door shut firmly behind her.

I now knew how he felt about female visitors. If he'd been bleak with her on the phone, now he was freezing.

There were three phone calls. Two were from friends of the Owner. One was for me. Mrs Sheridan required the services of Miss Rita Geddes, that afternoon at her hotel.

Miss Rita Geddes said she'd be there, thank you.

The Emerson woman stayed for ten minutes, and then came into the hall to ask if she could make coffee for Mr Johnson. Her expression, before she changed it, could be called grim.

I had switched a pot on for myself, and found some jazz on a portable radio, which I hoped no one wanted back in the sitting-room. While I got cups, she went to fetch milk from the cupboard.

33

She said, 'He gets a lot of letters, doesn't he? Are they still coming?' She had to shout a bit, so I turned the jazz down.

The second post had just come. I went out and scooped the mail up and showed it her. She put down the milk, and sorting through it, took out all the stuff that was handwritten.

'Do you suppose,' she said, 'that all the private ones, the ones like that, could get themselves lost for a day or two?'

'He'd notice,' I said.

'Give him a few at a time, then,' she said. 'But not all of them. In a week or two, it'll be different.'

I said, 'It's up to Mrs Margate, not me. I'll give him his lunch, though.'

The devoted correspondence took on a new meaning. I was safe as houses if the Owner was the bedridden organizer of a Gay Club.

The coffee was perking, and I poured it. She said, 'You've been very good. You work for Mr Braithwaite, don't you?'

'I'm a freelance,' I said. 'I'm with Natalie Sheridan this afternoon. So Mr Johnson will have to manage, I'm afraid, if his housekeeper doesn't come back before evening.'

'Of course, I understand that,' said Lady Emerson. 'I phoned the agency this morning to get a capable woman along. Someone with nursing training, who could take telephone messages and exercise Bessie.'

She hesitated, and then went to her handbag and lifted it. 'It occurs to me that, cut off from his bank, Mr Johnson maybe hasn't been able to thank you properly?'

She opened her bag.

'Oh, not at all,' I said. 'I wouldn't dream of it. He can always write me a cheque anyhow, can't he? The coffee's getting stone cold.'

I put the two cups on the tray with the spoons and sugar and milk, and she picked it up and went off to the sitting-room. I switched to the news and enjoyed a cup on my own, with some biscuits I'd discovered. I'd already found a place for the unwanted letters.

There didn't seem much sense to me in answering letters and not answering phone calls. But you never know what the boss class is playing at. Anyway, it wasn't my funeral.

The Emerson woman left fairly soon, and then someone called Ballantyne phoned, and I remembered just in time to tell him so that he could take the call himself, after I had plugged in the phone under his bed.

When I heard him ring off, I went in to unplug it, carrying the Oscar Peterson programme I was listening to while I was cooking. I didn't realize he was speaking until he asked me the same thing twice over.

It was something about the other calls. When I told him my pencil had broken he was distinctly not amused. He seemed, however, too fed up to go on about it. Or thought it wiser not to.

I hoped the capable woman didn't mind queer invalids who fussed about telephone calls.

The doctor came just as the steamed fish was ready.

Like all the Owner's well-brought-up friends, he greeted me as if he'd known me for ever, and asked after the housekeeper and Bessie, who came out and drooled over his trousers.

He seemed surprised to find Mr Johnson not in his bedroom, but opened the sitting-room door and went in with a broad doctor's smile. I heard the Owner calling him Henry. You couldn't tell, of course, whether anyone was on first-name terms with Johnson or not.

He was in a long time, and I ate the fish, since it was spoiling and I was hungry. After a while I thought I heard a voice in the hall, and turning the radio down, went out to find Henry leaving.

He did not, thank God, mention kindness to cripples, but just talked about Bessie. He'd had a look at the poor dear old bitch, and he agreed with the vet that she couldn't last, although it wasn't the time to tell Mr Johnson.

I said, 'He'll get more of a shock if she dies on him. Would the vet put her down?'

'He's been waiting to do it,' the doctor said. 'Should have done it, to my mind, when he had the chance. On the other hand . . .'

He stopped, and then said, 'Anyway, it's lucky you were here this morning. I'm sorry I've interrupted your lunch. It smells good. You keep cheering him up now, eh?'

Another bum. The way I felt, he'd be lucky if we just kept life ticking over, never mind bombarding the Owner with cheerfulness. And he'd be still less cheery when he found out I'd eaten his fish.

When I carried his lunch in, he didn't seem amazed to find it was based on four egg yolks. Asked what he wanted to drink, he suggested a glass of red wine each, and told me where to look for the bottles.

I'd seen them, actually, every time I took out the vodka.

I opened a chloride and poured him one, and then one for myself, and took it to the other coffee-table in the sitting-room, since he asked me. As the wine mixed with the vodka and I began to feel less unfriendly, I told him I was leaving for Mrs Sheridan's.

'Of course. You make her up, don't you?' he said. I had cooked him a good, nourishing dish, with cheese and onions and bacon as well as eggs in it, and he was working on it through his bifocals.

I was about to agree, when I remembered he and Natalie knew the same people. I said, 'She has her own man for that usually. Kim-Jim Curtis. I do her in London.'

'Kim-Jim Curtis doesn't mind?' he said. His wineglass was empty, and I got up and filled it.

'Kim-Jim? No,' I said. 'He recommended me to Mrs Sheridan.'

Johnson said, 'I suppose all make-up professionals know one another?'

'We all know *of* one another,' I said. 'We all watch one another's work, and use the same materials, and listen to all the new discoveries and everything. Some people do private work only, and some do magazine and society photographs, and some do general T.V. and screen work, and some specialize in characters or special effects.'

I broke off. He had had a lot of wine. He said, 'Go on, I'm not bored yet.'

He was just being cheeky, not patronizing. I like talking about what I do. I said, 'Well. Some people are rubber specialists, like Chris Tucker and Stuart Freeborn. That's working in prosthetics. Masks and noses and cheek pieces and everything. Karen Bauer does severed heads. Some like animal masks. Some people, like me, like doing work for impersonators. But I do a bit of everything.'

He said, 'You sound as if you like screen work more than painting up Natalie Sheridan.'

I'd had a lot to drink too. I said, 'I'd like to work for her for a bit. She knows how to dress. You can make a lot of her. And she knows a lot of people. That's useful, when you're a freelance. But I do sort of like the creative side. When you've got to find your own way through a problem. It's an awful new industry. There are lots of things you've got to think out and invent for yourself. I like that.'

'I can see that,' said Johnson. He gazed at a forkful of quiche. 'Is it such a new business? I thought you had families in the trade already. Like circuses.'

I'd forgotten he was an art college man. I said, 'That's true. I expect you know them. The Nyes. The Partleton brothers. Tony Sforzini and

36

his daughter. Mrs Sheridan's make-up man is one of the American Curtises, and they go back to the old M.G.M. epics. Of course, face paint is as old as Time, but it only really came into its own with the film industry.'

'That's the Kim-Jim Curtis you mentioned,' Johnson said. 'Does he stay with Mrs Sheridan?' Invited, I had given myself more of the chloride. 'What's known as a house-guest?'

'She goes in for house-guests,' I said. 'But he's the permanent one. Works like a dog.'

I remembered something. I didn't want to talk about Kim-Jim anyway. I said, 'You've got a problem with Bessie.'

'I have?' he said. He lay down his fork and pushed his plate away. He hadn't finished all of the quiche.

'She's been a great dog, but she's a ruin,' I said. 'It isn't fair, really. The doctor wants her put down.'

My hair appeared, twice over, straight in his glasses. It was quite a change.

'Oh?' he said, in his complete Owner voice. 'And did he mention which day?'

I said, 'Her legs are bad, she's half-blind and she makes messes all over the foyer. You have to say which day. The doctor can't and the vet's scared.'

'Thank you,' he said. 'Really, it's just as well you're going, isn't it? Who knows whom you'd feel compelled to have put down next?'

I got up and collected his plate. 'You didn't enjoy your lunch?'

'It was charming, thank you,' he said. 'Let me know when you leave.'

He had a short bloody fuse. I left him the bottle to get thoroughly sloshed with if he wanted, and let off steam with a good bash at the piano.

I had unwrapped the pot plants in the studio, and rearranged it all like a teashop. There were no grapes or chocolates left.

I fed Bessie, I supposed for the last time, and took her out to the pavement before I washed up. Then I got my shawl and my fishing case and went to say good-bye to Johnson.

Unfortunately, he had finished the bottle and was sprawling asleep on his face again. There was no way of telling if he had been going to give me a cheque.

I rubbed Bessie's ears, and then shut her in with her master.

I went off to my date with Mrs Sheridan.

She was staying at Claridge's but the doorkeeper and the desk clerks were well warned beforehand, and they treated me like a guest, even if I found myself in the lift p.d.q.

Natalie had got Ferdy's photographs and was taken aback, as I knew she would be, to find how well she could look on her left side. She wanted to ask me about it. And she wanted a special make-up for that evening.

As before, she was sharpish but business-like, which suits me all right. The maid Dodo, a dead ringer for Eleanor Roosevelt, stood around glaring at me, but that was all right too.

I didn't tell Natalie all my tricks, but I told her I could fix both sides again any time she wanted it done. And for that evening, I made her look stylish and different.

She asked me to stay while she dressed, and before she went out, she sat down and poured me a sherry, and told me what I knew already: that Kim-Jim was out of action for a short time, and she needed someone on call for her make-up.

'I like your work, Rita,' she said. 'I know you don't take jobs abroad, but it's only a plane hop to the villa. And now this film idea has turned up, I'll be in London for quite a few days yet, and I'd like to suggest an arrangement. Would you care to stay on call while I'm here? Will you come and work for me at the villa while Kim-Jim's away? If, of course, my fee is agreeable.'

It was what Kim-Jim had wanted. It was why he had arranged my engagement with his employer. I knew what he had in mind. People retire. People like the chance to pick the person who will fill their shoes after them.

A pretty innocent plan, and a generous one. For an American at the top of his profession, Kim-Jim was a pretty innocent guy. And he and I were good friends.

Just professional friends. We'd met only once.

An innocent plan.

The laugh of the year. I really thought, accepting Natalie Sheridan's offer, that it was Kim-Jim's scheme and mine, and had nothing to do with anyone else.

The plan to make a break. To go abroad for the first time in my life. To help Kim-Jim. To do the work I loved doing. To have a great time, staying with Natalie Sheridan, in her hideaway house in Madeira.

Of course I said yes. Nothing warned me. The only man who could have warned me had been in a wheelchair.

*

I flew to Madeira in April.

Madeira, so my mother said, was a place you used to take your aunty to in the winter.

It depends what sort of aunty you've got, but I wouldn't take one in April: not if she's easily shot.

You can't wear wool there in April either, so I had clothes to buy first, and a passport to apply for, and my accountants in Glasgow to visit.

A passport, because I'd never been overseas before. Britain for Rita, I'd sworn. I felt a traitor, going now. Not afraid, but a traitor.

I had a story all ready to spin my mother, but I didn't need it. When I got to the nursing home, they said she had gone a bit confused again, and I wasn't to mind if she was bad-tempered.

She wasn't, and she knew me, although she thought I was still at school. It wouldn't be Robina to be bad-tempered. We talked about hockey.

The rest of my things were in Troon, including my tape-recorder and radio and cassette-player, and all the make-up stuff I'd need for Natalie Sheridan. I went to pick them up, not liking the house without my mother in it, and had words with my Geddes aunt, as I always do.

That's one aunt I wouldn't take anywhere. She wouldn't go with me anyway. She has a motto as well: 'Your Dad, God rest his soul, would never have let you.' But she runs the house while my mother's away, and sees the gutters don't leak and the taps have washers on them. And takes messages for me, on the telephone.

The night before I left Glasgow, I went on the town in Byres Road with a bunch of old pals from show business. Two were girls I'd been friends with at school. One of them was a singer and the other had become a producer.

Put together, they earn half what I do, and that's leaving out my investments.

They can spell.

They liked these clothes I'd bought, and my hair. I'd had my hair cut and made a new colour. It finished up quite a nice shade of chrome with some blue in it.

They asked about the new job, and I told them.

Natalie's villa had a swimming pool, Kim-Jim had said. He never had much time to swim, but I wasn't to let her work me so hard. I would be there as her beautician, and anything else I did was up to me. The most I might have to do was book the odd plane or hotel, or phone up people with messages. There were English girls Mrs Sheridan could hire for dictating. Everyone else spoke Portuguese.

Phone up people with messages.

I was glad that Natalie had had no more chats with Johnson Johnson before she left London.

Ferdy, who was busy on the artwork for a big, glossy book on Sexual Strategy in Flowers, to be printed in Luxembourg, reported that Johnson was apparently still making great strides considering, and had mentioned something about a bill for phone calls to Troon and Glasgow and Lisbon, as well as blue and magenta stains in the bathroom.

I thought of the blond boyfriend, and the security men, and all those bloody phone calls and the perfectly good quiche I'd made him, and told Ferdy that if his pal Johnson was fussed over anything, he could get Lady Emerson to pay for it.

Once, on my way past from Claridge's, I'd seen a po-faced woman out walking Bessie past the flats, and another time, Bessie with Mrs Margate. Then, just before I went north, I saw Mrs Margate outside a coffee-bean shop by herself.

I didn't ask Ferdy, but it looked to me as if the capable woman had soon got her books.

And maybe even that old Bessie had got hers as well, if the Owner had crawled from his expensive new sickbed and coped with something apart from mail orders.

Male orders?

It was, luckily, none of my business. I was going to a new job, a rather special new job, in Madeira.

4

Abroad, it turned out, was very like Troon on an English Bank Holiday.
Waiting early that evening to be met at the airport, I couldn't understand
what anyone said, even when they were speaking English.

I expected Mrs Sheridan's car, but she had sent a hired driver who
stood about, with a peaked cap and dark glasses and a big placard saying
SRA RITA DA GODES.

It was some time before we found one another, even after the Arrival
Hall was quite empty.

To get to Mrs Sheridan's villa, I'd been told, you have to go from
the airport through Funchal, the main town of Madeira. You begin by
driving along the coast.

It was warm.

I expected that. The B.B.C. had filmed a programme about it, *Volcanic
Islands of the Atlantic*, and a pal had taped it. *Madeira the Floating Garden;
the Island of Gentle Summers and Mild Winters.*

Before my dark glasses got too dark to bother looking through, I
noticed a lot of blue water and red roofs and purple creeper, and a
harbour with the sun about to fall into the water.

Then the Mercedes turned uphill to cut out the town, and ran into
a lot of rutted roads with no walls and steep paths going up to farm
cabins, and finally into a side lane that seemed to lead nowhere.

There were a few trees and a lot of dry earth about, but no sign
of any houses at all, never mind a posh villa with swimming pool. It
wasn't the sort of countryside you would find Natalie Sheridan in, unless
she was making a documentary.

The sun went down, and I couldn't see much of anything any more.
The driver was nothing but a dim shape in front of me.

I gazed at it, waiting for him to slide back the partition and grovel.
I wasn't going to be ratty with him. Anyone can get lost.

Instead, he got out of his door and jerked open mine.

I think I still expected him to start making excuses. I took off my
dark glasses so that I could see him better, or as well as I could see
anything under the brim of this Humphrey Bogart fedora I was wearing.

41

¹ couldn't see him better because, under his hat, he had a stocking on.

I could see he was tall. I could see his uniform jacket was too small for him. There were four inches of shirt cuff and skin between his fists and his sleeves.

I said, 'You're not the man with the placard!'

I wasn't too put out yet, because the cuffs had cufflinks in them. The worst I was expecting was rape.

'*Senhora Rita da Godes?*' he said. 'You couldn't even read it, you illiterate bitch. You should be deported.'

In English. In educated, foul-tempered English with loathing in every vowel.

A nutter. I won't say I'm used to it, but if you're not in a home for the aged you meet them.

The rule is get out of it, fast. He was leaning in on one side, and the door handle was not too far away on the other.

I sent one hand along quietly, exploring for it. I may have hockey legs, but they're O.K. for running on.

I said, 'Great. Let's call the police. They'll deport me.' My fingers were two inches from the door handle.

He wasn't the kind to be humoured. He said, 'Stop bleating, my beauty, and listen.'

I was listening. The door handle was just an inch off.

I lunged for it and he lunged for me in the same moment.

He won. My hat fell off. Suddenly the car was full of him. His weight rammed me down, and his hand shoved my head back on the car ledge.

He was breathing hard. I expected rum or whisky, but his breath smelled of bacon and egg. Also something else. I couldn't quite place it.

'Scum!' he said. 'You and your partner!'

You get a lot of this in Scotland, if you have coloured hair.

I didn't know what he meant by my partner, unless he was thinking of Satan, which was quite likely. Religious cranks, having sex on the brain, can be the nastiest in that line when they finally work themselves up and over the edge, which a lot of them do.

I said, 'I got led astray by older people. I'll listen, if you want to talk to me.'

I can't say I meant to listen long. He must have been watching my eyes. I only glanced at the door, but a second before I tried to heave

42

myself over again, he changed his grip quickly. One of his hands collected my wrists. The other dived for the back of my collar.

Then it all got pretty lively. I hacked his shins, and tried to jerk my hands free.

He'd played that game before too. Before my heels half connected he had swung himself, saving his legs. And his gripping hand simply squeezed my wrists tighter, while the other closed on my collar and twisted it, until the cloth in front of my neck nearly throttled me.

'Sit, you stupid punk,' he said. 'And listen to me. You came here to meet Mrs Sheridan. You are going to see her. You are going to tell her you can't take the job. And you are going to get yourself out of the country. Back to the hole you crawled out of, you and your partner.'

Natalie. He was talking about Natalie Sheridan.

I stopped being limp. 'Are you nuts or what? Mrs Sheridan asked me to come here!'

'Because you arranged it,' he said. 'Because that trickster Curtis gave her your name and told her how good you were. The old, old con. First, Curtis dupes her, and then you climb in beside him.'

I stared at the blur of his face. I couldn't believe it. My partner in crime wasn't Satan. It was meant to be poor Kim-Jim Curtis.

I thought it was silly to ask, because nutters don't need to be logical. But I couldn't help saying, 'Why?'

Thinking about it all had made him tremble. It wasn't nice. He wasn't listening, either. He said, 'She'll tell you to publish and be damned. She's not worth as much as you think, you know. She's willed a lot of money away. Even if Mr Kenneth James Curtis gets her to marry him, there isn't a jack-pot.'

It was so weird I almost forgot the shrieks of my wrist-bones. 'He doesn't *want* to marry her!' I said.

The jerk on my collar made me gag again. 'You know his plans, don't you?' he said. 'You're a fine pair. You're a fine pair of blackguards.'

I wheezed, but he didn't shift his grip that time. I made a big effort, and tried to explain it.

I said, 'Of course Kim-Jim suggested me. He knew she'd like my work, and I'd like a holiday. As for the bloody woman's money, what's that to you? I don't want it.'

'I'm sure,' he said. He sat, holding me two-handed like Andy Pandy and I could feel the sneer from where I was sitting.

43

He said, 'You don't want the money? Then prove it. Prove it by going right back to London.'

I gagged again, but he paid no attention.

'Why should I?' I said. 'Give up a good paid job and a holiday because you're Perry Como? And,' said I rashly, because I was sore and angry and getting, by now, extremely annoyed with Abroad, 'who are you anyway? One of Mrs Sheridan's discards?'

I had planned, as the next move in the war, to crack my head in his face. He didn't give me the chance.

I no sooner got those words out than he socked me.

He used the hand from my collar, which half freed me. I rocked with the blow, as he had done. I did one better and half twisting round, fetched my hands, still in his grip, gouging into his face as he lunged over.

I wear a lot of rings when I travel. Big ones. A lump of grey quartz from Fior dragged across his stockinged cheek like a hay fork.

He exclaimed, and smashed my wrists down. The blow, as every bang does, untucked the wide band of my executive watch. It slid down, taking his fingers with it. I ripped my hand away and aimed with finger and thumb for his nose. My other hand was still free. I nipped the hatpin from my lapel and speared his fist with it.

He couldn't yell while I was twisting his nose, but he still had two limbs left, and a lot of superior weight, and he used it all. As the blows fell on my poor fatigued cotton top and what was under it, I hurled myself yet again at the bloody door handle.

It worked, in a way.

The door handle gave, and I tumbled head first on the ground, followed by my English fruit-cake.

That guy was trained. He took my legs in hard scissors hold, and got my hands in the same one-handed grip as before, except that we were both lying on the ground to one side of the car instead of inside it.

I yelled, and went on yelling, but not for long. The bastard took off his peaked cap and slammed it over my face, holding it with the flat of his hand so that I could hardly breathe, never mind yell.

I thrashed my head from one side to the other as best I could, but he only leaned harder. He said, 'This way, you get hurt. If you don't leave Madeira, you get hurt a lot more. When are you leaving Madeira?'

'Tomorrow,' I said. Naturally. I put on an agreeing face under the hat and hoped like anything.

'Tomorrow,' he said. 'You leave Madeira tomorrow, and you don't ever come back. You understand?' He lifted the hat a bit, and I breathed.

'I understand,' I said. 'Or I get socked.'

Unwise. 'Or you have an accident,' my chauffeur said. 'A fatal accident. As Kim-Jim Curtis will have, if he ever comes back. Tell him, will you?'

'I'll tell him,' I said.

We lay, breathing at one another. I was waiting for something funny, but nothing happened. It occurred to me that, if I hadn't resisted, we might just have had an exchange of snash in the back seat instead of a struggle.

Or maybe not.

He said, 'Tell Curtis that if he comes back, I'll kill him. I'll kill him. Nothing surer.'

I thought of explaining that Kim-Jim might be fading out of Mrs Sheridan's life, although Mrs Sheridan didn't know it; and then thought why bother. I thought of explaining that Kim-Jim didn't need anyone's money and neither, come to that, did I, much. He could phone my stock-brokers.

I thought that anyone who had done what this guy had just done wasn't worth wasting words on. All I had to do was keep agreeing, and then ring up his keepers.

Except that I didn't know who he was.

He was lifting the cap on my face, slowly, as if he hoped to read my expression in the darkness. As he lifted it, I saw it wasn't entirely dark. The car door still hung ajar where I'd left it, and a ray of light from inside was shining on him.

Shining on his arm with the shirt riding up, because the cufflink had snapped in the struggle. Shining on the skin of the arm, and on a couple of long purple scars that explained, in a way, all this rubbish.

Panic in Needle Park. The tracks of a drug-taker. And the smell of a drug, now I remembered it.

Heroin. You don't live where I live without coming across it some time. Or without knowing what it does to people.

I did a silly thing and started to struggle properly. I flung my weight about as best I could, but he was a strong man.

When his grip on my hands suddenly vanished, I hardly noticed, I was so short of air, and the pain in my wrists was so hellish.

I don't remember anything more, because that time, I didn't see my gent draw back his fist. I didn't see anything. I just felt the thud on my jaw, and on the back of my head. And from then on, I had no more problems.

I woke in bed later that evening in Mrs Sheridan's house, with Natalie Sheridan herself leaning over me. I was aching all over.

I knew it was Villa Sheridan, because the bed was in a smart single room, equipped from a powerful income. Also, my things had been unpacked and stood about everywhere. Including my special cat with the smile, my video tapes and my recorder. Bloody Dodo.

I knew it was evening, because Mrs Sheridan wore crimson silk, jet earrings and Arpège, for a change, and had a small drink in her hand, which she put down as my eyes came to rest.

She said, 'What a welcome to Madeira. Poor Rita. What on earth did they do to you?'

Her natural voice, I guessed, was clear and metallic. Ten years of hard work had brought it down to clear, warm and husky. Now it was sympathetic but bracing: buck up, Rita.

I lay still while I sorted her manner out. She had her hair done in a softer style than before, buckled at the nape of her neck and falling in a yellow silk tail. Her make-up was light as well, and kind of rosy. Motherly.

Her eyes were the eyes of a horse-trainer who has just bought a horse.

I said, 'Nothing permanent. I got bumped about by someone who thought Kim-Jim and I were after your money. I had to promise to leave Madeira tomorrow. And that Kim-Jim would never come back. Can I have a drink, please?'

She patted my hand, her rings flashing. 'When you've seen my doctor. He's waiting to look at you. Then you can drink all you want.'

The hand on mine became still. 'But I can hardly believe this. Tell me more. Who attacked you? Who could possibly make such a mistake? Kim-Jim and you!'

She drew back her hand, picked up her glass and smiled at me. 'If it didn't sound melodramatic, I'd say that I'd trust Kim-Jim with my life. And of course, anyone Kim-Jim trusts, I trust absolutely. So who were they, these idiots?'

I told her the story and she listened, sipping and sometimes looking into her glass. By the end, the glass was empty and she put it down and got up, walking slowly up and down the plush carpet.

She said, 'I can't tell you how sorry I am that this happened. It does, sometimes, you know. Public figures attract cranks. People form crazy attachments ... people I've never even met.'

She came and sat down, very gently, beside me. 'Rita. You've been scared and you've been hurt, and you deserve some sort of restitution. You think that if I call in the police and the consul, they'll track this lunatic down, and then we'll all be safe.'

I could see where she was leading, and it wasn't where I was going. 'I want the police and the consul on the trail of this guy,' I said. 'Or thank you, but good-bye.'

'And Kim-Jim?' said Mrs Sheridan. 'I thought he was a friend of yours? But for the sake of an unknown man whom no one can possibly find, Kim-Jim is going to have a reputation he never had before. A plotter. A gold-digger. Things that no more apply to him than they apply to you, but you'll both be branded. And so will I.'

She looked down, and I noticed that the black of her eye-liner was shaky. She said, 'Kim-Jim and I aren't married, but we don't live together like brother and sister. You must know that perfectly well.'

Garbage. I didn't say it. I just said, 'But if you don't go to the police, Kim-Jim will come back and be killed. Like I don't leave tomorrow and ditto.'

Mrs Sheridan smiled. She had very large eyes, and despite the duff job, they were compelling.

She said, 'The police don't handle everything. If you have money, you can see justice done, and without any publicity. Do you want to stay with me, Rita? If I show you how sorry I am that this has happened? If I promise that nothing like it will be allowed to happen again?'

I closed my eyes. My head ached, and I thought.

I wanted to stay. I didn't believe in Mrs Sheridan's 'anonymous crank'. Anyone who felt that strongly about her was already, surely, on her Christmas card list.

I had a feeling that I could trust Natalie Sheridan to root out my attacker.

And in case she didn't, I was prepared to do a bit of footwork myself. I wanted my own back, very badly.

I opened my eyes. 'Yes,' I said. 'I see what you mean. I want to stay, if it won't happen again.'

I hoped there wasn't chrome all over the pillows to spoil the finale. But she gave me a warm smile, and told me she thought I'd been perfectly dauntless, and that once the doctor had seen me, I was to order anything I wanted to eat or to drink, and not to think about anything else till tomorrow.

The doctor was bland, English and told me nothing except what I knew already about my own cuts and bruises. I had no concussion. A good night's sleep would cure all the rest. I waited until he was leaving to ask the question I'd forgotten to ask of my employer.

'How was I found?'

He finished packing his bag, closed it, and picked it up, smiling. 'What a shock for poor Miss Dodo. Mrs Sheridan's maid. She had just left for a walk when she saw the car. She thought you had driven straight for the gates somehow and killed yourself.'

I was slow. 'What gates?' I said.

He looked surprised. 'These gates. The gates of the villa. The car had stopped with its wheels at the wall, and you were lying in the front seat. No one could tell if you had been driving or not. The thieves must have had some good in them at least. They brought you where you could get attention. Pity about your camera, though. Tell Mrs Sheridan to get you another.'

I don't have a camera. He smiled, opening the door, and I smiled back, thanking him. The official story of the assault, put about before I'd even agreed not to report it.

How Natalie Sheridan got to be where she is.

I fell asleep. I was wakened by the click of the door and the appearance, looming over me, of Mrs Sheridan's all-American maid, a tray in her hands.

On the tray was a small cup of cocoa and an envelope, both of which she put on my bedside table. Then she stood holding the tray and just looking at me.

Her lips held apart a set of teeth like a weir. Whoever called her Dodo had a sense of humour.

At the same time, in the pecking order below stairs she was the tops. And below stairs was where I might hear some gossip.

The envelope was thick and expensive-looking, and I left it alone. The cocoa seemed worth talking about. I said, 'I don't know about you, but I could do with something stronger. Wasn't it a shock, when you found me?'

She lifted her eyebrows, which seemed to weigh a lot. 'Shock?' she said. 'I was a nurse for ten years, on Emergency. Drunks and layabouts, junkies and beaten-up deadbeats ... I've handled more meat than the Army has. If you want any liquor, Aurelio will have to go to Mrs Sheridan, and she's busy.'

In a house like this, there would be a butler. I didn't say that Mrs Sheridan had offered me anything. I just said, 'There's a bottle of Haig over there, and I'm fed up lying in bed. What about splitting it in the kitchen?'

Since she'd unpacked it, she knew it was there. And when she said, 'Well, there's no law against it,' and stood back, I smelt the whisky again on her breath as I stood up and aimed for my dressing-gown. The room went up and down quite a bit before I got it on, and I was quite glad when Dodo offered to carry the bottle.

Then I thought of the guy who had hit me, and ploughed on after her into the service wing, which proved to have a sitting-room in it for the resident staff, which consisted of cook, butler/chauffeur and Dodo. I got an armchair, a glass, a large whisky and a lot of horrified interest, but of information only a snippet.

I thought Natalie would have told them the camera story, but she had told them the truth, which meant she knew she could count on their loyalty. Later, I realized why she had had to tell them the truth, when I asked what had become of the car, and Aurelio said he had driven it back to where they had hired it from, and given the original driver a present to keep quiet about how it was pinched from him.

Aurelio was the Portuguese butler, recently acquired, and trained by brutal experience on the Algarve. He had dark brown skin and a black moustache and black hair that looked as if it wanted to run down in front of his ears, only Natalie wouldn't allow it.

I asked how the car had been pinched, and Aurelio said that the driver had been struck from behind and shoved in a Gents, and when he staggered out, the Mercedes was driving away.

It seemed to me that Mrs Sheridan must have paid quite a lot to keep that particular bruise from being reported, and I let myself wonder, for a minute, about the unopened envelope back in my bedroom. Then I asked if the driver had got a look at the guy who had bopped him, and nobody knew.

I got them to pour themselves another stiff double and steered them on to Mrs Sheridan's habits, if any.

Mrs Sheridan didn't have any habits. I'd put down Aurelio as true-blue loyal but I had hopes of Dolores the cook, born in Brazil and trained by all the consuls in Rio, to listen to her.

Dolores was hopper-active. That is, she moved like T.V. ping-pong at the fast rate, and had a squeak to go with it. I got all the scandal of Funchal and beyond, but nothing on Mrs Sheridan's love-life, even when the bottle was empty.

Dodo didn't open her mouth: just sat with her arms folded, watching us. I left after an hour, weaving my way stone-cold sober back to my bedroom.

Between my aching skull and my swollen jaw-bone, praise of Natalie Sheridan rang in my ears. *A fine lady, a kind and generous employer, Senhora.*

Please the Senhora, they said, *and always, she will show she is grateful.*

It was true. Back in my bedroom, I opened her envelope, and found she had been grateful to the tune of one thousand pounds. Which was about the right rate for the market, considering.

Dodo hadn't found the brandy I keep in my cat.

I got into bed, and drank it, and went out like a light.

The first thing that happened next morning was a phone call from Natalie, ringing I suppose through three walls, to ask how I felt. The thousand pounds, for which I thanked her, prevented me from being too truthful.

She said I was to have a pampered breakfast in bed, and she wouldn't need me till evening. I thanked her again, with the mirror this time in my hand. I had a black eye.

She rang off, and I wished I had asked her the time, and where my executive watch could have got.

Then I remembered.

Dolores hopped in with a breakfast-tray, and paused on the second bounce out to listen to what I was saying. She said that Aurelio's next trip to Funchal would be later that morning, and she was sure he wouldn't mind company. The time, it appeared, was nine o'clock. The weather, from the window, was warm but cloudy. Across the tops of a lot of palm trees and flowering bushes, as in the Glasgow Patanics, I could see the roofs of one or two other large villas.

Beyond was the sea. Grey-blue, as off Rothesay on a Glasgow Fair day.

I felt not too bad. I got into bed and dragged the breakfast-tray over my knees. My door suddenly behaved like a drum stand in the first set at Tiffany's, and I said, 'Come in,' cautiously, without moving my jaws.

The door opened, and in came King Ferdy, the photographer with the most subjects everywhere, including Madeira.

I don't know why I was so amazed to see him, except that when I spoke to him last, he was in London. I wondered if he had an interest in Mrs Sheridan's film. And of course, Madeira was the place for Sexual Strategy in Flowers, so long as creepers came into it.

This time, he was togged up in Brideshead Revved-Up; all cream flannel and open-necked silk; and his arms were full of orange flowers, which he dropped into my water jug.

I didn't see he had a camera under his beard until it was already in action, photographing me in bed with the flowers beside me. They

51

were funny flowers as well. Each had a great poking beak and a crown of bright orange spikes with a wee blue one sprouting in front of it.

By the time I saw what he was after, it was too late. I flung the teapot at him, but he was already shutting the lens cap and grinning.

'*Strelitzia parvifolia*. Birds of paradise, darling,' he said. 'Vulgar, vigorous, and their spelling is utterly ghastly. You've got tea all over Natalie's lovely carpet.'

'What a pity,' I said. 'I hope she doesn't send you a bill that's too big for you.'

My Scotch Bird of Paradise. I always thought he meant fancy birds with big tail-feathers.

'She won't mind. She thinks I'm the only photographer in the world who can make her look good on her wrong side, you unfairly gifted genetic mutation.

'Now,' said Ferdy, sitting on the side of my bed and sliding his hand as far as he could get under the covers, to show there was no ill feeling, 'now what about this nonsense yesterday? Someone tried to scare you off Natalie?'

I was glad Mrs Sheridan had told him the truth, and not the camera story. As well as being a goat, Ferdy is a guy who knows his world and can give sensible advice when he feels like it. He heard exactly what happened to me, and he listened to Natalie's reasons for not calling in the authorities.

And he agreed with Natalie.

He was quite firm, and perfectly reasonable. 'I know, darling. The call for revenge is burning in that stout little heart. But it's not going to do your career and Kim-Jim's a power of good to be labelled publicly as a pair of sex-fiends after Natalie's money, and that's what the media boys will make of it.

'I know,' repeated Ferdy earnestly, 'that you think I don't want Natalie's love-life dragged into the open because Natalie is going to lay me a lot of lovely golden eggs in the near future and, of course, you're right. But Rita ... She's going to lay you some also. And Rita, you do like eggs? Whites of, handy for hair?'

I told you. He's an idiot. I had hoped very much, as the gossip king of the western semiphore, that he would tell me what the kitchen wouldn't. Even supply a few names and addresses.

But he didn't know any. No one but Natalie, he said, knew exactly whom Natalie was laying. Apart, of course, from Kim-Jim.

I said, 'I don't want to be bumped off. I don't want Kim-Jim bumped off either.'

'My darling Rita,' said Ferdy, 'the fellow will have come to his senses and got on the first plane for Australia, I shouldn't wonder. Portuguese police don't like girls being beaten up and taxi-drivers coshed and eminent ladies' mid-life crises threatening to appear live on Cable.'

'And if he happens to know Natalie as well as we do, and is sure that she won't go to the police?' I said. It was my jaw that was hurting. 'Otherwise, why drive me all the way to Mrs Sheridan's villa, once he'd clouted me?'

'Maybe he thought you were going to flake out,' Ferdy said. 'Dodo said you looked just like –'

'– a slab of junked meat in Emergency.' I finished it for him, narkily.

Under every muscle in Ferdy's face and behind every whisker there was a laugh busting its guts to get out and shriek as he looked at me.

I took one of his Birds out of my water jug, and twisted its neck for it, but he just tut-tutted, picked it up, and put it in his top pocket like an umbrella handle.

He left, turning at the door to repeat his expectoration.

'Leave it to Natalie,' Ferdy said. 'She has what are known as Ways and Means. She loves your make-up, darling. Rely on it. She'll see no one knocks your socks off from here on.'

I didn't say anything. I didn't say that, driven to it, I could produce some ways that were quite mean myself.

I let him go. Then I got up, painted out my black eye, and went exploring.

Rich houses don't impress me. You get used to working out what's hired, hocked or might be negotiable.

Natalie Sheridan's was a medium-sized villa. There was a high white wall round it, with creeper almost covering the closed-circuit cameras, and solid electronic-locked gates, with a slight Mercedes-sized chip to one side of them.

Inside, it was all done in pink and grey suede and white marble, with flowering trees in white vats standing everywhere, and pink ruffled blinds to soften the sunlight. Kim-Jim's room was next door to mine, on the first floor.

I had a look inside, for sort of good luck, and it was just as I'd imagined it: neat and workmanlike with special places for all the things he was keen on: his record player and his world radio and his tapes.

On a chest of drawers, in the middle, was the yellow cat I'd sent him. I came out smiling.

His workroom was next to Natalie's dressing-room, and there again, the arrangements were efficient and American and streamlined.

The cupboards which lined the walls were full of packets and tubes and bottles arranged in date order and separated into their various uses: for cinema and T.V. work; for Mrs Sheridan and her friends. The make-up mirror was huge, with a special chair with a foot-rest in front of it.

There was a sink with a mixer-tap and another fitted for shampooing, and a standard hair-dryer and an infra-red stand for fuzzed hair. There was an incinerator chute. There was everything.

I had seen something like it once or twice before in a private house, but I'd never before been in charge of one. I understood, a bit, how he'd come to leave the struggle outside to serve Mrs Sheridan.

I left the room, and went downstairs to the other room, the morning-room and study where he sat, and where he did his secretarial bit.

Unlike the rest of the house, the study was not pink and grey but done up in pine panelling, with rows of books and a couple of filing cabinets. One of the two desks, heavy on onyx and leather, looked like Mrs Sheridan's.

The other stood to one side and had a tape-recorder on it, as well as a couple of telephones. Kim-Jim's desk. And now mine.

But this was also a sitting-room. In front of a real fireplace were two nice leather chairs and a good rug. And a T.V. with a video machine under it. And a cabinet full of cassettes.

Here Natalie Sheridan would sit with Kim-Jim sometimes, I guessed, if they were alone. Or here Kim-Jim would relax, watching films while Natalie entertained her private business friends, or her boyfriends.

Kim-Jim loved telly films. It was one of the things we had in common. I had brought a lot of tapes with me, most of them pirated or got for me on the side by my Byres Road pals.

Dodo hadn't found them, although she might have noticed that my pack of Modesse was a bit weighty. Dodo, whom I'd seen already when I carried the tea tray into the kitchen, was stony-faced according to custom, eyeing my drawstring pants of Old English Patchwork with the same look that she cast on my New Madeira black eye.

Dolores and Aurelio, bustling, were friendly. Aurelio would be glad, he said, to take me into town. What Mrs Sheridan's plans were they didn't exactly know, except that two men and an Honourable were coming to dinner.

After a bit they remembered the Honourable's name, which was Margaret Oliver.

A female Honourable. A female Honourable I had reason to know, because she was one of Ferdy's real bits of crumpet. A bitch called Maggie.

I was cross. I thought he was here to write a book on Sexual Strategy in Flowers, goddammit. What he'd already told me about pansies ought to have been enough to keep him going till Christmas.

After that, I came out of the service door and fell over him.

I fell across him because he was lying immediately outside the door on the furry wall-to-wall rug of Mrs Sheridan's sitting-room, requesting me to be his Sexy Flower Assistant and load his camera for him.

He had also freed Mrs Sheridan's parrot, or perhaps it was Kim-Jim's parrot, who was sitting on one of his shoulders, brooding over half a pound of unravelled cashmere and a bagel of bird-shit.

'She doesn't need you till later,' Ferdy said.

'*Screw the bitch*,' said the parrot.

I stepped over Ferdy's beautiful flannels.

'I'll pay you,' Ferdy said. 'Twenty a flower.'

'*Bugger the bastard*,' the parrot said.

I walked to the door. 'Not me,' I said.

'Who else is there?' bawled Ferdy. He got up on one elbow, and the parrot fell off.

'*Bugger the bitch*,' roared the parrot, fluttering off him.

'The Honourable Maggie. Your parrot knows her,' I said; and walked out.

The Bird of Paradise, I had noticed, still stuck out of his shirt pocket, with its neck broken.

I hoped it bit him.

As arranged, Aurelio dropped me in Funchal on his shopping trip.

Before we parted, he came with me to the house of the driver with the placard, and at my request, asked him questions in Portuguese about how his Mercedes was borrowed. By, of course, the camera thieves.

It was as well Aurelio was there, as the driver's wife wasn't keen to let me in, and kept shuffling about as if I was infecting the furniture.

In any case, we didn't learn anything new. He had been bopped on the head from behind, dragged into a toilet and his uniform pinched. End of story.

We came out, and I thanked Aurelio, and he went off with the car and his shopping-list, leaving me to explore the glories of Funchal.

It took me some time, I can tell you, to find the place where the Mercedes had parked with me in it. The town was steep, and crowded and foreign. There were a lot of striped buses, but I couldn't read where they were going. I got myself over a river and walked and walked and kept walking until I saw the view I had seen in the last of the light, when the car slowed down and stopped at the end of nowhere.

I might not have been sure even then, except for the tyre marks. And the fact that it was eleven o'clock on the dot when I got there, and something chirped from the grass.

My executive watch. You'd better believe it.

And beside it, what the telly crime man calls the marks of a struggle.

I never miss a crime series. I browsed all over the grass where the car had been, finding a few things that looked much the same in Troon and Madeira.

Plus the pin I had used to jab with. Plus a gold cufflink with a crescent engraved on it. Cannon would have been proud. I was proud.

I put it in my purse, and went off to find a taxi.

All the roads in Madeira seem to run down from the mountains. They make a big holiday thing of the sledges that once brought stuff to market. Everyone I know, just about, has sent me this postcard, showing the sledges like baskets with tourists in them, and the men who steer them in white, with straw boaters on. And here in real life they were. Big deal, Rita.

I wondered, now my fedora was bashed, if a boater would suit me.

There were a lot of flowers about, likely committing misconduct, but no taxis. In the end, I paid a boy to lead me to the nearest rank, which was at the harbour. I walked towards it, looking about me.

The Clyde is full of harbours. This one was quite big. There was a slipway with four fishing-boats on it, and a row of empty cradles for yachts, and some groups of tanned Portuguese perched on walls chatting in checked shirts and cardigans.

A wee white tunny fishing-boat was making out to the open sea through the entrance, rocking some nice yachts lying over at anchor. One of them, a tall white beauty with glittering brass, flew a British flag. I wondered what port it came from.

Outside the long harbour wall, a handsome cargo ship had arrived, big and clean as a liner, and covered with tackle. The flag at the masthead, a blue square with a yellow C on it, lifted now and then on the breeze.

It had got quite hot, and I could feel my cheeks glowing all round my sunglasses, and remembered I hadn't taken off my newly found watch, and therefore would have one brown and blue wrist and one white and blue.

As I thought about it, the digital pipsqueaked for noon, and the cathedral clock clanged.

There was a water-skiing kiosk. I didn't need to be back until evening.

I stopped with my hand on a taxi, and looked out at the sparkling water. Then I looked again, I don't know why, at the cargo ship.

The driver was saying, 'Where to?' but I didn't answer him. I said, 'That's a big ship. Does she call in here often?'

'Often. Where to?' said the driver.

I was thinking. I said, 'What is she called?'

Behind his moustache, the driver's face was getting red. He stuck his elbow out.

'Is called *Coombe Regina*. Is banana ship. You want this taxi?' said the driver.

Bananas.

'What,' I said, 'do you think I'm standing here for? You know the Funchal address of Coombe's Bananas?'

He did.

'O.K.,' I said, and got in. 'Turn round and take me two blocks beyond it.'

Cannon. Smiley. Move over.

The Madeira headquarters of the Coombe Banana Company stands among the banks, the consulates and the other good-looking buildings near Queen Amelia's Municipal Gardens in the Avenida Arriaga (I looked it up).

It is also near the highly geared-up cellars of the Madeira Wine Association, from which, it being lunchtime, warm-looking tourists were coming out in a steady flow with some of their Madeira wrapped under their arms and the rest of it no doubt already in their blood streams.

People were beginning to come out of Coombe's Bananas too, as I found when I paid off the taxi and walked back along the street on the opposite side.

57

It was a very fancy building, with double doors made of black curly iron and glass, leading into a tiled hall with plants in it. As the doors began to swing more and more, I could see that there was a reception desk and some armchairs further in, and a flight of white stairs on one side.

The bananas, I worked out, occupied the middle and top floors of the building, and the staircase was the only exit.

I worked it out because the crest of Coombe's Bananas, the yellow C, was embossed on all the upper parts of their windows, just as it appeared on their flag.

And on the cufflink of the guy I'd had this little disagreement with, in and out of the Mercedes.

The door opened and another typist came out. So far no one very important-looking had been struck by hunger. No doubt the top agents, or such as could afford good suits and cufflinks, were still taking phone calls from Southampton or Hamburg or Tenerife, or wherever banana growers and banana eaters find one another.

The door swung again, and a man in a cheap shirt and tie came out, carrying a jacket. He glanced across the street, saw me, and stared with such interest that he crashed into a woman with three children under four and another on the way.

All of them yelled at him except the one who wasn't born yet, and it taught me something. If I wanted to spy, blue and orange hair was a drawback. Telly Savalas didn't have it. I needed a headscarf.

I looked about. On either hand were touts with trays of embroidered hankies, standing firm in the way of outgoing customers of the Madeira Wine Association like battered steps in an off-season fish-ladder.

None of the hankies would cover the blue or the orange, and there were no likely shops that were near enough.

A man in a straw boater came along, this time on my side of the road. He grinned all the time he walked up to me, broke stride as he passed, and murmured something in Portuguese while pinching my patch-work. He then walked on, gazing backwards and winking. He was heading for a bicycle.

It happens all the time. He looked normal. He had a loop of rope round one shoulder, and a jersey slung over a creased white open-necked shirt. His trousers were white, and he had little boots on. He also had a big black moustache and black eyes.

He was one of the sledge-hammers who ran down the hill with the tourists. I said, 'Mind the bike!' and pointed behind him.

He grinned, showing awful teeth, but the sense got to him just a little too late. He turned to see where I was pointing, and fell over the bike.

I picked him up.

There is an art in letting a fellow know that, although you don't grudge a pinch, you don't want another one. We got it worked out, as I handed him his rope with one eye on the opposite doorway. He understood that I was Scotch, and staying in one of the villas, and would fairly enjoy coming on one of his sledge rides.

But first, that I wanted to hire his hat for an hour or two.

For a bet. For a fair sum of money. And if he wanted I'd bring it back later.

The distance between a come-hither and a friendly exchange between sexes is not so well marked in Portugal and her colonies as it is in Troon, for example, and it took a bit longer before we got everything straight. But we did in the end, and a handful of my escudos disappeared into his pocket.

Outside, the hat was plain with a brown ribbon round it. I wouldn't have minded knowing what it looked like inside, either; but he had it whipped off and fixed on my head before I could take a quick look. It had a nice concealing brim.

He was not all that pressed for time, it then seemed. His name was Eduardo. After five swings of the door and the exit of three girls and two men without cuffs, never mind cufflinks, I explained that he'd ruin the bet if he stayed, and I'd bring his hat back in no time to the sledge station. He kissed my hand in the end, and crossed the street grinning, nearly causing two old Austins to crash. I was so busy watching him, I nearly missed the Coombe door open yet again, and a tall man come out, for a change.

A tall, well-dressed man wearing a collar and tie, and grasping a briefcase.

A man with a lot of fine, dark-brown hair that kinked over his ears and at the back of his neck. Dark brown, but not black like Portuguese hair. And with it, a square face that had tanned to a shiny red-brown, making a pair of light eyes seem even lighter.

Then he turned his head, to check before crossing the road, and I saw that one side of his face was marked black and blue and red by a long, scraping graze. And that the hand holding his case had a bandage on it.

I took cover as soon as I glimpsed him, but even if I had been standing

59

full in the sun, I doubt if he'd have seen me. He was making for a sports car parked nearby under the trees. He flung his briefcase in, opened the door, and in a moment was edging out into the traffic, going away from me. I was surprised the noise in my chest hadn't stopped him.

The moment he was out of sight, I crossed the road and went into the hall of Coombe's Bananas.

Behind the desk, the girl was on her feet, just going for lunch, and not too keen to be bothered with tourists in men's hats who just needed to be told the way to their consul, but quickly.

Before she could walk to the door, I said, 'Excuse me. I have something to return to one of your company men. The one who's just driven away. Do you expect him back soon?'

She spoke English, but not well enough to do two things at once. She stopped putting things in her bag, and looked at me.

'No. He has gone to the airport. He will not be back. If it is for the company, I can take it.' She looked at a clock on the wall.

I said, 'No, it's personal, sort of. Do you have an address for him?'

If I was going to handle it, she was happy to do anything that would get rid of me. She said, 'He moves about; you will know. But I give you a card with the company offices.' She opened a drawer, and spread out a handful of pasteboard.

'And his full name,' I said. 'If you please.'

There was no reason why she couldn't give me it, and she did. A company card, with two addresses in the Caribbean, one in Liverpool and one in Rio de Janeiro.

And the name of the well-dressed man who had just driven off to the airport. Who had a grazed cheek where I had hit my assailant, and a bandaged hand where I had stabbed him.

He was well-dressed because of his position.

And he hadn't been lying when he claimed to know Natalie Sheridan.

The pasteboard I was reading told me that eventually, when I worked through the Portuguese writing.

The pasteboard which said, in full:

COOMBE INTERNATIONAL
Financial Director
Roger van Diemen

I suppose I thanked the reception girl. I remember she went out of the door ahead of me. I was still stuffing pasteboard into my bag, which was a sort of silver hoversock I was fond of, and thinking.

Of Mrs Sheridan, chiefly.

There were taxi ranks all up and down the Avenida, and I had just decided that I needed one when an estate car pulled over and a face I knew poked out of it.

Aurelio was quite cheerful. He called: 'You O.K.? The hat is wonderful.'

I'd forgotten the hat. I suppose he recognized what I was wearing. The back of the car was full of odd veg. and spillings, but no shopping. I said, 'Where are you going?'

'To the airport,' said Aurelio. People started hooting behind him, and he banged his horn a few times and bellowed a swearword before going right on talking.

He said, 'Good news: a nice cable, after you left. Mr Curtis is arriving from Lisbon. You like me to pick you up on the way back?'

'*Mr Curtis is coming back to Madeira? Now?*' I said.

'Sure,' Aurelio said. 'The plane's running late, or there would be problems to meet it. The cable just came.'

I stood there in the din, breathing. Then I hauled at the handle. 'Let me in. I'm coming with you.'

'Sure,' he said again. He wasn't worried, even when my elbow changed the gear. 'Take your time, Senhora Rita. No one comes quickly away when the Lisbon plane is late. The luggage. The crowds waiting to board.'

'To board?' I said.

'To board the same plane, to fly back to Lisbon. It turns round. When late, very quick.'

Very quick was how he was driving now, in spite of what he was saying. Weaving through the traffic in the direction the sports car had taken.

Roger van Diemen's sports car, taking to the airport Mrs Sheridan's friend Roger van Diemen, who hated Kim-Jim and wanted to kill him. And who, without a doubt, was about to board the Lisbon plane Kim-Jim was about to get off.

There was no way they couldn't meet. And there was no way that Roger van Diemen, seeing Kim-Jim arrive, was going to fly obediently out of the country and leave Natalie Sheridan and Kim-Jim together.

So a meeting between Kim-Jim and my banana nut case had to be prevented. And I knew who was going to help me.

I waited until we were on the northbound road out of Funchal. Then I spoke in a lovely clear voice to Aurelio.

'If you see a green BRM on the road ahead of you, try and pass it. It's got Mr Roger van Diemen inside, on his way to the airport.'

If I needed proof that Mrs Sheridan and her damned butler/chauffeur had been holding out on me, I got it then.

His hands went slack on the wheel, and couple of bullocks drawing a tourist cart nearly became Funchal McDonald's.

To do him justice, he didn't say, 'Who is Roger van Diemen?' or 'How do you know?' or 'What does that matter?' He only said, hollowly after a space, 'To meet Mr Curtis?'

'To take a plane out himself. I don't think he knows Mr Curtis is flying in. But of course he'll see him, unless you and I stop him.'

There was another long silence, but the car had steadied. Aurelio said, 'This morning, you did not know.'

'This morning, I was a softie from Troon. Now I know better,' I said. 'He's on mainline drugs. Why should Mrs Sheridan protect him? Because of what he could tell?'

'Mrs Sheridan?' Aurelio said. His tone said that he understood her, and I didn't. 'Nothing Mr van Diemen could say would harm Mrs Sheridan. Only, she wants to save him from himself.'

'But not the folk he attacks,' I said.

He glanced at me. He looked dead worried, and nervous with it. 'But that was terrible,' he said. 'Mrs Sheridan could hardly believe it. But what to do? To tell you would not cure the harm. Only to get Mr van Diemen out of the country.'

'So this flight away is her idea,' I said. 'Where is he going?'

He looked at the clock. 'Now, you are right, there is no flight from the airport but this one back to Lisbon. Why there, I do not know. Business, maybe. From there, of course, anywhere.'

'Barbados, St Lucia, Liverpool or Rio,' I said. 'Unless he's left his job, too?'

I could feel him give in. If I knew all that, I knew everything. He said, 'It is Mrs Sheridan to think of. You work for her too.'

'I'm not so sure,' I said. 'I don't say I don't see life in my line, but junkie lovers is something else. I got beaten up.'

'You got a thousand pounds,' said Aurelio, scowling at me.

I looked at him. He wasn't jealous. He just thought I was being unfair to Mrs Sheridan. It was clever of Mrs Sheridan to have told him what she paid me. She sure knew how to handle people. But of course, I had seen that already.

I said, 'All right. Let's save Mrs Sheridan some pain. How do we make sure Mr Roger van Diemen leaves the country?'

Buttling in the Algarve does nothing for the imagination, maybe because nothing is left to the imagination in the Algarve in the first place.

We arrived at the airport with nothing decided, and it was just as well, because between the scrum of people waiting to board the late plane and the scrum of people waiting to meet the late plane you couldn't have picked out a winkle, never mind a tall, well-dressed Dutchman with a ring-scar all down his left cheek.

The Customs and baggage bit for incoming passengers was barred off. But anyone with their health and strength and sharp elbows could get into the lounge, which was full of families, business men and tourists hugging polythene coffins with orchids in them, and neat carrier bags with Madeira in them, and large broken parcels with Whicker in them.

The chairs were orange plastic, which reminded me. I took my hat off, and fifteen people either smiled, or turned their children away.

There was no point now in hiding myself. Fright and politeness between them had got Aurelio halfway through the crowd, but no further. He knew half the people there. A scene in Portuguese would have been beyond him, never mind in English.

If anyone was going to stop van Diemen and Kim-Jim meeting, it had to be me.

Being four feet eleven is a bugger. Someone half-rose from his chair to wave at someone. As soon as his bottom was clear, I slid his seat out and then stood on it.

The jolt as he sat down again, on the floor, fairly rocked me, but I managed to stand long enough to see round the place.

I didn't much like what I saw. Through the glass windows all round the lounge there was a very good view of the control tower, and the airfield, and a TAP plane slowing down on it.

Also, there was a big outside balcony, to which welcome-parties bearing their welcomes were struggling, in order to look down at the welcomed and wave.

Among those making towards it, drink in hand, was this tall, well-dressed man with brown hair and a bruise on his suntan.

I got off the chair before I was pushed off, and fought towards him.

Four hundred Portuguese voices and several jet engines said that there was no way even my voice would carry. The Financial Director of Coombe's Bananas crossed the balcony and paused to lift up his glass. I picked up a packet of peanuts and lobbed them into it.

Tennis is one of my games. The bag drop-landed fair and square in his drink and most if it went up his nose. There was a short spell of whooping and choking, during which someone banged him helpfully on the back and a woman, passing, tut-tutted about the streams on his trousers. Then he got his eyes clear, and his mouth open to threaten ... and saw me.

Latins love drama. Behind me, the crowd had seen nothing. But as I battled the last two or three yards, the grinning crowd about van Diemen parted, and I found I had no trouble at all walking right through and staring up at him.

'Remember me, Mr van Diemen?' I said. I looked round at my audience and beyond them. The steps for the incoming TAP were in position.

When I looked back and up, I hit a violent glare. 'I certainly do not,' said Roger van Diemen. 'But you may be sure from now on that you will be remembered. You threw that object just now?'

He still held his near-empty glass in one hand, its cuff dripping, and in the other, a soaked mopping-hankie. He sounded bloody annoyed, but not frightened.

I said, 'You were lucky.' The door to the aircraft had opened.

'Lucky we didn't have flying glass everywhere, I suppose,' he said. 'There are children about, you know. I don't know what airports are coming to. Excuse me. I have to clean up.'

The tarmac began to look busy. An air hostess came out and stood to one side of the door, while another walked to the foot of the steps. A group of officials wandered out, followed by a fuel wagon and then by a luggage truck.

I stood plumb in front of the Flying Dutchman, and moved when he did. I said, 'You were lucky I didn't louse up the other cheek. What's the sentence for rape in Madeira?'

People had begun to walk down the steps from the aircraft. Now he had his back squarely to the balcony and I could watch it round one of his shoulders.

He said, 'Let me pass. I've never seen you before. What do you want? Money?'

The enjoyment round us went up a notch. Among the laughter and the exclamations, I risked another quick look behind him.

The last of a group of heads disappeared under the edge of the balcony, heading for the Arrivals area. Another bunch, in no hurry at all, were filing out and down the steps of the aircraft.

None of them was Kim-Jim.

Kim-Jim might be among the passengers that I'd missed. Or he might still have to disembark. I had to keep it up somehow.

Everyone wasn't off the plane. The air hostess still stood on the top step, smirking at someone inside, and a small man in some sort of uniform walked to the foot of the stairs with a wheelchair.

There was some chat between him and the airline man, and then they both stood, looking up at the exit door.

I had looked too long, and too hard. Roger van Diemen was looking where I was looking. At the TAP plane from Lisbon on the tarmac, with every passenger out but for one.

I had nothing left to throw. I couldn't get at his legs for a rugby tackle. If I dropped dead on the spot, Roger van Diemen was unlikely to remove his eyes from the plane, now he guessed why I'd held his attention.

Outside on the tarmac, there was an extra movement at the top of the gangway, and a steward began to come out, shaking hands with someone. And by the law of Rita's filthy luck, it was bound to be Kim-Jim who would walk out on the steps, so that Van Damned Roger would see him, and cancel his flight, and stay on in Madeira and take Kim-Jim for a ride in a Mercedes as well, but this time a permanent one.

I was rescued by Ferdy.

Ferdy of all people, who had heard Kim-Jim was coming and rushed to the airport to meet him and was told by Aurelio where I was. Who waded through the entire crowd behind me and lifted me up by my Old English Patchwork so that I dropped my straw hat and every face in the lounge turned in my direction, including Roger's.

I didn't listen to what Ferdy was saying. I was shrieking into his ear.

'Do something! That's my nutter! The van Diemen guy! Throw me at him or something! Kim-Jim's coming, and he mustn't see him!'

Ferdy grinned into my face. My toes dangled just short of his kneecaps.

'I know,' he said. 'Natalie rang him and told him to get out. And don't worry. Kim-Jim got smuggled off first. He's waiting in the VIP lounge. Roger won't see him.'

I could have killed Ferdy. For Mrs Sheridan's sake, he had held out on me. He knew who my attacker was. He had lied. He was a bastard.

He had maybe saved Kim-Jim's life.

I kissed him. I looked over his shoulder. The aircraft steps, I could see, were now empty.

Then Ferdy swung me right up, and I looked for Roger van Diemen.

He wasn't there. A sort of swirl showed where he had been standing. I said, 'The bastard has gone.'

'Shall I throw you anyway?' Ferdy asked hopefully.

He did, on to the counter, and was starting to raffle my hat when I got it off him and shoved until he agreed to take me to where Kim-Jim was waiting.

Overhead, the tannoy was apologizing for the late incoming plane and promising passengers flying to Lisbon that boarding would shortly begin.

I looked about all the way to the special room, but there was no sign of my vanished banana case. I hoped he was solidly in the Departure area, being unzipped by airport security. I wondered what had made him lose his cool all of a sudden, since the tannoy hadn't then called. Perhaps Nature had. Or perhaps ...

I said to Ferdy, 'Wait a minute. This banana guy knows you?'

'Everyone knows me,' said Ferdy. He saw my foot go back and said quickly, 'But O.K., my artist in non-toxic animal greases. He's seen me with Natalie. A big scene with me on top of a big scene with you was probably more than he could stomach. Could you stomach it, Rita? A big scene ...'

He talks like that all the time. I paid no attention, because he was certainly right. Roger the Lodger had spotted Ferdy and scarpered.

We went down some stairs. A kid came by in a sweat shirt with writing all over it that I didn't need to read, because I'd seen it before. It read:

JOIN THE ARMY
SEE EXCITING FOREIGN LANDS.
MEET EXCITING FOREIGN PEOPLE
AND KILL THEM.

The voice over the tannoy made an announcement in Portuguese and then in English. 'The TAP flight for Lisbon is now boarding. Will passenger Mr van Diemen please come to the gate?'

We were outside the VIP lounge. I stopped.

Ferdy said, 'What?'

I said, 'Listen!'

The parties who had come off Kim-Jim's plane were plodding out from the Customs Hall into the daylight, pushing or carting their luggage, and getting into taxis or cars.

A big Daimler with a guy wearing a peaked cap beside it hogged the entrance. Behind it was Natalie's estate car with Aurelio in it, waiting for Kim-Jim.

The tannoy, in Portuguese and English, asked for Mr van Diemen again.

Ferdy said, 'O.K. He got scared I'd come to spoil him. He'll wait till the last moment and make a run for it. He promised Natalie.'

I fumed, and he looked hurt. He said, 'If I hadn't shoved Kim-Jim in here, they'd've crashed into each other. Have a heart, woman.'

Overhead, Mr van Diemen was given a last chance, and lost it.

Ferdy, whitening a little, opened the door of the VIP lounge quickly and got us both in, shutting the door smartly after us.

'He'll get the next plane,' he said. 'Once he sees us all leave ...'

He broke off. Men are idiots.

'When he sees us all leave,' I said, 'he'll know Kim-Jim is here. You got him sneaked into this lounge. Now you've bloody well got to get him sneaked out. Under Mr van Damned's powdered nostrils.'

It was then that Kim-Jim's voice said, 'Rita?' behind me, and I turned round.

I'd forgotten why I was in the VIP lounge in the first place. I was so busy saving Kim-Jim that I'd forgotten Kim-Jim would be here.

I was terrified for him. I was so glad to see him.

Kim-Jim Curtis was no Adler; just pleasant-looking. He was tall, the way all my friends seem to be beanstalks, and had what was once roaring red hair, and light eyelashes, and blue, crinkly eyes with granny glasses in front of them.

He was fifty-two. And I don't know what he saw in a dwarf with punk hair and hockey legs.

Or I'm lying: I do. We shared a trade. We understood one another. And though we'd kept in touch, in close touch since the film we made, we'd never met again until now.

And it was the same, which was great.

I turned round and this guy was smiling down at me, smelling of cigarette smoke and airport biscuits and looking like an American out on vacation, as he always did, in his sharp doeskin blazer, and the fingernail specs, and this Japanese camera round his neck.

Kim-Jim always carried a camera. And usually, a miniature tape. Everything Kim-Jim did was recorded and registered, ready for use when next wanted. He was the best secretary Natalie Sheridan had ever had.

He lifted the brim of my hat, looked at my cheek, kissed it, and settled my hat back again. 'No stripes,' he said. He left his hand on my shoulder. We grinned at one another.

Ferdy said, 'I told you. She's in mourning. Listen. We've got the hell of a problem ...'

I thought we were the only VIPs in the airport's VIP room.

We weren't. Before Ferdy could get a chance to mention that the Demon Banana was still on the premises, this voice dropped in from behind him.

It said, 'Miss Geddes will solve it. Give her a dozen eggs, two bottles of vodka and a piano, and Miss Geddes will solve all your problems, and throw in a gland cocktail now and then for your endocrines. Good afternoon, Miss Geddes.'

I knew before I turned, and before I saw the bifocal glasses.

I remembered the wheelchair at the Lisbon plane.

I didn't know how, and I didn't know why. But it was, of course, the Owner.

Ferdy's pal Johnson Johnson stood by the hospitality table sportingly provided by the Madeira airport authorities.

He had a glass in one hand, and appeared to be freestanding, although there was a walking stick propped in the neighbourhood.

He was not, as last seen, wearing pyjamas, but got much the same effect with a pair of check trousers and an oatmeal sweater in a struggling cablestitch.

I had seen the pattern, done right, in the *Personality Knitting Quarterly*. I could swear to it.

The black floppy hair was the same, and the tight black eyebrows over a pair of bifocals girdered together like church toilet windows.

The bashed nose and lipless mouth were so ordinary that there would be nothing to see if you took his glasses off. Except, of course, for a lot of bad temper.

He had made a few strides, considering. His base colour had moved from Sallow nearly up to Pale Caucasian Man. The shark conversation hadn't altered.

Kim-Jim took his hand off my shoulder and said, 'You know Mr Johnson? He was on my flight from Lisbon. I was going to introduce you.'

'From *Lisbon*?' I said.

Ferdy's pal Johnson Johnson had put down his glass and was fingering bottles and watching me. 'We found ourselves sitting together. Vodka?' he said. 'Still? Or chloride?'

'Well, I'll be damned!' Ferdy said. 'If she doesn't want a vodka, I do. You didn't tell me you were coming over. What were you doing in Portugal? Wearing that pullover? I bet they've bloody deported you.'

'*Dolly*'s been here for weeks,' Johnson said. 'Had her papers to fix on the way. Sorry, Miss Geddes. Didn't have time to tell Mr Curtis I knew you. Didn't realize you were his Rita until the end of the flight. You like Madeira?'

'*Dolly*?' I said. Somewhere, I'd heard that name before.

The glasses flashed. 'Boats, unavoidably, are feminine,' Johnson said. 'You don't like Madeira?'

'It's all right,' I said. 'A bit crowded.'

Ferdy stood on my foot.

'No need to worry,' said Johnson. 'Mr Curtis didn't tell me anything I hadn't found out before. Can I give a lift to anybody?'

'My God,' said Ferdy. 'Is that your yacht in the harbour? Flying a British flag?'

'So Lenny tells me,' said Johnson.

I looked outside. The car with the uniformed driver was still waiting. I said, 'Is that your Daimler outside?'

'I hope so,' said Johnson.

The twenty-four hours I spent in apartment 17B came flooding back to me. Names came back.

'Where's Dolly?'

'Still refitting.'

'Why don't we send Lenny down to sail her out? He could take her to Tenerife and wait till you were ready ...'

And earlier than that:

'Mr Johnson! It's Natalie Sheridan. An old friend of Roger van Diemen.'

I walked up to Ferdy's pal Johnson, who was pouring vodka one-handed into four glasses, aided by Ferdy.

I said, 'Did Natalie Sheridan send for you?'

The spectacles turned round, with tonic fizzing all over them. 'Send for me?' Johnson said.

Ferdy held out a glass. 'Don't be an ass, darling,' he said. 'Natalie sent for Kim-Jim. But sending for Johnson is something even she can't manage quite, yet, poor dear. We hadn't a clue he was coming. Though we ought to have known, if we were yacht-watchers. As to a lift ...'

I saw what he meant, because I'd thought of it too. The Daimler had smoked-glass windows. You could hide Kim-Jim behind them. You could equally murder him.

I said to Johnson, 'How well do you know Roger the Gunman?'

'Roger van Diemen,' said Ferdy patiently, as if it wasn't obvious. 'He's been running about threatening to knock off both Kim-Jim and Rita. Believes they're after Natalie's money, or some such nonsense. Natalie persuaded him to get out of Madeira, but he won't go if he finds out Kim-Jim has arrived. And he's in the airport building somewhere now.'

Johnson opened his mouth. Before he actually said anything, I had thought of something else.

'He saw you!' I said to Johnson. 'That's why he didn't get on the bloody plane! Not because of Ferdy on top of me. But because ...'

'... of me on top of Ferdy on top of you?' offered Johnson, frowning.

Ferdy's face cleared. He said, 'Oh my God, that pullover's awful,' which he'd said already. Johnson, drinking, lifted his glass a little first, as though Ferdy had paid him a compliment.

Then Johnson said, 'I haven't met van Diemen in years, and of course Mr Curtis is welcome to a lift. How will he get from here to the car? Air hostess's skirt and blouse?'

Men really are idiots. I said, 'He's far too tall. Put him in a trolley with a rug over him, and take him round the far side of the car.'

The only one to object to that was Kim-Jim, who was embarrassed at all the fuss, and anyway didn't really believe, I think, that he was in any danger, which meant that the paint on my face was still holding out.

Then a porter had to be sent out for the uniformed Lenny, who brought us a rug and a trolley, and told Aurelio what was happening.

Next, just as we were loading Kim-Jim into the blind side of the Daimler, someone had to go back to fetch my straw hat, which had fallen off in the VIP lounge.

'Anyway,' Ferdy said, 'what's so damned important about that lousy hat?'

I explained.

Ferdy said, 'Well, come on. Aurelio'll drive you to the sledge station and I'll come and protect you from Eduardo. Unless I'm spoiling something?'

Johnson's man Lenny, getting on with it, packed the Owner into the passenger seat of the Daimler and skipped round the front to take the wheel. In the back, Kim-Jim was folded under the rug, sneezing at intervals.

The Owner's window slid down with a drone, and Johnson's voice said, 'Why don't we all go? Mrs Sheridan's butler can drive straight home now, and I can drop you both with Mr Curtis.'

Ferdy likes Daimlers. He has at least one of his own, but this was a newer model. He said, 'Don't you want to get in and rest?'

'It's quite restful, sitting here,' Johnson said. 'I'm not sure I'm fully up to explaining Mr Curtis and the rug, though. Why not get in?'

So Ferdy and I sent Aurelio home, and both got into Johnson's car, putting our feet on Kim-Jim as on Bessie.

The Daimler started off in frightening silence, like a stationary train when it's the next one that's moving.

I said, 'What about Bessie?'

'With the Great Old English Shepherd in the Sky,' Johnson remarked to the windscreen.

I thought he liked Bessie. I began to say so. Ferdy kicked me, but got Kim-Jim instead on the ear, which at least must have stopped him worrying over who Bessie was. I still found it hard to forgive Pal Johnson travelling all the way from Lisbon with Kim-Jim Curtis and not letting on that he knew me.

It depended, of course, on what Johnson's interest in tall, nice-looking Americans actually was. I wished I could rely on Kim-Jim to tell me. I could do with a really big edge on Pal Johnson.

Then Ferdy said, 'Stop!' and I thought he had read my thoughts and was going to kick me again.

Johnson's driver, better prepared, glanced in the mirror and then slewed the Daimler into the side and halted. Ferdy and I both stamped on Kim-Jim, who protested mildly between sneezes and got one lens out between Ferdy's ankles.

Ferdy said, 'Didn't you say you followed van Diemen in his own car? Where is it, then?'

Good thinking, as my maths teacher would say. Banana director with offices all over the world doesn't take a taxi to airports. He takes his own car, and pays someone to drive it back for him. We were just beside the airport carpark.

'Miss Geddes,' said the Owner. 'Describe Mr van Diemen's car.'

I did. When I finished, he apparently pressed a button, for Lenny the Uniform vanished.

Ferdy and I took our feet off Kim-Jim, who was having difficulty blowing his nose, and a moment later, Lenny was back, reporting to Johnson.

'The gentleman can sit up now, sir. Mr van Diemen has left the airport precincts. He returned to his car before the mechanic could drive it away. Said he had changed his mind about flying and would drive himself back to Funchal.'

Johnson said, 'Where does he stay in Funchal?'

Kim-Jim, struggling up, knew. 'There's a small apartment in the office block in the Avenida Arriaga ... Look, now it's safe, I don't need to trouble you. Why don't we just get a taxi and let you go on your ...'

'No trouble,' said Johnson. 'Anyway, there's the hat to return. We don't want to upset Miss Geddes's sledge-handlers. Or even Miss Geddes.'

Kim-Jim grinned. He had his arm round my shoulder. 'I see you do know Rita,' he said.

'Technically, no,' Johnson said. 'I have merely served my time, as it were, in the outer office of Missile Command. It appears the sledges are packing up for the night.'

The Daimler drew to a halt and Lenny got out and opened a door, through which I was sorry to see that the smoke-grey windows had been hiding a smoke-grey landscape which was getting steadily darker.

And right enough, that the wicker sledges were vanishing back to their stables, or perhaps, like Bessie, to the Great Old English Tit Wallow in the Sky.

There was no sign of Eduardo among the few guys still hanging about in boaters and boots, but I got out anyway, and so did everyone but Johnson. There was a short scene with Kim-Jim, who refused to get back into the car, being already worn and torn, so he claimed, below the minimum legal tread, and weeping mohair.

In fact, he had a point. No Demon car, we were quite sure, had followed us. And if Johnson had scared van Diemen off once, van Diemen wasn't going to appear where Johnson was, even if he wanted a sledge ride.

One of the boatered brigade said he'd give my hat to Eduardo, and would we like a free ride, which Eduardo had set up before he had to go down to his house, because his mother-in-law was having a baby.

I kid you not. And I believed it. Even the inside of his hat pulsed with Portuguese sex.

I wasn't sure whether I wanted a free ride, but Ferdy was all for it, and Kim-Jim didn't seem to mind. It would take about twenty minutes, he said.

Really, the sledges were just wicker boxes, with a bench across and a well in front to put your feet in. I had seen one set off as we arrived, down a walled path that was too bloody narrow, to my way of thinking.

A couple of guys in boaters ran behind. Their job was to steer, shoving the sledge by its high wicker sides and its back, and hauling the slowing-rope, and sometimes hopping on to a runner, one foot paddling or dragging.

The road surface was paved with oval pebbles, set cross-ways to the path, and to begin with, ran along the high wall of the Belmonte Hotel, with no doorways or crossroads to bother about. Later, it got busier.

So we got into this sliding basket. A couple of guys trundled it into position, and Ferdy and I sat down, with Kim-Jim between us. Then Ferdy said, 'Hang on. Always be nice to the Management,' and getting out, went back to the Daimler.

The two sledge-hammers stood like Twaddle-Jim and Twiddle-John, looking offended. They had cardies over their white togs, and I didn't blame them. Once the sun went down, it wasn't hot any more: more like Rothesay.

Ferdy came back, with the lamplight on his bald head and sideburns and smiling like Jaws. He said, 'Want to bet?'

I've lost money to Ferdy before. I looked at him.

Kim-Jim knew Ferdy as well. Every make-up man knows Ferdy. Kim-Jim said, 'I'm your man. If you want to bet, name it.'

'Us against Johnson and Milligan. A race to the bottom, five hundred dollars each side. Winning team takes all. Rita? You're rolling.'

I might be rolling, but I wanted to know a bit more before I let Ferdy split the risk three ways. I twisted round.

Johnson, who was risking all his money solo, unless Lenny was rolling, was already toeing the line, Lenny with him. Except that he wasn't using a sledge, but his folding wheelchair.

It gleamed in the half-dark, with his man Lenny's hands on the back, and Johnson's clasped on his lap like Mary Poppins. Fairy lights flashed on his glasses.

I weighed the odds, as Ferdy settled beside me.

Ours was the heavier vehicle, with three people in it, and two running behind it to help us.

Johnson's had his own weight and Lenny's, but had rubber wheels against runners, and would steer, of course, like a pram.

Our two guides knew the track, and their vehicle.

Johnson had just arrived. Johnson might act the Owner, but who was he? Just a scratchy rich crock and his nanny.

I said, 'Count me in,' and saw 17B's bifocals flash, as if he was going to hand me a pencil.

Then there was a lot of shouting, and someone stood on a bench, produced a big, dirty hankie, and dropped it.

Kim-Jim, Ferdy and I linked arms and braced our feet in the trough of the basket. Behind us, our handlers flung themselves into a long, racing sprint, and hurled our basket off down the slope like a slalom start.

They were supposed to come with us.

Instead, with a bursting crack, the rope which linked the two runners frayed and parted. And the handlers, staggering back, cannoned into each other and sat, as the basket containing the three of us gathered speed and launched off downhill like a rocket.

A rocket on runners, with no means of braking or steering. And embarked on a long, swooping descent to sea level.

The sledge hopped and we yelled out, in triplicate. Fading behind us, the remaining sledge-hammers yelled too, in Portuguese. Birds twittered above us in the gloaming. Lights bobbed about us: garden lights, window lights, and a thickening layer of lamps far below us, as suburb ran into suburb and then into the middle of town and then into the sea.

The slithering clack of the runners below us picked up speed. Became higher, and louder, and vibrated itself into a roar over the steep, polished cobbles. The wall beside me dropped away, and the wall beside Ferdy began, very fast, to become taller and blacker as we shot towards it.

I threw my arms round Kim-Jim's neck and flung myself to the rim of the sledge, dragging him with me. The runner under me scraped and groaned and flung off some angry red sparks before veering off with a whine to my side.

The black wall flicked over and past Ferdy's shoulder, and I heard a creaking bump and Ferdy's curse as his corner hit it. The sledge lurched, slewed, lurched, slithered and then gathered speed again, sliding this time half sideways. The cobbles flew past like the ice at Cortina, and I changed my mind about jumping out.

My teeth and kidneys knocked together and separated. My patchwork was full of clutching hands and my hands were full of Kim-Jim and Ferdy as we squashed together like the Three Muscatelles, panicking. Somewhere behind me, a hollow voice observed, 'Rita!'

God. I looked round.

God in a wheelchair, bouncing over the cobbles dragging Lenny behind it, his heels grinding into the paving. God with a stick in his hand, aiming to throw it to me.

Dog. Johnson's stick. I caught it, just as Kim-Jim beside me yelled, 'Ferdy!'

A corner was coming.

A sharp corner. A steep corner. And unless we all piled on Ferdy, we were about to climb the next house on my side.

We all leaned on Ferdy. The sledge began to slew his way, complaining. The corner began to unwind.

Halfway round, on Ferdy's side, a car was standing.

I screamed. Ferdy roared. Kim-Jim, with incredible presence of mind, snatched the stick from me and passed it to Ferdy, at the same time leaping on top of me.

The sledge, instead of making straight for the back of the car, made to crash into its side and would have done but for Ferdy, who fended it off with the stick crook.

We ground into the car, and off it again, gathering speed. We hardly noticed, because suddenly Ferdy rose up rigid like Adam going to God, while our grasping hands combed down his cashmere. Kim-Jim seized his ankles and hung on while Ferdy went on saluting and rising, and saying solemn words in an unusual voice.

Then there was a clatter and Ferdy collapsed on the wicker and slid back gasping and gulping beside us.

His stick had caught in the parked car's door handle.

What's more, the idiot had let it go. 'Unless,' he was croaking, rubbing his shoulder, 'you want a bloody runaway car behind us as well? Just say so. I can go back and fix it.'

The sledge, redirected, ran towards the entrance of the house on my right, up a step and away again. Through the half-open door you could see an old Singer sewing machine on the floor, with a lot of men sitting sewing around it.

Their legs were crossed. They couldn't get up in time to do anything.

A dog appeared and got out of it, fast. We jarred over a sewage cover, met a pot-hole, and skimmed a row of fluttering cords, guarding a ditch repair. Houses appeared on both sides below us, with doorways and people.

The road got steeper. On Ferdy's side, two fat women came out of a house and began to walk down the road, carrying shopping-baskets. They stopped to talk to a man pushing a bicycle, with a spade over his shoulder. I screamed, and they turned round slowly, still talking.

I saw the whites of their eyes as we came hurtling towards them. The women leaped for the doorway. The man had more presence of mind, or his bike wasn't paid for. He swung down his spade, and as we came towards him, bashed it hard at the wicker side nearest him.

Ferdy yelled, and the sledge swung out to the middle again. A cross-roads was coming. Beyond it, the incline became a drop, running down between street lights and lit windows and people. As the crossroads approached, a car drove sedately over, from my side to Ferdy's. A bus followed.

I wondered what God was doing, and looked behind. Much further back than before, the wheelchair flashed chromium as it passed windows. From the same light I saw Johnson still in it, with Lenny freewheeling behind. They were coming quite fast, and Johnson had a coil of rope in his lap.

The crossroads got closer.

Rope. He could fling it to us, and pull us out one by one, breaking our spines on the cobbles.

He could pass us, and cordon the road, catching the rope on the front runners and tipping us all out to fracture our skulls.

He could lassoo the rods joining basket to runners except that he hadn't the weight now to brake us. We should just pull him down after us until he skied up our backs.

He could lassoo the rods and anchor the rope to a lamp-post. The lamp-post might hold, but the basket would still tip us all out and likely kill us.

The junction was nearly on us. You could see it quite clearly, from the lights of a car about to cross our bows from my side.

We couldn't turn, the other road was too narrow. 'Yell!' said Ferdy. We yelled.

The car was an old Peugeot. It entered the crossroads just as we did. It slammed on its brakes. The bumpers raked all along my side of the basket. The man inside, I could see, was hysterical.

Then we were over the junction, and plunging down on the far side.

I looked back, once, at the Peugeot. And so saw the wheelchair, damn him, adroitly avoiding the car, turn safely as we couldn't turn. Turn into the nice, level side road and trundle off, leaving us to dive straight on and brave the chute Godless.

Twenty minutes, that ride is supposed to take. I wake up at night sometimes still, thinking of it. Just as, at work on a film, you learn what people are like under pressure, so I learned that much more about Kim-Jim and Ferdy.

That they were quick-witted, both of them. Steering by shifting their weight, they learned to make for anything that would slow the sledge without tipping us over.

A pail of water. A litter of cardboard and cabbage leaves. We made a few mistakes. We hooked the chair of a man being shaved outside a barber's shop, and we upset a lot of light empty crates that weren't empty, but had these fed-up ducks in them.

The cobbles behind us filled with complaining fat beaks like a football crowd. We had two in beside us, and a shaving-brush.

Ferdy was fit as a ballet-master. It was he who stood up and snatched two umbrellas, from where they hung upside down on an awning, with the sledge swerving beneath him. Until they blew out, they slowed us a fraction. Then he hooked a pail of cement with one handle, but that just spun us into the side, upsetting a man with a basket of cabbages. People were shouting by now, all up and down the Rua, and kids raced after us, throwing things, till we left them far behind, still running and squealing.

A *guardia* jumped in front of us at one point, blowing a whistle, and jumped quickly off in a flash of blue-grey, which was a pity, as he would have slowed us a lot.

A constant hooting behind us made me turn round. It came from a lorry.

It wasn't trying to pass. It was offering to throw us rope, out of each window.

The sledge swooped and curved. People scattered below us, dragging bikes and trolleys and babies out of the way. Beyond that were trees, and a major crossing, and the river. Beyond that, in fact, was disaster.

I turned my back on it, and knelt on the bucketing seat, and prepared to catch one of the ropes. Ferdy on his side did the same. Kim-Jim, his teeth clenched under his granny glasses, took our clothes in two powerful handfuls and grimly hung on to us.

The driver leaned out of his side of the lorry and flung the end of a huge rope to me. I caught it, and he let it uncoil itself.

On the other side of the lorry, the passenger leaned out and flung the end of a new coil to Ferdy. Ferdy caught it. The passenger, still in his peaked cap, was Lenny.

The two ropes began to unfold and Ferdy and I, balancing each other, bent to tie the free ends to the sledge stanchions.

For, while a sudden roping would have tipped us out on our heads, the lorry could match our speed, and then pull us up slowly.

It was brilliant.

I finished tying my rope at the same moment as Ferdy. At the same moment Kim-Jim swallowed and said, 'Folks. It's too late.'

And it was.

Ahead lay this big junction, swarming with vehicles. Swarming with whistle-blowing guys in white helmets and crossbelts who were having no effect at all on the traffic, which was on its way home to Mama and didn't want to know about sledges.

And if that wasn't enough, there was a lorry stalled on the junction before us.

A big lorry. The biggest I'd seen in Madeira, stationary, with its back to us, filling the whole of what I later believed to be the Rua do Bom Jesus.

'Bom Jesus!' in fact was what Ferdy said, or something very like it. There was no time for the coils of rope behind us to take the strain slowly. Even if the lorry behind us reversed, it would do nothing but send us flying into that great solid back of plate metal.

We hurtled down to the crossroads, and this huge bloody truck sitting there, blocking our path.

The truck got bigger and bigger. And longer. And higher.

The truck heaved itself up until the stars and the lights were blocked out, and we swooped screaming downhill the last yards into blackness.

Just before we arrived it got to its full height. It discharged its cargo. A curtain of green sugar cane dropped from its inside and spread, sliding and squelching on the roadway in front of us.

Screeching and smoking, the sledge hurtled down. It hit the soft, stringy mass, ran through it, ran up part of the uptilted truck, overturned in slow motion and turfed the three of us out, like a very slow catapult, into a bed of yielding green sweetness.

Sight and hearing briefly left me. I got to all fours. I heard the whole-sale intake of breath, as the Portuguese audience got over its fright and prepared its lungs for suitable comment.

I looked round, still on all fours, and saw Kim-Jim bent over, hunting his glasses, and Ferdy already upright and dancing a knees-up, his tanned head wreathed like Bom Jesus with cane leaves, and a struggling duck up his cashmere.

Out of the corner of my eye, I caught the flash, travelling uphill, of chromium.

'I have to tell you,' said Johnson, 'that you have passed the Madeira Visitor's Test.

'You will attend your Award Dinner on Friday. Crispy Duck with Dia-phragm Jelly. After which the sugar-cane owner busts your chops for you.'

He was sitting, a trace out of puff, in the wheelchair, with his hands still folded peacefully over his cardie. He added, 'Congratulations. Lenny is bringing the Daimler.'

Ferdy was crying. He leaned forward, the duck in his hands, and kissed Johnson. 'You got the rope?' he said. 'And the lorries?'

I suddenly felt pleased about ordinary things, like the Honourable Maggie.

'Don't thank me,' Johnson said. 'I'll be staying a few days at Reid's, if Miss Geddes wants to settle her phone calls. You could send the five hundred dollars there too, if you don't happen to have as much on you.'

Ferdy started crying again. Kim-Jim looked bemused through buckled glasses. I was so surprised and so cross I was speechless.

Men are what spoil the breed.

Men are bums.

That's what gives men a bad name: bums like Johnson.

He meant it, too. Before the next day was out, we all got our invites to dine with the Owner in a private room in Reid's Palace Hotel on the Friday. The words *Bring your Cheque-book*, being understood, were not actually printed.

I wasn't going to pay for my phone calls. I wasn't going to go to the dinner. I was fed up with the lot of them, for I couldn't get one of them to listen. I couldn't get one, even Kim-Jim, to believe that that runaway sledge was no accident.

Dead tourists are bad for the economy. Sledge-ropes as frayed as that had to be sabotaged. Sledge-runners as fast as that had to be doctored.

I had shoved the sugar cane off and looked at the runners myself, in the street lights, while the sledge was still upside down.

They were black with scorch-marks, but that was all you could see. If they had been sprayed, the slipperiness had worn off with the rubbing.

I wanted to go back to Monte, and find people, and ask a lot of other questions was well, but no one would let me.

Suddenly the Daimler was there, and money and names and addresses were changing hands, and the doors shut and the smoked-glass windows went up, and Ferdy and Kim-Jim stopped exclaiming at each other, and jabbering thanks and questions and whoops and howls at Johnson, and it got very quiet in the back seat as well as the front.

When we arrived at the Sheridan villa, Kim-Jim was actually asleep behind his squint glasses, and Ferdy had started to hold his spade-bashed body and grunt when he breathed, which I paid no attention to, as I had the mother and father of all headaches and my jaw hurt, and *I* wasn't grunting.

Johnson wouldn't come in to visit Natalie, and from the Good Riddance way the car doors got slammed behind us, I guessed his nurse-driver had voodoo'ed it.

Then when we got in we found the two male dinner guests and the Honourable Maggie were expected at any moment, and Natalie needed her face done.

She made all the right shocked noises over a digest of what had happened, kissed Kim-Jim warmly and sent him off to his room, and told Ferdy she was sorry about his bruises, but hadn't he better change, for this little dinner was quite important.

It came out that the little dinner was strictly for five, and that Ferdy was staying with his client Natalie, while his girlfriend, by her own choice or not, had a suite in a nearby hotel. Which was interesting.

I started to tell Mrs Sheridan while I was doing her face that her bananas friend was still on the island, but she knew that already from Aurelio.

Then I started to tell her that Kim-Jim and Ferdy and I had nearly been killed, and this guy van Diemen had done it, but she only got up, saying, 'Look, I'm busy now, Rita. I really don't think what you are saying is possible. But if it will make you feel any better, I'll check tomorrow where Mr van Diemen is. He probably got the next plane ... Is my hair done, or did you mean to smooth that bit?'

We did not discuss the fact that she had guessed all along that her bananas friend was the one who attacked me. She had paid a thousand quid not to have Roger bothered, and she didn't have my fat jaw to worry her.

Also, come to think of it, she now had Kim-Jim back. If I got scared and walked out tomorrow, she could play the reserve. I wondered when the reserve would tell her that he might not be playing.

Dinner was to be served in the formal dining-room, and Aurelio and Dolores and the non-resident help had set it all out with silver and napkins and candles. The smell of food reminded me that I hadn't had anything since my breakfast-tray.

I came to an arrangement with Aurelio. Then, on my way up to Kim-Jim and Ferdy, I paused to see the three guests arriving.

The two men came first, and together. From Ferdy, I knew that the silvery American with the rimless glasses and the matching hankie and tie must be Mrs Sheridan's American lawyer. His first name was Harvey. His second name, which I have to copy out, was Kazimierz.

The second man might have been harder to place. Short, and inclined to be tubby, with a European face but a Pacific tan. Hand-made shoes, bespoke shirt and dark glasses, even at night. And, if I wasn't mistaken, a hair-piece.

Fred Gluttenmacher, wealthy business man, who might, if well handled, put up the money for this film Natalie was hoping to get into. And Ferdy, he said, was hoping like mad to get into with her.

And finally, the Hon. Maggie. Nineteen, rich and high-handed, which was maybe why Mrs Sheridan enjoyed handling her. It showed that Natalie Sheridan wasn't afraid of young competition. It put Ferdy in his place by throwing a bone to him. It would light up the eyes of Fred Glitterbocker. And it drew the attention of the Hon. Maggie's important friends to the schemes and plans of Natalie Sheridan.

Maggie was quick on the draw, but hadn't the Sheridan brainpower or experience. The most important thing about Maggie is that she comes from a long line of debs who never got into trouble under anything less than a Duke.

Maggie had a feather boa, and a black Vidal cut and long, long legs leading to a velvet ra-ra and a coin-dotted transparent blouse, with the coins cleverly placed not to hide anything. She was small. She was slim. Her face, which I'd made up a few times, was O.K., with a cheeky, tipped nose. Her figure was smashing.

Maggie liked meeting people in trade. She would wait until someone got familiar, and then shoot him dead with light remarks about Sandringham. I saw her start work on the toupéed Fred Glitterbloggs, and Mrs Sheridan smile and tap her foot, waiting for Ferdy.

As I mentioned, I rather like Ferdy. I went along to his room.

Ferdy had had four straight whiskies since he got in from the sledge-run, and was mellow.

With Kim-Jim's help, I got him into his Pancaldi shirt, while Kim-Jim found a waistcoat and took his ducked ducks off. When we sent him downstairs, he had partly recovered. And anyway double vision, I thought, would do him nothing but good when he saw Maggie.

Once they were all in the dining-room, I found the trays Aurelio had promised me, and took them into the study, which was also Kim-Jim's sitting- and dining-room.

The fire had been lit, and Kim-Jim was sitting in one of the easy chairs waiting for me, with the green parrot grasping his shoulder and sort of combing his hair in a homey way. The parrot said, '*I guess there's just you and me left*,' and let off a lot of gunfire, still combing Kim-Jim's thatch lovingly.

I put the food down and said, 'Is he yours? I thought he came with the furniture.'

And Kim-Jim took off his buckled glasses and laughed, and said, 'Lee and Amy Faflick. You know? If you do, you'll know who to blame for the language. His name's Cone.'

'*My name is Bond ... James Bond,*' the parrot said.

'Do you teach it?' I said.

The parrot rubbed its face against Kim-Jim's. It knew him. He was fond of it. I supposed, when he left, he would take it. I lifted up the jug of wine Aurelio had given us, and poured some for us both, and put it down. The fire shone red through it, and through Kim-Jim's glass as he lifted it and saluted me.

'It learns,' he said. 'Don't tell me your secrets with Cone in the room. Do you think you'll like it here?'

He really wanted to know. But for him I wouldn't be here. It wasn't his fault that some freaked-out guy was fouling it up.

I said, 'Of course I like it. It's great. Your equipment is magic. There's nowhere I'd rather be, once we get rid of this bananas guy. You know, today wasn't an accident.'

He didn't want to talk about today. I suppose, like me, he was shaken, and he had bags under his eyes that you didn't see when the glasses were on.

Twenty years from now I'd have bags, but I could paint them out. Kim-Jim didn't use make-up. It was one of the things I liked about him. Just as I didn't really mind specs, unless they had twirps like Johnson behind them.

Kim-Jim said, 'I know you're worried. I wouldn't have come back if you weren't. But let me thrash it all out with Natalie. She's got a lot of clout, that particular lady. If anyone is really bothering you, she'll get rid of them.'

'It's you he's after,' I said. 'You shouldn't have come back. Why did Mrs Sheridan ring you?'

He had pushed the food away, but kept the wine. He had clean, work-man's hands, well-kept like the rest of him. I could imagine, whatever the job, he was never unshaven; never without every last item of his kit, all ticked and recorded.

He said, 'Of course she was right to ring me. She wanted to warn me. She wanted to tell me about you. She knew I knew about Roger. He's been treated for this addiction. In between times, he can be quite all right. She doesn't want to get him into trouble. Just to get him to go quietly away and get himself looked after till he's better.'

He continued, 'I see it like this. I brought you here. You're my responsibility. I'm sure there's no danger now, but I wouldn't be happy if you were here and I wasn't. And anyway, I have things to arrange.

Natalie doesn't mind. She thinks I've broken vacation to reassure you, and while I'm here, I might as well show you the ropes ...'

He grinned. 'I'll do that, of course. You don't need much showing. But if, in a while, you're quite sure you would like it, and she has got used to you too — why, then I could even wrap it up while I'm here. I could tell her I'm going.'

I said, 'She won't understand. She won't understand anyone wanting to leave her. If you tell her you're not coming back, you'll also have to tell her why.'

'I know. She's proud,' he said. 'I'll be careful, don't worry.'

He spoke of Natalie, as he always did, with a sort of old-fashioned respect, like a village chemist talking about a good customer. He spoke about everyone like that. I never heard him gossip, even about his own people.

From things he had let fall, I fancied he didn't see his work in the same way as his father and brother. Perhaps even he didn't have much in common with them, or his sister, or you would imagine he would never have left California.

I once thought it was because the family name was too famous, and he didn't feel up to it. Later, it seemed to me that he was just as good in his own way as they were, and that he had parted company with them for other reasons; but he never said what they were.

There were photographs of them all in his bedroom, beside my yellow cat. Great old Joseph, now in his eighties, scowling at the camera as if there was a director behind it. Clive, whose name every early science fiction buff seems to remember; who could turn an actor into a Chinaman or a werewolf with what the studios thought was pure magic.

Clive was Kim-Jim's elder brother, and as tall as Kim-Jim, but black-haired with a moustache that was red. Clive was wifeless at present, so the magazines said, although the picture upstairs showed him half-stripped beside a great swimming pool, with a gorgeous girl with blonde hair leaning over him.

And since he was in his mid-fifties at least, the chances were, I thought, that his hair, his moustache and his chest were all cleverly tinted. Like his sister Sharon, who at thirty-seven made a feature of early greying, with platinum streaks in her dark, well-cut hair.

Well-cut since she could surely afford it, with her T.V. make-up and her teaching, and her wealthy ex-husband, Paddy Proost.

Nothing wrong with Kim-Jim's family by themselves, maybe: but together, too much for Kim-Jim, who was quiet, and liked to deal with one person at a time.

As now, sitting by the fire talking about his work and mine. About tricky jobs we had handled, and techniques we had seen and admired.

About the sort of work I should be doing with Mrs Sheridan, and the kind of jobs I could hope to take when she was away. For Natalie had a private life, according to Kim-Jim, and liked to fix her engagements so that she could disappear – sometimes for only a week, sometimes for a month. And then I should be free, to take what work I wanted until she came back again.

Free to experiment, said Kim-Jim, in the make-up room here, or in her other houses. He had ideas for me: writers I ought to meet; directors who ought to see my work. When he bought his house in the sun, he would arrange it all. He would make me tapes of their names, and arrange meetings for me.

He had talked of his house in the sun before, but I had never asked him about it, in the tapes we exchanged, or our telephone calls. Where the house would be, and what it would be like, did not depend on him, but on his eye doctors.

Make-up is one thing you can't do with failing eyesight. You can, perhaps, read large-print books. You can see something at least on the telly. There's nothing to stop you from listening: to people, to music.

There is a lot you can do, with your friends, in the sun. But make up Natalie Sheridan isn't one of them.

I didn't want to ask him what the eye doctors in Lisbon had said. Maybe they hadn't said anything. He had to go back: he was still under treatment. But one day, as he had said, he would have to tell her that in so many months, his sight would be too poor for work. And that – if I was willing to stay – she should keep me.

And, other things being equal, I thought I would stay. I wasn't Kim-Jim. If I didn't like someone, I showed it. I admired Natalie, as he called her, as a professional, and I can always keep a professional relationship.

A personal one is another matter. Kim-Jim was worth two of Natalie. He should have acted like it. I certainly should.

Late in the evening, I remembered the video cassettes I had brought, and fetched them down from my room.

I didn't know Maggie had seen me until the first cassette was loaded and running, and Kim-Jim and I had settled down, in the firelight, to watch it.

Then the study door opened, and stayed open, and that high English voice sang out (but not to us), 'Darlings! Do come! The help are watching blue films on the video.'

I'd several times made her up for a ball. From Ferdy, she would know perfectly well why I was there. She also knew, I was dead sure, who Kim-Jim was, which turned that yelp into a dig against Natalie.

She wasn't worried about Natalie, or anybody. She leaned on the doorpost, with her eyes flickering with light from the telly, and was joined almost at once by the man Gluttenmacher, who laid a hand on some well-chosen coins. At a slower pace, Natalie's lawyer came also.

Then Natalie arrived, took a look and said, 'It's a free world. Kim-Jim loves horror films, don't you, darling?'

She turned. 'Where shall we have coffee? On the terrace?'

Kim-Jim had jumped to his feet with American politeness, but I wasn't going to have my viewing loused up. I went on watching.

Gluttenmacher took off his dark glasses. He said, 'What an extra-ordinary film!'

A royal command, under the circumstances.

Natalie pushed the door further open. Her voice was husky and smooth. 'Would you like to see it? Then we'll all have coffee here. Kim-Jim, Rita ... You don't mind, do you? Is it near the start? Could we just wind it back?'

Hell.

Kim-Jim said, 'Of course. Come in,' and knelt forward to switch off and rewind. The two men and Maggie came into the room, followed by Aurelio, who began pushing about chairs. Natalie's voice, in the distance, could be heard giving orders to a number of people including Ferdy, who seemed to have dozed off somewhere not very convenient.

Natalie came back in, followed by trayfuls of coffee and brandy meant for the four easy chairs now with the best view of the telly.

Kim-Jim and I sat on our desk chairs behind. The parrot, which had fallen asleep on its perch, woke and did a quick fail-safe check on its transport, stretch-pointing each wing with a creak, like pulling down eyelids.

It lifted its feet once or twice, ducked its neck, ruffled its feathers, and in a cloud of dandruff made a short, clear statement in Portuguese.

Aurelio spilled the coffee.

Kim-Jim jumped up, got a handful of tissues, mopped up the damage and tried to take out the parrot, which bit his finger and, fluttering sideways, began to walk up the curtain, looking at us. The door shut

87

behind Aurelio, and Maggie burst into Swiss-finished laughter. 'What did it say?'

'Roughly, "What's she got that I haven't got?"' said Natalie calmly. 'Aurelio, as you might gather, is much sought after. Shall we look at the film?'

We switched the lights out, and Kim-Jim pressed the button and sent my cassette for the second time on its way.

It wasn't a blue film, but it was badly made, and so had never been released. One or two of the players were pretty well known, and bits of their performances were worth looking at. And the horror sequences too had one or two things in them that were novel enough to have an effect on your stomach.

It was the kind of film I watched a lot of, and Kim-Jim did as well, while other people were looking at clean healthy things like football and racing.

Quite early on, it got home to Ferdy's girlfriend. The Hon. Maggie said, 'Oh my God, I shall vomit. My dear darling Natalie, what are your little brood thinking of? It's an *orgy* of nastiness.'

Kim-Jim and I said nothing, nor did the two men. Even Gluttenmacher seemed to have forgotten Maggie's top half. Natalie said, 'Ferdy's outside.'

'I couldn't *move*,' Maggie said. 'My insides aren't that colour. I deny it absolutely.'

'Christ!' said one of the men.

The story unfolded. There was a lot of interesting detail. If only Kim-Jim and I had been alone, it would have been great.

In fact, after a while, it wasn't too bad, because it really did seem to turn Maggie's stomach and she stopped saying anything, until Natalie noticed her swallowing and took her out to the powder-room.

The film came to an end, with the credits.

Kim-Jim put the light on.

Fred Gluttenmacher wiped his face, found and drank off his brandy, put on his dark glasses and then turned round. 'Natalie called you Rita,' he said. 'Rita Geddes?'

Film buffs not only watch unusual films, they watch the credits. Such as, Special Effects, Rita Geddes.

'I did it three years ago,' I said. 'Rotten film.'

'Of course,' he said. The lawyer had turned round as well.

Fred Moneybags added, 'You did the Hadley comedy series make-up. Didn't you? The impersonation sketches?'

'She still does it,' said Kim-Jim. 'You don't hear of her as you should, because up to now she wouldn't work overseas.'

They both looked at me.

'Why?' said the lawyer. He had a soft voice that went with the silvery hair and rimless glasses.

'You get mugged,' I said.

They laughed. 'And you come from Glasgow?'

'Troon,' I said. 'Next to Kilmarnock.'

It was a man from Kilmarnock who founded Reid's Palace Hotel, Funchal, Madeira, but they didn't seem to know that. They were dead ignorant.

But quite decent to talk to. We chatted to them, Kim-Jim and I, for quite a long time, until wherever she was, Natalie realized that the film must be over, and came in with Maggie.

The Hon. appeared quite restored. The Vidal hair shone like boot polish and she was carrying a shoe in each hand. She was also followed by Ferdy, definitely wakened, and bearing nightcaps.

'The Honourable Maggie!' said Ferdy, doing the courtly, as he handed his girlfriend her chaser.

'*And bugger the bitch*,' said the parrot.

In Ferdy's voice. You couldn't fault it.

Next morning, I sized up Ferdy's hangover and offered to be his Sexy Flower Assistant, provided he brought his Portuguese dictionary and helped me, as the crime series say, with a few inquiries.

I didn't trust anyone else not to suck up to Natalie and cover up Roger the Damned Van's tracks for him.

Ferdy had sucked up to Natalie too, at the beginning. He hadn't told me Natalie knew my attacker. But since then, he had joined the bleeding band of the attacked. He had a grudge to pay off.

He had also had, it seemed, a flaming row with the Honourable Maggie after he drove her back to her suite at the Sheraton.

In my opinion, the flaming row was probably caused by disappointment as much as by the parrot's slip of the tongue. I don't know how he drove there and back, never mind being expected to manage his buttons.

As a result, Ferdy and I had a sort of silent breakfast, helping ourselves in the morning-room.

I was silent because I was thinking. Natalie had already phoned me, through three walls, and I had reported to her in the study.

The study looked normal again, with the chairs in their usual places and the video covered. The cans on the parrot-perch had been refilled but Cone itself had been whipped out, I noticed.

At first, I thought Ferdy had broken its neck and stuck it in his breast pocket. I came across it later on in a big fancy cage on the terrace, copying the noise-patterns of the pool-pump, and the sound of Dolores being nice to the goldfish, and the sound of Aurelio being nice to Dolores. Cone couldn't tell them apart any more than the rest of us.

Natalie sat behind the big desk, shining, fresh and expensive in candy-striped linen, ticking things off on a pad as she told me about them.

There was an American magazine arriving that afternoon. Interview in the house; photographs in the house and the garden. She required me at one sharp for make-up. After that, I was free until five. Tick.

At six she was going to a drinks party. At eight, she and Mr Braithwaite and her lawyer were to dine at the Sheraton with her guest of last night. Fresh make-up, of course, and an evening coiffure. Had I got it? Excellent. Tick.

She would also like to say, while she remembered, that Mr Curtis had always been discreet when watching adult films, and she would prefer me to do this, if I must, when staff and visitors would not be involved. Tick and double tick.

I agreed. She was entitled. And her voice was still five pegs down, with no edge to it.

In fact, when she spoke again, it was almost social. She said, 'Which leads me to two further points. Mr Gluttenmacher was interested, it seems, in what he saw. He has asked me about you, and about Mr Curtis. Following that I had a talk late last night with Mr Curtis in which he told me what perhaps you already know. That his health may force him to give up his job with me permanently.'

She had her dark glasses on, with her eyes fixed on me from behind them. I didn't know Kim-Jim had had to tell her so soon. I did know the answer we'd agreed on.

I said, 'No, I didn't know. I thought he was just on vacation. What's wrong, then?'

She went on looking at me while she made up her mind. Then she hauled in a back-straightening breath, balanced it, and used it like celery.

'I think I should leave him to tell you himself. The point is, he believes you capable of taking over.'

'I don't know,' I said. 'It's make-up I'm keen on. Not desk-work.'

'I can hire help for desk-work,' said Mrs Sheridan. She took off her glasses and fixed me again with her showy blue eyes. 'That is the other point. I have always done a certain amount of film-making. You may know. Documentaries, of course.'

I did. I gazed at her. It didn't put her off.

She said, 'I shall be doing more. I shall need help. It will involve travel. And immediately, I have a large scheme in prospect. A four-part television serial on the life of the Empress Josephine. I shall write and present it. Some, but not all, of the scenes will use actors. Mr Braithwaite will be responsible for the art direction, and he and I will travel together, very soon, to look at possible sites, and take photographs.'

She paused, but I knew what was coming. I said, 'Who'll direct and co-produce? Is it fixed yet?'

It was, provisionally. And the two names she mentioned were good ones.

She said, 'I have asked you to think about a long-term arrangement, Rita, because Mr Gluttenmacher thinks, and so of course do I, that your work would be an asset to such a series.

'It would mean that, once filming starts, you would split your time between that and my personal service. Since Mr Gluttenmacher would be taking the financial risk, I have told him I should be agreeable. I am offering you therefore a permanent job, with the prospect of some very lucrative film work.'

Had he twisted her arm? Had she really wanted me? I couldn't tell. I wanted to say yes, fast, and get her to sign something. Instead I said, 'The film sounds great. But Mr Curtis should do it.'

She gave no sign of recognizing nobility when she saw it.

'Naturally,' she said, 'I have asked him. His health, he says, makes it impossible. You are interested, then?'

Chief make-up artist even on a prestigious documentary series was no peak in anyone's career. My name would come a foot and a half after the actors' credits, and wouldn't appear in the papers at all. But it would get me known in the trade outside Britain. If I wanted to work outside Britain. And some real plums might come my way next time.

On top of that, I should be working with Ferdy, who was good news, even when hung over. And who might tell me what the film was about.

I knew one thing about the Empress Josephine. She married Napoleon, and blew it. To people like me, Napoleon's career might be a blank.

But his one-liner 'Not tonight, Josephine' is the sort of thing that stays in your software for ever.

I didn't know where Napoleon lived, but it wasn't Madeira. I said to Mrs Sheridan, 'I'd have to go away with you? Now?'

I must have sounded unwilling. She used her smile. 'Not quite as quickly as that. We leave in two or three weeks. I want to start work where Josephine started. I want to look at Martinique.'

'Oh,' I said.

Her eyelids shut slowly, stretching like Cone, but she was still smiling when she opened them. From a shelf at her side she lifted an atlas like Atlas, heaved it open, and turned it round to show me.

'Martinique. That island there, in the West Indies. That's where Josephine lived.'

'Across the Atlantic,' I said.

She was following my thoughts. She was good at it.

'A long way from Scotland,' she agreed. 'Beautiful, though. A lot warmer then here. Flowers. Coconut palms. Excellent beaches. And a chance I think you're ready for, if you're not afraid to take it. And worth, Rita, a very good fee.'

She told me the fee. It was great. Again, I nearly said yes, but I didn't. I said I'd like to, but I had to think about it. I had a mother in hospital. I didn't know if I could get out of other things. I told a lot of lies, and she accepted them, and said that she quite understood.

She didn't really.

It was true about Robina, but I was thinking of other things too. About the nutter. About Kim-Jim in the months ahead when even a voice at the end of a phone might be nice for him. I didn't want to leave Madeira just yet.

But she had made it pretty plain. No film, no job with her. You don't offend the Fred Gluttenmachers.

I said it sounded great, and I should give her my answer as soon as I could, and I thanked her for her really nice offer.

She wasn't worried. She assumed I was mostly working to screw up my salary. She said, 'That's fine then,' and threw me a smile. She had already made her tick on the notepad.

I was at the door before she added something.

'Oh, by the way. I phoned the airport this morning. Our friend Mr Roger van Diemen has flown out. On the 7.15 for Frankfurt via Lisbon. I hope you're as pleased about that as I am.'

I was pretty pleased.

I was pretty pleased about everything, but it wasn't going to stop me. It wasn't going to stop me nosing about until, somehow, I got my own back on the absent Van Damn, and made sure that Kim-Jim was safe from him.

Safe from him, and from any bastards who worked for him.

I spent the morning nosing with Ferdy. It put me off flowers for life.

We borrowed Aurelio's station-wagon, and filled it with Ferdy's camera case and satchels and the text of Dr Carl Thomassen, the botanist, sexy or otherwise, who was writing the book Ferdy was illustrating.

We also put in a pair of steps and some bluetack and drawing-pins and a lot of green cord, for photographing flowers growing naturally in the wild but not in the right attitudes.

Then we added some gardening gloves, a lot of polythene bags and some wet cotton wool in big baskets, plus two sharp pairs of tacky-sewers for cutting wild flowers and photographing them growing wild in Natalie's workroom.

I asked Ferdy, during this, what he thought of Natalie's offer and he said, Grab it. Natalie Sheridan was not, I would notice, Mrs Tiggy-winkle, but she was a clever, professional lady used to getting the best as well as giving it. Anyone who worked with her was bound to be noticed.

About Kim-Jim, he was helluva sorry, but there were compensations. I could help him, Ferdy, load his cameras. And at last he would get all the dirt about Natalie, without having to extract it by water cannon.

I promised to tell him, if I took the job, the minute she took up with Andy Warhol. I was glad to see his hangover go. I felt quite a lot better myself. Ferdy did that to you.

We drove to the Rua das Dificuldades, what else, at the bottom of the Carro do Monte, or sledge-run, and found out that the sledges, when empty, were stacked in the Rua do Comboio with their ropes out.

Anyone could have produced an old, doctored sledge. Anyone could have put a grotty rope in, instead of a good one.

No joy from that.

On the way we stopped and photographed a Fetish Tree, which was bare. Dangling from it were a lot of unhealthy green globes like grenades. I supposed Ferdy was clearing the text with the Vatican.

We also nabbed a high-angle shot of a mimosa tree at the bridge by the dockyard. I let the steps rock, and got bawled out. I was looking at Pal Johnson's yacht, and wishing I'd taken up portrait-painting.

We drove up to the top of the sledge-run, watched in fear and trembling by all the Hammers, who thought we'd come back to sue them.

It turned out that the two guys who'd pushed off our sledge were on their way in a taxi to Ferdy, Kim-Jim and me with bunches of flowers and written apologies from everybody from the Delagacao do Turismo da Madeira downwards.

They were also briefed to point out that it wasn't their rope, and the sledge had been tampered with. And that their normal Sledge-Hammering safety record went back unbeaten to before the invention of wood.

Actually, I believed them, and after a bit, I could see Ferdy did too.

'O.K.,' I said, 'but what about Eduardo?'

Eduardo was at home, they all said. How could I think Eduardo was responsible, when Eduardo had been away, because of his mother-in-law's baby?

Which had arrived, I was interested to hear. A boy, nine pounds in weight and made by nature, Senhora, for a career on the Carro do Monte.

A bouncing boy, it would seem.

I thought I would like to visit Eduardo.

Eduardo lived at Camara de Lobos, a village built on its ear on the coast. We photographed a thing covered with sort of scarlet bananas, called a Coral Tree, and a thing with red drooping leaves called a Custard Apple Tree, and a thing like a green pin-cushion called a Dragon Tree.

At Camara, we got directions to Eduardo's house from a guy selling turtles at the fish market. The turtles were all rocking about on their backs with their wee mouths tight shut and their flippers out.

My wee mouth wasn't shut. Ferdy got me away, and we ran for it.

The sun was getting hot. The sea in the harbour was blue, and there were a lot of palm trees with shadows like mine. We jogged up a steep cobbled path and found Eduardo's wife sweeping the steps of a shabby, red-roofed white house, with five assorted kids and some cats playing round her.

From the size of her apron, Eduardo's mother-in-law's baby was nearly an uncle. I don't know how that man ever got time to sledge anywhere.

She didn't have any English, so we got out the dictionary. It ended up as a sort of committee job including the neighbours.

We needn't have bothered. Eduardo had never mentioned his hat. She didn't know anything about an accident at the sledges. Eduardo wasn't here anyway, but at his mother-in-law's on the San Vicente road. Drive west, and turn up to the right.

She gave us the address when we asked for it, once she understood the accident wasn't Eduardo's fault. She also took the money Ferdy gave her, for the children.

We said our *obrigados* and got down to where we had parked the wagon, which was full of pale blue clusters of Plumbago, which I thought was a pain in the back, and red Mexican creeper, and those seamless white lilies you see at weddings and funeral parlours; all covered with pages of the *Diario* to keep off the sun, which was going to bleach the chrome out of my hair if it got any hotter.

I had to get back soon. We looked at the time, and decided to try for Eduardo.

We drove along the coast past the bougainvillaea and the palm trees and the little houses with pots of orchids on the steps, and cacti, and zulus, and patches of pink and white flowering fruit trees, and, growing wild, clumps of red-hot pokers like Robina my mother grows. Grew.

We turned up the San Vicente road as directed, and it was snowing.

Ferdy, who spends all long car journeys singing opera in the original tongue, finished a very low part from Prince Eager, and started swearing instead as the wagon began skidding and squelching through cuttings as steep as the sledge ride, with snowy pine forests on top of them.

Around us suddenly were these Disney-type mountain peaks, with lower hills all ridged with terraces, as if someone had taken a palette knife round them. Joining them were ladders of little green steps, cut into the slope, with grey reed cabins dotted about, with their thatches bound neatly with willow.

Perched on the ridges were square buildings with black boilers beside them, sending up white steam beside faggots of cut cane.

Low down, there were plantings of cabbages, and bananas with potatoes between them, and thickets of lilies, their big fleshy leaves mixed with mummified Rangers.

The slush slid off into deep roadside gutters of rushing white water. The road got higher, and small peaks in valleys began moving past big peaks in the distance, with snow on them, and waterfalls like bits of frayed cotton.

The snow turned to rain and you saw there were farms about, and people working. Someone forking seaweed on to a patch. A lot of people moving about in a vineyard, with their black umbrellas hanging open upside down on the boughs.

Which reminded me why we were here.

I said, 'We ought to be near Eduardo's house.'

There was quite a lot of traffic. Lorries loaded with cane and bananas and workmen in round hats with earflaps and pom-poms came downhill towards us, driving round tumbled boulders, or it might be a wet black sheep with long legs like a goat. In the hiccough when Ferdy changed gear, you could hear a lot of birds singing, as well as the clang of sheep bells all over, and, of course, the sound of water pouring downhill like a dam busting.

I thought it was the hell of a place to have a nine-pound baby.

Eduardo's mother-in-law's house was nearly on the road, with a lot of kids walking up to it, pulling a sledge piled with green stuff, and no doubt starting their sledge training early. They all carried knives shaped like the Coombe's banana symbol.

The house was two storeys high, with an outside stair, and its grey thatch had weathered like tidemarks. The roof corners were pegged with clay pigeons.

We got out, and found the rain easing off, and the puddles deep, and yellow as poster-paint. The door was opened by an old soul with her head in a shawl, and wellies showing beneath her black petties.

I had an idea she was Eduardo's wife's grandmother, and was probably about Ferdy's age. Such things don't seem to strike Ferdy. She didn't like the look of my hair.

A lot of escudos improved matters, but she still wouldn't let us come in. She had no English at all, and none of her words were in the dictionary, being made, it seemed, entirely of bullets.

Ferdy, who wánted to get back to a Judas Tree, was all for chucking it in. We were saved this time by one of the children, wearing a dress over flared trousers, who stood embracing her cutlass and told us that Cousin Eduardo was at Monte, with the sledges.

Ferdy, who earns a fortune snapping the young of the wealthy, dropped to his hunkers, admired her dress, her trousers, her earrings, her hair and her chopper, and told her we'd been there and he wasn't.

She said that in that case, who knew?

In the end, Ferdy gave her a coin from his pocket and then, under mob attack, flung what he had to the other kids. Finally he drew out a large, healthy piece of paper money, and announced that he wished to lay something, in person, in the cot of the new little one.

It didn't get us into the house. They brought the newest little one out, all of eleven hours old, with a white felted cap pulled down as far as the snib of its freezing red nose.

It didn't pinch me, but it did look like Eduardo. I had even started to say so, when Ferdy put his arm round my shoulders, and nearly twisted me silly, which was just as well, when I worked it out later.

From the back yard rose a thick column of steam, and the noise of regular bubbling. I had planned to walk round the house, and even look into a window or two, but three men had come out, and a couple of younger women and a few more children and a dog, and it was like looking at a meeting of the God-fathers' Union, Members Only night.

We turned, shivering in our gear for Madeira the Floating Garden: the Island of Gentle Summers, and made our way back to the wagon, where the Floating Flowers were dying of winter.

We raced back down to the coast, to be in time for Natalie's make-up.

It was sizzling hot. All the hotel swimming pools were full of brown people. The palm trees shone like green varnished feathers, and all the flowers writhed about waiting for Ferdy in masses of pink and orange and yellow and purple.

No one had told us that there could be a forty-degree difference between the mountains and the coast in the spring-time. Eduardo's wife's parents needed their heads examined.

We got back in time, although there were moments when I thought Ferdy's flowers had a better chance of making it than we had. We howled down to the sea with Ferdy's bracelets jangling and his sideburns lifting like gullwings.

Among the cars that we passed was this little sports job, with open windows and water-skis strapped on the roof.

I wouldn't have noticed, if the sun hadn't lit up the driver. A tall, tanned young man with a mop of frizzed yellow hair.

A man I'd seen before.

Wearing black. Running down the fire escape of 17B. Sneaking into and out of Owner Johnson's posh bedroom.

I screamed for Ferdy to stop, and he wouldn't. He said he wasn't going to stop, even if I'd seen Eduardo. I began to say it wasn't Eduardo, and then thought what the hell.

I didn't need Ferdy. If this yellow-haired thug was on Madeira, I'd find him. If, on second thoughts, I even wanted him.

You might say I had enough on my plate over Kim-Jim, without taking up the Owner's private life as a hobby.

Really, I was only interested in Johnson's problems as a way of getting even with Johnson.

My aunty in Troon was dead right. I wasn't a very nice girl.

All the same, I decided, as I stepped trembling out of the wagon and helped Ferdy collect his wilting sex-fiends.

All the same, I thought. When I'd had lunch and fixed Natalie for her interview, I might see if she'd loan me some water-skis.

There were plenty of water-skis on offer, and flippers and everything. Kim-Jim told me to help myself and he'd square it with Natalie, whom I'd just tidied into her fourth and last outfit and who was being photographed by the pool, with Dodo on call just out of camera range.

Everyone else, refugees from the Magazine team, was indoors. Kim-Jim and the parrot were watching telly in such a haze of contentment that I just told him that the Great Sledge Disaster was still a mystery.

Now Roger the Demon had flown out, you could see he wasn't bothered. I was only glad he didn't seem to want to go back to Lisbon at once.

The parrot never looked round from the telly, no doubt because it was learning the sound track. Bits it already knew. *'Another fine mess you've got us into, Olly!'* it was bleating, as I shut the door.

Sunflower seeds and old films. I thought what a nice life it had.

Ferdy I left where he was, tarting up ageing flowers in Natalie's workroom and photographing them. We had had a row because I wouldn't help him, having spent the afternoon doing the same job for Natalie. Also, I knew he was cross because the Magazine had sent their own photographer, whom Natalie had accepted.

Which was their look-out, both of them. I got my gear and hiked down to the kiosk for water-skiing.

Proving, Rita, that you don't know when to let well alone.

There was a short queue: kids, students, beginners. The big hotels had their own arrangements. There was only one boat, and a longish wait in between. The guy who ran it spoke English, and I got talking to him. After a bit, he said, 'You ski a lot? There is a fast boat, not here just now.'

What I wanted was a fast boat that wasn't feeding a queue. And that wouldn't mind, for example, taking a turn past all the other ski stages, and having a look at anyone else in the water.

We agreed, not for nothing, that he would get the big boat to come back, and I'd have it. The kid he worked with ran off to organize it. I stayed on the stage, dangling my legs and chatting up the talent in bits of English and bits of mime, which was fine once they'd got over the shock of my hair and my two sets of lashes.

The kids were good value, and I'd already sold them the news that I'd a special boat lifting me, by the time the special boat came.

And I'll say it was something out of the way. A white Avenger launch which cut its way towards us like an electric saw, throttled down, went into reverse, and floated up to the staging, flipping its ski rope towards me.

There was nobody in it but a wee black-haired Portuguese guy at the wheel, who grinned and exchanged shouts with the ski-boss on the ski platform behind me. As he threw me the tow, I saw his shirt was tucked into creased belted trousers, which meant he didn't plan to enter the water very often, if at all.

By then I was in the sea, my skis sticking up in front of me. The speedboat guy said, 'O.K.?' smiling to me, in an accent you would cut in Sauchiehall Street, and before I could answer, never mind talk about where we were going, he leaned forward, still watching me, and set the launch moving.

He was good. That boat slid into its racing speed like a nappy going under a baby and I rose up on to my skis without a shake or a tremble. And we were off.

It was a sort of high spot, that, in the whole hellish business.

From the sea, Madeira really looked like an island of flowers, with the palms and the green, and the thousands of red-roofed white houses climbing all the way up the hillsides. The sea was bluer than ink, and the spray was warm and expensive-looking, and my knees and thighs and shoulders were behaving like best-quality bed-springs: strong and firm and elastic.

I hoped thousands were looking at me, and wished Kim-Jim were among them. And Ferdy. And even possibly Johnson and Natalie.

Except that Johnson, convoluting at Reid's and getting people to pay for their telephone calls, might object to the sight of his porter-bashing Miss Geddes skiing all round his yacht and pricing it. Which was one of the reasons why I was here. Singing, actually. I can't sing, but I was.

We skimmed out towards the sea, passing little boats, and big boats, and yachts. We didn't pass a yacht flying the Red Ensign because there wasn't one. The spot where I'd seen it before lunch was empty. If Lenny had sailed Johnson's boat in from Tenerife, he must have upped anchor and sailed it off again.

I did some fancy stuff, sheering from side to side. I jumped. I sang, between puffs. I yelled a few times to the boatman, freeing a hand to point in to shore, where from time to time you could see other skiers, not nearly so far out.

He turned round the first time, in case, I suppose, I was bawling to say I had broken my neck. After that, he just waved vaguely behind. I suppose he thought he could judge by the yell whether he was pulling a load of snapped bones behind him or not.

There are people who can tell by the sun where they are going, but nothing ever tells me but people. It was therefore with quite some surprise that I recognized in the distance the striped top of the fish market where Ferdy and I had seen the poor passing-out turtles.

Camara de Lobos, six miles out of Funchal. The Naval Club. Water-skiing.

I began to yell at the driver. Competing with me, music tootled out over the water. There had been a bandstand in Camara beside the church and the taxi rank.

I couldn't see the bandstand for this yacht, anchored well out, which was bang in my way.

This white yacht, flying club colours and a snazzy Red Ensign, with a short name on her bows I could almost see.

I didn't need to see it. I knew what it was. I took a huge breath and roared to the guy at the wheel of my launch, stabbing the air with one finger.

'Over there! Over there to the yacht! I want to get close to the yacht!'

And glory be, this time he turned round, grinned, looked where I was pointing and, spinning the wheel, put his thumb up.

He was bloody good. From the roaring speed he'd kept up, he slackened until there was just enough to keep me upright. He set a course for the bows of the yacht, and took me on a wide, gentle arc that brought me along one white, glossy side, round the stern and up the other.

When you got near, the name was big enough to read quite easily.

Dolly, it said.

And she was smashing. Whoever he'd bought her from had got it right. She had two tall pale masts, and brass railings, with a blue fringed awning over the cockpit. The curtains were blue, too, at the saloon window, and there were cushions and shining wood everywhere, and glittering gear and neatly coiled ropes.

She wasn't trailing a boat, and although there were clips on the cabin roof, the dinghy it was fixed for was missing. I looked, as I went round, but nothing moved. If Lenny had been there he had gone, leaving a companionway, I saw, down the offshore side.

An invitation to loot.

Not very clever, I thought.

An invitation to board?

I could never get my boatman to drop me off and pick me up again. He didn't understand English. And if he did understand, he would probably call in the *guardias*.

I couldn't make up my mind. My mind was made up for me. I suddenly swallowed the sea.

I swallowed it because the rope had gone slack. Losing power, I had crashed over sideways and was sinking.

I came up, choking, coughing and swearing, with the tow rope still in my grasp, and cursing the boatman for stopping.

Shaking the sea from my face, I saw the launch hadn't stopped.

On the contrary, the launch was now leaping off into the distance. Having cast off its end of the tow rope. And leaving me alone, in deep water, beside *Dolly's* heaving white beam, with the companionway glittering on it.

It was too neat by far.

I thought of the long swim to the beach of Camara de Lobos, and the dripping ride back in some taxi.

I thought, Sod you, whoever you are. You got me here. You can get me back to the villa in comfort. After I've seen your bloody yacht.

I grabbed the companionway and heaved myself on to it, and up three grained rubber steps, and on to a golden deck varnished like satin.

On the satin, someone was waiting for me.

'Miss Geddes. Please come aboard,' said the yellow-haired man from the fire escape; and clicked the bar of the bulwark behind me.

I said, 'If this bloody toy has a telephone, you can tell Mrs Sheridan her skis are here, and I expect to be brought back to the villa pronto.'

The guy looked down at me.

This time, he was stripped to the waist, and there was a lot of him. In the sun, his hair was blond and frizzed like crimped crêpe, as I'd seen it earlier that day in the car, and under the light, outside Johnson's flat. On his chest, the fuzz looked nearly white over the KM-4 Pinked Tan.

He looked hard and stringy-fit, with a freckled, banged-about face, and the sort of big hands you see in films, closed round a rifle, or giving someone a knuckle sandwich. Instead of black he was wearing white espadrilles and beach shorts and an identity bracelet, I suppose in case anyone blew him up.

I went on blowing him up. 'Was that your boat that dropped me just now? And nearly drowned me?'

I leaned my hand on the rail, while I glared at him. A foot away was the catch for the bar. Even if I didn't reach that, I could always flip over the rail. It was a long swim to the beach, but not a hopeless one.

He raised his eyebrows, which were as light as his hair. His lashes were white, and his eyes were resting on my wandering arm. He said, 'It was *Dolly*'s launch, yes. How lucky you managed to come aboard. I thought I was going to have to help you in with a boathook.'

I didn't want to be speared with a boathook. I shifted my arm off the rail. I said, 'I spoke to plenty of people on the ski stage. The villa knows where I went. I have an appointment at five with Mrs Sheridan. If you want something, say so. I haven't all bloody day.' After the long ski, I could feel my legs trembling, and I hoped he didn't think he had frightened me.

Which he had.

He said, 'Dry yourself,' shortly, and scooped up and flung me a towel. It was thick and Turkish and blue, and had JJ embroidered on one corner. As I hugged myself in it, I had a sudden affectionate feeling for Natalie Sheridan. Somehow, she'd been conned, too.

Then he said, 'You remember me?'

There seemed no point in denying it.

'Who wouldn't?' I said. 'If you run about under lights, and talk and smoke in a non-smoker's bedroom? That's dumb. That way, you'll never get picked to hand out the jotters.'

He had the same accent as Johnson. The accent my aunt would jump through hoops for. He said, 'I was trying to persuade him to throw you out.'

And that rang true enough. Flowers have nothing on humans. Give me a perverted gloxinia any day.

'You mean,' I said, 'you think we should get a divorce? And put the children in care?'

From under my feet, a peaceful voice floated up through a hatchway.

'Miss Geddes? You are Raymond's personal Everest, and he resents you. Don't push him too far. He'll just go away and come back with Sherpas.'

I couldn't remember what Sherpas were, but I didn't think I wanted Raymond to come back with them.

Raymond. A hell of a name. I looked at him and he said, scowling, 'You're to come down. To the saloon. Get a move on.'

'That was Mr Johnson,' I said. I said it with a slight question. So far as I knew, Pal Johnson, on sticks, was at Reid's in residence. On the other hand, he might have a twin brother.

Raymond said, 'Who else did you expect?' and I cancelled the twin brother and reinstated the Gay Club. Floating. Full of Portuguese skiing instructors.

I followed the unpleasant Raymond along the cabin-side deck, and down into the cockpit, and down again into a sunlit saloon full of pipe smoke and panelling.

The man leaning against the panelling and smoking the pipe proved to be Johnson Johnson.

He said, 'Raymond? I think we can do without you.'

Quite calmly. His glasses shone, mild as milk.

Raymond said, 'I don't think so.'

Johnson looked at him. 'You don't?' he said. 'What a pity. Then in that case, I go back, and you stay.'

Raymond hesitated. Outside, a distant roar got suddenly louder, and the floor rocked beneath us, and there was a light bump, while the roar dropped to a grumble.

Johnson added, 'If the fenders will stand it,' and after lingering a moment longer, the yellow-haired man turned on his heel and ran up the steps and disappeared.

He must have been in his mid-twenties. I've seen Commandos in training who looked like that. I said, 'I don't think much of your friends.'

The yacht swayed, and Johnson swayed with it, without moving. There was no sign of his stick. He said, 'You should see my enemies. Come and sit down. He won't hurt you, and neither will I.'

'You promise?' I said; and he laughed.

'As if we could. Of course. I beg your pardon.' He left the wall, and sat himself down on the long cushioned settee under the windows. He waved the stem of his pipe at the shore.

'Nice place. Lenny saw you climbing with Ferdy. What was it? A hunt for Eduardo?'

A few moments ago, I would have said, 'What's that to you?' but I was getting over my fright.

I was still annoyed at his Owner behaviour. I was bloody furious at this stupid kidnap. And no way would I risk being alone with Boy Raymond, ever again, here or anywhere else.

But I wanted to know what he was up to. And now I was here, I might as well try to find out before I fell out with him.

I said, 'You didn't need to bloody kidnap me to ask about Eduardo. What about a nice telephone call from Reid's?'

The bifocals flashed. 'But I thought you wanted to see *Dolly*? Would you like tea? Or something stronger?' Johnson said.

I seemed to be in the way standing up, so I sat down at the other end of Johnson's settee. I must have agreed to tea too, because it came, served by the little guy who'd driven the Daimler. Lenny somebody.

Without his peaked cap, he had brown hair streaked over his scalp, and a weathered face wrinkled by wind, and big ears. He was nippy, and wee, and not at all pleased to be serving me.

The Connie Margate, it would seem, of the *Dolly*. At least, the tea was great, and I would swear the scones were home-baked, and even the jam sponge. He noticed when the sugar bowl was empty as well, and went off to get more without telling.

The tea set was bone china too, but plain except for a thin band of blue, and the yacht's name was on everything. I said, 'Is it your boat?'

'My design?' he said. 'Only partly. But she was built for me.'

Christ.

He could read minds, like Natalie. 'You trained as an artist,' he said. 'I liked the sketches of Natalie. Do me one of Eduardo.'

There was a sketchpad at his hand, with a 6B pencil. He flipped them both on to the table.

I remembered the sketches of Natalie, wearing a similar towel but no bathing suit. I took up his pencil and let my own towel drop a bit, in case he thought I minded the comparison.

I didn't, actually. I never do. On things to do with beauty, it's my job to be realistic. I'm not jealous. Of other people's faces and bodies, anyway.

I wasn't afraid of doing a duff sketch either. I was as good as he was, I was bloody sure, at a likeness.

He looked at my face of Eduardo, and the outline sketch I'd done of his figure, with his sledgeman's hat and white shirt and trousers. He said, 'You think it wasn't an accident?' My drawing style, it seemed, was beneath comment.

'Well, my God,' I said. 'Your bananas pal threatens me and Kim-Jim, and next day, Kim-Jim and I are just about killed in the street. How could it not not be an accident?'

He appeared to get it. Lenny came to take away the tea, since I seemed to have finished it, and I hooked the towel up again. Johnson said, 'I told you I didn't know van Diemen all that well. Anyway he had left the airport just before you did. How could he have had time to have a sledge doctored? How could he know you'd go to the sledge-run?'

His voice had that patient touch I can never stand. I said, 'He could have seen Eduardo change hats with me from his window. He could have paid Eduardo to find and chat me up in the first place.'

'And getting the right sledge to you at the right time? How did he do that?' Johnson said. 'If, as I understand it, Eduardo wasn't there at the time of the race?'

Which of course was the snag. I'd swear the two guys who pushed us off were as amazed when the rope broke as we were. I'd found that anyone could shine up the runners and put in old rope. I hadn't found out who had actually put that sledge first in the queue.

Since he was waiting, I admitted all that. I added, none the less, that it seemed very funny that Eduardo had disappeared so completely. From his wife's home. From his in-laws. And the in-laws, I had thought, were distinctly against visits by strangers.

I could tell Johnson was going to disagree, and he did.

'I should have thought,' he said, 'a mark in their favour. Guilty, they'd be keen for you to meet Eduardo, and prove he was just a randy father of five who happened to have a perfect alibi for all the times he could have fixed up that sledge.'

I said, 'Then why not let us in anyway?'

His bifocals tilted upwards.

I said, 'Your Mrs Margate did.'

'The security men didn't,' Johnson said.

I said, 'It's pretty small, to hold that against me.'

'I don't. Nosiness gets all it deserves,' Johnson said. 'Would you like another dry towel?'

I have seldom met anyone I disliked more. I said, 'So you think it was an accident as well.'

'What else?' said Johnson. 'I think we should all forget it. Your unfortunate attacker is safely out of the country, nursing his septic hand and scarred face. Mrs Sheridan's reputation is unblemished. Mr Braithwaite can get on with his brothanical snaps and his girlfriend. And Mr Curtis can foster the romantic attachment which, I suppose, is the mainspring of your touching anxiety. Why not go on back to Troon, and set up house with him?' said Johnson Johnson.

Under the towel, I suddenly felt rather queasy. I looked at his glasses, but the orange glare from my hair hid his eyes.

'You *are* a friend of Roger van Diemen,' I said.

He studied me, with his pipe in his mouth. Then he took it out.

'But for Lenny and me, you would have been killed,' he said.

'And your pal arrested for murder. You didn't want that,' I said. 'But O.K., what if he does it again? To someone else? You don't know what addicts are like, or you don't care?'

'You think he's an addict? Of what?' Johnson said. Not excited.

I said, 'Nothing slight. It looked like heroin. That's what Mrs Sheridan's covering up, more than her love-life I should think. Don't tell me you didn't know.'

'I won't, in that case,' said Johnson. 'It didn't occur to you that Mrs Sheridan might be arranging for a cure in Frankfurt?'

I sat up. 'Is she?'

'Ask her, if you think it's any of your business,' Johnson said. 'I'm just pointing out that the affair does involve a number of fairly well-known grown-ups with big, important jobs who may even be capable of arranging their own affairs, if left to get on with it.'

'On the other hand,' I said, 'I'm the one who got roughed up and tipped down a hillside. Excuse me if I complain.'

There was a silence, during which smoke filled the space between us, and thickened.

'All right. You've complained. You don't like being roughed up,' said Johnson. 'So why not go back where you came from and leave them to it? If it's revenge you want, you've made them all dance quite a bit. Nothing more's going to happen now. How can it?'

I won't say I had never considered going back home. Or leaving Natalie and going somewhere that wasn't even home, such as that place in the sun with Kim-Jim. Where there would be enough work to keep both of us.

I still thought it would be nice.

But not yet, oh brother, not yet; not until I'd got my own back on Mr Roger van Diemen and pals.

And superior pals, especially Mr Owner Damn Johnson.

Just a few weeks ago, he'd been a rich bedridden crock I'd been cooking for. I didn't know how I'd got to be scared of him.

I wasn't scared of him.

I said, baldly, 'I'll stay if I want to.'

The smoke developed a hole, because he had exhaled sharply into it.

He took a fresh breath.

'Miss Geddes,' said Johnson. 'In a world full of contented, consenting subordinates, how is it that you and the blue-arsed fly have survived?

'I have no more to say. Lenny will assist you to leave. Unless you specially want it, I should like the towel back. It is one of a set.'

I suppose he thought he'd had the last word.

They sent me back to Funchal in the Avenger, with Lenny at the wheel. The man on the ski platform didn't seem at all surprised to find the launch under different management, and lost all his grasp of English the minute I began asking questions.

I got my things and left him, to find a cab to take me back in time for Natalie's next beauty fix.

But for that, I could have stayed away all night, for all anyone at the villa seemed to have noticed. The Hon. Maggie had appeared to patch things up with Ferdy and was in the workroom, Aurelio said, helping Mr Braithwaite with his flowers.

I bet.

The other thing that had happened was a hand-delivery of handsome thick envelopes from Reid's Palace Hotel. There was one for each of us, including me but excluding the help and the parrot.

Each contained an elegant summons to a dinner party being held by Mr Johnson Johnson in a private room at Reid's the following evening.

And that, one and all, was an invitation it was going to give me the greatest joy to refuse.

The funny thing was that it was Kim-Jim, whom the Owner had sneered at, who was cross, and wanted me to go to the party.

He wasn't going himself. Since he told Natalie about his retirement, he took, I saw, a fairly wicked pleasure in excusing himself from things that didn't interest him, and sending me in his place, if he could get away with it.

We spent that evening, he and I, with the video, since Ferdy and Natalie were at the Sheraton, cutting up Josephine over dinner with the money-man.

Between films, Kim-Jim kept coming back to the invitation; kept insisting that big dinner parties could teach me a thing or two.

I had already recited to both Kim-Jim and Ferdy how I'd been hang-shied by Ferdy's pal Johnson, and bloody ticked off for annoying the grown-ups.

Ferdy, who was on Johnson's side anyway, just jangled with laughter, and said that after buggering up his morning's photography for nothing, I ought to concede that Pal Johnson was right. Ferdy was satisfied, he said, that the Great Group Jeopardy Plot was just a figment of my imagination.

Which just meant that, now Maggie was back, he didn't intend to waste time Hemlock Chauffeuring. And that he liked to please Natalie, anyway.

Kim-Jim was gentler. But with van Diemen gone, he couldn't really believe there was any danger. Or that when van Diemen was here, his threats had been due to more than a fit of jealousy, heightened, poor guy, by drugs, and probably already regretted.

I could see that each of them, in his way, was quite impressed with the way Johnson had handled young Rita. I could see the 'young' attached to my name like a feeder.

The talk with Kim-Jim got so fraught in the end that I told him I would go to Reid's, just to content him. I even let him write the letter of acceptance, and discuss what clothes I'd wear.

The parrot kept saying *'Oh Cathy! Cathy!'* all evening, and attacking my ear. Kim-Jim eventually chained it to its perch, not liking to put it out on the terrace, where it would miss all the films.

We saw the last of the ones I'd brought, and a new one of his, and talked into the small hours.

About work. Sometimes I thought he was going to talk about something else, and then it seemed as if he stopped himself, because it wasn't time yet.

As long as he didn't plan to leave yet, there was no hurry.

Dodo came in once, without knocking, and it wasn't hard to guess what she hoped she would see. The movie we had on, as it happened, wasn't even blue, so it must have been an all-round disappointment.

It was irritating, but nothing more. When I went to bed, I slept like a log.

I was busy next day.

Natalie had a lot of dictating to do, which she did at a desk in her bedroom, into a tape-recorder. Then an English agency girl from Funchal came and audio-typed the letters and memos. Meanwhile I sat and worked, with Kim-Jim's help, in the study.

The phone rang a lot. I taped the messages that came in, and she told me later what to do about them. A lot of it had to do with the Josephine film.

Just before noon she rang down, through the ceiling, to tell me that I'd worked hard, and could have a swim before lunch if I wanted.

I had a swim, while Kim-Jim lay by the pool on an airbed and watched me. I was still there when the Hon. Maggie arrived, in a towelling robe and a shoe-string bikini, on Ferdy's invitation.

After ten minutes at the poolside, she took her bikini off, which hardly made any difference, except to Aurelio, who came into the garden eight times.

I stayed in the water and swam, and then went to Natalie's nets and practised serving.

I swim well and I play tennis well and Maggie looks great with no clothes on. Deuce.

Natalie joined us for lunch on the terrace. Maggie was covered by then, and no one fell out with anyone. After lunch it was more of the same, after a siesta.

In the late afternoon, I shaped and shampooed Natalie's hair, and piled it in folds, with wisps in front of her ears, for Johnson's party.

I didn't tell her, as I went on to make up her face, that I didn't mean to go to the party. I didn't tell anyone, and especially not Kim-Jim, whose passion about the whole thing was more than I could understand.

I got some white of egg from the kitchen, whipped like a tornado by Dolores, and fixed my hair as if I was going. I got into the painted tunic and trousers Kim-Jim had approved earlier, and put on scent and earrings and anklets and everything, and showed them to him in the study.

He was pleased. I felt a heel. I might have confessed, but Ferdy came in to say that Natalie was waiting, and I belted out to join her.

Kim-Jim called out, 'Good night! Have yourself a good time!' as I got to the car.

I thought he was talking to me, and only realized when I saw Ferdy outside the study door, grinning, that he'd stayed to say something to Kim-Jim.

Kim-Jim added, 'Don't do anything I wouldn't do,' and Ferdy posed in his ruffled St Laurent shirt with the telly flickering all over his face and said, 'I have news for you. Tonight, old boy, you are enlarging your scope. See you tomorrow.'

The parrot clucked. As Ferdy shut the door and came bounding out, I could hear it saying *I guess there's just you and me left.*

Natalie didn't think it was funny. Natalie was cool about having been made to wait.

I was pretty cool too, when I found out what Ferdy had been up to.

Ferdy sat in one of the let-down seats and grinned at me as Aurelio put the car into gear. 'Last-minute orders. No sugar for Rita,' he said.

'No party for Rita,' I said. 'Mrs Sheridan, I hope you don't mind. I didn't want to upset Kim-Jim. But Mr Johnson and I don't get on. If you'll drop me, I'd rather spend the evening at the Sheraton.'

Natalie looked at me, with the street lights catching her lid-frosting and her face-frosting as well.

She said, 'It's a little late for that, surely? You owe quite a lot, I should have said, to Mr Johnson's quick wits. It doesn't cost much to be courteous.'

I said I had thanked him. I also added, unwisely, that after all, I had looked after him in London. He would understand I didn't like parties.

Ferdy, who unfortunately had seen me at all too many parties, was grinning at me over his frillies.

He said, 'Do you know what, darling? Kim-Jim said you'd try to flunk it. And do you know another what? I gave him my solemn word you wouldn't.'

'Try to stop me,' I said.

He did. What's more, he succeeded.

Natalie, I will admit, told him once or twice not to be silly. She complained sharply when he manhandled me into the lobby of Reid's Palace Hotel in full view of a row of surprised bellboys.

When Ferdy picked me up in his arms and I bit him she stopped complaining and simply swept into the arms of the management, firmly ignoring us.

We were the last of Johnson's guests to arrive. The management were indulgent. Everyone knows Ferdy. Ferdy slung me over his shoulder and pressed buttons until the lift came down again. Inside it, he put me on my feet.

He said, 'I thought you liked Kim-Jim, young Rita. What were you going to tell him tomorrow?'

I said, 'That I'm more honest than you. That I think your pal Johnson is a poof and a bastard, and I don't see why I should spend a rotten evening with him.'

The lift had stopped, but Ferdy kept his finger on the close button.

He said, 'It's an argument. Carry a good deal more weight if he knew just how rotten an evening it was. Otherwise he might think you're just scared.'

'Twenty-five dreary bores, and Johnson and Natalie?' I said. 'Be my witness. You can tell him all about it tomorrow. I don't need to suffer.'

Ferdy gazed at me, with his mouth pouting out from the whiskers.

'I admit,' he said, 'that Maggie *desnuda* was pretty spectacular. But you don't need to admit it. The film finance boys will be there. And a couple of artists.'

'No,' I said.

'And the B.B.C. team planning that film on the Story of Malmsey, bless their wooden butts.'

'No,' I said.

'Help you look for Eduardo tomorrow,' he said.

'Yes,' I said. 'But if I don't like it, I'll leave after the coffee.'

'You'll like it,' he said.

I left after the coffee.

It wasn't actually rotten.

The food was good. I sat between a B.B.C. man and a guy whose paintings I'd seen in this gallery, and we ended up drawing all over the tablecloth.

Johnson wasn't particularly near me at the table, and only came up once during the drinks bit. The film finance guy I was with started to introduce me, but Johnson said it was all right, I used to walk his dog when I was younger.

I suppose it was meant as a joke.

The film man laughed and asked what my fee was, and I said Mr Johnson paid me in pencils.

Before the coffee, everyone drank the Queen's health and someone, who seemed to be the British Consul, stood up and made a dreary speech about how glad everyone was to see Mr Johnson restored to them, and how they were looking forward to the beautiful *Dolly* gracing their harbours for long years to come.

Then Mr Johnson stood up in the Owner's place at the head of the table and made a short, mildly funny speech which got a lot of clapping at intervals, and a round of applause at the end.

That's what happens, if you have money.

It was the time when they let you go to the toilet if you have to, and people were bobbing up and down.

I bobbed up, but not down.

I caught Ferdy's eye, but not Johnson's or Natalie's, and got the hell out of it.

It was a warm evening, and the flowers were giving out, free, a lot of scents that usually come in bottles.

I got back to the villa by taxi and let myself in, waving through the service wing window at Dolores, Aurelio and Dodo in front of the telly, watching T.V.E. Canarias.

The programme was *Elizabeth R: Horrivel Conspiracao*, the same that Kim-Jim was taping, which explained the presence of Dodo slumming. Anything royal, I guessed, would trap Dodo.

Running upstairs, I could hear the same thing quacking away in the study, mixed with Cone working hard on the Tarzan cry. Which, if they'd heard it, would fairly have baffled the Spanish Marauder.

I changed into this nice little wrap and came downstairs in my bare feet to wait for Kim-Jim at the end of the programme.

I went out to the terrace.

The sounds of Queen Elizabeth and Tarzan followed me distantly.

I thought of Kim-Jim's sight, and wondered how long it would hold out, and what he would do if he could only listen. When I heard his phone ring, I was enraged, because his time was so precious, and even when recording, he hated so to be interrupted.

He must have snatched up the receiver, for it only rang a couple of times. Queen Elizabeth got switched down or off, and stayed off. I wondered who could be ringing at this hour, and remembered that it wasn't late in New York, and Natalie got calls at all times.

If I'd stuck to my guns and stayed with him, I could have saved him the fag of that phone call.

I'd gone to the party, but left it.

A dithering berk. Neither a blue-arsed fly, nor a contented, consenting subordinate.

Rita girl, it's your life. Don't let other folk run it.

I went further down into the garden. There was this seat with a view. I could see the palms and the sea in the moonlight. The sea that went from here to Scotland.

I sat on it. I got thinking. I fell asleep.

I was wakened by lights on the terrace. Someone had switched the floodlighting on. And when I sat up, I heard a lot of well-dined voices twittering at one another and laughter rolling out from the sitting-room.

Maggie's, for one. And, I thought, Harvey Kazimierz, Natalie's lawyer. And Natalie. And Ferdy. And someone I could swear was Johnson.

I had nothing on under my wrap, and my feet were cold. I hopped through the grass to where I could see the French windows and Natalie's visitors standing about just inside or on the terrace.

It *was* Johnson. The party was over, and she had bloody brought him back for a night-cap.

Maggie was sloshed. You could see her, because she had on a dress made of sequins, with two well-placed straps instead of a top, which certainly explained the need to get brown all over.

Ferdy was singing the end of 'The Song of the Flea', with Maggie's scarf tied round his brow, and his frills unbuttoned down to his navel. The lawyer was talking to Johnson, who had unbuttoned his white tuxedo to show a woolly pullover, I swear, underneath.

Natalie's voice said, 'She'll have gone to bed,' in the voice she kept for guests who got stotious.

'Not without paying her bloody debts,' Ferdy's voice answered. And cupping his mouth, my famous photographer friend produced a full-throated opera bellow.

'RITA!' he screamed.

I swore. I tied a double knot in my wrap, and marched up the path to the light, skipping a bit because of the pine cones.

'And about time,' said Ferdy. He gazed at the wrap, with his capped teeth dividing his sideburns and gave a howl nearly as loud as the first one.

'Return match, Maggie! Last into the pool is a sissy!'

Natalie said, 'Have a drink, Ferdy. Do you really want Kim-Jim as well? Mr Johnson won't mind in the slightest if your silly debt waits till tomorrow.'

I noticed that the *Mr* was still sticking around, which was interesting. Aurelio was passing round drinks. Johnson sat down with his, politely remarking that of course tomorrow would do.

I don't suppose he needed the cash for the milkman. But there was a distinct impression that if someone paid him off now, he needn't see any of us again, which would suit him fine.

Natalie went off to fetch Kim-Jim, and I had time to look at the clock and be pleased that the Horrivel Conspiracao was officially over, anyway.

I went into the sitting-room and stood, because I wasn't decent when I sat, and took a drink from Aurelio's tray.

Out on the terrace, Ferdy and Maggie were throwing pebbles at something and cackling. Natalie came out of the study, shut the door and said, 'Aurelio, put the tray down. We shan't need you for a bit.'

The lawyer was still talking to Johnson, who wasn't paying much attention, his eyes following Natalie. Aurelio left, and Natalie said, 'Harvey. Would you come here for a moment?'

I had made her up. I knew better than any of the three of us that it wasn't paint that was making her colour all wrong: too red on the cheeks, and too white everywhere else.

Johnson said, 'Can I help?' and got up.

The lawyer's voice died away, and he began to get up too.

He was still slower than Johnson, who walked unevenly to Natalie's shoulder and touching the study door, said 'May I?'

He went in, followed by Kazimierz, and Natalie stood by the half-open door, staring at something. Outside, Ferdy and the Hon. Maggie had pushed each other into the pool.

I got my feet out of the carpet and walked to the study door too.

Natalie put her arm across it. 'Don't go in,' she said.

Inside, the parrot popped corks and had a cross fit of squawking. His chain rattled.

'Why not?' I said.

Natalie put her hand up and smoothed my robe lapel with her thumb, as if trying its quality. She went on holding it, and I stood inside it and waited.

She said, 'It's Kim-Jim. I'm sorry, Rita. He's killed himself.'

Just the facts, ma'am,' said the parrot. *'Just the facts.'*

I've seen shot people before, for real and in photographs. The forensic people at Glasgow are used to the likes of me ringing up for advice about a burn or a bit of hatchet work or a drowning. I did a decomposition once with mortician's wax and fuse wire and Kleenex. Drownings are worst.

He was dead.

Seen from the front, a bullet wound in the temple is no trouble. For a fresh one, corn syrup and colouring will give a nice sheen, and of course you don't see the back of the head, which won't be there anyway.

He was dead.

For older wounds, you use browner colouring, and you can get the powder marks for a suicide by striking matches and working the black round the wound.

There was black all round the entry hole in Kim-Jim's temple, but it wasn't made by matches.

I got into the study because Natalie couldn't hold me any longer and there he was. Neat, in his bespoke open-necked shirt and granny glasses, leaning a little sideways in the wing of his usual deep-buttoned chair by the fireplace. Swung round to face the telly.

Beside his chair was a table with an empty glass on it, and the control pad for the telly. And on the carpet beside one of his nice clean American sneakers was the small gun he always packed, American-style. He'd told me about it, long ago, and not been narked when I thought it was funny. He never got narked.

He was dead.

The leather arm of his chair was warm. I hung on to it, kneeling. Someone – the lawyer – said, 'Better not touch him.' Natalie spoke from the door, and he went out.

Natalie's voice went on talking, in short bursts, very much higher than usual, but inside the study it was quiet. The quartz clock ticked. From the corner where the perch was, you could hear Cone's chain as he picked his way sideways and back, stopping to frill out his feathers.

From the wall where the telly stood came a very faint whine, and when you looked, you could see the red light was still on, though the set was off.

'He switched it off from the control pad,' someone said.

Johnson, standing still by the big desk, so quietly I hadn't seen he was still in the room.

Kim-Jim's mouth was open, just a little. Sometimes, in make-up, you gave them just a trickle of blood from the corner, as if they'd bitten their tongue.

As for colour, there is a nice greyed base I have used. But it depends.

In heat like this, of course, the skin keeps its colour. Looks quite natural, really.

A voice – Johnson's – now at the door was saying, 'Give her a moment.' And then, after a pause, 'Should somebody break the news to the service people, and make some phone calls from the kitchen?'

There was some talk, then Natalie's voice and the lawyer's faded away. There was a breath of air as the door opened a little wider and someone came in again. Johnson said, 'Rita. We'll have to leave him.'

For a big man, Kim-Jim had a childish, soft sort of nose. His eyes were quite shut, with the short sandy lashes making shadows over his cheeks. His hair had a lot of grey in it, when you looked close, and was dull.

American hair is usually bouncy, and has lots of gloss. Maybe when you were dead, your hair got dull.

A hand took me under one arm and drew me up on my feet. Johnson said, 'You don't want to be here when the police and the doctor and everyone come.'

I didn't.

I walked with him to the door, and waited while he took the key from the inside and locked it on the outside, using his handkerchief.

Kim-Jim always carried two clean handkerchiefs as well.

The bastard. The bastard said that he'd kill him.

A thick whooping voice and a giggling voice, from the terrace. Ferdy, with his St Laurent frills and cummerbund wet as a dishrag staggering in from the pool and standing on the sitting-room rug saying, 'What's up? What's up, my British hearties?'

Maggie, also soaked, with her necklace glittering and her straps hanging down from her brown skin, was on all fours on the carpet. From the door, the lawyer said, 'I think you should dry yourselves. The *guardia* will be here soon. Mr Curtis has shot himself.'

'He didn't,' I said.

'*What?*' said Ferdy, not loudly at all. He took hold of the back of a chair.

The lawyer said, 'Mrs Sheridan is sending for help. Aurelio will bring us some coffee. I suggest you take your friend upstairs and dry yourselves. There are bathrobes, Mrs Sheridan says.'

The Hon. Maggie had stopped giggling. Her eyes, as she looked up, were streaked with eye-liner dissolved by the pool, but her Vidal haircut looked great. If she had been aiming at *Cabaret*, she had hit it.

She said, 'Ferdy? It's a gas?'

Natalie's voice said, 'It isn't a joke. He's lying there with a gun. He's dead. There's no note, but he killed himself.'

She came in from the service wing and crossed to take cigarettes out of the silver box on one of the sitting-room tables. Her hair was perfect, just as I'd put it up that afternoon, and there was hardly a crease in the Ricci green organza that I'd matched her eye-shadow to.

I remembered watching Kim-Jim study her, and then smile at me on his way down to the study. Smile approvingly.

I said, 'He didn't kill himself.'

Natalie's cigarette wouldn't light. Her lawyer took the lighter out of her hand and held the flame for her. Even his hand was shaking a little.

Natalie let out a lot of smoke and said, 'Suppose we sit down. Rita, I know it's hard, but you must listen. He died by his own hand.'

Someone's hand eased me down into a chair, and Johnson sat on the arm of it. The lawyer offered him a cigarette from Natalie's box, and when he refused, took one himself and sat down by Natalie.

Ferdy stood where he was, and you could see the drink draining out of him. The Hon. Maggie looked up at him, gasping, and when he jerked his head at the stairs, she collected her straps and ran across the carpet and up them. The service door banged and Dodo tramped out, looked across at Natalie and then followed Maggie up the stairs and into one of the bedrooms. I could hear her thudding about, collecting towels and coping with the start of wisteria.

Ferdy said, 'In there?' and walking over, pressed the study door handle.

Johnson said, 'We locked it until the *guardia* come. But it's pretty clear, I'm afraid. Gun beside him.'

Aurelio came in with a tray of black coffee. He was greeny-brown, and the tray was rattling. They all looked at him. You would think

I wasn't there. I got up and said to Natalie, 'You're covering up for your van Diemen friend. You all are. It wasn't suicide. It just looks like suicide. We had plans for tomorrow. He had plans for the rest of his life. *He was taping a serial, goddammit!*'

I got choked and broke off. Aurelio, who had been standing staring at me, moved on at a nod from Natalie, and served everyone. Johnson took a cup for me and put it on a table. I said, 'Someone got in and shot him. I'll tell the *guardia.*'

Natalie started to speak, and then stopped at a look from her lawyer.

Harvey Kazimierz. A little more silvery than usual behind the rimless glasses and above the bow tie. Stanford and Cambridge, Kim-Jim had said.

He spoke as if he had taken classes. But then all lawyers talk like that. He said, 'If there was any doubt, of course we should tell the authorities, but there isn't. No one could have got into the house. The front door and the gates were locked from the time we all left for the party until Miss Geddes came back. Aurelio and Dolores and Mrs Sheridan's maid were all together in their own sitting-room. After supper, they switched on a television serial, and they heard Mr Curtis do the same in the study. So he was alive then.'

'Unless it was on a time switch,' said Ferdy unexpectedly. He crossed the room, dripping, and pausing beside me, gripped my shoulder in one big hand and hugged me briefly, his chin on my hair. Then he walked to the foot of the stairs and stood nursing his coffee and staring at Natalie.

'I think it was,' said Johnson. 'But lots of people use a time switch anyway, just in case they forget to switch the tape on when the programme starts. What does it matter anyway? Mr Kazimierz is right. The house was locked up. I don't see how anyone could have broken in. And even if they did, Mr Curtis would hardly have allowed them to walk up to his chair and stick a gun in his face without some sort of resistance.'

'What about an upstairs window?' I said. 'Has anyone been round the house checking? What about someone with a key? What about someone Kim-Jim knew, who could get right up to him before he even pulled out a gun? Your bloody pal threatened he'd kill Kim-Jim if he didn't get out, and Kim-Jim is dead, and you're all pretending it was *suicide?*' I was shaking.

It was Natalie this time who put down her cigarette and said quietly, 'Rita. Come here and sit down.'

After a moment I went and took the chair beside her. Now the shock was getting less, her colour was coming back to normal. The Hon. Maggie, appearing suddenly on the stairs in a yellow bathrobe, with another over her arm, came down to where Ferdy stood and took his coffee while he put the robe on over his wet things, still looking at Natalie. He was quite sober now, and so was Maggie.

Behind them both, Dodo also came down the stairs and went and stood beside Natalie with her mouth clamped over her teeth. I could feel the blame pouring all over me.

Johnson, who had settled down in the chair I had left, was the only one who still looked a bit queer, but then he was, and had looked like that anyway after holding that stupid party.

If he hadn't held that party, I should have spent the evening here, and Kim-Jim would be alive.

Whether he had held the party or not, I should have spent the evening here.

A glass of something appeared under my nose. Brandy. Natalie said, 'Drink it, and listen.'

I took it from her.

She said, 'Everything you say is true. You and Kim-Jim were both threatened. The man who threatened you is not in Madeira any longer. And even if he were, he's a fool, but not stupid, any more than Kim-Jim was. If Roger van Diemen had gone into that study, do you think Kim-Jim would have sat in that chair waiting for him? Or for any stranger who came instead?'

'No one came into this house anyways, after you'd gone, Miz Sheridan,' Dodo said without warning over her head. She was looking at me. 'No one, that is, except Miss Geddes. And Mr Curtis was all right then. The phone rang, and he answered it.'

It was true. I had forgotten. As I went out into the garden, the phone had rung, and he'd turned down the serial.

As I went into the garden, leaving the terrace windows open behind me.

The bifocal glasses were watching me. Johnson said, 'Did you hear that, Miss Geddes?'

I nodded, looking at him. The brandy had done me no good at all.

He said, 'And did you hear him turn the programme up again?'

'No,' I said. 'I was at the bottom of the garden. But I left the terrace doors open. Anyone could have got in.'

'Excuse me,' said Dodo again. She stood like a minnyloth, six feet tall against the light, with shoulders to match. She said, 'No one came in from the garden after you went out, because Aurelio locked the doors again behind you. Miz Sheridan has valuable things in this house. I thought she would have told you.'

She paused and added, 'And no one came out of the study after you went into the garden neither. Dolores left the service door open near the end of the serial so's we could see when Mr Curtis came out. He liked to eat late, Mr Curtis, and he was going to pick up a snack in the kitchen.'

The Hon. Maggie, with the make-up now wiped off her face, crossed to the drinks table and poured herself a large tumbler of something, the glass chinking. The robe would have showed off her new suntan, but she clutched it about her like a blanket. She crept back to Ferdy.

Ferdy said, 'Then you could tell when he did it. If he switched off the tape.'

Kim-Jim always switched off the tape at the end of a programme. He liked to edit it while it was running as well. He would never use an automatic switch-off. Johnson said doubtfully, 'I suppose we could check,' and he and Ferdy went off to the study, Johnson taking the wrapped key out of his pocket. After a moment, the lawyer got up and went out too.

Natalie said, 'Rita. You say Kim-Jim was making plans.'

I tried to make her see sense. I said, 'He did a lot for you. He really did. It's the least anyone can do, to find out what happened. And punish them.'

She ignored it. She said, 'Rita. You know why he was retiring?'

I saw what she was trying to do. I said, 'His eyes were going. Yes, of course I knew. But he was prepared for it. He was getting a special screen, and tapes and everything. And there were things he was going to do for me. He wouldn't have taped that programme. Why would you bother with a bloody programme if you were going to kill yourself?'

The lawyer's voice said, 'The tape wasn't switched off. It went on recording until the end of transmission, and ran itself out. So he must have ... It must have happened while Miss Geddes was in the garden.'

They had all come back. Johnson sat down again right away, but Harvey Kazimierz and Ferdy stood together. The lawyer said in a quiet voice, 'You didn't hear a shot then, Miss Geddes? How long were you out?'

'No. I fell asleep. Until everyone came back,' I said.

Johnson said, 'Would anyone hear a shot from the service wing? With the door open?'

Dodo stared at me while she was thinking. 'I guess,' she said, 'that the television would drown out that sort of sound. And that parrot, he copies gunfire and barking and every other darned thing, so it wouldn't prove nothing if we did. But we didn't.'

There was a silence. Through it, there came the sound of wheels on the drive in front of the house, and two or three voices. A car door slammed.

Johnson said, 'Excuse me, Mrs Sheridan. You were saying something just now about Mr Curtis retiring?'

Natalie said, 'They're coming,' and stood up. She looked at me, and then at Johnson. She said, 'It's no way to say this, but of course, it's why it must be suicide. Rita is here because Kim-Jim was about to retire. He told Rita it was because he was losing his sight, as he didn't want to distress her. She says he was making all sorts of plans, I suppose for the same reason.'

She took a deep breath, and looked at me properly, as if she were sorry for me. She said, 'It was cancer, Rita, and serious. He didn't *have* a future. He was really fond of you. He saw you as his heir, in his work and in everything else. He wanted you secure in this job, and learning how to take your place in the world. And when he thought he had it all fixed, he killed himself.'

I repeated, 'Cancer. His heir,' like a zombie. I didn't believe her. He would never have told her that, and not me.

She said, 'In every sense. I witnessed his will the other day, Rita. He left you everything he owned.'

I felt funny. They all looked at me, and then towards the hall, where you could hear Aurelio letting people in.

'And so,' said Johnson, 'I think we should settle for suicide. For if we bring up the idea of murder, the only person with the time, the opportunity and the motive, ridiculous though it seems, is Miss Geddes.'

I saw Johnson's eye catch the lawyer's, and Kazimierz came over and put his hand on my shoulder. 'You can be jailed for a long time in a foreign country if they get the wrong idea. I think it was suicide, and so does everyone else. But you'll never find out, one way or the other, if they stick you behind bars. Will you leave it to us?'

A hint. A warning. A threat.

Whichever it was, I agreed.

They knew, I suppose, by the way I looked that they'd only put me off for the moment.

If they were going to stop me, they'd have to kill me, too.

Two days later, the Curtis family arrived from California to take the body back home for burial. It took two more days to make the arrangements, and for the Madeira police to decide that we could leave the island too if we wanted to.

I'm not sure, even yet, how I could have got through that time without Ferdy.

To begin with, he shed the Hon. Maggie like underwear. It wasn't really fair, as she was fit to turn into a total drunk alone at the Sheraton, and the boys she knew weren't going to help her do anything but drink harder.

Between them, Johnson and Natalie had her to meals and were nice to her, considering, and after a while she began to perk up. After that, it seemed you fell across her wherever Johnson was, and sometimes you would even find her looking for Johnson, who had been there a moment before but had rolled quietly away.

She had meant, I suppose, to use Johnson to make Ferdy jealous. Instead she was on the way to getting a crush on him herself. From what I'd heard, there had been plenty of dramas in her life before. She'd be lucky if this got the length of a drama.

I didn't mind, because it freed Ferdy to help me. Not to help me get over Kim-Jim's death, but to help me find out who caused it.

I'd expected everyone to be against me, as they had on the night of the shooting. I'd kept my mouth shut then, when the *guardia* came, and the doctor, and the consular advisers, and all the questions began. When they talked about suicide, I didn't speak. But when I went to Ferdy afterwards and said, 'O.K. I went to that rotten party of Johnson's because you said you'd help me find Eduardo. So now what about it?'

When I went to Ferdy and said that, I thought he and Natalie would be fiercely against my starting any sort of inquiries. But they weren't.

It was Natalie who gave me the number of the clinic Kim-Jim had been treated at, and let me check it with Directory Inquiries, and then let me phone them in Lisbon and get them to tell me what had been wrong with him.

It was cancer. Affecting more than his eyes, and eating him up. He had had a month or two to live, that was all. They were sending a formal report to the authorities and to his family.

I went off and sat in his workroom for a long time. It was still neat, because I'm a tidy worker as well. It had always been neat because he'd known he would never use it again.

All the stuff in these cupboards now belonged to me. His television, his cassettes, his radio equipment. His investments. The money lodged in the banks whose papers they'd found in his desk. I wasn't badly off already, but once the will was proved and everything properly wound up, I need never work again, even while Robina was still alive.

I hadn't gone through his papers myself, or anything he had. I'd left his room as it was, with the photographs. Only, I'd taken back my yellow cat.

It stood with mine, in my room, with the same knowing black smile on its face. My mother had one too, but not my aunt. Already, there were more cats than people.

Then Ferdy had come in and said, 'Look. About Eduardo. Where do you want to go? To his house again?'

I'd drawn up a list of what I wanted to do, and Ferdy did it with me.

Eduardo wasn't at home. He had left the sledges, we understood, and had taken casual work, they didn't know what. He had promised to come when he had a day off.

At the sledges, the story was different. Eduardo had been sacked for staying away once too often. Of course, he would get work somewhere else in the season. If not in a hotel, then at his father-in-law's. There was always work in bananas.

I remembered the cauldron. I said, 'I thought the family worked with cane?'

His brother-in-law did, they said. But his father-in-law – didn't I know? – was overseer of Combe's Bananas.

We had borrowed Aurelio's estate car. As he got behind the wheel again, Ferdy whistled. 'Rita, my Bird of Paradise. I don't see how he can have done poor bloody Kim-Jim any harm, but I begin to believe that the sledge-run wasn't an accident. Van Diemen paid your Eduardo to wreck us, and meanwhile got himself out. The chap's crazy.'

The sun fell on this vine called a Golden Shower covered with big orange trumpets and I could see the twinge on Ferdy's face as he drove past, but he didn't say anything. He hadn't even put his camera into the back. A good pal, was Ferdy.

He just said, 'O.K., let me guess. Up the hill to the baby farm? Or the airport first?'

We went to the airport first.

They confirmed that Mr van Diemen had lost an afternoon flight to Lisbon, and had rebooked for the following morning.

They confirmed that on the second occasion, the booking had been taken up.

They agreed that they knew Mr van Diemen well by sight. He came through all the time.

They couldn't confirm that the man who actually flew was Mr van Diemen. It had been a very full plane. The most they could say was that no one remembered speaking to him. It would take some time to trace the steward and hostesses on that particular plane, never mind find out when they might land again in Madeira. If it was important, perhaps Mrs Sheridan would write a letter? Or was this a police inquiry?

They had been pretty helpful, considering, and Ferdy had been brilliant but he had to sheer off at that.

What was clear was that there was no proof, at the moment, that Roger van Diemen had actually flown out the second time, and not someone else using his ticket.

The Coombe Banana Company's office were helpful as well.

As far as they knew, Mr van Diemen had left when he said. They hadn't heard from him since. They didn't expect to, until his next visit. Yes, he travelled regularly between all parts of the Coombe empire. If he had completed his business in Europe, he would probably be in South America or the Caribbean by now. The Liverpool office might be able to supply us with his movements.

'He doesn't sound crazy,' said Ferdy. 'At least, they're still entrusting all their bananas to him. I suppose in a firm of that size, someone would notice if the Financial Director had gone off his rocker. Maybe it's just lust for Natalie that does him in. Do I look crazy?'

'I thought Natalie was lusting for you,' I said.

I looked at him. He was frowning. I said, 'If that guy didn't fly out, he's still here.'

'Point taken,' said Ferdy shortly.

He was still frowning. I made an effort. 'So,' I said, 'if you make it with Natalie, for God's sake keep it quiet. You want to finish the flower book.'

'What do you mean, if I make it with Natalie?' Ferdy said. The frown had disappeared. He whooped. 'Rita! You care!'

The car turned off the coast road and began climbing again into the mountains. The sun went in. We passed another shower of dangling trumpets and then plunged into pine trees.

'Don't worry,' Ferdy said. I could see songs from Prince Eager climbing up inside his neck. The thought of sex always cheers him up and he's not the sort, anyway, to mope about anything much.

'Don't worry. From now on, I shall confine my practices entirely to flowers. Madeira, the Island of Sin. All the bloody bees'll come off with V.D.'

It didn't snow, but we ran into mist higher up, and it was no joke rounding the bends, with trucks and taxis and things looming up with their lights on. At one point we were held up for five minutes by a flock of sheep on the road, and then later on by a skidded lorry trying to get out of a ditch.

There was no mist around Eduardo's mother-in-law's house, and you could see the boiler boiling in the back yard with no trouble. I thought the sight of Ferdy getting out of the car and walking up to the front door was worth the Vicarage Cross, and told him later.

At the time, I couldn't get a word in edgeways because of the great welcome he was getting, and invitations to come in and see the baby the Senhor had blessed with so many escudos, and drink a glass of wine to his health.

We did, too. We walked through about every room in the house on our way to that baby, and met all its relatives, young and old through four generations, ending up with the baby's mother parked in bed like a double airship, cheerfully feeding the baby, and not from a bottle, I can tell you.

Ferdy's eyes glistened with sorrow from not having his camera. Then they stopped glistening as I noticed who was sitting next to the bed and dug him in the ribs.

'That,' I said, 'is Eduardo.'

It was, too, although he didn't have his hat on. He got up, wearing the same grin that went from ear to ear under this huge Pancho Villa moustache and said, 'But Senhora! So generous, so kind over the hat! And this is the Senhora's husband?'

I believe in attack.

'Eduardo,' I said. 'Where is Mr van Diemen?'

The smile met round the back of his neck. 'The Senhora knows Senhor van Diemen! But naturally, the Senhora and her husband know all of importance on Madeira. Eduardo is glad to have served her.'

'Where?' I said. 'We want to speak to Mr van Diemen. Urgently. Is he here? Was he here yesterday?' I waited, and then said, 'Eduardo, it would be worth a lot to me to know just what Mr van Diemen has been doing. An *awful* lot.'

Eduardo exchanged dimpling smiles with his mother-in-law and turned back, all attention.

'Mr van Diemen? This visit, alas, I have not seen him. Since we met, the Senhora and I, have I not been here, to look after my wife's family? They will tell you. Not a step have I stirred from the house these three days, except to go for the priest and the doctor.

'Mr van Diemen? No. But why come to me? There is an office in town, a big office. There you will get your answer.'

He produced this great smile, and held it. I gazed at him, and so did Ferdy, and so did everyone else in the room except the baby, who suddenly got filled to the brim and fell off the slopes.

A jet of milk hit the ceiling and fell like a tennis-court marker along and down Ferdy's tanned head and fawn whiskers.

Ferdy said, 'Rita?'

I knew it was awful and they were all lying and everything, and I was heartsick myself underneath it all, but I'd never seen anything so brilliant as the horror of Ferdy's face at that moment. Even though I shut my eyes and dug my teeth in my lip, I could feel the tears of laughter hanging on to all my lashes.

By the time I opened my eyes, Ferdy was laughing too, politely, along with everyone else, and wiping his head with his hankie.

We thanked Eduardo, drank our wine, and got out, leaving another pittance on the bed for the baby. In the car, I said I was sorry.

'It is the first time,' said Ferdy, 'I have been zonked in the eye by a Portuguese baby. You realize we can't prove anything?'

'I know. But we haven't proved they couldn't have done it,' I said. 'Van Diemen could have got Eduardo to do things for him. He must have, or Eduardo would have shopped him. They could have planned the sledge bit between them. They could even have planned –'

'Rita,' said Ferdy. The mist had cleared. He was driving quite carefully down back to the coast again, honking at bad corners and thinking. He said, 'Even if van Diemen and Eduardo were both seen outside the villa the night Kim-Jim died, how could they possibly have killed him? That's the real facer.'

'I know,' I said.

After a bit, he said, 'Then what next? Say the word. I'll do anything you want. You could try to get Eduardo alone, if you want to see what a really big bribe could do. If you think it's worth it.'

I said, 'I don't think he'd take it, even if the family weren't there. He's sort of a family man. I don't think he'd think twice about fixing that sledge trip. Or any other kind of stupid, dangerous trick. The thing is ...'

'You liked him,' said Ferdy. 'And you don't think he would deliberately set out to murder.'

I thought that was very decent, considering how, one way or another, they had soaked him. I said, 'I did like him.'

'I could tell,' said Ferdy. 'He's got your sense of humour. Well, what? What do we do next?'

'I don't know,' I said. I really didn't. And it wasn't fair to keep Ferdy dangling. He had his own work to do. I said, 'Natalie wants to get back to London.'

She had some meetings to set up for the film. Since Kim-Jim died, she hadn't asked me again if I wanted the contract, and I hadn't told her.

Ferdy said, 'Will you stay with her? With that money, I suppose you can do anything you like.'

'It's too soon. I don't know that either,' I said. 'But if she wants me, at least I'll go back to England with her. By the time she's ready for the next trip, I'll know what I want to do.'

'Plenty of work in London just now,' Ferdy said. 'The Princess's wedding. And they're doing a telly film drama series of that American book. Nice work there, if you want it.'

'I know,' I said.

We were nearly back at the villa. Ferdy drew in, and stopped the car, and turned and looked at me.

'Poor Rita. You bloody miss him, don't you?' he said. 'I'm not going to pry, but you know the questions everyone is asking. Sugar daddy? Future husband? Real daddy, even?'

The idea of Kim-Jim as my father made me snort, which I suppose was the idea.

All the same, in a way Ferdy deserved an answer. And Kim-Jim deserved that folk thought of him decently, as he had been.

I said, 'Of course he wasn't my father. And I didn't go to bed with him either. Ferdy, we'd only *met* once before.'

Ferdy's round eyes were gazing at me quite seriously between the earrings, and I tried to explain.

'He was just a nice, lonely man who needed to talk shop with a pal. I don't know why he picked me to leave his money to, except that he didn't have anyone else. I was sort of his cats' home.'

Ferdy didn't speak. I went on sitting, and he went on looking at me. Then he took a spike of my hair on either side and turned my face round, and grinned at me.

'What's this cats' home?' he said. 'Who named you the Scotch Bird of Paradise? King Ferdy, the world's best photographer. Who's going to take London by storm, and to hell with Madeira and the rest of the world's sweaty islands? Rita Geddes, the world's best make-up artist. Check?'

Ferdy can get very sentimental. Singing 'The Song of the Flea' really suits him much better. But he means well.

He started the car again then, and we topped this little rise, and we saw this long, good-looking ship, big as a liner, moving slowly out of Funchal harbour.

Flying above it, nastily, brazenly, jauntily, was the blue and yellow flag of the Coombe Banana Company.

We had had a fruitful morning. We had been very clever. I had got to like Eduardo even, once I'd seen him again.

But if Roger van Diemen had been on the island when Kim-Jim died, he was surely off it now.

Next day, the Curtises arrived at Reid's, nursed their jet lag, and then turned up for lunch at Natalie's for a sort of doom party, with everyone who had coped with Kim-Jim's death.

Ferdy said he wasn't going. Carl Thomassen, his Sexy Flower Book botanist, had flown in with the text, and he and a young friend planned to work on the diagrams. Underneath, Ferdy was being quite serious. The book was important, and he liked what he did to be perfect. As his assistants all knew.

Maggie said she wasn't going either, and then changed her mind as soon as she heard Johnson had accepted.

I didn't want to lunch, but Natalie said it was only fair to Kim-Jim's own flesh and blood. They might be, as she and I knew, among the wealthiest in the American entertainment industry, but still must feel a natural interest (she said) in anyone who had meant so much to Kim-Jim.

That was the nearest she had ever come to a jab over that will. Even then, there was nothing personal about it.

Kim-Jim's death had upset her. But she'd have shown the same kind of shock, I now saw, if Dodo had died. The services Kim-Jim supplied were, in her eyes, all part of the job.

And he in his turn had been the perfect servant-companion. He admired her. Instead of fighting his way to the top in the real world, he did it all at second hand, by smoothing the way for Natalie. And later, out of sheer kindness, for me.

I should have expected that will, if I'd understood their relationship better. He didn't want to remember his family. And he knew that to bequeath his wordly goods to the great Natalie was out of the question. Image-building, after all, was his business.

I didn't want to be stuck with his family either, but I went down to join the lunch-party in the end. On my own terms. Image-building is my business as well.

It didn't go as I'd planned.

They were having drinks when I came downstairs to the sitting-room and everyone looked up: the shining Mr Kazimierz and Maggie on a footstool beside Johnson and Natalie and two new guys accepting double martinis in basins from Aurelio.

Natalie looked at the stripes on my face for a moment, and then simply introduced me, smiling a little, in the quiet voice she was using to the newly-bereaved.

She said, 'We never know what to expect when Rita comes in. She's the most exotic thing in Madeira. Rita Geddes, Kim-Jim's great friend ... Rita, this is Kim-Jim's brother, Clive, and Porter, his nephew.'

It didn't go as I'd planned, because they were fantastic.

Clive was tall, like in his picture in Kim-Jim's room, and carried himself well; but not like a guy who'd gone to ballet classes. From the set of his shoulders and his handshake, I guessed that he spent a lot of time in pools as well as posing beside them, and probably played a hell of a lot of tennis as well. His Californian tan was quite something.

It was possible that, as I'd wondered, the black hair was tinted, and the red moustache was certainly touched up.

It didn't matter. What looks tarted-up on a middle-aged piece of flab looked fine on a fit, active man who seemed ten years younger than he must be. His eyes crinkled, sending lines to his ears like a protractor, and he had a small mouth, like Kim-Jim's, with the teeth dentally weeded out to make a nice smile.

He said, 'I guess you and I have a lot to say to one another, about Kim-Jim and everything. Back there in L.A., we know your work, Rita. We know the kind of artist you are. I'm real sad at what brings us together but I wanted you to know that we have a lot in common, and the Curtis family respect you.'

'I'll say,' said the nephew. 'Natalie, you didn't tell us.'

I didn't even stop to see if Natalie winced when Porter used her first name, I was so bowled over.

As I've said, Sharon Proost, nay Curtis, was a smart woman, as her videos show. Her son, Porter, wasn't just smart, he was gorgeous.

He was six feet two, and red-headed, with the sort of clinging half-curly hair that stays neat no matter what, like heat-treated nylon.

He had brown eyes like cufflinks, and a straight nose with a blunt end, and a small mouth that let you see two bright front teeth when he smiled.

He was wearing a shirt and tie too, but his shoulders bulged with muscle still growing. I supposed he'd be nineteen. Maggie's age.

I looked at Maggie.

I was surprised. Instead of eyeing Porter and Clive, or at the very least, staging a show for them, she was still firing the big guns at Johnson. I could hear her drawling voice, hopefully needling him, and see the intent look inside the eye-shadow. Her finishing school had been pathetic about make-up, although what she usually wasn't wearing from the neck down more than made up for it.

Johnson himself just wore that bloody polite look I remembered over his pyjamas. Above Maggie's Vidal, I could see the twin lenses trained on me, with a pair of black eyebrows sitting higher than usual above them.

A real Owner bally sick stare.

To hell with Johnson. I stared back, and gave a hullo look at Mr Kalimazoo and brought my eyes right back to Porter Proost, who was saying, 'Wow! I tell you, ma'am, there were some things Kim-Jim didn't mention ... Natalie, I'm sitting next to her.'

Mourning sort of slid out of Natalie's voice. She said, 'You're my guests. You must sit anywhere you like.' And I could see Aurelio put the drinks tray down and slip off to change the place cards without being told.

I bet I'd been put between Kalimazoo and the wall.

It was like having Kim-Jim back, almost. I sat between Clive and Porter, and they knew all the films I'd done, and about the comedy series, and my work for Ferdy and everything.

They wanted to borrow my video tapes. They fixed to send me tapes of their own, with work Clive had done for Gothics and M.G.M. Biblicals, and their father, old Joseph, for cops and classics.

They didn't talk about Kim-Jim very much, except to say he'd always been the quiet one of the family, and they hadn't been surprised when he decided he wanted to get out of the industry. They said to Natalie how very happy they were that he'd had such a wonderful time sharing her home.

Halfway through, Clive, realizing he'd been neglecting Natalie, began to talk to her about her filming, and Porter concentrated on me, with his teeth and his brown, teasing eyes.

He was a great talker. That time, I didn't think of Kim-Jim at all.

It was just about evening when they left, and I'd shown Clive and Porter Kim-Jim's workroom, and Porter had said he was going to be in London when Natalie was, and he'd like to see something of me, and Clive said that he knew the guys who were turning that American book into a film, and if I liked, he'd introduce me.

Natalie said, 'I hope you'll tell me if you're going to persuade Rita to do something else.'

And Clive's back-ache laugh-lines all vanished and he said, 'Mrs Sheridan, I'm so sorry. We thought Rita might need some work. But if she's staying with you ... That's great. That's marvellous. It couldn't be better.'

There was a sort of silence, while they all looked at me.

We were all standing in the hall, waiting for the cars to drive Johnson and the two Curtises back to Reid's, and Maggie and Kalimazoo back to the Sheraton. Behind us, Maggie was still firing at Johnson, and he was returning 17B replies, briefly, at intervals.

At this moment, she was saying, 'Doesn't the hotel or someone fix you with girls? Is this Lent? Or what's wrong with you?'

I would have thought more than twice before saying that, even tiddly as she was. But when the Swiss have finished with you, you don't care.

She got a one-word reply from Johnson. 'Satiety?'

Maggie said, 'I don't think you bloody can. What hit the ground when you crashed?'

'I'm all right,' Johnson said. 'Implant surgery. They gave me this irrigation system for grow-bags. Nine pounds of tomatoes, last year. That's your car. Do you think you can walk to it?'

She was crazy about him. I watched her lurch to the car, and wondered if I should tell her or not about Raymond.

Then Clive said, 'Then you're staying in private work, Rita?' and I remembered what we'd been talking about.

I said, 'I don't quite know yet. But I'll be in London. If Porter's to be there, we could meet sometime.'

Natalie, I suppose, was less than pleased, but she didn't show it. Only after they were all away, and I was alone with her in the dressing-room, making her up for a big party that evening, did she say, 'You liked the Curtises?'

'They were O.K.,' I said.

'Part of cinema history,' she said. And after a pause, 'So I gather you don't mean to retire?'

With the Curtises about, I was taking extra care with Natalie's face that evening. I said, 'I like my job and everything. You need to know about the Josephine film?'

She said, 'I would like to have it settled, of course. And I have offered you Kim-Jim's job. If you don't want it, I shall need to see about someone else.'

133

I didn't know. I said, 'Can I tell you in London?'

The way she looked, when I'd finished with her, she couldn't not agree.

Two days later, she was back in Claridge's, and Maggie was back in the London flat she shared with a girlfriend, and Kalimazoo was back in New York, and the Curtises were back in L.A. with the coffin, and inside it all I'd been hoping Madeira would give me.

Where Johnson was, I didn't know and I didn't care. He said good-bye to Natalie, but he didn't say good-bye to me. He was the one who told me to go home to Troon, because nothing would happen. Before we all flew out, *Dolly* had sailed from the island.

To find where Ferdy was, you only had to ask a Virginian Poke. With his botanical doctor in tow, he was completing his survey of flowers on Madeira.

There is no such word as brothanical.

Before I left the island, I phoned my stockbroker, and when we landed, I booked myself into the Hilton. Then I fixed myself two days of absence from Natalie, and flew north to Glasgow.

Senility's not a nice thing. Sometimes it hits quite young people, and sometimes it never gets to you at all.

Robina, my mother, was still quite decent-looking, except for this big conk we all have. But this time she wasn't just muddled: she didn't know me at all.

The nurses hustled me out after a bit, mainly because they hadn't seen my face stripe-painted before.

My aunt had, and left me in no doubt, again, how she felt about it.

I listened to all the moans about the nursing-home fees and what needed done to the house, and how the lower classes were boors nowadays. I paid all the bills she hadn't already paid, and arranged for the bank to pay more every month into her housekeeping. I went back to London.

Natalie was still having talks and didn't need me. I rang a few people to say I was around, and a lot of calls began to come in from old clients booking special occasion make-ups, mostly for the same days.

I rang one or two of the T.V. companies, and a man I knew who knew a man who was scripting the big melodrama they were going to do on this American book.

He said that he'd pass along the news I might be interested, but he'd heard that the Curtis family were going to work on it.

One of the T.V. companies said the same thing about their new thriller series.

I rang off feeling thoughtful. The Curtises weren't to blame. They'd just about offered to help, and Natalie had butted in with her bit about Owner's Rights.

All the same. The Curtis family had never worked in Britain before. It would be a bit silly if I moved out with Natalie to the West Indies, and came back to find they'd moved in.

I began to wonder if I ought not to stay in Britain after all. And let the Curtises have the Josephine film if they wanted it.

No hassle. It just meant that now, Rita, you have to make up your mind.

I looked at my two yellow cats in the Hilton, and thought I would help myself make up my mind by an afternoon in the country.

PETS INC was the name on the smart green and black board by the driveway, but you didn't need to read it, because you could hear them.

Kennels for pets and some breeding were all that Lee and Amy Faflick went in for when they started their farms in the fifties. Later, they got to be something else.

So I wasn't surprised at the tall security fence, or the double gateway at the entrance where you had to phone to be let in.

I'd rung for an appointment. Lee and Amy were in America, but I knew the guy, Jim Brook, who ran the English end of the business, and he came to let me in himself.

A plain-spoken guy with basin-cut brown hair, and an old jersey and leggings, he looked like one of your good local vets, which is what he used to be. Except that vets don't usually have big sewn-up scars on their forearms, unless they have to do with circuses, which gives you a clue.

The Faflicks didn't service circuses: they provided trained beasts for film companies.

Any time you've seen a Rin-Tin-Tin flick, or a series about pirates or cowboys or Mounties or otters, or an ad for beer, or choc bars, or petrol, or toilet paper, you can bet that the animals came from a farm like the Faflicks'.

Like make-up, it's big business now, compared with the old days. The first Brooke Bond chimps just came from a zoo. The Lloyd's black horse had been a circus high school act *and* a Black Beauty before he got led into banks and died in his thirties, leaving a helluva rich mare, I should think.

Companies like the Faflicks' don't keep all the animals themselves, since the Esso tiger and suchlike could be a worry to the cats and dogs, but they take fees for training and grooming them, and they'll act as importing agents when a *Raiders of the Lost Ark* wants more snakes and tarantula spiders than you get round the house.

Go to any television or film studio, and at one time or another you'll see the Faflick green and black trailer parked in the yard, with a box of rats or a camel being eased out of it.

I'd first met Jim Brook and Celia, the girl who headed the training team, on emergency call outside the B.B.C. when their kangaroo needed a quick cosmetic job done on a bitten nose.

The bite wasn't their fault, but the programme couldn't go ahead without disguising it. I'd been making up the rest of the cast, and had something in my fishing-tackle case that would do.

Since then, there had been a couple of other things, and I'd given them some free tips. Getting animals to look good on the telly is a bit like getting food to look good for a magazine: colour and varnish.

We talked about it, Jim and I, as we walked up the drive to the converted farmhouse they use. They do grow some of their feeding stuffs, and they have hay, but most of the fields round about were used for livestock, mixed where they would mix without doing any harm, but not too many of any one kind. One or two horses, one or two pigs, one or two cows, one or two sheep fabulously clipped, with no barbed wire in sight to ruffle their gorgeous Woolmark.

Two fields away, making a clanking sound, a man in armour was riding heavily round and round on a horse with tassels all over it.

There was no sign of Celia in the house, so we walked round, still talking, to the back.

The old laundry was the grooming shop, with rows of shears and scissors and curry-combs hanging from nails on the wall above the dog and cat benches, and a sunk bath in the middle where Celia, in a rubber apron and wellies, was just finishing shampooing an Old English sheepdog in a cloud of green bubbles.

At first, I thought it was Bessie.

Then I remembered the Owner's stupid crack, and saw that this was a young dog, anyway. It liked Celia and kept trying to lick her with a tongue like a Tongue. She said, 'Hi, Rita. Give her coffee, Jim. Be with you in minutes.'

As we turned away she called after me, 'What's with the suntan? Costa del Clyde in April?' and screeched, as she deserved to, as the dog got out and shook itself.

By the time we were on our second coffee indoors she came in, in her stocking soles with the apron off. The dog came in after her, already half dry and smelling of Liquid Fairy.

Celia said, 'Did you show Rita the elephant wash?'

He had. It was the same as a car wash only adapted. The elephants could work it themselves.

Somewhere a whistle blew, and the door noiselessly opened on a scrap of a dog who scampered to Celia's chair and, rising, pawed her knee anxiously.

'Oh, what a good boy!' said Celia. She picked the dog up and rose, making a fuss of him. To me she said, 'That's the kettle boiling. Any more Instant?'

She disappeared, carrying orders for two more cups and a refill of the sugar bowl, the dog's tail flapping under her arm like a duster.

'Tibetan terrier, name of Tiki,' said Jim. 'Owner lives with a deaf relative. Celia's trained him to tell when the kettle boils. And when the doorbell or the telephone rings. Clever tyke.'

'Clever Celia,' I said. Celia began her professional life as Consultant in Animal Behaviour to a pet food research centre, but Amy had brought her a long way since then. So had technology. I had heard the tapes they used, added to all the patient teaching, over and over.

You can teach anything nearly to anything. The Harvard Shrink Department say they can teach a pigeon to walk a figure-of-eight in fifteen minutes flat.

Celia came back with the coffee tray and the knight in armour, who took off his head, showing a lot of tight-curled yellow hair and a bashed and suntanned face I unfortunately knew.

'Raymond,' I said.

'You know each other?' said Celia, handing out refills. 'Can you sit down in that stuff?'

'No,' said Raymond. 'Miss Geddes and I met on Mr Johnson's yacht in Madeira.'

He stopped, with a buckle half undone, and looked at me, apparently struck by something. 'You're not here to choose his new dog as well?'

'No, I'm not,' I snapped through the noise of unknighting. It was like someone unloading a dishwasher. When he got down to the cutlery racks he sat and took Celia's coffee.

'Just as well,' he said. It could have been a threat: it was hard to tell. I would dearly have liked to know where Johnson was at this moment, but I wasn't going to ask this guy.

Then I realized what he was saying.

I looked at the landslide of white fluff asleep at our feet, and at Celia. I said, 'Don't say Bessie came . . . ?'

'From here? Yes, of course,' Celia said. 'Trained, too. Big stage career, that bitch had.'

'As Nana,' said Jim. 'The *Peter Pan* nursemaid. Used to carry the postman on his rounds every morning. Should have been put down long ago. The bitch, not the postman. But there you are. Well, now.'

He had glanced at the clock, but briefly. He was always busy. He said, 'Here's Mr Johnson's henchman come to look over dogs, and he finds himself dragooned into training a warhorse.'

'I volunteered,' Raymond said.

'You did. So what can we do for you, young Rita?'

Young Rita.

Hell.

And with Raymond present, double dammergung.

I said, 'Just advice. I've been left one of your parrots by someone living abroad. It's great, but I've nowhere to keep it. D'you want it back?'

Out of the corner of my eye I saw Raymond put his cup down, very carefully. Jim Brook said, 'One of ours? We don't usually keep them.'

'An old one. One of Lee and Amy's, I think. I brought a photograph of it,' I said.

Raymond was still staring at me. I brought out the picture. It was a colour one, taken for me by the man who photographs tourists in bullock carts.

Jim looked at it, and Celia got up and bent over it, too. Jim said, 'It's a St Lucia.'

'Red Data Book. That's a shame, honey,' said Celia.

Apart from its language, it was a perfectly ordinary green parrot, quite big, with a blue head and bits of red here and there. 'A what?' I said.

Celia sat down and took pity on me. 'It's a rare parrot,' she said. 'Comes from the island of St Lucia. That's in the West Indies. Eats bananas, so the banana people haven't been kind to it. As a result, it's in the

Birds and Mammals Red Data Book, the internationally agreed list of rare and endangered species.

'They don't get exported from St Lucia at all, and anyone wanting to move one from anywhere to anywhere has to go through hoops till kingdom come, explaining what they want them for, and why. Where is it?'

'Madeira,' I said.

'It's an old one,' said Jim. He held the picture up. 'Must have come in before the regulations. Before quarantine even, probably.'

'Quarantine?' I said. 'Six months in solitary, like dogs and cats?'

'No,' Celia said. 'Or at least. I'm pretty sure not. As I say, we don't have parrots now. But it used to be sort of house arrest only. That is, you could keep it in your house for the quarantine period, provided that it was in a special room, and it had no contact with other birds. A terrible fuss, but at least it didn't interrupt the lessons if you were training it. Is this one trained?'

'On film dialogue,' I said. 'It knows the catch-phrases of every old film you ever saw. Its owner used to watch them on video.'

'It might be more than that,' said Jim Brook suddenly. 'If the owner had had it a while, it might have come before the regulations from America. If it was a Faflick parrot, it probably did. So what was its name?'

'Cone,' I said. And a damned stupid name, although I didn't say it.

Celia and Jim Brook looked at one another.

'Then there you are!' said Jim.

I looked at him.

'Call yourself a film buff and don't know the name of one of the biggest studio bosses? Who do you think had that parrot in his office in Hollywood?' said Jim Brook.

Upon which, I got it.

Not Cone, but Cohn. I should have known. It hadn't stopped talking since its barmitzvah.

And that would be why Natalie had given it to Kim-Jim all that time ago, when she first bought a house on Madeira, and Kim-Jim had moved in. There hadn't been any import certificates and there would have been, if the parrot had popped in and out.

It had been another bit of proof, if I'd needed one, about Natalie's relationship with Kim-Jim.

When I'd asked her, she could remember nothing of interest about the parrot's past. Except that it had struck her, as she put it, 'that he and Kim-Jim deserved one another'.

She was perfectly content that it should pass to me, with the rest of the things he'd been fond of.

I said, 'If it's too much form-filling, maybe I should ask Mrs Sheridan to let it stay in Madeira. You could let me know if Lee or Amy would like it here, or on the American side. It's a piece of history, sort of.'

'That parrot,' said Celia, 'is coming here, if I have to threaten to walk out to get it. Yes, Jim?'

'If Rita doesn't want it,' said Jim Brook. 'And if she changes her mind, she can always get it back. You leave it to us. I'll write to Lee. And the regulations will be our affair. We do it all the time. O.K., Rita?'

I'd got all I wanted, and they were busy. I got up, and Raymond said, 'Run you back to town?'

He still had his leg-plates on. I said, 'I thought you had to see a man about a dog?'

'Oh, I've finished,' he said. 'Arranged a short leet for the boss, when he's back. I'll get my shoes.'

I let him go to get his shoes, and left while he was away. The taxi I'd ordered, thank God, had arrived and stood at the end of the drive.

I got the taxi to drive into the next sideroad and stop, until a red sports car came snoring out of the Faflicks' and roared up the London road, with Raymond at the wheel.

I gave him five minutes, and then the driver got me to the station in good time for the next train to London. He thought that young Hurrah Henrys that pestered a girl ought to be told off by the authorities, and I agreed.

I rang Natalie from the Hilton but she didn't need me that day or next.

Clive Curtis's nephew, young Porter, had dropped in, she said, and been very helpful. He might as well come along next morning and finish what he'd started, since he seemed to be at a loose end, and didn't mind.

I wondered what he'd started, and reminded myself what I'd already decided. It was time to make up my mind what I wanted.

I was thinking about parrots when the phone rang.

It was one of my nicer Debrett's cancelling an appointment, but asking if I would mind, as a personal favour, transferring it to a delightful friend, whom I would like very much.

It was for the following morning, at a Knightsbridge address not all that far away from where I was.

I agreed, and switched off the tape-recorder, and rang room service to get some sandwiches sent up. I had even picked up the paper to see what the telly had to offer that might be useful, when something about that appointment struck me as odd.

I never write appointments down. I always record them.

I played the tape back.

The address was quite ordinary: one of those grand terraced houses off Belgrave Square that always have horse shit lying in front of them.

The name had seemed quite ordinary too, until I remembered where I'd come across it before.

Lady Emerson, my new client was. The tough, good-looking mother of Joanna who had ordered Johnson about, and told me to sit on his Gay letters.

No friend, one would hope, of Raymond's.

I thought about it all for quite a while, and only realized afterwards that I'd missed *Lost Horizon* and the Shangri-la corpses again.

I got three more phone calls from people wanting special occasions, and one from a T.V. company and one from Porter, Kim-Jim's nephew, saying what the hell did I mean coming back to London without letting him know, and he'd got stuck with The Hag, but could I come out with him as soon as he was free tomorrow.

The Hag. It wasn't nice, but my heart fairly warmed to him. I said I would.

After that, Lady Emerson didn't seem any great deal, either then or next morning.

I had breakfast, and then I did what the cop thrillers always don't do, and taped and left in my room a full note of where I was going and why, for the police, in case my body turned up under the horse shit.

Then I packed my tackle-case, put on my white cotton blazer with drill trousers to match, and Jesus sandals, and a headband that showed both the blue and orange bits in my hair, and went off by taxi to Belgravia. In honour of the occasion, I had not painted stripes on my face.

The door was opened by a nice maid, in uniform. The hall was floored in black and white marble and there was a wrought-iron staircase with red carpet on it.

I was taken up to the drawing-room floor, and then further up to the private floor, and Lady Emerson's bedroom and boudoir.

The boudoir was more of an office, and not very well lit for make-up. I hoped she had a decent dressing-room somewhere. The maid shut the door behind me, and Lady Emerson got up and came forward.

As I've said before, she was a good-looking woman, with curling hair fading a bit at the temples, and a thin, longish face with good cheekbones.

As before, she was dressed more country-style than you would expect for someone being made up for a lunch date, although the silk blouse was a classic and the tweed skirt fitted her hips like an ad.

She said, 'Miss Geddes. You must have remembered the name. I'm glad you didn't mind coming. Perhaps a sherry, before we begin?'

'That's all right,' I said. 'Thank you.'

I looked about, while she fetched it.

It was a nice room, worn and comfortable, with an old writing bureau in the corner, its flap covered with papers. There were sweet peas on the table beside it, and photographs in heavy frames, groups and single ones.

One of them was of a thin girl in her teens: the absent Joanna of the drippy jam, maybe. One was of a girl too old to be Lady Emerson's daughter, but younger than me. Someone in films, maybe. She was as good-looking as that.

One was taken in winter, at a ski-jump. A competition, by the look of the crowds. The camera had focussed on the jumper, skimming off into the sunlight, sharp and clear.

Flying black hair, and goggles, this time, instead of bifocals. The pre-crash Owner.

'Here's your sherry,' said Lady Emerson, and looked where I was looking. She said, 'I ought to put those away. Come and sit down.'

We sat. Women are often nervous when they're about to be made up. I'm used to it. If they suggest a drink, I always agree. It helps them, and I don't mind.

Lady Emerson wasn't exactly nervous, so much as concerned, I thought, about how I was taking it. We talked about nothing. We talked about Madeira, and she suddenly took the bull by the horns and said, 'Well, of course, I know you were there: Johnson told me. And what happened. I'm very sorry about that.'

'That's all right,' I said. I wasn't going to talk to her about Kim-Jim.

She said, 'Johnson can be quite helpful sometimes. I hope you made use of him. I don't think he realizes yet, as I do, how much good you did, that time you stayed at the flat.'

I wondered what she thought I'd done in the flat, apart from walking the dog and saving the grapes from going bad. And getting up the Owner's blood pressure by suggesting he put down his life's companion.

I remembered the fuss about the phone bills and the bet over the sledge, and concluded she didn't know her bloody Johnson. I said, 'I enjoyed it.'

Which was not so far from the truth. Bossy Rita. Says my aunt.

'In that case . . .' said Lady Emerson, and stood up. She was frowning. She said, over my shoulder, 'Really, this wasn't in the contract. Come and do your own dirty work.'

I turned round and got up as well.

As I'd hoped, she did have a dressing-room. The door to it opened behind me. A black-haired man wandered out of it and, steering past the bureau and table, hitched himself on to a chair arm. After the photograph, I wasn't all that surprised to see who it was.

'It's all very well for you,' said Johnson Johnson. 'Hyped up on sherry. But I've got to do all this cold. Miss Geddes, I've kidnapped you again.'

It wasn't an Owner voice or a Maggie voice. More the ordinary style of the guy in the kitchen.

'So I notice,' I said. 'Can I leave now?'

'If you like,' Johnson said. 'But you'll miss my Black Belt throw and another sherry. I just wanted to tell you something.'

'What?' I said.

I wasn't worried. I could beat them both to the door.

'That I think you're right,' Johnson said. 'That I think Kim-Jim Curtis was killed. And that I'd like your help in finding who murdered him.'

12

I have heard of some revolting faces in my time, but *that* from a guy who had taken the trouble he had to pour cold water on all my suspicions ... that beat everything.

I stayed on my feet. I had no doubt what to do.

'Great,' I said. 'I'll go to the police with you.'

There was a short silence. Johnson, I saw, was looking over my head at Lady Emerson. 'I told you,' he said. 'I need a sherry.'

'Jay. You mustn't,' she said.

From the way she said it, he had to be an alcoholic.

'Yes, I must,' he said.

He didn't rush for a drink, but turned the bifocals without fuss on me.

'Look,' he said. 'Before you believe me, I have to tell you why I won't go to the police, and why I want your help anyway. Right?'

'Right,' I said.

'But you want to stay handy for the door. Frances, lady mine, could you turn that chair round? Miss Geddes? Would you feel safe in that? Frances used to be a great quarter-miler but she's got a tight skirt on, and as you have cause to know, I am still just held together by paperclips ...'

His mouth got wider. 'Anyway, I bet you left a message for Scotland Yard on your tape-recorder,' he said.

Bloody Owner. I sat down. I couldn't help it. So did Lady Emerson.

Johnson stayed where he was, looking rather uncomfortable on the edge of the desk. The Madeira sun had caught his face a bit and taken some of the deadness out of it, and his hair had more life in it. He didn't have cancer.

'Right,' he said. 'Begin at the end.'

He drew out the hand in his pocket and threw down two woollen objects. They lay on the carpet, and I looked at them.

A pair of gloves. My gloves. The gloves I'd left at 17B when I'd walked Bessie. I said, 'Where were they?'

'I hid them,' said Johnson. 'Just to see if I was right. And you did get lost, didn't you?'

The bastard.

I could feel Lady Emerson looking at my face. She said sharply, 'What are you saying to her?'

'Look at the palms,' Johnson said.

The double bastard.

She did, turning them over to look at the embroidery. An 'L' on one, and a 'R' on the other.

Johnson got up, and taking the gloves from Lady Emerson, laid them on my lap and took a chair opposite me.

'Drink, and listen,' said Johnson. 'Without her gloves, Miss Geddes doesn't know her left hand from her right. She can't find her way to her own home, never mind how to reach an address she's never been to. That's why she doesn't drive, and why she goes everywhere by taxi.'

I hated him. I drank my sherry, because it was spilling. He hadn't finished.

'Without a tape-recorder, Miss Geddes can't accept telephone messages, because she can't write. Separated from her notes or her diary, she can't make phone calls because she can't remember the numbers for long enough. The notes she makes are mostly drawings, because she can interpret them quickly, whereas she reads words very slowly indeed, or not at all.

'She can't with any ease master books or newspapers, therefore the television is her main source of information. There are, of course, lots of others. She has learned what is likely to stick and what isn't.

'Miss Geddes is used to being regarded, as a result of all this, as of below average intelligence. Her intelligence is in fact higher than average. The result is that she has learned also to become extremely resilient. Her reactions are amazingly fast. She is a hard worker, and a perfectionist.

'She is creative, with a sure eye for colour and design, and quite brilliant in a job which happily makes the most of her talents, without giving away her weaknesses.

'As a one-woman business, she has hedged herself about with accountants and other professionals who handle her affairs. And handle them very successfully. Even without Kim-Jim's legacy, I imagine she could live off her investments, if she wished, to the end of her life.

'She is, you see, a successful, intelligent young woman, as well as a bloody courageous one, who has merely had the misfortune to be born with a disability.

'Miss Geddes is word-blind. She suffers from what is officially known as dyslexia, for which there is no absolute remedy.'

He stopped.

No one spoke. My heart was wagging my head up and down, and my blood had gone into patterns all over my face and head like a sort of prickly moquette.

I could have stood it better if Kim-Jim's death hadn't happened so recently. I did stand it, though. I couldn't speak, but I didn't go for him. Or burst into tears, or anything.

Lady Emerson said, 'Well, now you've delivered your lecture, I don't suppose there's any reason why we shouldn't have another good slug of sherry. I'll bring the glasses. You pour.'

She took mine from my hand. As she carried it over the room, she said over her shoulder, 'I don't know why he imagines nobody else has ever heard of these things. I know two dyslectics. Boy and a girl. It's not as rare as you'd think. But he's quite right. It does need courage.'

She came back and handed me my glass, and sat down with her own. She said, 'What do you do in the summertime? Ink your palms?'

'I wear rings ... Who are they?' I said. 'The ones you know?'

'They're young. They live in America, where the schools tend to look out for that sort of thing. Over here, teachers often don't understand.'

'No,' I said. I had spilt some of my sherry again. I put it down and said, 'All right. That's what it's like. You know all about it. So what?'

This time, he had brought back a drink for himself. He put it down, sat down restlessly on the arm of the chair he had just left, and hitched up a hip to get at his pipe and tobacco pouch, his eyebrows requesting permission.

Lady Emerson said, 'If Miss Geddes doesn't mind, I think I'm going to leave you to tell her the next bit on your own. I don't think perhaps that was very fair to her.'

'Yes it was,' I said flatly. 'But I don't see how it matters.'

She got up, still carrying her drink and looked down on me. 'Oh, I can see that,' she said. 'He's showing you that you would be the better for a partner. And that if he knows all that about you and wants you to help him, then you must be more of an asset to him than you know.'

She looked at Johnson, who had his head bent over the ritual pipe ceremony. She looked at me. 'I shan't be far away if you want me,' she said, and left the room.

I said, 'It doesn't make sense unless you're the police, or unless you're on Roger van Diemen's side. And so far, I know you know van Diemen. I know you tried to tell me the sledge thing was an accident. I know you tried to stop me going after Eduardo and making a fuss about whether Kim-Jim's death was a suicide. And none of that puts you on the side of the police. Or on my side.'

'You think not?' said Johnson. He finished lighting his pipe, and shaking out the match, found somewhere to toss it. Then he put the pipe stem in his mouth, his elbow cupped in his hand, and watched me quietly through the smoke.

After a bit he took his pipe out and said, 'You're quite right. I didn't want you to start a witch hunt, but not to protect Kim-Jim's murderer.

'I *do* know Roger van Diemen. He *has* become addicted to drugs. If he's committed murder, then he must be punished, like anybody else. The trouble is that there are two sets of witches in this story, and by crashing about after Roger, you were in danger of warning off mine. Because Roger is the common link.'

'How?' I said. I seemed to have drunk off my sherry. I put it down.

'Financial Director of Coombe International, with its own fleet, and offices all over the West Indies, and in Europe and South America. Come on,' said Johnson. 'It's a script conference. What do you think he could be up to?'

I thought, thumbing my headband and staring at my toes in the Jesus sandals.

The smell of heroin. The blue and yellow flag of the *Coombe Regina*, slipping out to her next port of call with her refrigerated cargo.

Bananas. And drugs.

I said it aloud. I said, 'You're going to tell me you're with Necrosis.'

'Narcotics actually,' Johnson said. 'That was shrewd.'

I said, 'Not really. Hash and heroin are always coming into the Clyde. Everyone knows one parlour junkie.'

'And you? Do you take it?' he said.

'I've tried most things,' I said, which was true. I tried most things once, and then dropped them. The central thing I hadn't tried was none of his business.

He set down his glass, which was half empty. 'Then try this,' he said.

'I said Roger van Diemen was the link between two witch hunts. One arises out of the series of assaults on you and Kim-Jim. The other is concerned with the very early stages of a plan to use Coombe International as a way of smuggling drugs out of South America.

'The other top brass in the company are not involved. Van Diemen is just, in classic language, the inside man with the job of setting up the system. We want him, of course. But we also want the man outside, his partner, or more likely his boss, who buys the dope and puts up the money and will eventually make the whole thing work.

'We know about van Diemen. We don't know who the other is. We know he's working at present through a chain of go-betweens and is contacting van Diemen very little. We think that's because van Diemen is busy fact-finding just now: collecting all the data they'll need to construct the final operation.

'What I am waiting for therefore is the next stage, when van Diemen finishes his tour, presents the big fellow with the results and then discusses the final plan with him.

'They have to have a meeting at that point. If I keep on van Diemen's tail, we'll have our first real chance of finding out who his principal is. There may be enough evidence to put them away at that stage, or we may have to go along with it for a bit longer. But at least we'll be on the way. And since all that is going to take a bit of time, it's pretty important not to have van Diemen worried beforehand.'

Johnson stopped. He put out his hand, lifted his glass, drank, and put it down again. 'Do you buy it?' he said.

'No,' I said.

'Well, thank God,' said Johnson. 'For a moment I thought you were going to conform there. What's worrying you?'

I said, 'Lots of things. Van Diemen knows you. He flipped when he saw you at Funchal. The Necropolis people ...'

'Narcotics,' Johnson said.

'... the Narcotics people'd be stupid to use you to tail him. And there's Kim-Jim.'

Johnson stuck his pipe in his mouth, got up and transferred himself a bit stiffly into the chair itself. 'Yes, I know. Go on,' he said.

I said, 'If Roger van Diemen is on the point of making millions, I don't see how he should have bothered to risk arrest, risk losing his job, risk letting this drug-ring boss of his down by fooling about with all that stuff in Madeira.'

Johnson unfolded his pipe-holding arm, and laid the hand holding the bowl on his knee. He said, 'I think he knew it was a risk, all right, from the way he dodged away from me at the airport.

'I think perhaps he couldn't help himself. He really seems to be infatuated with Mrs Sheridan. He really seems to have thought that you and Kim-Jim were taking his place, and would cheat her. He may even have worked out that whatever he did, his boss would try to get him out of it, because as far as the dope business goes, he's irreplaceable.

'Added to which, he's on drugs. He took a cure, but it doesn't seem to have lasted. So you can't look for normal behaviour.'

He gave me, briefly, a glance I remembered from the Owner days.

He said, 'And you can't look for evidence against him either. There isn't any. If you want Roger van Diemen shopped, there is only one way to do it. Wait for me to get him first on the dope charge ... You've forgotten what you originally asked me.'

'No, I haven't,' I said. 'Why should the Narcissus ...'

'Narcotics,' said Johnson. Patiently.

'... why should the Narcotics Department use you? He knows you.'

'Come on,' said Johnson for the second time.

In a world where people always try to tell you things, it was a change to be asked.

I thought. I said, 'Because he'll argue the same way. If you're hanging about, you can't possibly be an agent of anyone.'

I had another idea. My headband snapped, and I took it off. I said, 'But all the same, you could be after his blood for what he did on Madeira. Off your own bat. Outraged ex-friend.'

'I couldn't,' said Johnson. 'I've protested Roger's innocence all the way through. You were extremely cross about it.'

I stared at him. 'That was why?'

Another thought. 'Then was that why you tried to persuade me to drop it? So he wouldn't think I was after him either?'

'Well, it worked,' Johnson said. 'Not that I frightened you off. Not that anything could frighten you off, I imagine, unless Scott Joplin rose from the grave with your legwarmers on.

'But since Kim-Jim's death, you haven't actually run about calling it murder. From van Diemen's point of view, you've got all you want, and a nice inheritance. He may not be the chap you'd most like to meet in a taxi, but with Kim-Jim gone, he can't feel threatened by you any longer.'

A sort of silence fell. I was thinking again. I said, 'Do you know where he is?'

'Yes,' said Johnson. 'Of course. Any Coombe's office will tell you where Mr van Diemen is at any given moment. Regular as All-Bran. He looks after a big empire, and there'd be questions asked pretty quickly if he started dodging the mandatory meetings.

'He travels all the time, and that, of course, is how he'll find it so simple to collect the data he needs. Different sides of Coombe's business are split off into different departments and sometimes even subsidiary companies. The bottom line on everything will find its way to the central computer, but for detail, he'll have to pick up local records.

'My guess is that he'll do that on his regular visits. He'll look at the likeliest crews, the handiest plantation managers, the possible container men and drivers and storemen and make up a scheme and a dossier. As I said, it's going to take time.'

'And the meeting?' I said. 'Where do you think they'll hold that?'

His pipe had stopped drawing. His head bent, he poked at it for a while, slowly; then, collecting it in one hand, used the other to drag off his bifocals. He looked up and straight at me.

I've seen more movies than most. I know an act when I see it. I knew, too, we'd come to the crunch.

He looked worn. He looked pretty convincing. He said calmly, 'In the West Indies.'

I said, 'And where's your yacht? Where's *Dolly*?'

'I thought you'd never ask. Crossing the Atlantic,' Johnson said. 'Crewed by Lenny, with friends. Raymond flew to join him early this morning. I'd be on board before you got to Martinique with Mrs Sheridan.'

He didn't have to say any more.

He had told me why he couldn't go to the police. Now he had told me why he wanted me to help him.

Because of all people, I had a cast-iron excuse to be in the West Indies. All over the West Indies.

Of all people, I had the motivation to get even with Roger van Diemen.

Of all people, I was likeliest to louse up his whole bloody programme unless he kept me there, under his eye. For whatever happened, I was going to get Kim-Jim's murderer.

The only problem was, whether I could believe Johnson's story. Or whether he was just a rich crock recently dropped on his head, never mind what he'd told Maggie.

I should go to the West Indies for nothing, and Clive Curtis and Porter would stay in London and mop up my clients.

'Two to one against,' said Johnson, apparently reading my face. 'You're a distrustful blighter, aren't you? What would convince you?'

He found his glasses in his hand and put them back on. It was an improvement.

'You tell me,' I said. 'I seem to be doing all the work here.'

He said, 'Thought you'd been lectured enough. It's better if you think it through and work out the pros and cons for yourself. Work out the ...'

'I know what pros and cons are,' I said. 'The cons have it.'

'And nothing would persuade you to believe me?'

'Why should I rack my brains? It's your problem,' I said.

'I'll make you a promise,' Johnson said. 'Whatever works out or doesn't, I'll find you Kim-Jim's murderer. And I'll see he's dealt with.'

Kim-Jim.

I'd never find the truth about Kim-Jim in London. Whether I believed Johnson or not, it had nothing to do with my real problem.

Either I gave up and stayed; or I tried to find Roger van Diemen.

And Johnson would help me, if he thought I believed all he'd told me.

I stared at the varnish on my toes.

Johnson said, 'There's another thing. This will only work if van Diemen thinks you've lost interest in him. So it wouldn't be wise to pass on what I've told you.'

'No,' I said. I wondered if Porter was lunching with Natalie, and when exactly he would be free. Of The Hag, he had said.

'So just in case,' Johnson said, 'I've got a thing for you to sign.'

He had got up and was rooting on Lady Emerson's desk among the papers. After a moment he drew something out and brought it over.

'Here we are,' he said. And spread it before me.

It was a three-page document, printed closely in black on stiff white paper, very smooth, with heavy black words at the head of it.

Johnson laid a pen beside it and walked to the drinks table.

'Take your time,' he said. 'The top bit is what matters. I'll read the rest of it to you, or Lady Emerson will do it, if you'd rather. Would you like more sherry, or would you like to get legless with vodka?'

He took a long time to find and pour out the vodka, which was just as well, for it took me a long time to work out what I was looking at.

It said OFFICIAL SECRETS ACT. And underneath were three pages of promises that I was expected to make, and to keep, or I'd go to prison.

I had pals who'd passed the exams for the Foreign Office. I knew what they signed.

The vodka came back, in Johnson's hand, and I took it. He stood, holding a glass of his own. 'I suppose I could have faked that,' he said. 'But I didn't.'

I believed him. I looked up at him. I said, 'What if I sign, but don't come with Natalie?'

There was a pause. Then he said, 'No problem. It's entirely your choice.'

'I'll sign it,' I said.

He stood, holding his glass as if he'd forgotten it.

'And come to the West Indies?' he said.

I made him wait for the answer to that. He did wait, without speaking or drinking.

'Yes,' I said.

There was a pause. Then he touched me lightly on the shoulder with his free hand and kept it there for a moment. 'Good girl. Wait there,' he said. 'You'll need witnesses. I'll get Frances.'

I waited for them to come back.

I sat, while Lady Emerson came in and read the document through aloud, clearly and quietly, and I tried to follow the words on the page.

I signed it, and nobody cheered, or slapped me on the back.

Lady Emerson took the drink Johnson poured her and sat, her eyes fixed on him. Then she said to me, 'It was his idea to ask you. He said you would do it. But don't let him push you beyond where you want to go.'

Johnson said, 'Frances. She and I are after the same thing.'

'I know,' she said. 'But she doesn't know what a bastard you can be.'

I was surprised.

'She does,' said Johnson. 'Can't stand women singing on water-skis.'

He didn't smile when he said things like that. I was getting the hang of him.

He had told me a lot, maybe some of it true. But I knew for sure he hadn't come clean with everything.

Neither had I.

It wasn't deuce. We were sort of on the same side.

But we were even.

Ask me something about Martinique.

Ask me something about Madeira, and about Martinique, and about Paris.

Paris, because that's where I went with Natalie after she'd finished her business in London. She had a political article to do, and she dictated it to her French secretary after making a thousand phone calls, and meeting people over lunch and coffee and drinks, and skimming through piles of cuttings already waiting for her on her desk.

She had a flat near the Etoile, and I stayed with her, taping phone calls, fixing her hair, arranging her dress appointments and re-kitting my make-up to match with the gathering pile of outfits Dodo was packing, on hangers and in tissue, for the Caribbean.

The Great Natalie had taken perfectly calmly the news that I was accepting her offers. The permanent offer of Kim-Jim's job. And the chance to work for her team on the Josephine film.

If she preferred what Porter was doing for her, she didn't say so. If her backers had hinted that Clive Curtis would be an even bigger catch for the film, she ignored it and stuck to her word.

I was impressed.

And I must say when, after talking to Johnson, I met Kim-Jim's nephew Porter later for drinks, and supper, and more drinks, and coffee, and what could have been a lot more if I hadn't had some practice in dealing with Porters, he wasn't put out in the least to hear I was staying in Natalie's employment.

If the job had come his way or Clive's, that was fine, he said, so long as I didn't want it. They picked up jobs if they looked like some sort of fun. But Christ, I must be out of my mind if I thought they could stay with the British climate.

Clive and Old Joe lived where the sunshine and the studios were. L.A., San Francisco. Clive had already offered Natalie the loan of Grampa Joe's beach pad in Barbados. Next to Claudette Colbert. But Porter guessed Natalie was hardly pushed for places to rent or to borrow. What it was to be famous.

Porter wore sandals as well, of the kind that drop off if you want to play serious footsie under the table. Ferdy does it until he's kicked, and all his pals at other tables jeer and throw bread rolls at him.

With Porter, you had to stay with it or quit. It was like eating with a tiger that's just had its dinner and wants to beat Concorde from a standing start at the next traffic lights. Stunning looks, muscle and energy, all pointing in the direction of bed.

But he didn't get there. Not that night, into my bed, he didn't.

Then we left for Paris, and came back to London after a week, and stayed there for another spell while Natalie taped three interviews, dictated some articles, and spent a fortune on trunk calls to everywhere.

I began to think that, whatever was going on in the West Indies, if anything, it would be over before I got there.

I remembered that Johnson had thought the opposite. What Mr Damned Van and his pal were setting up was going to take time.

I remembered another piece of advice, and took time myself to phone one or two pals, and also to take a taxi to Tavistock Street and add a few things to my account there. Following a few other telephone calls, my make-up hamper had come down from Troon, with my travelling mirror in its big four-foot box.

Not that I expected to need it all yet. Now I was just tagging along while

Natalie and her producer were looking at possible locations. Adding local material and local views to the historical facts. Looking for colourful places, and colourful personalities. Sweet-talking the authorities: the administration, the police, the tourist boards into laying on services, side-stepping regulations, putting up money, if she was lucky.

I'd seen it all happen on home jobs, like the island film I'd done with Kim-Jim. You could get set-ups in parts of the British Isles which were as bloody, for local Hitlers, for hardships, as you could get anywhere overseas.

Not just mental challenge. Physical challenge as well.

Film buffs and circus artists.

All part of the entertainments industry, brother.

13

The island of Martinique lies in the French West Indies between Florida and Venezuela, and is only fifty miles long.

It is volcanic, like Madeira.

The guide books say its real name, Madinina, means Island of Flowers, which also makes you think of Madeira, and goes to show that flowers have been on to a good thing for a very long time, including not only beds but Jacuzzi baths.

In Martinique, the only physical challenge comes from the female talent, which has done more for Europe than Rose's Lime Juice.

Owners of Martinique ladies include the French King who picked Madame de Maintenance, and, of course, Napoleon, who married Marie-Joseph de la something, whose middle name was really Rose, but who got labelled as Not Tonight Josephine.

At the airport the bookstore was full of *Le Monde* and *Paris Match* and everyone spoke French, including Natalie, which was lucky as there was no Ferdy to meet us as expected, and she had to get her own car to the hotel.

The Bakoua Beach Hotel is twenty minutes across the bay from the capital, and the view would have cheered up anyone except a person demanding a message from Ferdy and finding there wasn't any, although we had been in the thoughts of the United States Consul, the Préfet de la Région Martinique and the President of the Martinique Tourist Office, according to the envelopes the desk clerk handed to Natalie.

We went to our rooms, which had telly sets, and I expected a bit of peace while Natalie made a hundred telephone calls, but I was mistaken. I had just torn out the telly programme, which included *Hulk*, which I translated without any trouble, and *Une Rue Sesame*, which I could guess, and *Incroyable Mais Vrai*, which I was working on when Natalie tapped on the door and said we were off to the Tourist Office.

The President had offered her a car and a guide to go north right away to St Pierre, where Josephine's Dad was a big shot, and back south to La Pagerie, the sugar plantation once run by Josephine's family: just what she wanted.

She intended to go, she said, without waiting for Ferdy, who could make his own arrangements when he came, *if* he came. Tick.

I was sorry for Ferdy.

The Tourist Office was in the capital, Fort de France, which you could see on the hill over the bay behind the cruise ships. We got there by ferry.

Close to, the town turned out to be dead busy, with Peugeots and Renaults and Toyotas and people steaming round a grid of boutiques and stores and banks and offices, with palm trees everywhere, and more purple creeper. There was a cathedral, and a park with a statue of Josephine in it.

The sky was blue, the sea was blue, and it was boiling. Natalie had a big hat on over her permanent champagne-colour suntan. Not wishing to be flash-fried, I was covered in cheese-cloth.

French things had no tariff on them. I followed Natalie into the Tourist Office with my dark glasses pointing longingly towards a streetful of shops that beat Josephine for appeal, in my vote.

However, Natalie was paying my salary and I was carrying her cameras, so in I went.

And crashed into Natalie, who was standing stock-still on the threshold, having her hand half-kissed by the President of the Tourist Office, who had stopped to see what Natalie was staring at.

I peered round her elbow myself.

After the dazzle outside, it was hard to make anything out in the President's Room, except some classy French chairs and a rubber plant. And behind the rubber plant, hanging like headlights, a pair of baleful bifocal glasses.

A pranky bastard, the Owner. I won't say I was learning what to expect of him, except that I now knew it was apt to be unexpected.

Natalie exclaimed in English, 'But what a surprise! What are you doing here?'

The President finished her hand off, straightened and murmured in English, 'Ah, you know one another?'

The rubber plant said proudly, 'I am speaking. At the Rotary Club of St Lucia. It meets at the Green Parrot on Fridays.'

Then everyone moved together inside the room, which let me see properly.

It was Johnson all right, though he had changed again. Since London, his skin had turned to Bronze Tone or even Light Egyptian, and his hair was quite glossy. Mrs Margate or somebody had turned him out in fairly well-pressed Navy-type whites, with white drill shoes and stockings.

He had got up in quite an ordinary way, and was adding, 'Mrs Sheridan? Miss Geddes? Are you here for the film? How splendid to see you.'

'Of course, my dear man,' said Natalie. 'You were going to bring *Dolly* over. Is she here?'

The Tourist President bowed us into seats, his eyes passing quickly over my hair, but his smile getting no smaller. 'Mr Johnson,' he said, 'has sailed from Tobago especially to bring me something, before his so-welcome speech to be made in St Lucia. You know, I have no doubt, Mr Johnson's great skill as a painter?'

Tobago?

'Yes, of course,' said Natalie, also smiling. She crossed her legs, causing a slight pause in the conversation.

'Then,' said the President, taking his eyes away and getting up, 'I shall, with his permission, show you the so-beautiful example of his work which he has been so kind to give me. To hang in the office of our Prefecture. In return, as he has been so kind as to say, for the many happy days he has enjoyed with his yacht in our waters. See.'

And from behind his desk he lifted an oil painting, done from the sea, of the bay with its shuttered white houses, and the green tropical hills rising behind.

It was good. It was bloody good. It had also been done from real life. Which, since the paint was dry, meant that it was the work of a previous visit.

'Conté crayon, worked up in the studio,' Johnson said, obviously deafened again by my thoughts. 'Not my line really, as you know. But it's a change from portraits now and then.'

Natalie said, 'It is beautiful. M. le Président, you are fortunate. You don't know, Johnson, how much we've all been hoping you'd feel like painting again. Perhaps you managed something on Tobago?'

I sat back from the painting, keeping my face straight, and wondering how he would take his promotion to Christian-name status.

He didn't seem to notice it. He said, 'I've got a sketch block on board, but Ferdy's a hard task-master. I didn't get a lot done.'

He turned obligingly to the President. 'Mr Braithwaite, the photographer, is compiling a book of flower portraits. I can imagine how much he will find to enjoy on your beautiful island.'

Sexual strategy, I noticed, wasn't mentioned. He didn't look at Natalie, either.

If you knew Natalie, you could see her working on her self-control. But her voice, when it came out, was quite normal.

'I was expecting Ferdy here to meet me,' she remarked. 'To visit St Pierre and La Pagerie. He didn't mention his plans?'

If you believed Johnson, neither Ferdy nor his botanist pal Dr Thomassen had mentioned their plans. Johnson had left them on Tobago, he said, still extremely busy.

'What a pity,' Natalie said. 'In that case, I see I shall have to deal with Martinique on my own. I suppose it is best to get to these places by car?'

'One may go by sea,' the President said. 'Although, as you know, I have a car and a guide for Madame, whenever she cares to leave.'

'I'd take the car,' Johnson said. 'You'll enjoy the drive to St Pierre. Do that first, and catch the rain forest on your way back to La Pagerie. Which is really worth seeing. Museum. Church where Josephine was christened, 1765. Her cradle. Famous love letter to her from Napoleon. Sugar mill, ruins of. Come back and have dinner on board. Miss Geddes going with you?'

The President clasped his hands. 'Miss Geddes? Ah!'

Natalie raised her eyebrows.

The President said, 'This car I have, it will take yourself and the guide, who is a driver. A third is not so comfortable.'

The hair. I could see Natalie working out why I'd been censored, and agreeing.

'But that is quite all right,' she said. 'I have no need of Miss Geddes on this trip. Rita, the cameras?'

Johnson and I left her there, putting the President through his paces over the film while the little car, and the guide, waited patiently.

They must have had quite a job to find a car so small it wouldn't take three. As I walked out into the sun with the Owner, I remembered the President's glance at my hair. He hadn't been surprised.

I said, 'Well, what else did you bloody tell the Tourist Department? That I was on coke and laid beach boys for money?'

'Roughly,' said Johnson. 'I wanted a chat. If I can find Lenny, we can go out to *Dolly*.'

I pulled myself together and got my brain working.

Of course, Lenny would be here. Lenny and pals had sailed *Dolly* across the Atlantic from Madeira. Lenny and pals, including Raymond.

I said, 'Is Raymond here?'

'Mary-had-a-little-lamb country. Raymond is always here,' Johnson said. 'At least, at the moment he's stocking up for Lenny's rum cocktails. How's your vodka addiction?'

I was answering him when I found he had disappeared. I looked about and found I was in the middle of a shopping street. You wouldn't have thought it possible to lose interest in duty-free French scent, but I had. On the other hand, if Johnson had been wearing any, I should have known where to go.

Then he reappeared in a doorway and said, 'Then what about sours?' and I followed him, still talking, into a dark, empty space with low music playing somewhere, and planters' fans twirling miles up in the ceiling, and what seemed to be paintings all over the walls as far up as the eye could see.

A gallery. Naturally. Where a painter sells paintings if he needs a new set of cups for his yacht. I don't suppose the Nemesis Department throws its money about.

Narcotics.

A dark man sitting behind a desk said something cheerful in French, and Johnson said something cheerful back and made for the stairs talking, apparently to me, about daisies.

As well as paintings, there were sort of rugs hung on the wall, and long bits of net and whiskery rope, all done up in patterns.

He stopped on the stair. 'Macramé. Knotted sisal. A folk art, now highly fashionable. Wear it, drape it, fish with it, or use it in your chip pan. Raymond, two daisies.'

I should have known. At the top of the stairs was more gallery, and a door leading to a wee office, and inside the office, three people in various attitudes of slump, sitting at a table littered with half-empty glasses and jugs of melting ice and newspapers.

One of them seemed to be a taxi-driver, slowly lowering what I hoped was orange juice. Beside him, sure enough, lolled Raymond, his yellow hair all fuzzed in the heat like crimped yak, wearing a safari jacket and shorts over nothing.

His expression when he looked up was relaxed. Then it tightened, as if he was missing his armour. 'Miss Geddes,' he said.

'Where's Lenny?' said Johnson.

There was an opened newspaper between me and the third person, who couldn't therefore be Lenny, especially as the paper was written in French.

The third person, not putting the paper down, said, 'Oh everybody, listen,' and began quoting, in French. I got it later, and copied it out.

'Terry,' murmura Jacinda, 'tu ne crois pas qu'il serait possible qu'on se marie avant ton départ ... un mariage secret, je veux dire? Personne n'aurait besoin de le savoir sauf nous ... mais je serais ... je serais ta femme.'

The third person read it all out, over-acting something shocking.

It was a woman. Behind the shaking paper, I couldn't see her, but I knew her voice. I looked, shocked, at Johnson.

'Barbara Cartland,' he offered.

The paper came down and it wasn't Barbara Cartland. It was the Hon. Maggie, in black Vidal haircut, moon glasses and a tietop and green pants over nothing.

The Hon. Maggie, who had got herself asked by the Owner to help Lenny sail from Madeira. Lenny, Raymond and pals. Lenny, Raymond, and Maggie, switched from photographers and in hot pursuit of bums in bifocal glasses.

A West Indian Rum Daisy consists of gomme syrup, curaçao, lemon juice, soda water, and a hell of a lot of rum.

I had two, and sat sulking while Maggie read out all our horoscopes. I was Taureau and Johnson was Poisson, which he sure bloody was.

I was still sulking when Raymond and Maggie went off with the driver to buy extra food for Natalie's dinner party. The taxi, when I looked into it, was full already with what they had bought that morning, consisting mainly of rum and a crate, I bet, of French duty-free perfume.

I had lost interest in Johnson. He was a block ahead, talking about volcanoes, when he noticed I wasn't with him. I had almost got into Albert's when he got back to me and wheeled me round. He said, 'What's your favourite scent?'

I haven't got one, but I know what the most expensive one is. I told him.

'Got it on board,' he said. 'Present from Bessie. Come on. Policy talks.'

I didn't believe him, but I trailed beside him, receiving a lecture on eruptions, all the way to the sea. It was still boiling hot and his glasses, I was glad to see, were steamed up.

Some charter company people, who seemed to be pals of his, had whistled Lenny over from *Dolly*; and the white Avenger launch I remembered so well was floating at their dock. *Dolly*'s other boat was tied up beside it, waiting for what Johnson referred to as the Rum Babas.

He could, of course, afford to be calm about Maggie, considering Raymond's particular leanings. He was apparently calm about the taxi-driver as well.

Lenny handed me into the launch and out of it like a picket letting somebody through for his hankie. As I got shown to a cabin to tidy up, I heard Johnson say, 'Absolutely no whisky, boss. Miss Geddes will vouch for me.'

Although it didn't show, he'd had one daisy more than I'd had. I remembered the empty chloride and Lady Emerson's house. If he had a problem, it was none of my business. My business was to pin Kim-Jim's murder on Roger van Diemen, without getting let down by drunks.

The cabin was finely fitted and fresh and comfortable, and designed by the same hand that painted that picture. Before I left it, Lenny tapped on the door and brought in, with Mr Johnson's compliments, a thing like an Easter Egg containing about fifty quids' worth of the scent I had mentioned.

I looked at it, waiting for the rabbit or ten knotted handkerchiefs but it stayed looking like fifty quids' worth of perfume. Lenny, breathing over me, unclamped his teeth again and snarled, '*And*, Miss Geddes, if I can just mention ...'

I wasn't surprised. I know when aggro is coming. I stared at him. I don't believe Ferdy when he says my hair counter-attacks like a cockatoo's, but I felt it begin to stand up.

But whatever Lenny was going to mention, it never came. Johnson called his name once, quite nicely, from the saloon, but with a note behind it that sent Lenny's feet to the door, never mind lifting his hair.

I got to the saloon myself, and accepted a seat on the same handsome settee that I'd sat on in my bathing-suit in Madeira, and remarked that the perfume was great.

I didn't know what else to do. A Gay Yacht loaded with bottles of all known makes of perfume is something again.

'Never without it,' said Johnson. 'Comes in handy as bribes for their girlfriends and mothers. Will a fish salad do? Raymond and Maggie are eating on shore.'

A mind-reader is something else also. Raymond and Maggie.

'I wish,' said Johnson, 'that you'd let me call you Rita. My name, unfortunately, is just Johnson.'

He took a look at my expression and added cheerfully, 'I'm sorry. Awkward to have the same wavelength. But useful at times. Let's have a glass of wine, to please Lenny, and talk about Roger van Diemen.'

He had hauled off his tie, and slung his jacket aside. His arms were brown, and his throat inside his shirt. We weren't on the same wavelength really. I'm not that much of a fool. He was clever. And my thoughts are easy to read.

A great team. An open book and a lush.

And he read me thinking that, too. I saw him.

We had our meal outside, under the awning, while the yacht rocked to her anchor and the sunlit water sent dazzling lights everywhere.

We talked for thirty minutes. Or Johnson talked, while I had two helpings of cold crab with palm heart salad, and fresh pineapple with cream, and coffee with Poorer and Fewer, and two glasses of wine.

What he said made me thankful that Natalie hadn't delayed our trip any longer.

His tour of Coombe's finished and his investigation complete, Roger van Diemen was now in Barbados.

The signs were that his report was in the hands of his boss. And the chances were that the next thing that would happen would be the meeting to launch the new dope ring.

Eating, I kept my eyes down and my thoughts, I hoped, to myself.

Barbados. An English-speaking island, not a French one, and about a hundred miles or more to the south. Natalie and I had slept there last night, after the long flight from London. We had slept there, and Roger van Diemen was somewhere on the same island.

Johnson said, 'So what I *don't* want you to do, is go after Roger yourself. He'll know I'm around, and you're around in the area, but if we show no special interest, he'll keep out of our way.

'This time, I'm sure he won't trouble you, and I don't think he'll be anxious to dash from the islands. If he moves, it will be because he's been told where to go for the meeting.

'My guess,' said Johnson, 'is that the people he's working for will meet him where he is, in Barbados. It's the busiest island, with a huge through-put of casual traffic. And a nuclear bomb could go off in Bridgetown without anyone hearing, never mind noticing, once Caurry-fista has started.'

'Caurry-fista,' I repeated. Barbados is full of descended Scots. I didn't know they had left-handed processions.

'Rita. *Carifesta*,' said Johnson. 'The Caribbean Festival of Creative Arts. A two-week regular binge of Euro-Creole culture shared by thirty countries in and around the Caribbean, and hosted this year by Barbados.

'Jazz and folk music. Books and poetry and handicrafts. Drama, ballet, films and cooking. Carnival. Fighting. There will be syringes in every gutter and everyone will be bananas. Roger and his pals will hold their billion-dollar meeting, and we shall tape it.'

The Lone Ranger and Tonto. 'You and me?' I said. He'd had more wine than I thought.

'Not if I can help it,' he said. 'That stuff you've brought is meant to keep you out of trouble, not get you into it. You did collect it?'

I nodded. He meant my fishing-tackle case, which was sitting in the Bakoua Beach Hotel with a Bakoua straw hat on top of it.

I don't know how he got the wavelength that time, but he suddenly said, 'By the way. What colour *is* your hair under that dye?'

I thought everyone knew. 'White,' I said. Naturally.

'Naturally,' he said. He had picked an expensive pipe out of a rack of expensive pipes and was filling it. 'This doesn't worry you? Or sailing?'

'No,' I said. 'On the film I did with Kim-Jim, everyone was sick except me. You didn't say what happens after the meeting. You bug it, you indemnify Roger van Diemen and his boss, and you arrest them?'

'Identify,' Johnson said automatically. The pipe had caught, and he was shaking the match out.

'Well now, that's another matter. Remember Charlie Chan. The Thin Man. Fu Manchu, come to that. To arrest people, you need evidence. To catch them actually handling some dope would be nice. But whether we pull it off all in one move or not, it'll be simple once we know who we're dealing with.'

There was too much smoke about. I didn't trust it. I said, 'Would they buy dope so soon? Before the Coombe scheme has started?'

'If it's on offer. They'll have some other outlets. They'll need a cash flow to set this up as well. A world-wide network of fruit- and drug-stores takes some financing,' said Johnson.

I thought it would be nice if he went on talking. 'And where would they get it from? South America?'

'Colombia, or points north and east,' Johnson said. 'Most of it comes in the first place from there.'

'By boat?'

'More often by plane, up to now. Small planes usually aimed at the American market. Straight to Florida, with a refuelling stop somewhere halfway.

'Unfortunately for the smugglers, it's getting too risky. One or two rings are still operating, but the rest are casting about for other ways. Hence the Coombe idea.'

I said, 'Aren't planes searched?'

'Airport staff can be bribed. The Pipers and Cessnas may not even go to an airstrip, but crash-land on a beach. A written-off plane hardly makes a dent in the profits in this business. Unless you're talking in loads of nothings, there's no point in all this trouble.'

'And that's what the Van Damned guy is in it for?' I said.

'Perhaps,' said Johnson. 'They may be blackmailing him too. That's very common.'

'And when you catch them all retarded, you expect him to confess? To killing Kim-Jim?'

'Red-handed,' said Johnson.

'I don't care what it is,' I said. 'Will you make him confess? And if he doesn't, how will you prove that he did it?'

'I will repeat the promise I made you in London,' said Johnson. 'Whether he confesses or not, I will personally pursue the murderer of Mr Curtis and see that he receives the fate that he deserves. Word of a Necrosis Officer.'

'Narcotics,' I said.

'There you are,' said Johnson.

He looked pleased.

I thought. I said, 'What was that about sailing?'

'I was coming to that,' Johnson said. 'But let's see first where we've got to. Point one, there's a meeting coming off soon we want to know about. You're not involved. Keep clear of it.

'Point two, as a result of the meeting, there may be some hanging about waiting for a drug consignment. If they've bought the stuff already, they'll want to shift it quick to raise funds to run the new scheme with.

'Like the meeting, we don't know what island they'll pick, but *Dolly*'s very well tricked out with radio, and she has every excuse to wander about. After the meeting, I hope to know where to wander to.'

'And never mind the Rotary Club of St Lucia?' I said.

'The Rotary Club of St Lucia,' Johnson said, 'is the flagship of my plans, as you would hear if you stopped interrupting.

'Three, I have a floating engagement to speak in St Lucia, which is a mere twenty-five miles south of here, and from which I can fly in an hour to Barbados. Therefore I am setting sail for St Lucia tomorrow.'

'Josephine was born on St Lucia,' I said.

'So she was,' said Johnson. 'Although a Martiniquaise, I am told, would dispute it.'

I said, 'Natalie meant to go there. With Ferdy.'

'So I should expect,' Johnson said. 'But Ferdy, unfortunately, is snapping Birds of Paradise in Tobago. For you, I understand.'

'With the Toboggans,' I said.

'Actually,' said Johnson, 'the Tobagonians. Don't let's get into a rut. Do you think Natalie would agree to come sailing with me to St Lucia?'

'Yes,' I said. 'And if you promise to paint her, she'll marry you.'

Johnson coughed. 'I don't think,' he said, 'I could risk upsetting Raymond. Which reminds me. He'll be back soon, and there is something I want to show you. But meanwhile, can I rely on you? If Natalie comes, you'll come and protect me from her?'

It was, of course, the only way he could be sure I wouldn't muck up his programme for Roger.

I said, 'If you'll protect me from Raymond and Lenny.'

It was the only real flash of Owner of the day.

The bifocals turned full on me. 'If either of them shows you one shred less than the fullest courtesy,' Johnson said, 'you will report it to me, and I shall keel-haul him. And that means ... Oh, never mind.'

I knew. It was a Newcastle boating song. But I didn't bother mentioning it.

14

Exactly as Johnson planned, we set sail, all six of us, for St Lucia on *Dolly* next morning.

He may not have had to marry Natalie, but the appearance of that terrific painting had done wonders for their relationship. If she wasn't angling to get her portrait painted, she would never have turned up for dinner the night before in the one-shouldered Italian silk that was one of her most impressive dresses.

She had decided to sail on *Dolly* even before she climbed the companionway and found the saloon all done in orchids and candlelight, and the British Consul there, with his wife, and someone grand from the Prefecture.

Lenny, in a white jacket, served herb soup and lobster and soufflé, while Raymond in a tuxedo poured French wine as commanded by a gentlemanly Johnson in ditto.

I wore culottes and this jacket with epaulettes on it. Maggie wore a bikini under a crinkle gauze top with a neck-ring. The crinkle gauze lasted until we had digested our dinners. Then we all went overboard for a swim, bathing-suits in all sizes being provided by *Dolly* and stored, I shouldn't be surprised, next to the scent stocks.

During the meal Natalie talked about this cock-fight she'd seen, and the ruins at St Pierre, where the volcano killed everyone except this guy who was sitting in jail, and who made a fortune afterwards appearing in circuses; which goes to show it's an ill eruption, as Johnson said.

And about waterfalls and tree ferns and stuff in the rain forest, which gets four hundred inches of rain a year, putting it upsides with Glasgow and making it hell for the cameras.

And, of course, about Josephine, whose mascara, I could see, was going to look like the tree ferns unless I was careful.

While we had our coffee, Johnson hired a boatload of Martins to sing us Beguines from the water. There were cigars and stuff.

About then, when we were all pretty mellow, he started using Natalie's first name.

He was already calling me Rita. He had said his name was Johnson, but

I didn't call him anything while the others were there. Maybe there were some wavelengths of his that reached me, at that.

Natalie loved it. She kissed Johnson's cheek, and delivered a small speech, and threw some orchids across to the Martins, with a bunch of ten-franc notes taped on to them. She had style, had Natalie Sheridan.

We left *Dolly* at midnight and were back on board eight hours later, with our bits of luggage.

By nine we were sailing. My Bakoua straw hat toppled off when the mainsail went up, and Natalie and I were encouraged to go below, where I oiled her gorgeous skin round her perfect bikini, and then larded myself all round my swimsuit.

Every now and then the bottles would slide one way or the other, and you could hear a lot of rattling and running footsteps up on deck, where Lenny and Raymond and Maggie were doing what Johnson told them.

Real, genuine Owner stuff, I can tell you. He lay back in the cockpit with the gear lever under his fingers, and never raised his voice once. He didn't have to. He owned the bloody ship.

She was beautiful. I'd got used, now, to the way she looked below.

Johnson's own bedroom, the master stateroom, was at the back of the ship.

I'd only seen glimpses of it. There were two beds in it. Everything was fitted and padded and carpeted, and there was a bathroom off. You got to it from the cockpit, which was this sunk-level sitting-place in the open air. It was lined with cushion-topped lockers, and the wheel and the gear lever were there.

Tiller, Johnson says.

There were also a lot of dials for the engine, which was under the floorboards, and which you could turn on, Johnson said, if you were late for a date and the wind was wrong.

From the cockpit, you went down steps, past more lockers, to the saloon, which was for eating and lounging in. Flowers, cushions, books, a radio, a stereo: even a telly let into the panelling by the bar. A table that folded out, for a dinner party. Another table that let down for maps and charts.

Everything was hand-finished, and there was a lot of brass about in the way of clocks and barometers, shining like gold. There were fitted cupboards and lockers everywhere, and hidden lighting, and a thick carpet with toning curtains and cushions, all done in wasteful, fadeable blues.

The two long deep-cushioned seats could be made into bunks, and you

167

could hang hammocks for two people more. There was a toilet, off one corner, with an actual bath in it.

Through from that, a passage led you past a single room on one side, and a bright fitted kitchen on the other.

Galley, Johnson says.

At the end of the passage was the neat, two-bedded room that I'd been in before, when Lenny pounced on me. And in front of that, reached by a hatch, a small room for a hand or someone to sleep in.

If you used that, and two hammocks, ten people could sleep on *Dolly*, five of them in beds. Bunks.

Bunks with merino blankets and perchance sheets and tailored covers that matched the fringed curtains. And wash in washrooms that had American towels and handmade soap, and mirrors, and boxes of tissues and cupboards full of suntan lotion and tooth paste and shampoo and sting cream and elastoplast. And Tampax. Man of the world, Johnson was.

Man of the world, and stacked, with a yacht valued in hundreds of thousands.

A stacked heel.

And since galleries don't pay this kind of money, or Government departments, *Dolly* must be financed, as I was, from vanity. From what people would pay to look better. In my case, to look well in photographs. In Johnson's case, to look well for ever, stuck on somebody's wall.

The work of Mormon, as my aunt would enjoy saying.

How she would be impressed by Johnson. Two heels, but only one of them stacked. Financially, anyway.

Sailing is different from being in a motor boat. Natalie knew all about it. She knew when to duck when Johnson remarked, 'Ready about,' and this bloody great pole began swinging over.

The boom, Johnson says.

She knew how to lower the morning papers and lift her elegant legs out of the way when Raymond or Maggie made a dive for the thing that twirls the ropes round and tightens them.

The winch. The sheets. To hell with Johnson.

And when Lenny came up from below with chilled Buck's Fizz and coffee and flaky buns, and then took over from Raymond and Maggie – she knew how to pump Johnson about *Dolly*, in a way so idle you'd hardly notice it.

She supposed, said Natalie, that they'd find they had quite a lot of friends in common, in Antigua and the B.V.I. and so on. *Dolly* must know every inch of these waters.

The British Virgin Islands, the millionaires' playground. I'd made up quite a few golden ladies who went there. If Johnson was one of the golden layabouts who played with them, he wasn't admitting it.

No, he remarked. He'd had the yacht quite a long time but only used her occasionally.

Natalie was surprised. You could sail the world, she imagined, with that amount of electronic equipment. But perhaps he was keen on gadgets?

I knew what she meant. There were Sci-Fi dials all over the cockpit and behind some of the cupboards below decks. Seventy thousand pounds' worth, according to Raymond.

Johnson had his eye on the sails. 'I used to need them for racing,' he said. 'Very scientific, these days.'

It wasn't often Natalie made a blunder. She had sense enough not to add to it. It was Raymond, collecting plates, who said crossly, 'You'll race again.'

'Oh, I expect so,' said Johnson, peering over the sidedeck. 'And if not, I'll use her for painting. Good as a wheelchair, a yacht. Raymond, get the binoculars for Mrs Sheridan. There's Diamond Rock coming up, and I'd like her to see it.'

He knew the coast. We all watched, shading our eyes, while Johnson produced jolly snippets and instructive snippets about what we were passing, and Natalie gave him all her attention, while the blue sea sizzled beneath us, and the morning sun shone and shone from a cloudless blue sky.

Then Martinique fell behind, and the currents began to kick a bit, and Natalie went below, to freshen up her suntan-oil unaided, she said, and Maggie lay on the side deck with half her bikini off, and began again on the fast, sexy double-talk she had been throwing at Johnson ever since Ferdy dropped her on Madeira.

I thought he'd freeze her, but he wasn't interested enough. He gave her the kind of polite answers I'd heard him give in 17B, in his pyjamas, with a kick like a mule somewhere behind them.

Then, although I didn't see signals passing, Raymond suddenly appeared again with a chart, which he spread out beside Johnson. A moment later, Raymond was at the tiller and Johnson's stateroom door was swinging gently behind him.

Raymond said, 'Do I have to call you Miss Geddes?'

I had given up trying to wear the Bakoua straw, and had settled for a check napkin under a blue berry with a red pom-pom on it, which Johnson said he'd pinched off a coconut.

'Yes,' I said.

'O.K., Miss Geddes,' said Raymond 'God gave people punk hair to cover something, I take it. In a minute I'm going about, in the hope that Maggie's boobs will slide off under the rail, and Natalie and I will be alone together. Are you capable of following a few simple orders?'

'Don't answer that,' said Maggie's voice. 'He wrote the Kama Sutra's bloody appendix. He *is* the Kama Sutra's . . .'

'If you don't mind being wrecked. More than usual, that is,' I said.

I'm not stupid. Even if I turned out to be stupid, all I could do was sink his bloody boat, and he'd deserve it.

'O.K. Listen, Miss Geddes,' said Raymond nastily.

I had my left ring on my left hand and my right ring on my right hand. We went about, and we didn't sink.

Later, I tightened the mainsail.

Later, I went forward and freed a sheet on the jib.

Later, I climbed the mast, and swayed above the blue of the sea, and watched flying-fish sparking up, and dolphins roll, and below me, *Dolly*'s white coach-house roof and long, satiny deck, with the sun twinkling away on the brasswork, and on the tray of rum and pineapple fizzes coming up, carried by Lenny.

I slid down and Natalie said, 'How agile of you. You are making us all feel quite sick. Have a fizz, darling. If anyone deserves it, you do.'

Johnson had long since reappeared. Across the cockpit, his bifocals glittered peacefully. He said, 'God, guns and guts made Miss Geddes. Raymond, try her on jet-skis.'

'Here?' said Raymond. 'She'd end up in Mexico.'

'There,' said Johnson. 'St Lucia. Mr Christian, ladies and gentlemen, we are making landfall. Three cheers for the navigator. Third dial from the left.'

It *was* St Lucia, straight ahead. Birthplace of Josephine. Green and lush and mountainous and romantic. A place I shall never forget so long as I live.

With good reason.

We had lunch at anchor in Marigot Bay, where they shot *Doctor Dolittle*.

I could hardly believe I was there, in this deep blue lagoon in the hills, hidden among flowers and a forest of coconut palms, just like the photographs I'd seen, where they had all this pain with the snail.

Kim-Jim had known the people who did the pink snail, and also the make-up for Rex Harrison. From Kim-Jim too, I knew that the Curtises had expected to look after Sophia Loren when she came here for *Firepower*, but the deal had misfired. It was the contract that Clive got after that, Kim-Jim said, that got him into really big money.

Martinique is a department of France. St Lucia batted about under the French a lot as well, but after changing hands thirteen times, ended up as an independent state inside the British Commonwealth, which is fine if you can speak pidgin French, and are not having enough trouble with pidgin English.

There were half a dozen other big yachts in the anchorage, and some small ones, and quite a lot of boats dodging about, and people swimming. A hotel on the other side of the inlet had a ferry service. There was another hotel hidden behind flowers on our side, where Natalie and I were to stay the night. Nothing but Bounty-grove greenery and white beaches were to be seen anywhere else, apart from the road-end jetty and Customs.

Paradise.

Johnson had already been on the radio-telephone to Castries, the capital of St Lucia, seven miles up the road, to arrange a welcome committee for Natalie, and transport to take her Josephine-hunting next day. Asked about his own plans, he just said it depended on the Rotary Club, and he was going to give them a spin in the morning.

Natalie, after a late night and a long morning of sunshine and sea air and two rum and pineapple fizzes, was happy to let someone else do it all. When Johnson mentioned that he had been on to the Deputy High Commissioner at Castries, and there was no word of Ferdy, she just looked resigned and said in that case she would take herself off Johnson's hands and book into the hotel before she made any other plans. She was sure they could all do with a siesta.

I suppose if anyone needed a siesta it was Johnson, but since neither of his nurse-companions was around and Maggie's siestas aimed only at sleeping with people in the most energetic sense, he didn't seem to be bothering.

Indeed, while Natalie was gathering her things together and Raymond began lowering the boat to take us ashore, Johnson said to me, 'Unless you really want a rest, why not come back and try the jet-skis once you've dumped your stuff? Unless Mrs Sheridan needs you?'

Mrs Sheridan, it turned out, didn't need me. She thanked Johnson warmly for the ride, arranged to have him and Maggie and Raymond to dinner at the hotel in the evening, and got athletically into the boat, followed by me and the luggage.

Fifteen minutes later she was in her hotel room and I was back on the hotel jetty, with a towel and a Hurricane Hole T-shirt over my swimsuit, and screening cream everywhere else.

Instead of Raymond, Johnson had brought back *Dolly*'s boat for me. And instead of bringing it back to the hotel, he was tying it up at the road-end, where blacks in coloured shorts were lounging on the verandah of the Customs hut.

That landed me with a walk, and it was bloody hot, but he had the jet-skis. I set off, jogging, across the strip of grass between the two jetties.

A Toyota jeep, screaming down the only road, just missed the hut and two palm trees and stopped in a shower of dust and white gravel as Johnson strolled up from the boat and I arrived, dripping and crusted with cream, from the shore.

'Baked Alaska,' said Johnson.

A woman got out of the Toyota, carrying a box with a towel over it.

She spoke to the blacks by the hut and they laughed. The Customs officer came out and laughed too. She had on long baggy shorts and thick socks and shoes and a stiff cotton blouse rolled up over her arms, which were dark brown and the kind that you connect with champion women golfers, vintage 1920.

Her hair was short and strong and dead white, and her face was like Humphrey Bogart's, with a long, weedy cigar sticking out of it.

She marched up to Johnson and spoke to him.

'You getting your effing dogs from someone else nowadays? How come your boyfriend's so effing choosy?'

'You know Amy Faflick?' said Johnson.

I was too amazed to answer.

'Ever since she fixed that kangaroo's nose for us. Nice worker, Rita,' said Amy.

The cigar waggled up and down. She took it out, spat, and put it back again between her big yellow teeth. She smiled at me. 'Hullo there, girl. I hear great things about you from Celia.'

God knew what age she was, but her voice was as English as on the day she married Lee in the States and started the business that ended by feeding every studio in the world with performing animals. I'd met Lee as well, but it was mostly Amy who dodged over to keep an eye on Jim and Celia and the English end of the business.

I said, as if I didn't know, 'What are you doing here?'

'My God, what do you think: hatching effing parrots,' said Amy. 'You got that bird of poor Kim-Jim Curtis's? Want to donate it for breeding?'

'Don't listen to her. That parrot's worth fifteen thousand on the versi-colour market,' Johnson said. 'Anyway, it's Hollywood mad. It'd lay all those chicks on the casting couch. What brought the parrot numbers down here, Amy? The black market? The hurricane?'

Amy's cigar had gone out. She put her box on the ground and delved in her shorts pockets. Johnson held a cigarette lighter, already lit, in front of her. She bent forward, used it, and puffed.

'Always were too damn quick for comfort,' she said. 'Yup. People pinch pretty birds. Nice things, St Lucian parrots. Friendly. Bright colours. Talkative. Numbers already well down before the hurricane. Now only a hundred left. In the world. Here. The World Wildlife people are bothered, but look at their effing funds. You got a boat that could take me over there?'

'Via *Dolly* and a cold drink. You can sell Raymond a dog,' Johnson said. 'And so you're helping conserve the parrots for the Wildlifers?'

She jerked her head over her shoulder. 'Lee and I have a place anyway, in the rain forest. We added a cage or two for them. Breeding in captivity. Sick-nursing if need be. Sort of busman's holiday, when we're fed up with the farm. The boy who runs it's quite good, and we usually have a few beasts of our own that we're working on.'

She picked up the box, and it squeaked.

'Such as?' said Johnson. He lifted a bit of the cloth and I wondered, madly, if it would be budgies.

It wasn't. It was a cluster of darting pale furry things with long legs.

'Effing gerbils,' said Amy, dumping the box in the boat and swinging a booted leg over. 'Get a pair and they breed like reporters. Taking them to the hotel zoo. Couple of white peacocks and a monkey and a snake that's eaten its mother. You got Curtis's job, Rita? Where's the White Huntress?'

I hadn't heard that name before either. I said, 'She's in the Hurricane Hole. She's researching for a documentary on the Empress Josephine.'

'Huh!' said Amy. 'Needs to go to effing Soufrière then. Malmaison Estate. It belonged to Josephine. Quite near my place.'

There was a pause. Johnson didn't say anything, but he was grinning. The outboard puttered, and we swung in towards *Dolly*, with Lenny waiting above.

'Oh hell, be neighbourly,' said Amy, scowling round her cigar. She took it out of her mouth and addressed me. 'Tell the Sheridan woman I'll take her to Soufrière after her siesta, if she can put up with the Toyota. Tell her not to try anything on me, though.'

'Try anything?' I said.

173

Amy heaved the box up on deck and followed it, nodding to Lenny, raising her free hand to Raymond, and gazing critically at Maggie, who was sunbathing mono on the aft deck.

'Hates effing women,' she said. 'If you haven't noticed, it's because she needs you for something. Had a cat like that several times. Always had to be top bitch.'

'You must show me your cats some time,' Johnson said. 'Lenny, tell Mrs Faflick what drink you think she ought to have.'

I left them, to try the jet-skis, which is just a motorized sort of sledge with a handle, that lets you ski without needing a motor boat. Raymond gave me a lesson, and I got it almost right away.

You would think I'd had enough of sledges, but I hadn't. It was great.

By the time I got back, Johnson had disappeared for his siesta, Maggie had disappeared to another boat, and Amy had taken Natalie to Soufrière in the Toyota.

She had left the gerbils behind, which was fair enough after an hour's solid drinking out of Lenny's repertoire. I hoped the road to Soufrière was a straight one.

According to Natalie, hostessing dinner back in our hotel later that evening, the road to Soufrière was what politicians were modelled on.

She looked quite pale under her make-up, but rallied to give us an account of her trip in the Toyota, and these two peaked volcanic mountains called the Pitons, and the drive-in crater between them, with bubbling sulphur pools and bus parties from package-tour day trips.

She had approved of Amy's underground jungle outpost in the mountain, and had spoken to several parrots.

She did not expect, she said, a great deal of Castries tomorrow morning, which, like every other place so far as she could see on this island, had been burned down so often that very little charred Old French and Old English Colonial was still left standing.

She covered a yawn about ten o'clock, by which time we were all slapping at things Raymond referred to as No-see-ums and I, for one, didn't want Josephine tonight any more.

Johnson and his crew left shortly after, and buzzed over the lagoon to where Dolly was lying in a fuzz of lit mosquito coils and drunken mosquitoes.

Maggie was with them. I went to bed happy.

It seemed only fair, next morning, to give Johnson a lift north to Castries in the car that came to take Natalie to Government Buildings. After that, she was going north-east to Morne Paix Bouche, to the estate where, if you believe St Lucians, Josephine got herself born.

I wasn't getting to go to Government Buildings, even though I was wearing decent white pants and a pin-striped cotton jacket and my hair was nearly lying down, because Lenny had made Roman Punch, which needs the whites of ten eggs, goddammit.

I did go with Natalie and Johnson as far as Castries, though. I had been given some shopping to do. I thought she was joking when she said she needed some Bee-Wee dollars, but she wasn't. It's what they call East Caribbean currency, and I had to get to a bank.

I had also been approached by Raymond to bring back a bag of anything that would keep Amy's abandoned gerbils alive without encouraging their fertility. The gerbils were still on *Dolly*. The zoo, it turned out, didn't want them and Amy wasn't answering her telephone.

The rodent population of *Dolly*, to my mind, was Johnson's problem, but I said I'd do it, for Amy's sake.

Johnson, it appeared, was in for a dead busy morning. He needed dropping off by Columbus Square, at Johnson's hardware store, for which he said he had a natural fondness. He also had a call to make down in the bay at Vigie Creek, and another at a bar-restaurant called Rain's in Brazil Street, to meet a guy called Somerset Ma'am, as he explained in the car to Castries.

The road from Marigot to Castries, although shorter than the road from Marigot to Soufrière, is much the same as regards politicians, and Natalie's share of the conversation got smaller and smaller.

No one was surprised when, on a hill just short of the capital, she got the driver to draw in and stop. The reason was, she said, to pick up some screen-printed cloth while she remembered.

I followed her into the place and bought a bag for myself. It had a Bird of Paradise printed on it, and made me think of Ferdy. It was when we were back in the car, and about to zoom down into Castries – that we got this great view of the town, and the big bay in front, and all the shipping.

Including this big, clean ship like a liner, flying a blue flag with a yellow C on it.

'*Coombe Caroline*,' said Johnson, in an interested voice, from under his binoculars. 'Nice boat next to it, too.'

He handed me the binoculars.

It was *Coombe Caroline*, all right. Sister ship, naturally, of *Coombe Regina*, out of Madeira.

St Lucia, the banana Independent Commonwealth State. Part of the bloody empire of Roger van Diemen.

I handed the binoculars back.

'You didn't look at the big twin-screw diesel,' said Johnson. 'You'd have been interested.'

I looked. It was a long white private cruiser, flying the American flag. There were a lot of awnings up, and I could see the blue of a swimming pool. Without the binoculars, I couldn't read the name. I couldn't read the name anyway.

It had caught Natalie's attention as well. As it vanished from view, she turned to Johnson. 'Do you know that ship?'

The bifocals were trained on our driver. 'I bet our friend here does,' Johnson said. 'Sir, would that be the *Paramount Princess*?'

The driver's teeth flashed.

'Yes sir,' he said. 'Yes sir, that would be the *Paramount Princess*. All the Windwards, they know the *Princess*. Old Joe Curtis's boat, bought from the studios. One real boat, she is, sir.'

'Rita?' said Johnson. 'I thought you were never sick?'

'I'm not,' I said. 'But I think we should stop. That was Ferdy Braithwaite at the side of the road. And Clive Curtis and Dr Thomassen with him.'

You could tell Natalie was restored by the edge in her voice. 'Then *certainly*,' said Natalie, 'let us stop. Do you suppose that Ferdy's prolonged absence is now accounted for? Could he possibly, for example, have been sailing on the *Paramount Princess* from Tobago?'

Johnson, I noticed, was tactfully silent. Ferdy, on the other hand, accepting a few sharp inquiries through the open car window a moment later, was not in the least cowed.

He and his good friend Dr Carl Thomassen had turned the flowers of Tobago inside out, one way or another, and had photographed the Buckoo Reef, the scarlet ibis and everything except, he said, Man Friday. They had gone from Speyside to Scarborough, and there, what had they seen?

'Robin Hood?' ventured Johnson.

Ferdy's capped teeth appeared between his whiskers like a footprint. Carl Thomassen, his botanist friend, a small pale guy with poached-egg eyes and a face somewhere between Herbert Lom and Andy Hardy, never stopped smiling anyway. Clive Curtis, Kim-Jim's brother, didn't smile at all.

He just inclined towards the car, with his suntan and his black hair and his red moustache, and remarked, 'Dad was in Scarborough with the *Princess*, Mrs Sheridan. He was real glad to give a lift to Mr Braithwaite and

176

the Doctor, although, of course, he was a little disappointed that the Curtis family couldn't help with your film, my brother Kim-Jim having been with you so long.'

He gave me a small, pearly smile. 'But I guess that's the way it is, with the young generation coming up. Young Porter tells us competition is competition, and if you don't like the heat, get out of the kitchen . . .

'Mrs Sheridan: my Dad, Old Joseph, would be real privileged if you would come aboard and take lunch, or visit with him, seeing you're here.'

'Why, that's very nice of your father,' said Natalie. 'But I see I'm late at Government Buildings already. You know what these arrangements are like . . .

'Ferdy, Rita has one or two jobs to do for me, but she can fill you in on my plans. Then perhaps we can get together this evening. Really, there is quite a lot to arrange.'

The vibes would have knocked out an elephant, but seemed to pass over Clive. Clive said, 'Then if Miss Rita isn't going with you, why don't we take her aboard after she's done her shopping, and Mr Johnson as well, if he's available? Then she and Ferdy can do their business in comfort. It's quite a nice little ship my father has there, as Ferdy will tell you . . .

'You haven't met my father, Kim-Jim's father, Miss Rita? Or my sister, Porter's mother? They sure would enjoy meeting you.'

I could feel my hair lying down, and my insides. It was Johnson who took my arm in a grip like a Kirby and said, 'How very kind of you. Rita and I would both like to come, very much.'

I tried very hard not to go and meet Kim-Jim's family.

I came out of Barclay's Bank with my bag full of Bee-Wees and every intention of going straight back to Hurricane Hole.

Instead, I walked into Johnson, newly out of both Johnson's and Rain, where he'd had two Reverend's Downfalls, he said, and if I didn't need guiding to the *Paramount Princess*, he did.

I said, 'You go, then. And if you find time between parties, tell me when you're going to do anything about Roger van Diemen.'

He stood, rocking on his heels, not upset in the least, with his hand in his pockets behind his binoculars and his floppy hat pushed to the back of his head. The sun had gone in.

'Raymond's on *Dolly*,' he said. 'Standing by the R.T. I've just phoned him. You're scared of the Curtises?'

I thought of the photographs beside my yellow cat in Kim-Jim's room in Madeira. The glowing old man. The over-sexed middle-aged Clive by the pool. The classy Sharon, with her streaked hair, and her good-looking brat Porter, with the curled ginger hair and flashing teeth.

The Curtises were big shots, each with his or her own tidy fortune; known all over the world. The only one out of active life now was Old Joseph, and you could see he was on the bread line. The *Paramount Princess*, with a crew of twenty-five, Johnson said, and a swimming pool.

If the Curtises took against anyone, they were powerful enough to be nasty.

I imagined they would fairly take against Roger van Diemen, once it was known what he had done.

Johnson had promised me the killer of Kim-Jim. If Johnson wanted me to go on board the *Paramount Princess*, it was for a reason.

It started to rain. Between the rows of parked cars and the glass and concrete stores, people moved into shelter. The rain hazed the woolly green hill at the top of the street. It bounced off an ice-cream handcart and a Chinese-food van. Women sitting by barrows of cottons flung coloured prints over them, and crouched next to each other, talking in twisted French under big dripping umbrellas.

Like parrots.

Rain ran down my face, and splodged Johnson's glasses. He hadn't moved, and I hadn't answered him.

I said, 'Yes, I'm scared of the Curtises.'

He said, 'It's quite a good reason for facing them.'

I said, 'I don't know about that. But if I'm going to get bloody soaked, it might as well be on the Curtises' boat, and not on your crummy canoe.'

'Good girl,' he said, as he had once in London.

That was all. We turned and walked round into Jeremie, and the rain stopped, and the sun came out again.

I thought, as everything steamed, Next time, I'll be nicer to Raymond.

By the time Johnson and I boarded the Curtises' ship, men in white coats had put the awnings back and dried off the drips, and two of the loungers by the pool were already occupied, one by a blonde and the other by a brunette, who both had the same idea as Maggie about not getting bikini marks. The only untanned bit on them was round their wedding-ring fingers.

Johnson looked at them with great interest but neither looked back. I wondered which of the Curtises had exhausted them. Or, of course, there was always Ferdy and his botanist pal, straight from the flower beds.

We didn't get to stay in the sun. The sort of chief steward who had met us at the companionway took us down a flight of stairs and along a carpeted corridor to a door that had 'DEN' written above it.

Johnson went in while I was reading it, and I nearly lost him, following, the cigar smoke was so thick.

The Den, which was twice the size of *Dolly*'s saloon, was done out in Old English, all buttoned leather and oak and pewter tankards. Three sides of the room seemed to be bar, and the other had a T.V. screen fixed to it, showing a video of the Empire State Building with Fay Wray on it.

Shades of blue light from the telly flickered on the faces of the three people watching it, glasses in hand, sitting in deep leather armchairs chained to the floor, with a table in front of them.

One was Clive, all done up in cashmere trousers and matching pullover, which was dead sensible as the air conditioning was freezing.

Another was Sharon, Porter's mother.

The photographs hadn't shown her thick creamy skin, or how angular her nose and jaw and cheekbones were, in her broad face that photographed so well. But the black hair was still nicely streaked, and she sat like an actress, in a trouser suit with patterned silk facings, and a matching scarf at the neck.

Their father, Old Joseph, sat in the middle.

Unlike his son and daughter, he didn't drag his eye away from the screen when we entered, and King Kong flickered all over his face while Clive got up and began making introductions.

Old Joseph, you would say, had fought old age the way he fought the Warners and Sam Goldwyn and Louis B. Mayer and all the rest of the men from Europe who needed to get to the top in the movies. He'd forced make-up, and special effects, and all the know-how of illusion to grow up alongside the cameras, and sometimes outstrip them.

The fight itself had kept him young. He was more than eighty, and he could pass for twenty years younger.

If you looked at the thick, cropped grey hair and not the bent spine. If you looked at the pouched eyes without glasses, and not the loose, spotted skin that disappeared down inside his open-necked shirt.

Sharon Proost said, 'Pa. Your guests are here.'

For a moment, it looked as if he would ignore us. Then, pulling in his lip-corner, he laid his drink on the table, put the cigar in his mouth, leaned forward and pressed the T.V. control pad and, as the screen became blank, said, 'I see them,' and looked up at me.

He took the cigar out of his mouth. 'You brought the punk girl,' he said.

'Pa,' said Clive. 'This is Rita Geddes. You remember.' And he mentioned the titles of a couple of films I'd worked on. Early, and not very good ones.

His father picked up his drink without taking his pouched eyes off me. 'Nope. I don't remember,' he said. 'What part did she play?' The drink was in his right hand, and he made no effort to shift it.

Sharon said, 'She's in make-up, Pa,' and stirred to the extent of patting the leather seat beside her. 'I'm Sharon Proost. We're real worried about my son, Porter, and Porter's uncle and I plan to have you give us all the advice that you can. We know how you two hit it off in Madeira and London.'

I sat down carefully. 'Porter isn't here?' I said. Johnson was still standing beside Clive. I daren't look at him.

Pa Curtis laid down his empty glass and snarled. 'Porter's laid all the flesh here: what's to keep him? Gone off with the titled riffraff to the Mediterranean, most likely. I tell you, Sharon, that boy's friends are never going to come on board this ship again.'

He looked up at Johnson, as smart as a young man. 'You snort, fella? Or mainline? Keep the ship full of grass? You're the painter fella with the ketch, ain't you? Johnson?'

'That's right,' said Johnson. He smiled at Sharon and sat down, with style, on what had been Clive's chair. He said, 'No, I'm only into cheating the income tax. But I enjoy one of these occasionally, if Mrs Proost doesn't mind.'

He waved his pipe at her, and I saw her pricing it, and his clothes, and his accent.

She said, 'Of course. Clive, Mr Johnson hasn't anything to drink.'

Johnson smiled at her and at Clive. I'd never seen so much of his teeth before. He said, 'Johnson. Silly first name: same as my last. I think Rita and I would both like a Tom Collins. Actually, I'm sure you've no need to worry about Porter. A charming boy. Perfectly behaved on Madeira. What about London, Rita?'

It's stupid to lie when you don't need to. 'I don't think he's on coke at all,' I said. 'Bennies, in London, but that sort of crowd always do. He never took anything while I was there.'

I could see them all looking into my eyes, and I looked back, with my proper-sized pupils. Pa Curtis said, 'Oh.'

He sounded disappointed. He sounded actually bored. He added, 'Well, do we eat today?'

Two Tom Collinses on a tray stood at my shoulder, ready for serving. I saw Clive look at them, and then at his father. He said, 'Whenever you want, Pa.'

Pa Joseph got up and went out of the door. The Tom Collinses hovered, untouched, then the barman caught Clive's eye and melted away, still carrying them. I hoped they wouldn't be wasted.

Johnson, having indicated that he wished to wash his hands, which I felt was an outright lie, departed in one direction with Clive, leaving me free to say the same to Sharon. But in my case, it was no lie, I tell you.

She left me in the doorway of a toilet like Glasgow City Chambers, with a sharpish piece of advice about where to put anything I wanted got rid of.

I lost my way, coming out, and had to be found and guided past a lot of cabins. I heard Ferdy's voice quite distinctly coming from one of them. He was using some quite botanical words, with short spaces between.

I thought he might have been talking to Dr Thomassen, but when I got to the Little Dining-room, the other half of the Sexual Strategy in Flowers Book was there, between the blonde and the brunette, who had put caftans on.

Another girl in a towelling robe came in halfway through the first course, followed after an interval by Ferdy, looking as if he needed to be plunged into water with his stem crushed.

No one said grace.

The food was high-class French, and none of your West Indian rubbish, with two cold courses to start, to give the chef time to catch up with Pa Joe's inner clockwork.

Joe and the girls ate without talking. Clive asked Johnson about portrait-painting and Johnson shamelessly told him, dropping names that made even Sharon lay her fork down.

Dr Thomassen, whose hair had got very bleached in Tobago, so that he looked more like Andy Hardy than Herbert Lom, gave a long account of the Cocoa Damselfish, and what the liver fluke would do to our insides if we swam in fresh water on St Lucia.

The captain of the *Paramount Princess*, who looked as if nothing more could happen to his liver, sat at the end of the table in snowy white uniform, with his cap on the carpet, and had two helpings of everything while trying hard to catch the eye of the blonde.

After a bit, Johnson and the skipper started a long, technical talk about reefs and shoals and currents and the mess the Pitons made of the wind situation west of St Lucia.

Sharon stopped trying to hold a conversation with Ferdy and said to me, 'I should have thought you would have had a good living in England. What's the attraction? This rich wimp with the glasses? Natalie Sheridan? I thought she was hetero.'

'She is,' I said. 'And Mr Johnson got spoiled in a plane crash. I'm just here for the money.'

I added, 'Don't you get enough work over here? I could speak to Mrs Sheridan.'

I saw her cheeks flatten. Before she could answer, Clive said, 'Go on, Rita. Give us the dirt on Mrs Sheridan. Who's the favoured cat now? What's with that conductor?'

'No buses on *Dolly*,' said Johnson, sliding into my dialogue. 'I wish I could pinch your cook, though. We're eating agricultural lupins on my boat. I won't say my table was the talk of Cowes, but one acquires a certain reputation. Poor Lenny,' said Johnson regretfully. 'He won't like it, but I'm going to have to ask him to go back to plain estate work.'

All I got in the way of warning was a blinding flash of bifocals. I hadn't been going to say anything anyway. I hoped Lenny wouldn't sue him. I waited to hear what he was on about.

Unaffected by anything going on around him, Old Joseph Curtis opened his mouth and made a statement.

'He plays blackjack,' he said.

Clive looked at Ferdy, who looked at the skipper, who looked at Dr Thomassen.

The gem of information, it seemed, referred to Johnson.

Johnson's glasses looked embarrassed. He said, 'As I said to Clive. Only now and then.'

'Then why don't we have a game? You have time for one, I guess?' Clive said warmly. 'If the ladies don't mind. We can take our drinks and coffee along with us.'

I couldn't believe it, but it happened.

Suddenly the table was empty. All the men filed out, talking, plus Sharon to complete the seven. Back to the Den, to make up a game of blackjack for Old Man Joseph Curtis.

Of the three girls left in the room with me, no one seemed surprised. Two of them got up, talking to each other in American voices, glanced at me, and went off in the direction of the cabins. I followed the third girl on deck where the steward brought coffee and sweets and magazines and as much sugar as we wanted.

I lay under a beach umbrella, eating and thinking, with my dark glasses on.

I wondered if Johnson had ever played blackjack in his life before, and what he could afford to lose.

I fell asleep.

'Hullo,' said Johnson.

I opened my eyes. He was sitting on the edge of a lounger with his hands dangling between his knees, looking at me.

He still had all his clothes on, including his shirt. The rest of the deck was empty. The sun was blazing down. I said, 'Where's everybody?'

'Waiting for the loss-adjusters. You don't waste your batteries, do you?' said Johnson.

I wasn't going to tell him he looked tired. He did look tired. I said, 'Well, I didn't know you expected me to hang around a Yukon gambling bolero. What are you having to hock?'

'Bordello. They settled for my address-book,' said Johnson. 'Actually, everybody's retired for a siesta except Ferdy, who collapsed somewhere from metal fatigue. Someone'll come in a minute to show you to your cabin.'

'My *cabin!*' I said. 'I'm going back to the Hurricane Hole. To wait for Natalie.'

'Well, no. That's what I came to tell you,' Johnson said. He was frowning. 'We've got this series of poker games started, and Joe isn't keen to break off, even though, as you know, I really have got to get on to Barbados.'

'You have?' I said. When Johnson frowns, you have to be careful.

'Of course,' said Johnson. 'But that's all right, because Joe was going to Barbados anyway. A ball at Government House. The Curtises have a genuine invitation from the Governor. They showed it to me. So instead of a nasty rough beat on *Dolly*, you and I are staying on the *Paramount Princess*, and Joe is taking us all to Barbados. With Natalie. Clive has been ashore and invited Natalie. She'll be on board as soon as she's finished Josephining.'

I said, 'Lenny? Raymond? *Dolly?* Our clothes are at Hurricane Hole. And I didn't get the food for the ...'

'Everything,' said Johnson, 'is taken care of. I've been ashore. A car has gone off to Marigot, to settle up at the hotel and bring back your gear and mine. Raymond and Lenny have been told, and will sail *Dolly* to Barbados with a pal or two. Amy has called at the boat, and solved that other small problem.'

'And Maggie?' I said.

'Well, that was the outcome of the poker game,' Johnson said. 'Ferdy got Maggie back. She's coming on board as well. Seven radiant women and six magnificent men, counting Joe and the skipper.

'It's going to be a busy night. Ferdy's promised to run us a demo tape on the home life of the bottle-brush tree. I'm going to bed.'

'You're gassed,' I said.

'No. Tired but happy. You'll like Barbados,' Johnson said. 'Have fun. Do anything you feel like doing. Leave everything to Christian and His Stamp-Collecting Friend, who, you will recall, have the concession.'

'All the same ...' I began.

'No. All quite, quite different. Keep your fingers crossed. Right hand ring over left,' Johnson said, and went away.

So the call to Raymond had told him something. The time and place, I had to suppose, of the meeting of the top hamper in Roger van Diemen's great drug and banana scheme. The meeting which, it was now pretty clear, must be going to be held in Barbados.

And that was me being warned off.

What a pity.

*

We all met, seven women and six men, on board the *Princess* after the siesta and prepared, in our various ways, to spend an evening and a night together.

I thought afterwards that even Natalie was slightly surprised by the peculiar life-style of the Curtis family.

It wasn't just the figured walnut and lace tablecloth and napkins and silver of the Large Dining-room. Or the spotlit paintings of the Grand Salon, with its piano and its feather-stuffed armchairs chained to the carpet. Or even the amazing plumbing in her bathroom and mine.

It was the sort of grim determination behind it all.

Whatever Clive had said to Natalie when she agreed to come on board, it had changed the coolness between them.

To Sharon she was smooth as baby oil. They greeted one another, chatted, and parted; and from then on, Sharon's share of hostessing was neatly passed over to Clive, who was intelligent, amusing, flattering and never left Natalie's side.

To the swinging chicks, who were never introduced, but just referred to by sort of tacky pet names, Natalie paid no more attention than anyone else, talking across them at dinner as if their seats were empty.

In fact, it was quite hard to overlook them, as they each wore a dress at least as nude as Maggie's had ever been, with jewellery filling the spaces. Their make-up, as might be expected, was faultless.

They didn't look any better than Natalie. I had taken a lot of trouble to make sure of that. I knew every tint on her face would be analysed, and the sort of brushes I'd used, and the make of everything. I'd even locked up my sables when I finished. It may have been stupid, but they have been pinched before now.

Natalie chose to wear a rose taffeta dress with a low waist and crystal pleating that she had bought in Paris. She looked terrific.

I love my work. I love people who are made like Natalie: who let me mould them and paint them into something beautiful.

I was proud of her.

I have to say that Maggie didn't look bad either, because she had strolled across to Natalie during drinks, tapped her on the arm and said, 'You don't mind if I borrow the girl, do you? I can't do anything with my face after that bloody crossing.'

It wasn't a shock. She'd hardly thrown me a sentence on *Dolly*, mainly because she was working so hard to get Johnson. I guessed the present act was because I'd seen her not get him. I wondered how he'd told her she was back in with Ferdy, and hoped he'd told Ferdy.

He apparently had, because when Natalie, after a pause, agreed to loan out my services, Maggie walked straight across to Ferdy, knocked the glass out of his hand and said coldly, 'Hello, stranger. And whose *herpes* have you been collecting since I saw you last?'

I was interested to see that hardly anyone paid any attention, they were all so busy working on their own angles. The only man with tact to match Natalie's was Dr Thomassen, who started up a gentle conversation about card-sharping that kept Joe awake until it was time to change for dinner.

I had a thing I'd bought in Paris myself: a sort of baggy black satin suit that unzipped to the navel, with a collar under it. I didn't have a lot of time after doing the others, but I spray-spiked my hair and put quite a lot of stripes on my skin, sort of tiger-style.

Nobody said a thing except Johnson, who came out of his cabin looking normal and said placidly, 'My God, I'll tell your Probation Officer. May I lead you to the Large Dining-room?'

We entered together, which is why no one said a thing.

I was annoyed with him. I had expected him to arrange an assortment. Discretion is all very well, but I was dying to know what he'd found out about the banana meeting. He might have the concession but I was, after all, a bloody partner.

At dinner, we got French wine and brandy, and Old Joe asked Natalie who she knew, and checked off the answers.

After dinner, the poker school, including Johnson, departed for regions unseen, while the rest of us watched films and went on drinking. After a bit Natalie went out to see, she said, what on earth the gambling was like, and came back an hour later smiling, with Clive, and a rich-looking bulge in her bag that hadn't been there before.

She went to bed when the engines started, but although various people drifted in and out, went up on deck for a smoke, or tapped the never-ceasing flow of booze in the Grand Salon, the game still hadn't finished in the small hours, and I went to bed too.

To hell with Johnson.

I have never been anywhere where so many doors opened and closed between three and five a.m., perhaps because I had never been anywhere where there were absolutely no locks on the doors.

I was sent the chief engineer about two a.m. without even having booked him, and by the time he'd got past my chair under the handle and into the light of my torch, I was getting more worried about his engines than anything else.

After making sure I wasn't just shy he did however accept a refusal and leave quite cheerfully, which was more than could be said for Dr Thomassen, who was shocked to find me there at all and had thought, it appeared, that this was the chief engineer's room.

In that I thought I could see Ferdy's touch.

An hour later, sure enough, along came Ferdy's touch.

As ever, we had a fair struggle, and then as ever he took no for an answer and sat for another ten minutes drinking my bedside whisky and howling with laughter and telling me all about Carl Thomassen, on flowers and off them, and trying to get me to tell him who Natalie had been sleeping with since he left us.

I asked how the poker game was going.

Ferdy said that he thought that Johnson now owned half the *Paramount Princess*, and he, Ferdy, hoped it wasn't the half with the girls in it.

I asked him if he'd got over his spat with Natalie and he nodded, wiping his whiskers. Ferdy has very large features, and there is always a lot to wipe.

'Boring, bloody Josephine. Let Natalie do all the dirty work, my little Toucan. Supportive independence, it's called, if you can get away with it.'

Ferdy's gypsophila. He always got away with it. His house in Barbados was already rented to Natalie, and he had persuaded the Curtises to lend him theirs, next to Claudette Colbert, where he proposed to set up house, he said, with Tulip Thomassen and the Hon. Maggie.

Shades of 17B. Ferdy always fell on his feet, on someone else's expensive carpet.

And what, he now added, about helping him carry his cameras round with Tulip tomorrow, twenty quid a sexy flower?

I said, 'But what about Natalie? She was on the R.T. before dinner calling a board meeting of the Josephine buffs for tomorrow. Fred Glitterbocker's flying over.'

'Gluttenmacher. My darling Rita,' said Ferdy. 'Not letting Natalie think that she's won is as important as actually winning. Leave Natalie to me.'

I said, 'Ferdy, if she sacks us both, can I get a *permanent* job on your Sexy Flower Book?'

Which was a mistake, because it reminded him of his usual routine, and I had to quite hurt him before I got him out.

I gave up waiting for Johnson. I pulled the chest of drawers in front of the doorway that time, and forgot to set my watch alarm, so that I had some trouble letting the steward in with my breakfast in the morning. I felt great. I felt sad. I felt hungry.

There were flowers and cold orange juice on the tray. The sun poured hot through the porthole on to deep-pile carpet and silver and armchairs. I showered and put on a loose cotton top and pants and went up on deck in my bare feet.

It was eight o'clock and I had the ship, swabbed and scoured, to myself, apart from quiet gents in white coats asking in a murmur if I would like an iced something on deck.

The *Paramount Princess* was like a Model T Ford. It was like an old Las Vegas pleasure palace. It was old-fashioned.

I thought of the captain, doing his duty, and hoped that someone would wake him and the chief engineer, in time to walk about with their uniforms on when we came to Barbados.

Barbados, where Roger van Diemen was.

I knew which was Johnson's cabin. Like mine, it wasn't locked.

It didn't have a chair under the door-knob, either. With the uncanny instinct of the plastered, he had got himself stripped and on to the bed, with a towel round his waist. He was in his favourite position, on his face. His hair was all over the pillow, and his glasses had dropped from his dangling hand on to the floor.

I went forward, heaven help me, to pick them up.

I was curious, anyway, to see what sort of shape the plane crash had left him in.

In spite of all that stuff with the sticks and the wheelchair, there was nothing wrong with his legs. They were American-colour, as if they'd been on the sea or in the snow getting tanned for years and years, but not this winter.

So I looked above the towel.

The forensic people always gave me a cup of coffee when I'd been studying something, and joked with me because I never really got much upset.

It's not that I'm funny. But to imitate wounds, you've got to know what you're doing, and when you're thinking and drawing, the reality of it all doesn't get to you.

I'm not a doctor. I couldn't diagnose what all the operation scars were, or what the bumps and hollows meant. Except that this wasn't a matter of a few broken bones from a seat-belt, or a cracked rib or shoulder-blade.

These injuries were internal. I thought of the wheelchair, bumping down the cobbles on Madeira, then didn't think of it.

Sole survivor of a plane crash.

Sole survivor, perhaps.

Plane crash, my arse.

I covered him with the blanket, to spare the breakfast steward, and got myself out of the room.

An open book and a cripple.

Rita, you're on your own, girl.

The captain woke in time to get us into Carlisle Bay, Barbados, later that morning, and I drove with Natalie to the St James district, the classy bit of the west coast where she had rented this beach house from Ferdy.

We drove on the left. Barbados is the Oldest Democracy in the Western World. Barbados is half Martinique's size, and so British it isn't even volcanic. I felt deprived.

I had left without seeing Johnson. Natalie had been waved off by a small bunch of Curtises, whom she was meeting anyway later at the Governor-General's gig, to which, no surprise, she was also now going.

I had done the civil bit too, because I probably wouldn't see them again. After the party, said Clive, they might take themselves north to Florida. Old Joseph didn't care much for the West Indies in mixed weather.

My brochure said that the temperature stayed at a steady eighty all the year round in Barbados, and the way the sun was shining didn't look very mixed to me. But maybe the dice or the girls needed changing.

Ferdy's villa was casual, like Ferdy, and you could tell by the way Dodo stood waiting to greet us, like a Total Pole, that the daily help had been a shambles, but she'd licked them into shape all right.

She and I exchanged naked glares and I went off to my room to sort myself out and unpack. I'd locked all my boxes this time, before I left for Martinique. I took my cat out and put it beside the air-conditioning unit, and it grinned back.

Then Natalie made fifteen telephone calls and went off to the Coral Reef Club with a hard hat and her hair tied back, to pick up her backer Fred Glitterbags who had actually flown in that morning. They were going riding together.

Her lawyer, I found out from Dodo, was arriving on the next plane, with her accountant. In the early days of a film, this is a good sign. Number-crunching was about to begin.

I told Ferdy when he called an hour later, needing some help with a few Bachelors' Buttons, twenty quid all in. Dr Thomassen was there, with a sheepish expression and a car and a driver.

According to Ferdy, Natalie could hang about and wait for her meeting until he was good and ready.

In fact, as I found out pretty quickly, he knew all about it, and didn't have to parade until Kazimierz did, which was in a room at the Coral Reef Club at four.

I was free anyway until that meeting ended. Then I had to make over Natalie for carnival-time at Government House, leaving some time in hand to do the same for one or two of her friends in the neighbourhood.

So she had ordained, tick. It was fair enough. A few extra faces, since I wasn't, in any way, being her secretary. It would do her relationships a world of good, and it didn't harm me. Rita, Interfacial.

I considered Ferdy's offer. I was free. Until *Dolly* arrived, Johnson was stuck on the *Princess* anyway. And meanwhile, as Ferdy's camera-loader, I could get to see the island. The flowers. The banana plantations.

I slammed on my French pom-pom berry and climbed into the car. Then I took it off again, because Ferdy had brought me a Nelson straw boater to wear instead.

The place they were taking most of the photographs was just off the east coast, near the Atlantic shore. But Barbados is only fourteen miles across, and that was no problem.

To please me, Ferdy told the driver to go from Speightstown by way of the Scotland district, but I didn't meet anyone I knew, and it looked tropical, like everything else. There were some little hills in the middle.

I asked Ferdy where the banana plantations were, but he said we weren't passing them, and Barbados was mostly sugar cane anyway: where did I think all the Bajan monkeys came from?

It turned out that Bajan meant Barbadian, and Bajan monkeys were drinks made from rum, and that if I was dead keen to see bananas, there was a new plantation somewhere I could get shown over tomorrow.

I was dead keen. Dr Thomassen, his eyes like oysters in his pink suntan, said he'd arrange it.

Ferdy, remembering his duty as a resident, pointed out as we passed it, the ruined half-plaster plantation house built by 20th Century-Fox for *Island in the Sun*. He'd found stills from the film in the Curtis home. Harry Belafonte. James Mason. Dorothy Dandridge.

Lovely make-up job, he said.

I didn't listen to what he went on to say. I'd heard about it already that morning.

From Old Joe Curtis.

It was the only conversation I'd had with Kim-Jim's father, from the moment when he'd looked up and said, '*You've brought the punk girl.*'

There was no special reason, I suppose, why we hadn't talked. We never sat together at table, and he was off playing cards the rest of the time. Or if he wasn't, Sharon and Clive were on either side of him, like a bath with grab handles.

But after that visit to Johnson's cabin on *Paramount Princess*, I'd felt a bit dim with no company, and padding through the Grand Salon tumble-twist carpet, had found and sat down at the piano.

Halfway through *Bop Till You Drop*, Old Joe had come in.

I didn't know I had an audience until my toes slipped off the loud pedal and I spun round on the stool, massaging them.

He was there, sunk in one of the stuffed brocade chairs, with his weedy ankles crossed under his bathrobe, and his cigar sending up smoke past his crew-cut grey hair. 'Ry Cooder. You sure are no great piano player,' he said. 'You see my *Dorian Grey*?'

I hadn't thought he would remember who I was, but he had.

'We didn't have what you've got,' he added. 'Your foam latex and Old Age Stipple and Scar-Em and contact lenses. Lon Chaney used chicken membrane for his blind eye. If an actor couldn't cry, he sniffed ammonia. If we wanted to make an old man, we used Pan-Stik and pencils and acting. If we wanted to make a monster, we used imagination. You know what that is?'

'You taught us all,' I said.

'They know my work over in England?' he said.

I didn't say I came from Scotland. I said, 'The film libraries are full of it. They teach it in film school and make-up classes. Why do you never come over?'

He puffed at his cigar for a long time. Then he took it out.

'Europe?' he said. 'Europe's for losers. They know me here. America's been good to me. This is where I belong. Do you know, on this island we're going to ...'

And he'd told me about 20th Century-Fox, and the film, while I shut down the lid of the piano.

To hell, oh to hell with growing old.

Ferdy said, 'Rita? Short of sleep, darling?' And I was back, being driven past Farley Hill and down to worn mushroom-shaped coral rocks and mounds of sea-grapes and the big waves of the Atlantic coast, and the park that Barclay's Bank had laid out free for the islanders, out of their spare Bee-Wees and, no doubt, Natalie's.

The hotel Ferdy took us to was serving fried dolphin and pickled banana and egg-plant slices and soused bread-fruit and pumpkin fritters and breaded flying-fish and coconut bread.

I was quite sorry when Ferdy, suddenly remembering why we were there, came bounding back with the driver to drag us off to this tropical garden

But actually, that was great, too. It had humming-birds and monkeys and doctor birds in it, and birds like sparrows with yellow stomachs, and flowers like lobsters and snails and shrimps and candles with red wax curled round them.

Dr Thomassen stood quite still with his forehead bulging, making suggestions, while Ferdy skipped and twirled and leaped and climbed like Neurosis. Narcotics. Nureyev.

We had the most trouble with a powder-puff tree. Then Ferdy had to pack it in to get back for his Coral Reef meeting, but said O.K., if I insisted, he'd take me through Bridgetown.

Bridgetown is the capital of Barbados. Bridgetown is very like Troon, except filled with black people in the shades you get in a natural Icelandic sweater, and the policemen have pith helmets on. The Barbadian national colours, I was sorry to see, are blue and yellow.

Bridgetown is so busy anyway, that driving through during Carifesta you hardly noticed the visiting nationals from all the other Caribbean countries at first.

The ordinary Bajans didn't seem to mind the Carifesta jamming the halls and the streets, but just stood about talking, and going in and out of bars and department stores.

I was interested, of course, but that wasn't why I wanted to go through Bridgetown. I wanted to go through Bridgetown to see what was in Carlisle Bay since we left it.

Being in the grip of his post-photographer's tension, Ferdy had given up being a guide in favour of asking me for the third time whether I'd seen him change the exposure for the hibiscus, which I had.

It was Dr Thomassen who noticed and pointed out our late floating hotel, the *Paramount Princess*, still at anchor and hardly swaying in spite of all the athletics going on in the cabins.

And there was the *Dolly*, also in from St Lucia, which made Ferdy stop knotting his whiskers and sit up, his mind switched from exposures to Maggie, the perfect photographer's cure, to be taken as often as necessary.

I was glad for them both. I wasn't sure whether or not I was glad for myself.

Because beside them, large and solid and powerful, and flying her blue and yellow beastly house-flag, was the *Coombe Caroline*, in for bananas and bunkers and mayday.

Mayhem, Johnson says.

We were both right.

Because the first person I saw, when Ferdy dropped me off at his own house, was Roger van Diemen.

Thank God, before I went in, I went round the back of the house and looked through the window, because I thought Natalie might be with her lawyer, or even horsing about still with Fred Moneybags. It wasn't four yet, and she wasn't expecting me.

Instead, the shutters to the back sitting-room were half open, and inside was Natalie, changed for her meeting into a pastel dress and jacket with a puritan collar, walking about twirling her rings, which was much the same as Rome burning down.

The person she was angry with I couldn't quite see at first, then he shifted edgily into view.

Roger the Damned One. Wearing a well-pressed cotton safari suit, instead of the trousers I'd spilled drink all over at the airport, but with the same hot, light eyes and brick skin and hair crinkling up over his ears with the heat.

The scars of our little tussle in the Mercedes had gone, but otherwise he looked just as beastly.

He didn't like what Natalie was saying, either. He said, 'I'm sorry. I can't accept that.'

'My dear man,' said Natalie. They were both speaking quite softly, and it was a strain, actually, to hear, although I was inside the croton hedge right under the window.

'My dear man, I'm not trying to make a living out of you. You can have your jewellery back. If you can't bring yourself to remain friendly to me without climbing into my bed, then I'm sorry. But for your sake as well as mine, it really has got to stop.'

He said, 'You didn't say that before.'

'No, I didn't,' said Natalie. 'But that was on Madeira, where you were very silly indeed. You were lucky not to find yourself in prison on a murder charge. But for me, you would have been. I really don't feel I owe you anything, Roger.'

She stood still and faced him. He had never moved, since he walked where I could see him.

He said, 'You don't, do you? If it hadn't exposed you, you would have seen me go to prison quite happily. You might even have put me there. How long do you think you can get away with it, Natalie? How long before someone turns the tables and sells you out? One of these days, that girl with the orange hair will make a killing out of you.'

Natalie abruptly crossed her arms and, hugging her elbows, paced to the other side of the room and back. The lines I took such good care to fix for her had broken through all over her face. She said, 'She doesn't know anything. My God, look at her. I feel like St Lazarus.'

'Do you think the Curtises are to be any more trusted?' said Roger. 'Or that photographer? Or this Gluttenmacher you're so friendly with all of a sudden? What do you think I could do, if I wanted revenge? I've never told anyone. Anyone. I'm the only person who won't let you down.'

He looked as if he really meant what he was saying. He was a nutter all right, but Natalie wasn't afraid of him.

She laughed, and unfurling her hands, smoothly picked up one of his arms and pushed the tailored sleeve back.

I could see the needle tracks from the window.

She let his arm fall. She said, 'Roger, I wouldn't trust you to do my laundry.'

He had gone absolutely white under his tan. She was a bitch. If I didn't know what a bastard he was, I would have felt a pang for him.

He said, 'And if I talk? I could, you know.'

'I'm sure you could,' Natalie said. 'Your word against mine. I'll come and visit you in the home they put you into.'

They stared at one another, then her eyes went past him to the clock.

She said, 'So shall we leave it at that? Rita will be back, and I have to get to my meeting. I'm sorry, Roger. It's been a ridiculous conversation, but you forced it on me. We had a nice time, but it's over. Go and take a cure somewhere, and make another start. In another job, away from the tropics.'

She picked up her bag and a document case and walked to the door. 'Dodo!'

In a moment, Mr van Damned would be out. And when he got into his car, the girl with the orange hair was bloody well going to be behind in a taxi. And wherever he was going, so was I.

I bent low, and scrambled out of the crotons.

Then I stayed bent low, because someone's hand was on the back of my neck, holding it down like a fork, with someone's knee on my ankles, so that I couldn't move.

195

'*Bloody hold it*,' said Johnson's voice. 'He's followed.'

I held it. I heard van Diemen's voice again, and then Natalie's, telling Dodo something, and then a slammed door and footsteps in the front, and the sound of a car starting up. A pair of shutters opened up in Natalie's bedroom overhead.

Johnson released me.

The nerves in my neck shrieked, and so did my ankles. He hadn't used force, just pressure.

He said, 'Sorry. This way, quietly,' and disappeared into the depths of Ferdy's garden. Out of earshot of the house, I fell over him, sitting on the grass among a clump of red ginger-flowers. I recognized them.

'Sit down,' he said. 'Overmanning in the machine room. Dangerous thing, private enterprise. What brought that on? Did you come into my cabin last night?'

The blanket. As Amy Faflick said, he was too damned quick. I sat down, and saw that my face had already answered him. The open book.

'O.K.' he said. 'Crippled centre, but lots of tough cookies round about to make up for it. Don't follow him, don't talk to him or you'll gum up the works. What did you think of what you heard?'

'That you could start a murder case with it,' I said. 'If you'd taped it.'

'But we didn't. And Natalie?' Johnson said.

He seemed to have heard it all. I was full of ideas.

I said, 'She could be the person you're looking for. She could have begun the affair with van Diemen; even started him somehow on drugs, and then got a third person to blackmail van Diemen into bringing Coombe's into their network. This meeting at Coral Reef could be the meeting you're waiting for.'

St Lazarus. I could hear the bite in my voice.

Johnson showed no special surprise. 'It isn't,' he said. 'Because Roger van Diemen isn't going to it. Because she's thrown him out, Natalie's actually cleared herself. Remember, no van Diemen, no dope and banana network.'

He paused. 'Do you want to stay with her? She may change. Ask you to alter your hair, for example.'

I said, 'She won't get rid of me. Neither will you. When is the meeting?'

'I'm waiting to hear. Tonight, perhaps.'

I looked at him. He said, 'I can't trust you, can I, not to try and find it?'

'No,' I said.

'Bloody hell,' he said. With feeling.

I watched him. After that little game in the crotons, my opinion of his chances had gone up a bit, but as far as I was concerned, it was a split concession now. He wasn't going to fall down on this job if I could prevent it.

He was twirling a bit of feathery ginger. He chucked it aside, and looked back at me. 'Well, you can do something. I expect you'll be tarting them up for the Carnival Ball. Are you free after that?'

I was.

'Well, suppose,' Johnson said, 'that Raymond calls with a car to take you out on the town, and you just happen to have your fishing-tackle outfit with you? All of it?'

I could feel my smile stretching. I said, 'No problem. Where d'you want me to do it? On *Dolly*?'

'No,' Johnson said. He made to get up, swore, and succeeded.

'No, it's life in the fast lane for you. The Hackney Carifesta team's quarters in Bridgetown.'

'You're not joking,' I said.

'I never joke,' said Johnson. 'Now shut up, and listen.'

For some things, it helps a lot to be wee, and have hockey legs.

I was always the one who got sent up the tree or under the shed for the ball. I had one teacher who used to complain that, but for a few Victorian commies, I would be up there cleaning his chimneys instead of wasting his time at a school desk.

The Brighton Beach is a chalet hotel built on the shore at Oistins, just south of Government House and along the coast from Bridgetown.

The central block faces the road, and has the reception desk in it.

Through that, or by a service passage further along, you get to the chalets themselves, which are one-storey concrete apartments, each with its own kitchen and bathroom and bedroom, and a sitting-room opening on to a porch.

The chalets are joined by dimly lit paths, and are set among flower beds, and lawns with slatted sunchairs on them.

By day and by night, quite a few of the chalets are taken by people who haven't come for the swimming or the sunbathing, but to spend a weekend with the girlfriend, or a few days off with some drinking pals, or to do some serious gambling, or pull off an even more serious business deal with no questions asked.

Briefing, by Johnson.

He was with me somewhere in the dark that night, but I couldn't see him.

It was Raymond's hand that led me to the chalet whose garden was next to the beach, and whose lit windows were already covered with curtains behind the glass screens.

A very small bush can cover me. Raymond found one, near the beach steps with a good view of the porch, and settled me into it. Then he found a place for himself.

People came by, on their way to the central dining-room, and came back. Two couples went down to the beach, and only one came back.

A security man with a torch came, shining it in a bored way all round the garden, and putting it off, hitched himself on the corner of the chalet porch rail.

Two lots of footsteps came down the passage, and turned out to belong to a clerk, showing a drunk the way into the chalet.

The drunk, a man in a flowered shirt over dark trousers, took his time fishing out a couple of notes for the boy, leaned confidingly on the security man's shoulder and staggered into the porch, holding the key to the chalet.

The light from the sitting-room shone on his face, as he opened the door and went in. He had a rum bottle in each of his pockets, and his face was covered with a Carifesta plaster mask in the shape of a cockerel, behind which he seemed to be crowing.

The door shut, and the security man shook his head and switching on his torch, wandered off.

In the chalet, a side light suddenly came on from the bathroom, followed by one from the kitchen, to one side of the door. Both windows were protected by louvres, and the light only showed in thin lines between slats, and from this wee grating covered with bug wire in the kitchen.

There was a sound of distant chinking; then the rectangle went dark, and half-bright, and dark again.

'Swinging door into the sitting-room,' Raymond said. 'Van Diemen, we know, has a monkey mask.'

Two people came round the passage, went into the porch and knocked on the door of the chalet, which opened almost at once. Both wore carnival masks and both seemed to be sober. I got a glimpse, as they went in, of their clothes. One wore the same as the first man: a flowered shirt and dark trousers.

The other had on a ground-length shift and high heels. From the way she managed them, there was no doubt she was a woman.

The door closed behind them.

Silence, or sort of. The chickadees buzzed and the frogs whistled. The sea sighed on the beach. Beyond the darkness of the living quarters, the sky gave off a glow from lit gardens and dance-floors and restaurants, and the far-off murmur of music and talking sounded just like another sort of sea.

Someone brushed by my shoulder and spoke to Raymond.

'You should go round the back,' said Johnson's low voice. 'The bedroom curtains are open. The plant, I have to report, has been equipped with scrubbers.'

Raymond, in the lowest of voices, said, 'Wow!'

'Three wows,' said Johnson placidly. 'Call girls, coloured expensive. I took a photograph. I'll give you a peek in the dorm.'

'Three?' said Raymond.

'Quite,' said Johnson. 'And Roger still has to come.'

I thought he was being thick. Roger van Diemen wouldn't be interested in coloured call girls, whatever the other two fancied.

I remembered he wasn't thick, and put my mind to it again. What he meant was, Roger still had to come. And another man.

The other man came first, walking quickly with no one to guide him. He stepped through the porch, rapped, and was admitted. The light shone on him for a second only, and showed nothing but the same uniform: the loose shirt which could have covered anything, the dark trousers and a mask.

'I'd like to . . .' said Raymond, and half rose.

'No. Wait,' said Johnson.

I hadn't heard anything, but a moment later, footsteps echoed in the passage. Crisp footfalls belonging to a tall man in a floral shirt and a monkey mask who knocked at the same door, and waited, and then went in, rather slowly.

'Roger van Diemen. The entire Board, I would guess,' Johnson said. 'Go and look now, if you're quick. The security man will be back in a moment.'

The security man came back before Raymond did. He stood swinging his torch outside the porch, and looking idly about him. Like Johnson, Raymond made no sound coming back; but I saw his shadow lingering in the passage.

Then the security man moved away, on his patrol, and Raymond slipped over the lawn and arrived beside us. 'They've drawn the curtains,' he said. 'If they exist. I think you were having a wet bloody dream. What about getting up close?'

'They're bugged,' said Johnson.

'And if they spot it?' said Raymond. 'You brought her. Why not use her?'

Men.

I was over the lawn before he had finished the sentence, and into the porch among the breakfast chairs and the bougainvillea. I crouched down in the shadows and listened.

It wasn't as good as Ferdy's villa, because the glass and curtains were closed. A lot of the time, I couldn't hear what they were saying at all, and then the woman or one of the men would speak sharply, and I caught a few phrases.

The voices were blurred and none of them was familiar. I couldn't even pick out which was Roger van Diemen. The woman could have been anybody.

It was the fault of the masks, of course. We have the same trouble with make-up. You can get a great likeness, stuffing the cheeks and adding shaped teeth and false jowls and everything, but it's no good if the actor can't speak through it.

There was another thing, too. If I heard too much, I couldn't remember it.

But of course, Johnson had thought of that. Raymond suddenly was beside me.

He didn't speak: we were too close to the window. But in the glimmer of light through the curtains, I could see him pointing.

I looked.

He was showing me the grating. The small netted grating, now dark, in the kitchen wall. Through which nothing, of course, could be heard. But which, when the door to the main room was open, might just give a glimpse of the people inside.

It was quite low. I could see it without climbing. I carried across a tub of portentias, and stood behind it, and watched.

I watched for quite a long time. I could still hear the murmur of voices, but not what they said. Once, Raymond shifted his position a little under the window and I saw the creeper shake, and go still.

There was no sign of Johnson. The security man strolled round the corner, flashing his light, then putting it out, took up his favourite position at the end of the porch rail, and began to roll a cigarette.

I crouched behind the tub. At the other end of the porch, the creeper was motionless.

Inside the sitting-room, the way they were speaking became different, and jerky. The passage beyond the end of the chalet suddenly became striped with light, as someone in the chalet moved out and into the bathroom.

Above my head, the light went on in the kitchen.

As before, it only showed in the cracks between louvres. But the ventilator had become a square of pure light. A little window into the kitchen. A little window which might let me look through the kitchen door, if it happened to open. Which might give me a glimpse, if the angle was right, of four men and one woman without their masks on.

Except that, with the guard standing in front of me, I couldn't rise to my feet and have a look.

Above my head, a fridge door slammed, and a voice said, 'There ain't nothin' here. Ice or soda. I'll try the godammed shelves.'

A tap ran, and I could hear other cupboard doors rattling. Someone had got bored, or thirsty, or both, and was searching the kitchen.

The meeting was very likely over. Soon the man with the thirst would give up, and switch off the light, and open the door to the sitting-room and I wouldn't see who was there, because I was squatting here like a dummy on the floor of the porch.

After which they would come out, one by one, and fall over us.

To hell with it.

The guard had his back to me. He was licking his cigarette paper, and feeling in his hip pocket for something.

I stood up, in full view if he turned, and fixed my eye to the ventilator.

I was just in time. I saw a hand turn off the tap above a full jug. I saw a tummy in a flowery shirt cross the kitchen and put a hand on the door and shove it open. I saw the man, full length now, carry the jug into the sitting-room. And as the door started to close, I saw the other three men and one woman, sitting round a littered table with two bottles of rum and some glasses on it.

One of them was Roger van Diemen, his dark brown hair curling wetly round his broad, reddened face.

The other four were the folk who had summoned him there, including the woman in heels, and the man who had come in from the kitchen.

The dope runners, according to Johnson. Whose boss had strong-armed or sweet-talked the Financial Director of Coombe's into distributing their goodies for them, along with his bananas.

It would have been a great moment, if I had recognized them.

I didn't, because everyone except Roger van Diemen was still wearing a mask.

The security man struck a match, and I slid down to a furious crouch, as above me the grating went dark again.

All that bloody trouble for nothing. And until the security man decided to wander away, I was trapped where I was, and so was Raymond. Easy meat for the five when they decided to leave, and the light from their open door floodlit his creeper and my bougainvillea.

I remembered the girls in the bedroom, and hoped the gents in the masks had as well. If they were supposed to be there for an orgy, then the more artistic they made it, the better.

Unfortunately, it turned out to be the fastest lay outside A.I.D., and in five minutes, flat or not, it was over.

The guard stayed where he was, looking about him and enjoying his cigarette. Inside the apartment, there was a sudden banging of doors, and a lot of high-pitched giggling and clinking of glasses.

A girl shrieked with excitement and the security man, his cigarette glowing under his folded arms, turned his head and gazed at the chalet, a dirty grin on his face.

And that was it. As he looked, the door half-opened on a crowd of masked heads and hookers, and a flood of light beamed out to within a couple of inches of where I was crouching.

I was bloody trapped.

Given half a chance, I might have managed to do something, such as clocking the guard with the tub and rushing past him into the garden.

I didn't get to do anything, because of this digital watch.

Anyone who likes going in crowds, such as to church or the flicks, knows that when the wee hand gets to twelve, everybody's digital pips.

This is called human error, there being a knob to push to stop it pipping in company.

After a lot of early advice from sound engineers, I always silence my watch on a film job.

I had silenced it. It wasn't my fault that at that moment it started to cry because its batteries had bloody expired.

A digital dying would make a great Disney serial.

There are these quacking noises, while the display has a serious fit. Then it starts to go blind. That is, a sort of mist creeps over its face and you think it's gone, and it was one great, gallant guy to leave the tent in this weather.

But you're wrong. It's not beaten yet. A quack, and there is its face, staring at you like a cat in a well, and shrieking, goddammit.

A digital can take half an hour to expire.

At the first quack, the security guard turned round.

At the second, I stopped trying to bash the watch on the tub without making a movement, and ripping it off, hurled it into the darkness, where it fell and lay sobbing.

The crowd of flowered shirts and masks in the doorway stopped dead. The security man, getting me into focus behind the portentias, put his hand to what was undoubtedly a gun at his belt.

He never touched it. A furious, and familiar, voice roared from the garden.

'You, Cordella girl? Is you a walkin' duppy? You come right here. What yuh Ma say, yuh societ wid dis guy, he a guard? Evahbody do agree. Evahbody en show up here wid me, tek you home. You chase after men, soul, you get dirty like sin. You get throw in hell. I en cay wuh nobody say, *you en come here!*'

He didn't have to yell. I was there already, dashing past the guard and across the grass to the steps down to the beach, where there stood not only this indignant Rastafarian with Johnson's voice, but a whole crowd of other blacks, jumping up and down and adding their voices to his.

And out of the corner of my eye, I saw a sudden shiver of creeper and a dark form leaping the porch fence behind the guard's surprised back, that meant Raymond was away as well.

The black figures swallowed me up, laughing and shouting. Through them, I could see the guard hesitate, and look behind him. For a moment, one man stepped forward from the crowd on the threshold, urgently, as if he meant to lead a rush after us.

The man in the cockerel mask, who had arrived first.

Then he stopped, and turned back, and said something to the others.

The guard looked at him, and said a few words, and the cockerel mask replied with a snap.

No one blew whistles, or raised the alarm, or summoned help. The guard made no effort, after the first moment, to touch his revolver. Instead, he began to walk towards us, waving his arms and telling us to clear out to the beach, with his eyes straining, trying to pick me out again after that one flying glimpse.

With Johnson and myself unseen in the middle, the mob retreated good-humouredly to the shore. In the middle of the noise I could hear Johnson's voice, still happily scolding.

'Yuh goin' get one load of licks, girl. Yuh a fret on yuh folks. You lose out bad, you muchin' dat man. Lukie, you ever hear anyt'ing so yet as dat guard an' dis li'l girl? No, soul. I so dam fed up. I don' tek um easy. This girl like um so bad, I has to get she a husband. You, girl. You, Cordella ...'

The guard stood on the beach steps, looking at us. The light from the chalet porch abruptly went out, as the party on the threshold went back inside and closed the door. The twenty or thirty blacks round about us continued to move along the beach, as the shore wall of the Brighton gave way to the shore wall of the hotel next door, talking, singing and dancing on the smooth sand among the crabs.

The one turning cartwheels in a bowler hat, sleeveless T-shirt and tasselled garters was Raymond, I was pleased to see, with his wax nose and all-over No. 11 Mulatto still intact.

On the other side, in a swirl of laughter and cross-talk, I saw Johnson coming towards me, his round black glasses glittering under the brim of his stiff knitted hat.

His nose was his own, but covered like the rest of him with Egyptian No. 2. His eyebrows were pasted down with mortuary wax, and a scrub of crêpe hair thoroughly altered the shape of his jaw and his lips. I was as proud of him as I had been of Natalie.

My own make-up was everyday Bajan, with a wig of short black fuzz to cover my hair, and a prosthetic mask I'd brought from England.

I had had the mask made because he had asked me. I had also brought a box of wigs. Among them was the one I wore every day, of orange spikes.

He hadn't asked me to do that. He had only said, speaking in Lady Emerson's comfortable room, that I had already proved a splendid target because of my hair, and it might be quite a nice idea if there were two of me.

Wigs on top of spiked hair are not easy. I had the wig made, and thought about it. Then before I left England, I went and had my hair bleached and cropped, and put the wig on it.

Johnson had admired it earlier this very evening in the Bridgetown headquarters of the Hackney Carifesta delegation. I'd no idea then that I'd ruin everything.

I stood on the beach and said, 'I blew it. I'm sorry. I didn't know the watch would do that. And they kept wearing their masks. It was a bloody disaster. Now they'll change their plans.'

'So they might,' Johnson said. 'I shouldn't worry. Worse things happen at sea.'

He didn't sound wild, or fed-up or anything. He sounded breathless, and a bit high.

Raymond came up, all over sand and out of breath, and said, 'Sir, may I shake by the hand the greatest living Bajan-speaking Englishman? You're a genius.'

'I know,' said Johnson.

'You had me sweating blood when that thing went off.'

'I know,' said Johnson.

'They could have caught her,' said Raymond.

I stood there like a shrimp plant, with them talking over my head.

'Not before so many witnesses,' Johnson said. 'But once the top brass are safe, they'll come after us.'

'Well, you'd better look after Rita,' said Raymond. 'There's a truck out front for this lot. They've a concert to go to. I'll go in that; I wasn't spotted. And there's someone round front, on the offchance they can follow the masks as they leave.'

I said, 'Then you might see who they are after all?'

Johnson said, 'A faint hope. They'll be jumpy, and we mustn't push it too far. We need proof, remember. We want them to go ahead with their plans. Don't worry. Next time is the biggy, and no one will blow it ...'

'Right,' said Johnson. 'Rita. They're going to search that truck in a moment. And this beach. Let's get on with it.'

Under his knitted hat was this fearful Rasta wig. Under his fringed satin shift was an even more awful red frilly shirt, and a locket.

'Meet,' said Johnson, 'a member of the Trinidad Collapso Band, playing this evening in the hotel beach patio right there next door. Who's got a turban?'

Someone, giggling, came up and reversing Johnson's satin, slipped it over my blouse and skirt. It came to my ankles.

Someone else, delving into a pocket, dragged out a matching pink turban and tied it over my Afro.

'Now. It's a silly question,' said Johnson, 'but tell de troot, doh. If put to it, can you play a steel drum, my gel Rita-Cordella?'

Johnson didn't fool me that time.

He wasn't frowning. He meant it.

The Trinidad Collapso Band all wore red frilly shirts and seemed to be expecting him.

He went straight to an oil drum at the back, picked up the sticks, and when I refused politely, took a grip and threw himself into the next number. And whatever else, he'd done *that* before.

I watched him ripple his way cheerfully through three bits of reggae, including a rendition of *House on Fire* with solo bits in it, and then found a pair of congos looking lonely, and had a bash on my own.

I didn't do so badly at that. With all those rows and rows of oil drums murmuring musically away you could hardly hear me, but I heard myself, and it was great. It was like having six daisies. Or three Bajan monkeys. Or drinking your way, like Ferdy, down the whole daiquiri list.

After a while, they got Johnson out to the front of the stand and he sang a whole long collapso in the same accent he'd used at the Brighton Beach, getting screams and applause between verses; and at the end, a fat black woman climbed up and kissed him.

Soon after that the band took a break, and he came over with two plates of barbecued chicken legs and these drinks made of rum and cane juice and lime, and said, 'Big Lou says if you play mainstream clarinet as well, you're on any time. Enjoy it?'

'You're bananas,' I said. Joke. I took the plate. I was starving.

'Had to put off a little time. Let's talk,' said Johnson. He returned the wave of the bandleader, took a swig of his drink and walked me round the back, through the dark part of the patio.

'Raymond's got a car waiting outside. You'll change in it, and he'll drop you near Natalie's, and slip your case to you later. Ferdy says you wanted to see a plantation?'

I'd wanted to track down Roger van Diemen. I'd now seen Roger van Diemen, and much good it had done me. 'I don't mind,' I said, with my mouth full.

'Right. Because as a banana expert, Dr Thomassen is visiting one in the morning, and will take anyone who wants to go. Such as Maggie or Ferdy or Natalie plus or minus lawyer, plus or minus Fred Gluttenmacher Moneybags.'

'And Roger van Diemen?' I said. 'Without the monkey head? What did Raymond overhear in that chalet? Or doesn't it matter now?'

'It doesn't matter now,' Johnson said. 'But it was useful. Don't worry. Raymond picked up your watch, because it and you may be worthy of many pale blossoms yet. It told us what not to expect.'

'Such as?' I said. I had nearly finished the drink. It was great.

On the beach, the sea was still whispering in long ghostly rollers, and overhead the stars looked like large-grain sugar in a black bowl, and all round us in the shadows, big fancy flowers were puffing out different scents like the ground floor in Harrods.

Where Johnson and I were standing, you could just smell sweat and spirit gum and rum and barbecued chicken.

He put his empty glass down, and his plate, and straightened slowly.

'Well,' he said. 'Prediction. A general move out of Barbados. The *Paramount Princess* is going on to Miami anyway. Natalie's backer, accountant and lawyer all leave tomorrow afternoon, and Natalie will have fixed her Josephine details with Ferdy and be keen to get away, and let Roger stew in his own banana purée.

'Ferdy and Thomassen expect to finish by latish tomorrow, and are talking about taking their stuff back to London, via St Lucia. If they do, Maggie threatens to stay on with me.'

'And you? And *Dolly*?' I said.

Johnson took his dark glasses off and clenched one of their legs thoughtfully in his teeth.

'I rather felt,' he said, 'that *Dolly* ought to hang about, and go wherever Roger van Diemen was going.'

I said, 'I want to come with you. But what do I do if Natalie leaves?'

'Well,' Johnson said, 'that's the last item, as you might say, on the birthday chart. Would it ruin your life if Natalie were to sack you tomorrow?'

I gazed at him. 'Because I won't cut my hair?'

'Partly,' he said.

'Because she's converted Fred Moneybags to the idea of handing the film to the Curtises?'

'Partly,' he agreed. 'And maybe one or two other things you haven't heard about. All in a good cause. You don't need the money. And Natalie really occupies the only prime slot in Natalie's life. And that way, no questions asked, you can come on *Dolly* with Lenny and Raymond and me.'

'And Maggie,' I said. Absently. I was thinking of what he'd just been saying.

And maybe one or two things you haven't heard about.

He had put his glasses back on, but I had seen the gleam. I said, '*Wait a minute.*'

'You said I could,' Johnson said defensively. 'Borrow your orange wig. Divert attention from the target.'

I began to raise my voice, and dropped it again. 'I *was* the bloody target,' I hissed. 'In a bloody black Afro wig. Who was wearing mine and what was she doing?'

'He,' said Johnson. 'Lead trumpet-player with the Brixton West Indian Band. Four-feet-eleven, and smashing legs. We borrowed that feathered thing you've got, with the bloomers.'

It was new. I'd never even worn it yet. I was keeping it for a good thing. My feathers. My bloomers. My wig.

'And what did he *do*?' I said. In spite of myself, my voice went up at the end.

'Nothing much,' said Johnson soothingly. 'You were jet-skiing in some-body's swimming pool. No one got close enough to see anything but the hair.'

'And the clothes,' I said. 'That bloody outfit cost ...'

'Put it down to expenses,' said Johnson. 'You'll find the outfit and the wig in the car. If you're asked which swimming pool, say you don't remember. They'll assume you were sloshed.'

'Nobody wore *your* hair?' I said. 'Didn't you need an alibi? Nobody took your bifocals and your best cashmere jersey and painted the statue of Nelson? So you can come back to this bloody town and I can't?'

'Thought you didn't want to,' said Johnson. 'Curtis country.'

'Curtis country for *one film*,' I said. 'That's all. O.K. – she chucks me out of the Josephine film. There'll be others.'

'That's my girl,' said Johnson. 'And I promise you, you'll live your wig down. There's the car. Tell Ferdy what happens tomorrow. And I'd better warn you. Young Porter flew in.'

Porter. I wondered if they'd be pleased to see him on their floating old-fashioned gin palace or not. I wondered if I should be pleased to see him or not. It was hard to ignore him. For someone, he'd be a real capture.

Maggie, for instance. If Ferdy moved out, and Johnson wasn't moving in.

The car was waiting and Johnson, supporting the patio wall, looked like a Rasta running out of collapsos, or maybe even into them.

There was nothing I could do about that. I said good night, and got into the car, and changed, and went back to Natalie's.

My orange wig had a black hair in it, which might or might not have come from Brixton. My feathered outfit, when I dragged it on, was still soaking wet. I looked like Mother Goose.

Dodo, who was the only person in the house, gave me a long stare while the curtains slowly drew back over her choppers.

'My!' she said. 'You been raped, or laid an egg out there?' And watched, grinning like a frog, as I marched upstairs to bed.

I was sacked on the banana plantation, which is where Natalie came across me next day.

Ferdy and Carl Thomassen came for me in a taxi next morning before she was up, and there didn't seem much point in hanging about to ask her permission.

I told Dodo I'd be back before lunchtime, and nipped out to the taxi with a copy of the *Advocate-News* over my spikes, because it was raining, and my bowler would have got spoiled.

Johnson, unexpectedly, was inside the taxi as well, looking perfectly blank behind his bifocals, and I caught sight of Maggie sitting next to the driver.

Ferdy and Carl, who had been at the Governor-General's ball like everyone else except me, were still suffering from a surplus of chat, and contented themselves with reading the *Advocate-News* while it was still on top of my head.

Ferdy was interested in the case against Isaac Harbansingh, better known as John Bull, but Johnson had spotted this headline saying *Aussies Make Light Work of Worcestershire*, and that was it, the whole of Barbados being cricket-crazy including the taxi-driver.

After a serious exchange of views, the driver remembered that the Voice of Barbados was relaying the fourth day of the English-Australian Test, and turned on his radio for us.

His driving got so peculiar, in between Johnson trying to demonstrate spins and Ferdy shouting him down and the driver contradicting them both, that we had to draw in by a cane-field to hear it.

All the West Indies are mad about cricket of course. The English teams used to be brought out here for free. On banana boats.

The thought can't have reached Maggie, but she did turn round a hung-over face at that point and say, 'J.J.? Bananas?' And Dr Thomassen looked at his watch and jumped and said we'd better go, the manager would be worried.

It turned out that he was going to read a paper to the Windward Islands Banana Growers' Association on cheaper ways of keeping bananas from ripening before they get to the shops.

Unless it meant dipping them in cocaine, it didn't seem to have much bearing on what I was there for, and I stopped listening. Then we finally passed all the board houses on stilts, and the half-cut forests of cane with the rain drumming on it, and came to this neat double gate, with the bloody Coombe flag flying above it.

It was a model plantation newly started, which meant that the green-banana trial was in full swing, and hadn't been messed about by hurricanes, or eruptions, or Test Cricket, which was why Dr Thomassen was keen on it.

The rain stopped, and we got out and tramped through it.

Ask me about bananas.

Banana plants look like little palms, with shiny green leaves like paper, cut at the edges by the wind. Wee bananas grow pointing down, till they're made to curl up by the sun. Every plant has a single stem with a shower of up to a dozen banana hands on it, growing one on top of each other inside a blue plastic bag.

The bags keep insects off, and prevent the bananas from rubbing against one another.

When they're still green, but ready for harvesting, the stem is cut off every plant with a coyote, and the banana bags slung on a cable which takes them to the packing station for washing, cutting and packing in cartons and transferring by conveyor belt into the hold of, for example, the *Coombe Caroline.*

I supposed Johnson knew it all already, but he asked questions as though he didn't, and the manager, or Dr Thomassen, answered.

The manager said that it was a pity we'd just missed the firm's Financial Director, Mr van Diemen, but he'd had to fly off to St Lucia.

He showed us how the irrigation ditches were being trenched, and told us about pruning, fertilizing, soil pests and leaf blight, but I hardly heard.

As soon as I could, I said to Johnson, 'What happened about the Rotary Club of St Lucia?'

A woman went by with a single coyote on her turban, and another with a basket of washing. Ferdy and Maggie had found a railway line and were flagging down a little train carrying cartons.

Johnson said, 'There's one on Barbados was well. Meets at the Hilton on Thursdays. Also the Freemasons, the Foresters, the Mechanics, the Elks, the Gardeners, the Oddfellows and the Shepherds. Raymond and I thought of joining the Oddfellows. Let's go over to Ferdy.'

'But what about —' I said. He was already strolling away from me, his pipe in his mouth.

He turned and took it out. He said, 'I know what you mean, but the weather forecast for tomorrow is lousy. Look, isn't that Sharon's son, Porter?'

It was Porter, coming towards us in a yellow Italian blouson with white virile trousers, his watch-band flashing gold chain mail in the watery sun, and his hair red as a Flamboyant Tree.

He was looking mainly at Maggie's legs, swinging on to the carton truck, but wrenched his attention back to me as he got near. 'Hullo there, gorgeous!' he said. 'And Ferdy, and Mr Johnson, sir. I hear you two were the sensation of the Governor-General's ball, while Rita was off doing her water display.'

I thought he'd made a mistake. But Ferdy grinned and answered and I realized that Johnson *had* been at the ball: whether before or after the little adventure at the Brighton Beach wasn't clear.

I wondered how, under the circumstances, he'd got the energy, and supposed I should have been grateful that someone else had fixed my alibi for me.

On the other hand, here was Porter, sliding his hand from my neck to fold me in a comforting arm and saying, '... over there, the old cow. Darling, she really is furious, and we thought the best thing we could do is take her off your hands to Miami.'

'Who? What?' I said. You allow Porter's arm to do things, and his hand takes unfair advantage. Ferdy, who is in the same league, was watching with admiration.

'Natalie,' said Porter. 'I don't know who she had a row with last night, but she seems to have decided that Barbados is a waste of time, and now she's finished, she wants to get out of it. Gramps offered her a berth to Miami. And that Boy Scout with the hair-piece.'

'Fred Gluttenmacher,' said Ferdy. He jumped off the truck, frowning. 'Natalie's going back to the States? What about Rita?'

Before Porter could answer, someone called in the distance.

We all turned round, including Porter, who let his arm fall, a bit to my relief. In the distance, where the cable was trundling into the packing station, stood a tall, slender blonde in dark glasses and embroidered linen and pale hand-made pumps. She called again. It was Natalie.

Porter said, 'We'd better go over. That's why she's here. It's a god-dammed shame, the old cow; but that's show business.'

We had all started slowly to move, but at that, Ferdy stopped.

He said, 'Are you telling me that, after giving Rita Kim-Jim's job, and getting her to take on the Josephine film, Natalie is booting her out?'

Ferdy was and is a great name in photography. Patience wasn't much in Porter's line, but he made an effort. He said, 'I guess I shouldn't have jumped the gun. Maybe Natalie's cooled down at that. She just got all up-tight, and there was nothing any of us could do. She wanted Rita out, and Uncle Clive in.'

'She's offered Clive the film?' Ferdy said.

'I'm afraid she has, sir,' said Porter. 'But of course –'

'Never mind,' said King Ferdy, and pulling ahead of us, stalked through the banana groves and up to Natalie.

To do her justice, she tried not to have a scene on the spot.

The manager had gone, sent politely on his way by Johnson and Dr Thomassen, who were the only ones to have kept their heads, so far as I could see.

Maggie, eating a banana, was looking from Ferdy to Johnson and no doubt wondering where she was going to sleep if the Curtises withdrew their villa.

Natalie said, 'Certainly, I have something to say to Rita, but it will keep until we are in the car.'

'It won't,' said Ferdy. 'Are you sacking her?'

'Really, Ferdy,' said Natalie. She had done her own face that morning, but it looked very nice, with the lines under her eyes painted out. She said, 'I know you and Rita are friends, but this really isn't your business. Rita? I haven't much time.'

'Well, if you haven't much time, maybe you should tell me why?' Ferdy said. 'I thought we were doing a film together?'

'Are we?' said Natalie. 'I don't remember your joining me on St Lucia or Martinique. We have managed one meeting here, it is true. But now I find you with Dr Thomassen again. I think you, too, will really have to make up your mind whether your book or my film is the more important.

'Meanwhile, I have done all I want to do in the West Indies. I have other business awaiting me. If you are still at all interested in this film, I hope to be in London shortly.'

'But as of this moment, you're sailing away with the Curtises,' Ferdy snapped. 'What's wrong with Rita?'

I pulled myself together. It was great having Ferdy fight my battles for me, but enough was enough.

I said, 'Come on, Ferdy. It's up to Mrs Sheridan and me. No need to get your film involved. Tell you all about it later.'

I tried to get round him, but he stood in my way. He said, 'If she goes, I go.'

Johnson said, 'That's bloody silly.'

Ferdy's bald bit got very red, and all the skin you could see round his sideburns.

He said, 'I got Rita into this. I'm not having her thrown out by one ambitious patronizing bitch and doing nothing about it. Get a piccaninny off the banana farm to follow you, Natalie. Only thing he won't be able to do is fix your nose for you. Nor will Clive Curtis. I'm glad for Rita's sake, I can tell you. You don't deserve her.'

It was like the night of Kim-Jim's death. Natalie had gone perfectly white, so that all her make-up stood out like a diagram. She said, 'I had expected to deal with this in a normal, civilized way, but you make it ...

'... Oh, my God.'

It was funny that I should have thought of Kim-Jim.

Not that it was any one of us she was looking at, or someone she knew, or anything.

She was just looking over our shoulders, at the clear blue plastic bags, swaying and bulging, creaking their way to the packing shed.

Each bag full of up to two hundred bananas, weighing up to seventy pounds altogether. You could see them, hand upon hand, greenly clutching one another.

You could see them in all the bags swinging past us, except one.

I've seen first-rate severed heads made of wax. You can also make them of styrophor moulded with ceramic plaster, sealed with liquid plastic and coated with greasepaint. You paint veins on the eyes, and get the teeth from a dental mechanic. You can buy a greeny-grey base called 'Blithe Spirit'. It's meant for the comedy, but it does for dead heads just as well.

In the studio, it's really absorbing.

On a banana plantation it's not quite so good.

When the severed head in the blue bag is real. And when it belongs on the shoulders of a Brighton Beach Hotel security guard.

We all stared, but no one spoke but the Owner.

'Salami,' said Johnson.

I still got the sack, after that; but it was in a subdued sort of way, and by mutual consent.

The murder having nothing to do with us, we weren't held up while the manager was sent for, and the police.

It had happened before, someone said. A drunken brawl in a rum-house, or over a woman. It might not be anyone on the plantation at all.

From the constant view of the back of Johnson's head I was reminded that this was supposed to be a face I'd never seen before, and I knew nothing about it.

The act of parting from Natalie passed like a kind of dream, I had so much else to think about.

It actually was a parting, too. Dodo had already packed and taken her things on board the *Paramount Princess*. Natalie had merely dropped in to tell me I was dismissed, and should remove myself from Ferdy's house as soon as convenient to Ferdy.

I said I was sorry it was ending like this, and she said the same, and she'd left a cheque in the sitting-room. She wished me well for the future.

Behind her back, Porter pulled a face and blew me a kiss and mouthed some sort of promise. I nodded and grinned. I could still feel his fingermarks.

Johnson had got the cricket-mad taxi to wait for us, and we dragged Maggie from the crowd round the severed head and got into it.

I hadn't looked at it again. I said, 'It probably was someone on the plantation. You could cut a head off with a coyote.'

It was a squeeze in the back, and Johnson's arm had to go round my shoulders.

He said, 'It's either cutlass or machete. But on the whole, I rather go for coyote.'

His fingers played on my far shoulder. 'Rita, you're free. Maggie, you're going to be sick. Ferdy, I've got an empty boat, and you've got an empty house somewhere. Let's go to one of them, and get drunk.'

Considering everything, he did have good ideas.

At Ferdy's suggestion, we went to Ferdy's house, which smelt of Natalie's personalized scent, and quite a bit of my scent from *Dolly*.

The help had gone, which was just as well. Using Ferdy's recipe books, we worked our way down four more items in his daiquiri list. After that, instead of having lunch, we all went to bed. I went to my own room, and Ferdy and Maggie, I suspect, to Natalie's.

Wherever Johnson went, he was up first. I was second, and wandering into the kitchen in my bare feet and shirt tails, found Johnson cooking himself scrambled eggs with his bifocals looking solemn under his hair. He was wearing a kimono I recognized as belonging to Ferdy in his John Weitz Japanese mood, and his feet were bare, too.

It was a bit like 17B all over again.

He must have thought so as well, for he said, 'I've saved you the whites. Shut the door while I award you a prize for not having a fit of the vapours. You weren't to blame for that killing.'

An open book. I said, 'They must have thought I was his girlfriend. They must have thought he let me in close to the building.'

The eggs curdled. Johnson spooned them on two bits of buttered toast, put a plate under each, and shoved one along the breakfast bar to me.

'Cap the seeps from the daiquiris. Knives and forks beside you. He wasn't a hotel security man, he was one of theirs, anyway. My guess is that they planned to get rid of him in any case after the meeting. Making a hand of his head was just a warning and a deterrent to others. Nasty people.'

He had got himself a glass of milk, and he looked at me over it.

'I asked you if you'd mind getting the push from Natalie. How would you feel about getting it from me?'

I went to the fridge and got myself milk as well. There was silence from the rest of the house. If he thought it was safe to discuss this with Ferdy and Maggie around, then I supposed it was safe.

I said, 'You mean, now we're coming to the dangerous bit?'

'Never crossed my mind,' Johnson said. 'Thought you might trust me to go in for the kill without you, though. I'm taking *Dolly* to St Lucia, and Roger van Diemen was flying there this morning. Also, incidentally, Carl Thomassen, I am told.'

'I haven't retired yet,' I said. 'Who else is sailing with you?'

He had got his pipe out, and was hunting for matches. 'Raymond and Lenny, of course,' he said. 'Ferdy wants to take some photographs, and I don't mind taking him. Which probably means Maggie as well.'

I sat looking at him, and he set the flame to the stuff in his pipe. I said, 'And if it's dangerous, why is it all right for them to go?'

Johnson flicked the burnt match into the sink, and leaning both elbows on the table, looked at me with the pipe in his mouth. Then he took it out.

'Because they're not dangerous to me, and you are. Trapping a faceless gang of drug merchants is one thing. It's quite another not to give the game away when they turn out to be people you know. As now seems very likely.'

'Who?' I said. I didn't want any more scrambled eggs.

'You saw as much as we did. Three men and a woman,' said Johnson. 'You didn't hear, as we did, what they talked about. The Coombe plan, of course. But their immediate worry is that they've got a load of cocaine to get rid of. And van Diemen's network isn't ready.'

'So?' I said.

He puffed gently and removed the pipe again. 'So they decided to make their own arrangements, and send the cocaine on to Florida.'

I played with my fork, and there was a short silence. He didn't break it.

I said, 'The *Paramount Princess* is going to Miami. You think I'll give you away, if those people in masks were the Curtises?'

'I shouldn't think so. I expect she's sailed by now, anyway,' Johnson said. 'But I thought you should realize that van Diemen's partners may very well be people you think of as friends. People whom van Diemen knows too, or they wouldn't have troubled to keep their masks on in front of him.'

'Unless they don't know each other either,' I said.

'It's possible. But at least one of them must have been on Madeira. At least one of them must be on his or her way now to Florida. Someone may possibly land in St Lucia, to keep an eye on what van Diemen is doing.

'We know who's on the *Princess*, and where she's going. She'll get quite a reception at Miami. If she's full of cocaine, there will be a full-scale inquiry, and the link with van Diemen and Coombe's will probably come out without too much trouble.

'My part of the job is watching Roger van Diemen, and anyone else who has decided, for various powerful reasons, to move from Barbados to St Lucia.'

I said, 'Last night at the chalet, I said they might switch their plans. And you agreed.'

'Yes,' said Johnson. He continued to smoke, quite calmly. 'They've a lot of cocaine. They have to put it somewhere.'

There was another silence. I said, 'And you're afraid, if I come on *Dolly*, that I can't keep quiet about all this?'

'I'm not sure,' Johnson said. 'You couldn't trust anybody.'

'Except you,' I said.

'Um,' he said. 'I'm afraid you'd have to trust me. Actually, I know you

216

don't much like Lenny or Raymond, but they wouldn't see you stuck either.'

He paused, and said, 'And on top of that, I must tell you that it would be dangerous. People who cut people's heads off are usually not short of weapons, and the will to use them. Also St Lucia is a hundred miles to the north-west, and there's a bloody storm coming up.'

He sounded cross, and I suddenly knew why, but I didn't say so. I said, 'I think you are saying that I can come if I want to. I want to.'

'Want to what?' said the Hon. Maggie, peering round the kitchen door. 'J.J., Ferdy is having what he calls a little *crise* of the *foie*. Any suggestions?'

Johnson tapped out his pipe, and picking up his empty plate, carried it to the sink. 'Third of rum, third of whisky, third of absinthe,' he said. 'It'll blow him into the middle of next week. Then we carry him down to the *Dolly*. If you've both decided you're coming, that is. I want to sail in two hours.'

Maggie laughed. 'It's a pipe-dream,' she said. 'D'you know how long it took the three of us to do all the paperwork last time?'

Johnson smoothed the folds of his kimono and walked primly towards the door.

'Supplies and paperwork long since set up by Raymond and Lenny. Do you imagine,' said Johnson, 'that this is a sudden decision? With the Rotary Club of St Lucia stamping their feet there in the Green Parrot?'

We sailed out of Carlisle Bay at half past six, just before sunset, waved off
by a number of tiddly holiday-makers from the Holiday Inn, and by a select
number of properly dressed parties from the Royal Barbados Yacht Club
who used (said Johnson) to play bridge with him, but could still apparently
afford the fare to Barbados.

To the people who stood stirring their planter's punch and asking why
the hell he was leaving at night, Johnson replied, waiting for the rope that
Raymond was throwing him, that he had a date in St Lucia, and *Dolly* would
be a damned sight safer in Rodney or Castries than here.

Which was apparently true. I asked Raymond, as I was helping him to
stow the dinghy on the saloon roof.

After the digital watch, I didn't expect to be Raymond's favourite
passenger, but he was less rude than I'd expected, maybe because there
seemed to be so much to do. Also, remembering the handstands in the
Mandarin cap and the tassels, I realized that even Raymond had his
moments.

You couldn't actually say the same for Lenny, who hardly said a word
as he showed me where to stow the satchel of clothes and my make-up kit,
which was all that I'd been allowed to bring with me.

All the rest of my gear, and my fifty quids' worth of scent, were back in
Ferdy's house, by kind permission of Ferdy.

And that was another thing. Ferdy was to share the master stateroom,
it turned out, with Johnson.

I had a bunk in the double cabin in the front of the boat. Sharing with
Maggie.

With Raymond brutally outcast to the single cabin, and Lenny aggres-
sive, and Maggie after both Ferdy and Johnson, it looked like being a great
voyage. With a storm blowing up.

No one bothered to tell me what that meant. 'Take a pill,' said Johnson
abstractedly, when I asked him. 'We'll be in St Lucia by teatime.'

He was lying, and he knew he was lying. But I didn't find that out till
later.

Ask me about tropical storms.

The last one to hit the West Indies came from well down the African coast. This one had to be corny. It started where we had all started. From a little disturbance somewhere just south of Madeira.

By the time Johnson and I were playing in the steel band, it had become a tropical depression, moving westerly.

He knew that too, because Raymond heard all the broadcasts and told him.

By the time we were at the banana plantation, it had become a tropical storm, moving slowly west at the rate of fifteen miles an hour. In thirty-six to forty-eight hours, it should reach the Windward and southern Leeward Islands on its way to Central America. Giving *Dolly* an easy sail of a night and a day to get into St Lucia before it hit us.

Unless, of course, it weakened first.

Unless, of course, it strengthened, from a tropical storm to a hurricane.

Hurricanes can travel across an area 400 miles wide, and produce wind gusts of over 125 miles an hour. Hurricanes in one day release the same energy as a 420 megaton hydrogen bomb.

Don't ask me about hurricanes.

All I knew that evening was that there was a lot of movement in the sea, and that nobody lay around the cockpit cushions drinking, or admiring *Dolly*'s lights on the water, or the glow of Barbados disappearing behind us.

Instead, Johnson stayed almost all the time at the helm, his glasses flashing green in the binnacle light and saying things periodically to Lenny or Raymond or Maggie which caused little bursts of action, with rubber soles thudding on deck, or the buzz of a winch, and a bit of puffing and swearing.

Ferdy had been given the charts, and would occasionally come up from the saloon with his glasses on, which I had never seen before, frowning over a folded bit of paper, which he and Johnson would peer at.

Supper came early and was taken in relays down below, except by Johnson, who ate at the wheel and drank what looked like Perrier water. Nobody heroically took his place, so I assumed he was taking first shift, and would go to bed later.

It wasn't like the sail from Martinique to St Lucia at all, being at night, and busy, and four times the length, and having Ferdy with us instead of Natalie, which was a definite improvement.

The change to Owner was something I found I could put up with, as well. Nobody called him Johnson any more; just skipper. Someone had to be the boss, and he was it.

I tried once or twice to help with what was going on up on deck, and just got in the way, so I went and got hold of Lenny and said if he didn't mind my breaking all his bloody dishes, I'd clear the table after the last relay and wash up.

I heard him go and ask Johnson, but the helm must have approved, because Lenny came back and showed me where to put everything, and thanked me.

Quite soon after that, he disappeared to his cot in the prow and after a bit Maggie, too, looked in to say she had been told off to sleep for a spell, and would I kindly keep out of the cabin.

She sounded as if she'd rather like to have told me to shut up the clash in the galley as well, but no doubt decided that clean pans were worth suffering for.

I finished with some trouble, because every now and then the ship would shudder, and everything that could jump, jumped. I already knew the signal for going about, when the ship suddenly leaned the other way, and everything that could fall, fell.

The radio was on, and through the noise of the wind, and the ship heeling her way through the sea, I could hear announcements, in level, distinct voices. Twice I heard Johnson's voice, pitched differently, apparently speaking on the radio-telephone.

I was glad we had a radio-telephone. I was glad we had radar, and a direction-finder, and an echo-sounder and even an automatic pilot.

Lenny and Raymond and Maggie had sailed *Dolly* across the Atlantic, not Johnson.

Maggie might know about boats, but I didn't know her track record for stamina. Ferdy might be light enough on his feet, but I doubted if he really knew much about boats.

And Johnson might be skipper; might have raced his bleeding boat or other people's all over the world, but all he had actually sailed since his gruesome smash-up was a calm twenty-five miles out of Martinique.

I hung up the drying cloths and went up into the cockpit and said to Johnson, 'I reckon you're going to need a cook.'

He looked down from the sails, his glasses glittering green like a comic strip. Which was another thing, with all these ropes and draughts and elbows about.

He said, 'I keep a spare pair with my socks,' and smiled like a kosher cat at Raymond, who was sitting beside him, not understanding, and looking peevish.

Johnson added to me, 'All right; you're it. Flasks and sandwiches. Raymond will show you where to put them. And breakfast from daybreak on demand. If it gets rough, we rig lines on deck. You don't come up without clipping your harness to it. You obey me, or Lenny or Raymond.'

'Hey,' said Ferdy. For sailing, he had put on a gung-ho navy hugger and jeans, and natty gold pirate hoops in his ears, matching his two rings and his necklace. 'Hey, you give orders to Lenny or Raymond. I bags Rita.'

'You don't know the ship,' said Johnson calmly. 'You're just the photographer. We'll let you know when we're on a good tack for the *Yachting Monthly*.'

I said, 'What's the forecast?' and Johnson said, 'Weather.'

They were busier than they seemed. I went below, and raided Lenny's stores in the galley, and struggled with my catsuit in the head, and sneaked into my cabin to change into a cotton-knit shirt and pants, and a sweatband to keep my hair on.

Maggie was sleeping with her mouth open and gunpowder-green circles under her eyes. You couldn't tell if it was Ferdy or Valium.

I nearly got into my bunk, but on second thoughts set my rescued digital alarm, and curled up instead on the saloon seat.

I slept, too, and missed the changeover, when Johnson went below and Lenny came up to take the helm. Raymond came down, and woke Maggie, and stayed to eat three of my club sandwiches and down some coffee before he went up and took Lenny's seat.

The wind was a lot stronger, and so was the bouncing on *Dolly*, which made the sails jar and jiggle. Raymond's voice yelling orders was drowned out by the noise down below. The radio crackled and spat. At one point, Maggie came down, her hair soaking, and tuned in to Radio St Lucia, which was just signing off at 11.15.

The Meteorological Office at Hewanorra, it announced, had just made it known that Tropical Storm Chloe was now moving west at wind speeds of up to 70 m.p.h. Residents of St Lucia should tune in for further news at six a.m. tomorrow.

She didn't say anything: just stood pulling at the dripping point of her hair. I said, 'There's some fish paella in the dinner-pail thermos. And coffee or punch.'

Her mascara had all streaked in the spray, so that she looked surprised, like a doll. 'You cooked it? That's good.'

I didn't need the pat on the head, but it was no time to be fussy. I gave her a spoon and a plateful and said, 'How far away is the storm?'

'About six hundred miles. We should be O.K.,' she said. 'Look, Ferdy ought to come down. Tell him you're serving food.'

I was halfway to the steps when she added, 'Don't you think?'

Tropical Storm Chloe, the great equalizer.

It turned out that Ferdy's mind was running more on rum punch than on food, but I'd plenty of that as well, and he duly came down. He then came into the galley to inspect the paella, and we were comparing notes about squid when someone rapped on the doorpost and said, 'Be quiet a minute, will you?'

You do what you're told, when you're in the path of a tropical storm. I felt my heart thud. Ferdy stepped quietly outside, and I followed him.

Johnson was up, and bent over the radio-telephone, with Raymond and Maggie beside him. It wasn't producing storm warnings: just a great roar of quacking static. Every now and then, Johnson would move a switch and speak into it himself, but if he'd got any response once, he'd lost it.

He straightened after a bit. 'No good. Where's the chart?'

'What?' said Ferdy.

Maggie answered. 'Boat in trouble. Holiday cruiser. We can't get proper details.'

'Where?' said Ferdy.

Johnson looked up. 'Between us and Chloe.'

'Anyone else around?' said Ferdy.

Johnson said, 'Look for yourself. There's the radar.'

There was no one else around. Not with Chloe approaching, there wouldn't be. The arm swivelled round, bleeping every time it passed this speck to the east.

Ferdy said, 'How long will it take us to reach her?'

'Into the wind? We'd have to motor. Drinking fuel, of course. But I think we could pick her up and still make it. Anyway, we can't leave her,' said Johnson, with finality.

Which of course we couldn't. Not a powerless boat, with those winds approaching.

On engine, in rising seas, *Dolly* stopped being a lady. She stopped doing her best to skim along on one glossy ear, and rolled and pitched and wallowed, with her propeller fizzing out of the water, and her bottom coming down on every fourth or fifth wave with a thud.

Johnson steered, his shirt stuck to the nylon of his oilskins, tipping her up and round and over the waves like a sculptor.

After a while, my back ached with the jarring, and I saw Raymond watching Johnson uneasily.

I remembered Maggie's method and, handing myself off the woodwork, struggled down below and came up with the rest of the sandwiches in a bag, and something to cut them with, and some mugs and a quart flask of coffee.

Lenny said, 'Here. Let me, Miss,' and handed them round, while Raymond put his hand casually on the wheel and said, 'Rita's specials. Take one while you've got the chance.'

Johnson gave up the wheel without comment, and slithered over to where he could brace himself better against the ship's bucketing. I admired him, rather, for admitting defeat, although Raymond wasn't nearly as good at the helm as he was.

Ferdy ate half the sandwiches, and then hopped down and fetched us some punch, which was a help too. Then Johnson leaned forward and called, 'I think we have her in view. Let's have some light.'

The rain had stopped. In the dimness of the cockpit, Raymond had his binoculars up as well. His wet yellow hair had gone like brown varnish.

Then we all saw it: a collection of lights tossing up and down like dropped stars beyond us. Raymond flicked on a switch.

A brilliant searchlight sprang from *Dolly*'s prow. And there, heaving and wallowing in the distance, was the disabled ship, a motor cruiser with no engine power.

Not a boat you'd see in Monte Carlo, or visiting with the Royal Barbados Yacht Club. A biggish, shabby boat, probably under charter, with rust on her sides, and a good deal of chipped paint, and some people in oilskins and some in soaked cottons waving to us. I counted five or six, and other faces at the portholes below.

They were flinging their arms about and yelling in a foreign language. They looked pretty happy to see us. I hoped they also realized what Johnson had done for them. And right away began to wonder how much it would slow us down, towing this thing behind us to harbour.

Johnson said, 'We'll send Lenny over. He may be able to fix their engine.'

Mind-reader. He took a loud-hailer from Lenny, and began addressing the other boat in what seemed to be its own language. Spanish, perhaps.

The other boat answered, and as the two ships bounced towards each other, fenders began to appear, and a rope spun through the air, to be caught and made fast for winching. Warped together, the cruiser and *Dolly* got closer.

On the other ship, they'd found a loud-hailer as well, and the captain, young and tanned and bare-headed, came to the rail of his own ship and used it.

He spoke English too.

He said, *'We board on your ship. You try to stop us, we kill you.'*

People say that kind of thing in films. It doesn't happen for real. We were all standing or kneeling on *Dolly*, in the cockpit or on the side decks. We just all went on standing or kneeling, and looking at this guy making threats at us.

Except Raymond. He believed it. He moved.

There was a crack; a whine; and a shower of splinters jumped into the darkness from the mast at Raymond's side.

We all saw the red flame come and go on the opposite deck. There were a lot of men standing there now. Twelve, perhaps. And most of them held, pointing at us, these long shiny rifles that give producers such headaches.

Like the severed head, it was quite different when it was real.

'The next time,' said the captain, 'you be killed. No person move.'

We were so close now, we could hear him without the loud-hailer. Without moving, Johnson spoke.

No drama. He just said, 'There's a hurricane coming.'

We were near enough now to see the captain's white smile. 'One tropical storm. Is nothing. We have one good engine.'

Their ship had never been in trouble. Their distress call had been a hoax.

I looked at Raymond, at Lenny, at Maggie. None of them looked at me. They all stared, as if silly, at the rifles.

Johnson said, 'Rita, keep still. You, sir. What do you want?'

The captain was smiling again.

'I think,' said the captain, 'we have no rum. You have rum a bordo? We come a bordo and you give to us your rum. You move, we shoot.'

Ferdy said, 'To hell with that.'

He was a big man, with the feet of a footballer. He knew we were six against twelve. Being the sort of man he was, sheer blind fury at being assaulted by wogs was more then enough to make him forget it.

He was also, of all of us, the one nearest the controls for the idling engine.

As he spoke, he plunged forward. He kicked the big Mercedes-Benz into gear. He scooped up the sandwich-knife and, rising, hurled himself at the poop warp.

It was one of two, and even if the knife had sawn through, *Dolly* would still have been held by the other, or for as long as it took to aim rifles.

As it was, he didn't even get the rope frayed. Somewhere in all the noise, a rifle popped. A lot of extra wet suddenly appeared on Ferdy's smart hugger. He let go the knife and lost balance backwards, down the shallow steps into the saloon.

I saw the honeycomb soles of his shoes, and his eyes, looking scared as he fell. I saw Maggie move to help him and stop, and so did I. The voice from the other ship said briefly, 'Engine off. Or else.'

Johnson put it off quietly and stood by the wheel, half blocking my view of the gunmen. The sea slapped and jumped between the two ships. They touched fenders, and shuddered, and heaved up and down.

'We board on you,' said the other captain.

Since they didn't mind how much the two ships battered together, they jumped from their rail to *Dolly*'s with no special trouble.

Eight of them came aboard. They hadn't come up against soap and water for a long time, and they were pretty funnily dressed, some of them, but they weren't in want, to look at their rings and their watches.

I had heard, right enough, of freelance enterprise in the Caribbean. Present-day pirates, high on hash, who cruised about the rich playgrounds, robbing the fancy yachts.

I wondered what on earth a bunch of Spaniards could be hoping for, from a yacht like the *Dolly*.

I supposed, with their distress signal as bait, they were out for anything they could grab. And there was plenty of gear on the *Dolly*, if they knew how to dismantle it.

I thought it was a pity that they had shown us their faces, although, on the other hand, killing the six of us would be quite a risk.

I realized, as the boats lurched and banged, that they didn't even have to kill us, as Tropical Storm Chloe was approaching at fifteen m.p.h. to solve their problem for them. I am never sick at sea. I began to feel sick at sea.

I had forgotten to think of rape, until the first two or three jumped on the side deck, and one of them took hold of Maggie, and ripped all her buttons off, down to her all-over tan.

It was the worst thing that could have happened, because it made our men flip. Lenny forgot everything and went for Maggie's attackers as if she had been a bloody virgin, and so did Raymond.

The pirates didn't shoot Lenny or Raymond. They just clubbed them with the end of their guns and left them, half in, half out of the cockpit. Then they lifted up Maggie and threw her on to the cockpit cushions while

225

the captain jumped in and sat down beside her, with his rifle pointed at Johnson's oilskin.

The man who had spoken on the loud-hailer was quite young: not more than twenty-five, and his face was wide across the cheekbones and looked more Indian than Spanish. I put its colour at Max Factor Bronze Tone Latin Men. He had on frayed denim shorts and an expensive sweater shirt, with a necklet and a couple of rings that didn't come out of Woolie's.

He looked at me, grinned, and looked back at Johnson. Behind him, Maggie was silently fighting off one of the explorers, who was interested in getting the rest of her clothes off. A number of men shoved past us all and down into the saloon where, finding Ferdy in the way, they slung him where I couldn't see him, somewhere off the passage.

I heard him grunt as they did it, and saw Johnson's head turn as well.

Ferdy was alive, then, but how badly hurt, you couldn't tell. You couldn't imagine the planter's punch and the sandwiches all lying there, doing him no good. And the tongue staying inside his own mouth, that used to have such fun at the end of its leash.

But you couldn't have imagined Kim-Jim lying shot, either. You looked at people in mortuaries, but they didn't belong to you.

The captain was getting bumped by the struggle behind him with Maggie. He snapped something in Spanish, and then something else, and the guy she was fending off got up and then staggered back as she kicked him.

The boat was rocking so much that if you didn't hang on, you would spend your time rolling about the floor. The captain freed one hand from his gun and, turning round, slapped Maggie's head hard.

I heard her teeth jar, and saw her eyes roll up. She wasn't quite out, but as near it as made no difference. The captain shouted in Spanish, raising his voice more this time, and a man appeared on the rail of his own ship, stuffing something into his pocket, and vaulted over, shouting something in reply.

He came down into the cockpit, still talking, and I saw Johnson's eyes hadn't moved from him.

I don't understand Spanish. I hardly understand English. But I understood the word 'Chloe'.

Whatever else was said, it made the captain stop and think. Then he rapped out an order, and the guy who'd just come hauled some twine out of his pocket, and a knife, and tied Maggie's hands and ankles together.

Then he lurched over to the side deck, pulled down Lenny and Raymond, and did the same to them, leaving them on top of one another on the cockpit floor. After that, he went down below.

I could hear his voice, talking to the others. I could hear the ship being searched: cupboards being wrenched open, dishes and glassware jolting out and breaking.

Raymond was going to have a bruise on his face. I knew exactly how long it would take to develop, and all the colours it would go. I wondered what colour my face was. Johnson and I were the only two who hadn't been touched.

The captain looked at us both and said to Johnson, 'Orange hair. This your piece?'

'Yes,' said Johnson. 'What do you want? Money? There is a safe in the wall of the stateroom. Through there.'

I had seen two men go through that door already, and heard the sound of breaking wood through all the other noise. We pitched and pitched. The captain had a grip of the edge of the cockpit with one hand, while the other held the gun trained on Johnson.

Johnson said, 'The key's in my pocket, if you'll let me get it. There's nothing else on board. The ladies don't carry jewellery.'

I could see what colour Johnson was. He had looked fairly bleached when Raymond took the wheel from him, and he'd been thrown about like the rest of us ever since.

I hoped he hadn't seen the same films that I had. I hoped he wasn't going to produce a gun from his pocket, because the captain would so enjoy shooting first.

I hoped he wasn't going to lure the captain into coming forward, and then try and grab him as hostage, because that needed the guy who used to go skiing, not the guy who had just left his wheelchair.

On the other hand ...

The bulkhead was batting me backwards and forwards, and my teeth were jarring, like Maggie's had. I said to the captain, 'Don't shoot. He's kidding you. He gave the key to me.'

I moved away from Johnson and gave a nervous smile. It was no trouble. I said, 'Don't shoot. It's not my fault. I didn't want to come anyway. I'll give you the key.'

The captain smiled. He had rotten teeth. He would need wallies before he was thirty. He would need wallies, but he would be alive, and maybe I wouldn't.

Johnson said, 'You silly bitch: you'll get us all shot.' He was shouting above the wind, and it sounded nearly natural. He was bloody quick. He said to the captain, 'The key's here. Tell one of your men to come and . . .'

I didn't have a key, but I had a nice silvery coin with a bird on it, in a little pocket too small for a gun.

I said, 'Catch!' and tossed it to the captain, and dived, as his eyes flicked, for the gun.

I didn't get it.

The gun fired itself into the deck. Behind me, Maggie yelled something to Johnson.

Without his glasses, Johnson's face could be seen sometimes to wear an expression.

I saw it. It looked resigned.

Then he flung himself on to the captain, and the three men who had been watching with interest from the side deck jumped down on to him. The captain laid down his rifle and said, 'Hold him.'

They held him against the edge of the cockpit seat, and the captain did the kicking.

I saw the first blow sink into the odd, sunken places in Johnson's side, and the second into his stomach, and the third into his ribs. Heavy sneakers aren't the same as bovver boots; more like a rubber truncheon, slamming over and over in the same places.

A baby's bootees would have felt like bovver boots to someone as badly damaged already as Johnson. And they didn't stop when he flaked out, either.

It was my fault. The only weapon I had to hand was the thermos of coffee, but it was scalding. I got the captain straight in his Bronze Tone Latin face. I was trying to take the cap off the paella when the rest of them turned on me.

It wasn't like the Mercedes on Madeira. It was pretty rotten. It ended with a rabbit punch on the back of my neck. I joined the other three on the floorboards, and blacked out.

19

I woke with a screaming headache, a stiff neck, and the impression that someone was tossing me in a wet blanket in the middle of a pipe band parade.

Opening my eyes did nothing to correct it.

The deafening wailing and rattling and thudding continued. It was pitch black, and I was rolling backwards and forwards among something that could have been heaps of soggy cushions. I felt dead sick. I felt dead.

It was the problem of finding somewhere to be sick that made me keep my eyes open, and work out where I was.

There wasn't much trouble, once I put my mind to it. In the cockpit well of *Dolly*, sliding about with several unconscious people in total darkness, with no engine on, and no sail, and a storm going on around me.

The thugs who had left us that way, and their ship, had all vanished.

It didn't accordingly seem to matter very much where I was sick, but I did stagger as considerately as I could to the side, and got there in time.

I was aware, as the sandwiches and the paella and everything else disappeared into either the Atlantic or the Caribbean, that I was walking without twinges, which I was vaguely glad about, until I remembered how pleased my aunt would be as well.

I remembered Maggie and, with equal vagueness, hoped she'd got off with it too.

Then I remembered Ferdy. And Johnson.

A voice at my feet said, 'Rita?' and gagged, and added, 'Are they gone?'

Raymond. I wondered why I couldn't see him, and realized I really could see nothing. There were no lights on *Dolly* anywhere. None on her busy dials. None even on the binnacle.

I said, 'They've gone. And their boat.'

I suppose people used to the sea always think of their yacht first.

Raymond didn't ask about people. He must have been lying, working out the way *Dolly* was rocking. He said, with a sort of bleary surprise, 'They've left her hove-to.'

It was Greek to me. But I understood him when he added, 'There's a knife in my pocket.'

Of course. He'd been tied up. I knew how he felt.

I groped my way to him, and found the pocket he directed me to, and sawed his feet free first, to let him get to the side. Then I undid his hands.

I said, 'Raymond. Chloe. What time do you think it is?'

'There isn't any bloody light,' Raymond said. I could hear him clicking on switches in the bulkhead. He kept forgetting to hold on, and staggering. He wasn't really awake yet.

I said, 'The storm. Is there a torch somewhere?'

He was so slow, he must have been half-concussed. But he climbed down off the cockpit seat and tried to kneel and undo the locker underneath it. Then he realized what he was kneeling on and said, 'Christ . . . ?' as he felt the humped cloth lying about him.

We couldn't do anything without the torch. Help Lenny, or Maggie, or Ferdy, or Johnson. Get the radio going. And the engine. I wondered, if the engine ran out of juice and everyone else was overboard or dead, if Raymond and I could sail *Dolly* into St Lucia.

And find the bastards who'd done this to us.

And kick them bloody to death.

I shoved Raymond out of the way, and hauled open the locker he'd been fiddling at, and threw out everything in it until I found the torch. A big box torch with a battery in it that lit *Dolly*'s cockpit like daylight.

Lit up the back of Lenny's head, with blood drying brown among the scanty hair, and his wrists lashed behind him against the neat blue jersey.

Lit up the long cushionless bench with Maggie lying on it, in the shreds of her shirt, with the brown of her leg showing through her pants. She was bound exactly as she had been when I last saw her, but not awake any more.

I kept the light on her until I saw her chest rise and fall, and then turned it to the man on the floorboards behind Raymond.

Raymond hadn't seen him yet. Awake at last, he knelt in the light and taking my knife, cut Lenny's bonds and turned him gently over.

Lenny snored. The crusty, salt-bitten face was unmarked, and as we watched, his mouth moved about, though his eyes were tight shut.

Raymond's own mouth slackened. He let Lenny's head down, and got up and bent over Maggie. He said, 'Chloroform, I think. Otherwise, we'd not be waking up together. And Maggie has hardly a mark on her.'

'Ferdy was shot,' I said. 'They dragged him down below. I don't know if he's all right.'

'*Shot!*' exclaimed Raymond. He grabbed a rail, swung, and took a lurching step to the saloon stairs.

I think he stopped because I didn't move. And then he turned and looked where I was looking.

He didn't yell out again. He just said, 'Jay,' in the middle of an incoming breath, and went down on all fours beside Johnson.

Jay. By itself, it was a nice name.

I went a little nearer. My light lit up everything. Raymond, and the wheel, all tied up with rope, and the owner of *Dolly* lying pitched on his back underneath it.

Because his yellow reefer was waterproof, the blood hadn't been able to get through it, and just shone underneath in big lakes and smudges. Where the nylon ended it had streamed out, and then followed the roll of the boat like a weather chart.

His face, carried up and down and from side to side by the bottom boards, was unmarked. He had a five o'clock shadow. It grows on dead men as well.

Our boarders hadn't touched his hands, or his limbs. Just his body.

Raymond said, 'Rita. Can you sling a hammock, really fast? And get sheets and the first-aid box. The one in his own room has morphine. And call me.'

Not another Kim-Jim. Or not yet. Raymond looked up at the noise my throat made, and said, 'We'll do it, soul. Don't worry. Be quick though.'

I had to come back for the torch, because I couldn't get into the saloon. Raymond was cutting off the streaming reefer, but he gave me the light. When I called him a moment later, he came without protesting. I suppose the sound of my voice had something to do with it.

I couldn't get into the saloon because there wasn't a saloon.

It is something burglars do, when disappointed. They wreck, tear up and befoul.

These particular burglars had done all of that. They had loaded everything that was moveable into the middle of the room: curtains, cushions and bedding, books and maps, cloths and napkins, every plate, every glass, every cup, even the table itself, and had methodically torn it all up and smashed it.

They had also made very sure that it would never be used again. The smell was awful, even with the wind scouring round from the broken door.

The silver had gone, and the liquor store, the T.V., the radio, the record player. So had the navigational equipment that I had been so pleased to notice: *Dolly's* £70,000 worth of electronic aids, from echo-sounder to radar to radio-telephone. What could be pinched had been pinched. What couldn't, had been smashed.

We would never get that six a.m. storm bulletin from St Lucia Radio now. Or any other.

The chart drawer had been emptied as well. The charts were confetti, and the drawers themselves smashed, every one. There was nothing left of the elegant saloon of the Martinique dinner-party, with its orchids and crystal and candlelight.

The galley was the same, and the bathrooms, and each of the cabins. We climbed through them, concerned now only with looking for Ferdy, and found him on the floor in the room Maggie and I had been meant to share.

There was a bullet-hole right through Ferdy's shoulder, and he showed no sign of waking. In the smaller space, the smell of chloroform was quite distinct. The raiders had decided to enjoy themselves without any interruptions from us.

There were no useable sheets, just as there was no morphine. The first-aid box had been given special attention. I gave Raymond the light to go back to Johnson with, and before he went, stripped off my cotton-knit shirt and slung it to him.

It was better than nothing. He neither looked at me or away from me while I did it. It simply didn't matter.

I used my own handkerchiefs to stuff into Ferdy's shoulder, by the dim light from the cockpit, and his own bigger one to bind it round with.

There was no way of making him comfortable. I jammed him into the wreckage of the bed so that he didn't roll with the movement, and shifted anything I could see that could hurt him. I didn't even have brandy. The longer he was unconscious, the better.

Before I scrambled and slithered my way back to the cockpit, I took off my cotton trousers as well, which left me in briefs and nothing else but an oilskin jacket and an orange wig with a sweatband.

Striptease time. In the cockpit, the light glimmered on Raymond's bare back and shorts. Everything else he had worn, added to my cotton knit, had been wrapped firmly round Johnson's messed-up body. And Raymond's own oilskin, I saw, was going on top for good measure.

I dropped my bundle of cotton beside him. There was no way of telling if it would be any use. Our boarders had made just about as good a job of stripping Dolly's owner of what supported life as they had of his lovely ship.

Dolly shuddered, and the light was suddenly full of glittering water, striking Raymond on the back and shoulder and splashing Johnson's black hair. The cockpit cushions had gone. And there was no hammock to put him in, even if we could have risked carrying him over the smashed glass and china in the demolition area below.

Raymond said, 'Now. You'll have to be his mattress, love; just for a minute. Put your back to the weather and support him. Interior springing, it's called.'

What he was organizing, very quickly, was a rough sling, made out of my pants and his skipper's cut reefer, and jammed from locker to locker across the cockpit corner.

It would support Johnson's back. It would free me. It was, I should have thought, a job that could have waited until Raymond turned the engine back on and got *Dolly* bloody sailing.

Then I remembered. Seagoing people always think first of their boats.

I didn't want to hear the answer, but I asked in the end.

'We can't motor?'

'Empty fuel tanks,' said Raymond. 'And the sails are all missing. They really have thought of everything.'

'I don't know why they didn't just open the sea cocks,' I said.

'But that would have been murder,' said an unexcited voice, distantly, on my knee.

This time, it didn't surprise a name out of Raymond. He only went red, and when Johnson didn't open his eyes, touched his hand.

'It's all right,' Raymond said. 'The yobs have gone. It'll be daylight in a couple of hours. We'll have you in St Lucia in no time.'

Dolly rolled. When you knew to listen for it, the grinding crunch from the saloon sounded like a Corporation tip in an earthquake.

Johnson said, 'Sure.'

He was absolutely motionless, but he didn't have to say any more. The first sense to come back is your hearing. He knew, all right.

He still hadn't opened his eyes. Raymond drew a deep breath and said, 'O.K. Tanks, sails, supplies, navigational gear, all kaput. Ferdy's shot through the shoulder: no danger. Maggie and Lenny are O.K. but haven't come to, yet. Rita and I are about to see if we can sail on bar poles. If the storm moves at an even rate, we'll still be in St Lucia before it.'

'Hurricane,' Johnson said. He half-opened his eyes, fatally, to see if Raymond had got it, and the torchlight got to his nerves.

You can't let people be sick lying down. Raymond's big hands were careful, but the boat wasn't. Afterwards, its owner flaked out again without

233

comment. Between us, we got him sort of shawled in the half-hammock. Without his glasses on, he looked unreliable.

'Hurricane,' he'd said. I said, 'The Spaniards heard something about Chloe.'

'That would be it,' Raymond said. 'Tropical Storm Chloe, now granted hurricane status. Rate of progress therefore unknown. Sunrise just before six. Time now, nearly four-thirty.

'We don't know where we are, or where St Lucia is. We don't know if it's downwind, and if we can get there without sail before the hurricane does.

'We don't know if we're in deep water, or near a lee shore with shallows. The winds aren't normal, so we can't rely on their direction to tell us anything. Because there's a hurricane warning, there won't be any other ships about.

'What's the good news?' I said. I had put off the big torch to save its battery.

'Don't hold your breath,' Raymond said. 'We might get clear patches, before sunrise or after, that would let us get our bearings. We might get a land sighting in daylight. Chloe could be approaching at the same pace, or slower. It could have changed direction. If we're in its path, but in deep water there's a slim chance that we could ride it out. We haven't got a sea-anchor, but we could make a drogue of smashed wood.'

The boat rocked and jolted, and the sling beside us moved with it.

I said, 'How long does a hurricane take to pass?'

'Too bloody long,' said Raymond shortly.

On St Lucia there were six hospitals, and a lee shore. I said, 'Ferdy might know these waters. He's had his Barbados house for ages. And what about Lenny?'

'Yes,' said Raymond. 'Manpower undoubtedly the next move.'

I felt him shiver. I wanted to go and check up on Ferdy, but I prodded Raymond instead with the torch. I said, 'Look. See if there's something to put on in the other locker. Where this came from. They haven't cleared it out.'

Behind our backs, things were still shifting about in the cockpit and Raymond turned, using the torch. Among the rubbish was Lenny, sitting up. He said, 'Oh, my Gawd,' with his hand on the back of his head.

We all knew the feeling. Raymond said, 'Over there,' and levered him over to the side; then went back for Maggie, who was stirring.

She opened her eyes, saw him leaning over her, and said, 'What?'

Raymond said, 'All present and correct, but the skipper's had a bad go and the boat's disabled. On your feet, my angel. We've got some problems.'

It was still dark. The hurricane was still on its way. But at least the manpower had doubled.

And what was more important, they were the sailing buffs in the team.

Maybe there was no way of saving ourselves. But if there was, I'd put my money on Lenny and Raymond. And possibly even on Maggie, who was a survivor if ever I saw one.

It struck me to wonder, once she was on her feet, which of our two injured men she'd be most concerned about.

Lenny's reaction, kneeling by Johnson, had been to swear: real nautical stuff that went on and on with hardly any repeaters.

Maggie just gazed, without wasting energy. Then she wrenched the torch out of Raymond's hand and plunged below, Lenny following.

They weren't down very long. When they came back, Lenny wasn't swearing. He just looked rather like the head in the blue banana bag.

On the other hand, Maggie had got her voice working. She said to me, 'Ferdy's fine. The way you've got him, he'll be all right till daylight. We'll need the lamp up here to get the boat seaworthy anyway.'

She hesitated, looking at my skin under the reefer. It was then that I saw there were tears on her cheeks. She said, 'Are *you* all right?'

I could hardly believe it. As Ferdy's nurse, my status had upped. I said, 'Oh, yeah. Another dull night.' Since, suddenly, she seemed almost human, I added, 'I told Raymond, but I don't think he looked. They've left stuff in the locker.'

Maggie didn't waste any time either. Before I stopped speaking she was on her knees, shining the torch into the space where it came from.

'Flags,' she said. 'Raymond, that's your new shirt, boy. What do you fancy? There's a G Flag, a Red Ensign, lots of International Code ... racing colours ... four-flag hoist ... No. We might need that. And something for Rita, for God's sake. You know you're black and blue, girl?'

I knew. I could also feel what was happening at the back of my neck. I caught the flags she threw me. They were coarse and clammy, but I packed them in under my oilskin.

As my aunt would say, it would be the price of me, to be washed up on some darkies' beach wearing bunting.

Maggie was still searching, without much success. No alcohol, no emergency first aid, no beach towels. 'Brushes ... cans of stuff ... engine waste ... turpentine.' She sat up. 'Turps and engine waste?'

From where he was working, on the edge of the light, Raymond looked over. 'No matches, but J.J. had a lighter. Rita love, go and look. In his back pocket, I suspect. It'd let us make flares in a can, for what it's bloody worth.'

I understood. Even if we'd had distress rockets, who would see them? He'd already guessed, from the weight of the sea, that we couldn't be close to land.

However, if a lighter was wanted, I'd get it. I scrambled back to the cockpit in my briefs as Maggie finished repacking the locker and turned back to where Johnson was lying. The torchlight jerked all over, and steadied.

I heard her say, 'I thought you were awake. We need your lighter. How is it?'

'Moderate to hellish,' he said. 'How's Ferdy?'

'Lost a lot of blood but he'll be O.K. Still out,' she said. 'We couldn't really see what's what, without any lights. Your lighter. Where do you keep it? I'll hold you, and Rita'll get it.'

I got the lighter without having to move him much, and this time he stuck it. Maggie said, 'Once it's daylight, we'll rig you up something below.'

Carefully, nobody had actually said what had happened below, as if he wouldn't have noticed the reek, or the noise of the rolling wreckage.

I said, 'There's enough smashed wood to make a few torches to work by. I could make a start in the saloon.'

'My God, would you?' said Maggie. 'And keep an eye on poor Ferdy? If you could heap the worst of it, and batten it somehow.'

'It sounds charming. Poor Rita,' said Johnson. 'Is anything working at all?'

Maggie glanced at him, and then at me. 'What about the water pump?' she said. 'There were pewter mugs somewhere.'

I went below, and had a look, and found one dented mug, and a pipe that would give me some water.

We all drank some, beginning with Johnson. She had been right again. He had needed it badly. I took the sixth refill along to the sleeping Ferdy.

He was going to need it too. Unlike the rest of us in the open air, he'd had a real dose of chloroform. What with that and his shoulder, he was going to have a nasty awakening.

I worked for half an hour, staggering backwards and forwards in the saloon, with a makeshift torch stuck in a tin can.

I could hear talk on deck, and hammering, and the others moving about. At one point I saw Maggie let herself down into the cockpit and then into the big stateroom which had been Johnson's. After a bit, I realized she was clearing his room as I was clearing the saloon, except that a lot of stuff was going overboard, with Johnson's sanction.

My head was still aching, and I was tender all over from cannoning into obstacles of one kind or another. But I had cleared a working passage through to the front of the ship and shored up some of it when Lenny came down to give me a hand, and to sort out stuff Raymond needed on top.

With his help, I got some quite heavy stuff moved, and secured it. Like Raymond, he was good to work with, and had lost all his aggro, the way that happens in disasters.

Ferdy woke soon after that, yelling blue murder because he thought we'd all been shot as well. He didn't seem to mind that I wasn't Maggie, but drained his mug of water and then, stretching shakily, sat himself down and collected me beside him with his good arm, to prove that we were both really alive, he said.

He must have been in real pain from his other shoulder, but his good hand played with my neck and my ear in a familiar, friendly way that I never resented in Ferdy, and that seemed such a nuisance with Porter. Even his bristly chin and his whiskers were comforting.

He talked nonsense for a while, and then got me to tell him what had happened, and about the boat, and about Johnson.

At the end, he was quiet for a bit. Then he withdrew his arm and said, 'If he thinks it's safer, he'll persuade Raymond to stay in deep water, rather than risk our lives getting him into St Lucia ... Rita, you're a shrewd little Scotch cookie. Is he badly hurt?'

'Yes,' I said.

'Burgee at half mast,' said Ferdy, and swore suddenly. Then he got up, and without listening to me, lurched his way through the pitching boat to the cockpit stairs, where he stuck, looking up at his skipper.

'You mean,' said Ferdy, 'that the Rotary Club of St Lucia have sent a tornado to fetch you, and you're hanging about?'

On Johnson's glassless, black-bristled face appeared a mild copy of Ferdy's indignation.

'Not at all,' he said. 'Just held up by the traffic.' He and Ferdy stared at one another, and then Johnson closed his eyes.

'He comes and goes,' I said. 'There isn't any morphine. Maggie's trying to fix some space in his cabin.'

I helped Ferdy up the steps and into the cockpit and called, 'Maggie!'

She came to the door of the stateroom, and gazed at the one-armed photographer with the most. She said, 'You absolute ass. Bulldog

Braithwaite. Too many of Rita's films. I've never seen you perform an unselfish act in your life. Why begin now?'

Her eyes were sparkling, and he looked pretty cheered up, in spite of everything. He said, 'I was working up to the sequel. Let's begin the sequel. You and I get stranded on a desert island. And the skipper and Raymond, if you insist.'

'And Rita and Lenny,' said Maggie. She had turned bitchy again, and the crisis hadn't even peaked.

Raymond said, 'Skipper!'

He said it in such an odd tone that at first I thought something had happened to Johnson.

Then Johnson opened his eyes, rather slowly, and looked up, and I turned and saw that Raymond wasn't studying him at all, but was standing on the cabin roof, peering into the darkness ahead.

He said, 'I think I see a ship's lights.'

'Nonsense,' Ferdy said. 'It's a mirage. You'll see camels next. You'll see water next, I shouldn't wonder.'

Maggie said, 'Shut up, Ferdy. Raymond?'

Lenny's voice said, 'Yes, Miss Maggie. I see it too. Shall I do the flares now, sir?'

'Flares, torches, everything,' Raymond said. 'Starting with the big one up the mast. It's not a small boat. It's big enough to have radar. We'll be on her screen. All we have to do is show we're in distress ...'

He looked down. His face was quite different. 'J.J.: it looks hopeful. Pretty nurses and brandy.'

'It's a hospital ship?' said Ferdy light-headedly.

She was not, naturally, a hospital ship. She had, however, seen Raymond's signals. In quite a short time it was clear that she had changed course and was making towards us. We had no binoculars, but we all watched her coming closer and closer.

It was again Raymond who, as the gap narrowed, jumped on the tossing coach-house roof with our precious torch, and began sending rapid signals. *Yacht Dolly, adrift without power, on passage Barbados St Lucia.*

Out of the wind, a light flickered in answer. 'What does it say?' Maggie burst out.

Raymond looked down. 'That she'll take us in tow. Into hurricane shelter on St Lucia. Remain hove-to and they'll try to board us.'

'That happened to me once before,' Ferdy said. 'Could it be the same bastards? Come back for the gold in our fillings?'

238

It wasn't an old rusty boat; you could see that. But all the same, I felt the same qualm as Ferdy.

It was Raymond who answered.

'I don't think you need worry. We know them.'

'It's the *Paramount Princess*, storm-delayed on her way to Miami.'

20

The transfer to the *Paramount Princess* was a cinch, although even for five fairly nippy people there were a few interesting moments. Ferdy, who is no Stook, yelled regularly every time something strained his injured shoulder, but otherwise performed as if at the Aldershot Tattoo.

Johnson soon lost interest in the proceedings, having been pumped full of pain relievers sent over from the *Princess* earlier.

To avoid the problem of trans-shipping him, we had all been in favour of being left on board *Dolly*, with a few home comforts such as the *Princess*'s entire stock of blankets and alcohol.

The captain's horrified reaction to this suggestion got to us even through a loud-hailer, and the gloom of the two men he sent to stay on board *Dolly* clinched the matter.

With heavy following seas, towing *Dolly* too fast would only swamp her.

Towing her too slowly would place the *Paramount Princess* and all the money inside on the wrong side of St Lucia at roughly the same time as Hurricane Chloe.

If there was the slightest doubt about getting into harbour ahead of Chloe, the captain made clear, he would cast off *Dolly*'s tow without a second thought, and make full speed without her.

The captain was green, and there was a controlled air of panic on board the *Paramount Princess*, whose crew, you could tell, didn't care for sailing in hurricanes. There was no crumpet in sight, this being the time of night when the Curtis family and its passengers were apt to be firmly below in their own or someone else's bunk, no matter what the crisis.

There were exceptions. One was Sharon's much-loved son Porter, in bathrobe and suntan, who took one look at what Maggie and I weren't wearing and zig-zagged happily over, with much the same idea as Chloe.

Also, surprisingly, the tubby shape of Fred Gluttenmacher, the man behind the money behind Josephine, with his hair-piece up like an air-sock and his athletic legs spread apart under an initialled dressing-gown and a mat of hair with a locket in it.

The last rubberneck, more surprisingly still, was Dodo the Teeth, Natalie's to the death and hence no pal of Ferdy's. Unlike the others, she was fully dressed with her life jacket on, for which you couldn't blame her, considering the way we all felt about her.

A couple of pills and some brandy having cleaned Ferdy out of his few emotional blocks, he gave Dodo a thump on the back and a smacking kiss in passing, which more than threw her. She recovered in time to jerk her head at Johnson and say to me, 'And what's the matter with *him*?'

I'd had a brandy as well.

'Drink,' I said. 'You should see what he's done to his ship.'

I knew I shouldn't go to sleep because of the hurricane. I knew I ought to see that Ferdy and Johnson were all right. I knew I ought to get rid of Porter, or I was in for a strenuous night.

In the blessed carpeted dryness below decks, I looked at the armchairs creaking about on their chains and didn't want to do any of these things.

It was Maggie who did them.

She went out and came back several times, and the last time got hold of me and said, 'O.K. The wrecks are going to be fine; the chief steward's looking after them, and they've radioed the hospital at St Lucia.

'I've told Porter he can have us both together tomorrow on the water-bed, and he's gone back to tearing up telephone directories. Lenny and Raymond propose to take turns in the wheelhouse and sleep in here between times, which I should think the insurers of *Princess* as well as *Dolly* ought to be happy about. You and I are going to bed.'

On board somewhere were the rest of the Curtises: Clive and Sharon and Old Joe himself. I hoped he was strapped into his bed. I wasn't so much bothered about Natalie. I was finding it hard to bother about anything.

Maggie and I shared a cabin. Finally. We had a sort of lurching shower each, and as I got into bed, ignoring the night-gear provided, I remembered what I wanted to find out. How the *Princess* had known to come after us.

'She didn't,' said Maggie. 'Dramatic irony. She was on her course for Miami when she got the same distress signal that we did. She's here because she answered the hoax call from our hoods.'

I was too sleepy to say so, but I thought it would have been funny if the *Princess* had got to the hoods first, and what Natalie's reaction would have been, to find twelve guys with guns in her room, demanding recreational sex and her diamonds.

I thought I was still thinking about it, when Maggie shook me awake.

It was daylight. Full daylight. Late morning daylight.

Maggie said, 'St Lucia. We're coming into Marigot, just ahead of the hurricane. The skipper's so-so, and Raymond wants to get him out before

241

Chloe hits. The Victoria Hospital at Castries are sending an ambulance. Do you want to go into Castries with Raymond and Lenny?'

I held on to the sides of the bunk. Everything was swinging. Two of the drawers were out of the dressing-table. I said, 'What about Ferdy?'

Silly question. Ferdy was Maggie's business. She was taking him to be patched up, and then to meet up with Carl Thomassen. If Ferdy and Thomassen wanted to fly their stuff home when the storm was over, she might just go with them. Raymond didn't mind. And Johnson, said Maggie, didn't exactly need a crew any more. She was brisk again. Like my aunt.

I lay thinking.

Natalie was on board, but I wasn't her employee any more. I was here because Roger van Diemen had flown to St Lucia yesterday, and Johnson was following him.

But Johnson had been knocked out of the game. Which left me, and maybe Raymond and Lenny. Or maybe not Raymond and Lenny. I doubted if they gave a damn at the moment for Roger van Diemen.

Unlike Maggie, I quite cared what happened to Johnson. In turn, he had his job to do, and if he couldn't do it, someone would step in, surely, after the storm.

And if nobody stayed with it, I would.

I said, when Maggie asked me, that I wouldn't mind going into Castries in the ambulance. I borrowed someone's shirt-tails and pants, and was on deck when the anchor went down. The ambulance hadn't yet come. But, the R.T. informed us, a car was leaving the hotel for Castries, with room for two passengers.

Maggie and Ferdy decided to take it, and leave the proper ambulance to take care of Johnson. Considering all the bends in that bloody road, it was probably sensible.

I got a good-bye kiss from Ferdy that did us both a lot of good, and delivered a tongueful of brandy where it was rather nice. Then Maggie helped him, still talking, down to the launch.

I watched them chug to the jetty. I watched them pass a yacht I thought I knew, and I stood, clutching the rail, and gazed at her.

I knew her. I knew every line of her. I was looking at the broken struts and stripped booms and battered sides of the white and beautiful *Dolly*, her two tall masts arching backwards and forwards against the dark sky.

Her temporary crew had departed. Once the queen of the harbour, she now rocked to her own anchor in shallower water, tipsily threadbare, like someone's old mistress.

She had made it. I was glad.

The wind in the anchorage was wild and freakish. The deck of the *Paramount Princess* was dirty, with no sunchairs in sight, and the pool itself dry except for the swaying puddle left by the rainfall.

No white-coated attendants asked if I'd like an iced drink. No topless girls lay about, dreamily reading. I could hear the captain on the radio-telephone, his voice ragged and snappish, and see Raymond's blond head beside him.

Clive Curtis said, 'Well, Rita. You've had quite an adventure. You're going to Castries with your skipper?'

We owed our lives to the *Paramount Princess*. Coals of fire, after our behaviour to Natalie, the Curtis family's principal guest. Or a gesture I needn't feel too grateful for, since they'd pinched my job from me. On the other hand, but for them, Johnson might have been done for.

I said, 'You took a real risk for us. I'm glad you got here before Chloe.'

Clive gave a small smile; then the red moustache snapped back again. 'Win some, lose some,' he said. 'I doubt if Pa would have agreed to it, till he heard the guy was too sick to play cards. That's one Limey sharper you've got there.'

A woman's voice said, 'You think he had to cheat to get the better of you?'

Clive's sister Sharon, walking to his other side, didn't spare me a glance. She added, 'When the hell do we get off this hulk?'

Clive said, 'There's the hotel, over there. We're waiting for this painter guy's ambulance.'

I said, 'I think I'll see if Mr Johnson is ready.'

Before I'd gone a step, a voice below me called, '*Ahoy Paramount Princess!*'

I saw the captain peer over his side deck. I looked over the deck rail as well.

Bobbing on the water below was the Customs launch from the jetty, with four men and Amy Faflick standing in it.

Because of the wind, she had taken the cigar out of her mouth, which looked less like Humphrey Bogart's and more like George Raft's. Her white hair whipped like new standing rigging.

Instead of the baggy shorts, she had on trousers like fireman's canvas, taut with draughts. And on the planks beside her was a square box with a towel over it.

She spotted me.

'Rita Geddes? Where's your effing fair-weather sailor?'

I wondered which one she meant. 'Johnson?' I said. 'He's waiting for the Victoria ambulance. We got boarded.'

'Horses' asses. I know all that,' said Amy. 'Heard you on the ham radio. I'm your ambulance.'

Raymond came to the rail. 'Amy?'

Bears obeyed Amy Faflick. She turned the same sort of stare on Johnson's boyfriend. 'There's an effing hurricane on the way,' she said. 'All hospital services on stand-by. No ambulances. I volunteered to drive your stupid party to Castries. What's wrong with the silly sod?'

'Wait. I'll get him,' said Raymond. I watched him two-step off below, not sure whether to follow him.

Clive came up, and seamen opened the rail and fixed the companionway. Even when made fast, the Customs boat jarred up and down. Three men moved forward and, balancing, prepared to board the *Princess.*

I'd thought, if I thought at all, that they'd have made some sort of stretcher. Instead, Lenny suddenly appeared on deck, one hand grasping the rail and the other supporting *Dolly's* owner under the shoulder. Raymond, lurching forwards, took a grip of his arm on the other side. Johnson winced.

He wasn't quite Blithe Spirit, but he was a weird colour, with the sort of lines you put in with a maroon pencil.

Someone had shaved him, and some staff work had produced a spare pair of bifocals, which made his face look less a disaster area and more like a stockbroker's.

He was concentrating so much on the effort to walk that I didn't think he would see me, but he did. He pulled a face, and then forged on to the head of the companionway.

There, he said, 'Amy? Made a mistake with my body language.'

'Made a mistake with your effing crew,' Amy said. 'Can't you move quicker than that? There's an effing hurricane due.'

She watched him down the steps with pure anxiety, and let off a string of obscenities as soon as he was safely in the boat with Lenny and Raymond.

Then I joined them, having added my thanks to the speeches Johnson and Raymond had already made to the captain and Clive and his sister. Old Joseph wasn't about.

The three Customs men were still on the *Princess,* but their boatmen didn't mind giving an emergency lift to the hospital party. Engine roaring, we smacked our way over the lagoon.

Weightless and deserted, *Dolly* bounced on her cable. Johnson looked at her.

Behind the bifocals, anything might have been happening. But when he spoke, making an effort against the wind, Johnson's voice had very little expression in it. 'You saw her, Amy?'

'Stepped aboard with the Customs on the way across. And off again,' Amy shouted. 'Cross between a breaker's yard and a cat box. What were your boarders searching for? Cufflinks?'

Raymond called, 'Mrs Sheridan had worn her jewels in Martinique. They maybe thought she was aboard. Amy …'

'Amy, shut up,' roared Amy. 'He's bugged-out. I see it. What if his effing guts pack it in before he gets treatment?'

'Let's just try,' snapped Raymond. The launch jarred and jolted. His eyes were bloodshot, and so were Lenny's. I was the only one who'd had a decent night's sleep.

Day's sleep. It must be lunchtime. I drew a breath, and yelled, 'When is Chloe due?'

You had to bellow, because of the drone of the launch, and the creaking and banging of boats, and the noise, like steam under pressure, of thousands of jostling palm trees. And this other roar, like crowds at a football match, which filled the sky and had come quite suddenly, along with an extra darkness that took what light there was out of the air.

I looked up. So did everyone else. You could see the pale faces on every boat, and on shore, and on the jetty.

Birds. Birds of all sizes and shapes streaming over our heads from the east, screeching, wailing and croaking their warning.

Amy glanced up. 'There's your answer,' she said. 'Front edge of the cloud in just over an hour …

'Birds. Effing quitters,' she added.

The boat slid alongside the jetty and Amy planked her basket on top and clattered up with the rope and made it fast. 'Now,' she said. 'Wee fella at the top; Raymond at the bottom, and ease our dumb sailor friend up. This'll effing teach him not to answer distress calls in future.'

Amy drove the big Toyota herself, with an unforthcoming Johnson packed with cushions in the back seat, and the other two sitting beside him. I sat beside her, and watched the coconuts ripping off the palm trees.

It was seven miles to Castries, once you got to the top of the road; and half an hour to do it in. Easy.

Amy turned on her crackling radio, and we listened to all the advisories, in English and then in French patois. Among the rest were flash-flood warnings: keep away from beaches and rivers.

And finally, an announcement. In ten minutes' time, all electricity would be cut off on the island.

Johnson said, 'I think that's far enough, Amy.'

I didn't know he was awake. No one showed any surprise. The Toyota's wheel spun under Amy's ferocious brown claws, and the car hurtled straight for the palm trees, turned on its axis, and exploding through several gears, set off like one of her tigers in the exact direction we'd come from. Her cigar waggled.

I said, 'Why?'

Raymond and Lenny both looked at Johnson, who looked straight back. Amy said, 'Road blocked by effing trees. That's right, isn't it? Can you stand this, buster? There's an hour of it.'

She was addressing the Owner. Johnson said, 'It's genius, Amy. Keep going. I'm full of Henry's depth-charges.'

'You look it, buster,' said Amy. 'You look as if you're running on deaf-aid batteries.'

The car rocketed on, leaving me none the wiser. They knew something I didn't. We weren't going to the Victoria Hospital. We were actually approaching the end of the road that led back and down to the yacht harbour.

We were approaching it, and going to pass it.

We weren't going to pass it. In the middle of the road, among a tangle of palm leaves and some bouncing coconuts, a short figure was planted, waving its bare knobbled arms. Amy braked.

Grampa Joe Curtis thrust his mottled face in the window and yelled, Are you goin' to . . .'

He broke off. 'Hell: you're the painter fella who bust up his ketch?'

'Johnson. Yes, Mr Curtis. The road to Castries is blocked. Mrs Faflick's kindly offered to take us to her home near Soufrière. What's your trouble?'

It was the longest speech he'd made yet. At least it told me where we were going. Once I would have asked why.

Old Joseph's sharp, elderly eyes passed over Raymond, registered me and ended with Amy.

'You got room for one more?' he said. 'Hotel's full. Bedrooms full. Folk sittin' in each other's laps all over the bar an' the restaurant. Time for the Happy Hour, they'll need to hold a mass marriage. The only one of us with a bedroom is that bloody dame Sheridan.'

Johnson said, 'Amy? It was Mr Curtis's boat that rescued us. We do rather owe him.'

'Sure, there's plenty of house-room,' Amy said. She leaned back and opened the door. 'Any more of you? Take one or two.'

Old Joseph held up his arms, and we pulled him in. Under his smart, tailored rainsuit in stone-colour, his bones were like pencils.

He said, 'Get goin'. That storm's on its way. Clive an' Sharon an' Porter want to live in a refugee camp, don't let's spoil their fun. You drive on, ma'am.'

She started up, shuttled through the gears again as if weaving concrete, and drove on, and south.

There are said to be 385 bends in the road between Castries and Soufrière. By now, the gale seemed all set to straighten them. Amy drove the twenty-nine miles from Marigot as if it had.

By the time we got to the fishing village south of Marigot, we had seen the first of the cabbage palms crashing. Green creeper, unfurled from the stays of telegraph poles, looped and flew in front of us, like adverts from low-flying aircraft.

The sea was white and grey and roaring, and the sky was going black.

Between that and the next village my main job was to keep the windscreen clear of the torn fronds and branches that kept hitting and packing it. Leaf-pulp and crushed fruit on the road made the wheels whine.

Smells streaked into the car, and dashed out of it. The warm vanilla smell of a copra factory, and the sweetness of cane, and the schoolroom smell of sulphur from the Pitons, like green sugar cones through the cloud ahead.

At the next village, the river was already flooding yellow-white over the bridge, wrapping the uprights in ragged sheets and bits of bleached cotton.

We crossed between walls of spray, and ran into a torrent of rain. It hit the road with the sound of tearing cloth and covered the windscreen like glycerine.

'Jesus,' said Grampa Joe. The rain, whirling in through my open window, thudded on top of everybody, and every time the trees thinned on our left, the heavy car rocked and shuddered.

The radio crackled on, almost drowned out by the row from outside, and now and then produced a row of its own of quite a different sort.

Grampa Joe sat with a cigar shaking in one hand and his lighter trembling in the other and said, 'What in the name of sweet Jesus are those dumb clucks doin'? *Singin'?*'

Johnson roused himself to the extent of opening one eye. 'National song of St Lucia,' he said. 'Ferdy Braithwaite would sing it to you.'

I wondered where Ferdy was, and if Maggie had got his shoulder fixed up, and if I would hear him sing Prince Eager again. I didn't much want to hear him sing Prince Eager again, but I missed Ferdy.

Amy said, pleating the wheel, her eyes half shut against cigar smoke, 'England's greatest gift to St Lucia. *I'll* effing sing it to you.'

I saw what she meant as she bucketed along, her voice raised in chorus with the radio voices, her lipless mouth keyholed round her cigar and her words smashed by explosions of coughing.

> 'Sons and daughters of St Lucia
> Love the Land that gave you birth
> Land of beaches, hills and valleys
> Fairest Isle of all the earth
> Wheresoever you may roam
> Love, oh Love your island home.'

There were two more verses.

I can't sing, but I joined in; and so did Raymond, once we got the hang of the tune.

I sang; and thought, What the hell have I got to sing about?

The last time I sang was on my water-skis in Madeira, when I was made to board *Dolly*. The rich, superior yacht with the rich, superior Owner.

I knew *Dolly* now, as I didn't then. I knew every stick of wrecked, filthy *Dolly*. After one night, she was part of my life.

I had left Madeira; I had left London with only one purpose. To pay out the man who killed Kim-Jim. Rita's one-man crusade.

Now I was what I had always resisted being in private life: part of a team. For a moment, on board the *Princess*, I had thought the team had gone, and I might be on my own. And instead of feeling free, I'd felt the opposite.

I suppose it was a landmark.

And so, in a car racing a hurricane, with Ferdy hurt and Johnson the way he was and bloody violence behind and ahead and all round about me, I sang.

It was old Joseph who said finally, 'You seen a career counsellor about that caterwaulin'? Do us a favour? I got an anxiety disorder about hurricanes. I like peace to worry.'

'We're there,' said Amy, and braked.

We let Amy get down first; and when she yelled we got out, collected our disabled, and staggered into the tropical Tube-station which was the Faflick branch of Pets Inc. at St Lucia.

The only thing we had time to notice, in the semi-darkness under the roar of the trees, was that it was the best place in the world to stay through a hurricane.

It was built into the side of one of the Pitons, hollowed out of the crag so that all you saw on the face of the hill were the doors and the shuttered windows, and other great double doors, stretching further than we could see on either side.

Some of the doors had empty cages fixed in front of them, giving on to the big paved front yard. There were more cages under the trees, also empty. The Toyota's garage was a little along from the house, and also scooped out of the hillside and strongly structured.

Raymond helped put the car in, and barred the door against the tug of the wind while Amy struck a match and led us into her hot, lightless sitting-room, where a couple of dogs made a fuss of us.

On the table were three stout candlesticks, with several candles in each. She lit them, and we saw we were in a comfortable, low-ceilinged room full of chintzy cane furniture and piles of magazines and out-of-date newspapers with dog bowls on them, and some nice but chewed rugs.

It was rather like Pets Inc. in England. You could imagine Celia or Jim Brook walking about quite easily.

But there was no one else here except the dogs and the caged guests and Amy. She had let her lad feed the animals and then get off home, because of the hurricane. She could reach the indoor cages herself through the house if she had to, but they shouldn't need any attention.

She directed old Mr Curtis to a bedroom, if he wanted to wash and lie down, and showed Lenny another, for Johnson. She went off, with Raymond, to find and switch on the emergency generator. She seemed to have selected Raymond as having the highest combined I.Q. and muscle power, which was probably right at that.

Somewhere, a jenny started up. An inside door banged. Amy strode in, flicked down a switch, and blew out the candles. The chintzy armchairs got brighter and the air conditioners started to buzz again.

Then there was a crash like the end of the world, and Hurricane Chloe struck.

From beginning to end, a hurricane can punish one area badly for something like six hours, or three hours until its eye reaches the area, and three hours afterwards. The worst damage happens at the time the eye is passing and afterwards, and there are severe gales and squalls for a lot longer than three hours after that.

The noise is stunning.

If you know you're safe, you can go to bed and stuff your ears and get hold of a sleeping pill, as Old Joseph did.

If you need to lie on your back, as Johnson did, then you are as well to do it, while you have the chance.

Lenny made himself earplugs from bread rolls, and kipped down in the same room. I said to Raymond, 'Why don't you do the same? If the house caves in, I'll wake you.'

He looked down at me. 'You really into congos?' he said.

Cartwheels, he'd turned. With tassels on.

'Learned from Leroy Horsemouth Wallace,' I said.

The freckles on his cheeks stretched. 'O.K.,' he said. 'You and Amy let your hair down over your cocoa. No house with Old Joe's wallet in it can fall very far.'

I went to tell Amy that she and I were sitting out the hurricane on our own. I found her in the kitchen, finishing off the sort of cook-out that would keep a cavalry regiment and its horses properly fed in battle conditions, assuming the supply line has snapped.

She told me how to help her, and we finished it easily between us. Then she said, 'There you are. They're a nice enough lot of young fellas, but my God, show them a saucepan. You keep dogs?'

I didn't.

'Don't need a warm fuzzy. Quite right. Did the right thing about J.J.'s old lady, though,' Amy said. 'Poor old Bessie. See, these dogs are young. They're nervous. You keep beside them, if I'm busy. So long as you're calm, they'll be all right.'

She meant well. I always did like her.

The storm banged and howled dimly outside, but we were safe from it. Shack people had to keep their windows open and live in the gale, because it made the house safer. Underground as Amy was, she could keep her shutters closed.

At her suggestion, I went round and checked them while she got the Hurricane Hole Hotel on VHF16 to tell them that Mr Joseph Curtis was safely at Faflick's, in case anyone panicked.

I didn't know she had a ham radio, till she showed me it. Apparently the first thing to blow out in a hurricane is the telephone system. Then it's up to the hams to feed the central emergency unit, and the airport and the hurricane base in Miami.

There were only one or two hams, and if the lines came down, she was going to be busy. Meantime, it was past lunchtime, and we were hungry. We piled chicken creole on two plates and had a sort of picnic lunch in her office, which had no outside windows and was quieter, especially with the door shut.

We didn't talk about the storm all that much. Amy's animals often work for the same show people I do. We have a lot in common.

She knew this man in Beverly Hills who did tucked jowls and capped teeth for rich dogs, and I knew the guy who trained the U.S. Coast Guard's search-and-rescue squad pigeons. He taught them to spot bright colours floating in water, and press on a buzzer.

As I've said before, pigeons are clever. 'Like gerbils,' I added.

There was a silence filled with horrifying noises from outside, during which Amy's cigar glowed bright red in the middle of her Humphrey Bogart face.

At length: 'Cool, man,' she said. 'But I can't tell you anything.' She paused. 'Ain't an effing law, though, that says you can't guess.'

The basket of gerbils was in the room we were in, with the towel still in place over it. I got up and brought it over.

They're nice. I used to keep them myself. Kangaroo-active. Plushy as Chad Valley toys, with double-sewn eyes you can't choke on.

Almost hidden under the hay and general litter was the knob of the buzzer. Beside it was a bit of boiled egg and a dog biscuit. After they'd done what was expected of them, her gerbils had got their reward.

Like pigeons, gerbils can be taught to press buttons. In their case, when they sniff narcotics.

The basket had come aboard *Dolly* the first time I had visited Marigot harbour, and today. I wondered if, the night I found Johnson lying asleep in his cabin, a search might not have produced a little stranger in his luggage as well.

I said, 'I have a theory. I think that the folk who boarded *Dolly* and wrecked her were dope runners.'

'Oh?' said Amy. The cigar smoke hanging about her leather face reminded me of smoke-clouded bifocal glasses.

I said, 'I don't think they were searching for drugs.'

'Oh?' said Amy.

'No. See those boats smuggling drugs from Colombia, who attack an innocent ship, throw out the owners, transfer their load to her, and sail her themselves to Miami, pretending to be Fidel Castro delivery skippers?'

'Bona fide,' said Amy absently. 'One of those?'

'Yes. Except that because of the storm, they couldn't sail *Dolly* to Miami. They had to go for the nearest safe harbour. And that was Marigot, where everyone knew *Dolly* wasn't in the hands of a delivery skipper.

'So they smashed her up but left her seaworthy, knowing that someone would tow her in, and the Customs would never think of ransacking a boat in that state. Then when the boat was deserted, they could take the cargo ashore and hide it somewhere.'

'Clever,' said Amy. The light shone on her white hair, and a row of nice smoke rings. 'But I don't see anyone unloading drugs from *Dolly* just now. The eye of the storm, thank God, is passing south of St Lucia. But it's still got to pass.'

'But later?' I said. 'When do the winds die?'

'They don't,' Amy said. 'But we should be down to an effing gale, say, by sunset.'

She went on smoking, and looking at me.

'You think it's silly,' I said.

She said, 'Did I say so? You worried about that son-of-a-bitch Johnson? He'll live. He's too angry now to do anything else. Ask him about the gerbils. He'll probably tell you.'

I lay back with my sneakers apart, in my borrowed pants and my borrowed shirt and my flattened orange wig with no make-up. 'But you won't tell me.' I said. 'You won't tell me if they smelt drugs this morning on *Dolly*?'

Amy got up. 'Cat,' she said. 'You'll find out soon enough. Meanwhile, there's work to be done. Let's clear these dishes and see what Chloe has got to say.'

At four o'clock in the afternoon, the eye of Hurricane Chloe passed to the south of St Lucia. By then all communications except by ham radio on standby power had been knocked out, and Amy had been at the instrument for an hour, relaying messages, and talking to the meteorological office at Hewanorra.

During this time, and the hours that followed, three-quarters of the banana plantations were ruined, the roofs were peeled off the copra and sugar factories, churches and schools were reduced to their skeletons, and forests of palms were blown down.

Amy sat, and relayed messages.

She knew me. She didn't ask me to relieve her. I brought her strong tea, and sandwiches and whisky, and when one by one Lenny and Raymond and finally Johnson came in quietly to stand and watch, I fed them too.

Old Joe, asleep on his pill, snored without waking. The last time I went to the kitchen, I heard Amy say, 'She knows about the gerbils.'

In the office, Raymond had taken her place at the radio to let her relax with her drink. Johnson, carefully propped on the edge of the desk, was leafing through her notes of floods and road blockages. He put them down.

'If they're your gerbils, they've probably been moonlighting,' he said.

He turned to me. He didn't look like a write-off. He looked the way anyone might look who had broken a couple of ribs. Slightly cautious, wholly filled up with pain-killers, and otherwise placid. Too placid, perhaps.

He said, 'I don't plan to be beaten up, but there may be some rough stuff this evening. You don't need to get mixed in it.'

Men. 'How do I keep out of it?' I said.

'No problem. Just stay here with Amy. Teach her tricks,' Johnson said.

The shutters shook and shook, and the door rattled and rattled. It was five-thirty, and nearly official sunset.

Time for Chloe to wane. And the banging we could hear wasn't all Chloe. It was caused by a pair of fists hammering on Amy's front door. And added to that, you could now hear the sound of shouting, half carried away by the gale. The shouting of a strong, impatient voice. A woman's voice.

The voice of Dodo of the Teeth, who stood on the threshold when we dragged the door shuddering open, bawling the same thing over and over, while behind her stood the malicious, grinning figure of Old Joe's grandson Porter.

'Where you-all bastards got her?' Natalie's companion was yelling. 'Where you-all put my poor Miz Natalie?'

She caught sight of me. 'You, you no-good nothing! If you harm a hair of her head, I swear by my Daddy, I kill you!'

'I didn't think they still said that,' Johnson said. 'But Amy, do bring her in ... Rita, I'm helluva sorry.'

I knew what he meant.

I was too late.

It had begun, and I was mixed up in it.

21

The news that Dodo slung at us all in such fury turned out to be true.

When, in the fading hours of the hurricane, she had gone to her mistress's room in the Hurricane Hole Hotel, it was to find that Natalie Sheridan, syndicated political journalist, divorcee, economist, maker of sharp documentaries, and late employer of Rita Geddes, had totally vanished.

The idea that the quickest way to find Natalie was through the ham radio at the Faflick Pets Inc. near Soufrière was Dodo's own.

It was sensible. She knew Old Joe Curtis was with Amy already. Porter had found an abandoned car, and against the hotel's urgent advice, they had set off in the last of the light. It had not been an easy journey.

If she had found only Amy and Joe, Dodo would have downed a rum punch, confided all her troubles to Amy, and been content to have the terrible news transmitted, efficiently, to the right authorities.

Instead, she saw before her the four familiar faces of those in whom Miz Natalie had been so disappointed.

Including the undersized creature with the unfortunate hair whom Miz Natalie had befriended, and who had deceived her. Conspired against her. Prepared to blackmail her even, it had been said.

Being already the richer for one suspicious death in Madeira.

I saw it all on Dodo's face even before she accused me of kidnapping Natalie, and even of luring old Mr Curtis into my lair.

She demanded to see them both. We had to wake up Old Joseph to convince her that we weren't selling him for money or spotted lampshades. Then she demanded to be shown over the rest of the house, in case we were concealing Miz Natalie.

Porter lay back on the sofa, shut his brown eyes and giggled. He looked high on something. But perhaps it was just relief and amusement.

He was giggling at Dodo. He was giggling at the rest of us too, if you watched him. His grandfather knew it: threw him a look like a laser beam, and then went back to extracting our news of the hurricane.

What had happened to Natalie didn't interest Old Joe. Except that it had struck him, if not Dodo, I thought, that Porter might have had something to do with it.

Amy, used to behavioural problems, had chosen to take the agitated Dodo firmly round the entire settlement, to see for herself that Miz Natalie was not on the premises.

I went along too, at Dodo's request, and the dogs came without invitation.

Actually, I wanted to see Amy's animals. So, it seemed, did Raymond and Johnson. When she opened the door off the scullery that led to the long, stone-flagged path of the zoo, the two men came through and walked along with us.

It made me uneasy. I thought, for a man who was supposed to be in the Victoria Hospital, Johnson had already been on his feet longer than he should, and that either Raymond or Lenny would have stopped him.

All they had done, so far as I could see, was supply him with one of Amy's training sticks, which he was using to take some of his weight. And, I suspected, stuff him full of pain-killers again.

For the rest, the zoo was a nice antidote to Dodo, in a way. One side was just wall, with sinks and hoses and bales of stuff and shelves of jugs and cartons and bottles.

The other side was wired and partitioned to hold all the various creatures the Faflicks were curing, or training, or breeding. In different cages, Amy had little monkeys, and opossum, and a pile of fers-de-lance, which is the poisonous snake of St Lucia.

And in a huge cage, three times the size of the others, were the green and blue St Lucian parrots, hopping, swinging, nudging each other; swivelled in sleep; or intent, stabbing and prodding, on their grooming routine.

They were big, argumentative parrots. The noise they made was like the noise of that skyful of birds, fleeing the hurricane.

Amy was used to the questions people asked.

'They don't talk,' she said. 'My talkers have private apartments. Now, you silly bitch, what's the matter?'

Unshaken, Dodo followed Amy's gaze to one of the dogs who, from prancing and sniffing and wagging her tail, had suddenly broken out into barking. The second one joined her.

'Excuse me,' said Amy. 'Would you care to walk to the end on your own? I have to get back.'

She didn't wait. She caught Johnson's eye as she passed him, and ran. Raymond had already turned back and was sprinting along the zoo alley to the house proper.

Natalie's maid said, 'Is something wrong?'

'A tree falling, perhaps. Rita will show you the rest,' Johnson said. He didn't run, but he turned and limped fairly grimly after Amy and Raymond.

Dodo looked after him, and then wheeled and gazed at the rest of the corridor, which ended in a blank wall. She said, 'Is there another building through there?'

According to Amy, the hillside was dug out for half a mile with concrete storerooms and workshops, some interconnected and some not.

The zoo had no outlet. To get to the storehouses, you had to go out through the house and enter by separate doors from the yard.

Which was what the others had gone to do.

Whatever was going to happen, I wasn't going to be left out of it. I didn't excuse myself. I just left Dodo standing, and turned and ran back to the house.

At the connecting door, Johnson was waiting for me. 'I thought so,' he said. 'Was Old Joe in there with you?'

He hadn't been.

'Really?' said Johnson. 'Then he's vanished as well. It's like the Bermuda Triangle. You didn't unlock the snakes?'

I hadn't.

'In that case,' said Johnson, 'let's make sure, for God's sake, that nothing happens to the divine Dodo, at least.'

Upon which he locked the connecting door to the zoo, and ignoring Dodo's muffled cry, gripped his stick and led me out after the others into the darkness and the wind.

I had thought, and I supposed Amy had thought, that someone had designs on the Toyota. By the time we got outside she was standing, Raymond at her side, shining her torch on the double barred doors of the garage.

They were closed, which didn't satisfy her. I was surprised. I was innocent. On Amy's insistence, Raymond opened the garage and we all trailed inside, to make sure that nothing was missing.

The Toyota was safely there, and a truck, and a lot of equipment. Behind them all was a door, leading away from the house and the zoo. Talking and flashing her torch, Amy opened it.

Raymond stayed holding the doors, but Lenny followed Amy, and so did Johnson and I. Boughs and palm fronds and bits of bushes whirled through the big doors, and I wondered why Raymond wasn't closing them.

Pitched to carry over the racket, Porter's voice teased us from the door. 'Busy, cats? You know you locked in one angry lady? I've just released her.'

With Amy, that put him into the opossum class. 'Well, that's great,' she said. 'Now you effing go back and stop her coming outside and forgetting she doesn't know the first effing thing about hurricanes.'

Leaning on the door, his clothes trembling and flapping, Porter was enjoying the torchlight. He called, 'I think the old bag is right. I think you're all planning to run off with Natalie. I'm not moving my butt.'

'Then bring it with you,' said Johnson mildly. 'We don't know where Mrs Sheridan is, but we think someone's breaking into a storehouse. There's a string of them, so Mrs Faflick says. If we cut along here, we may surprise them. .'

Porter grinned, his hair vibrating. 'Sir,' he said. 'That's a load of crap. The dogs would be barking.'

'They stopped because they were told to,' said Johnson. 'The person holding your arm is Raymond. He thinks you should come along with us, too. Amy, wonder-woman, get the jeep out.'

She put the torch down and began to do what he asked. A scuffle began and ended in the doorway. Amy started the engine, checked that the doorway was clear, and began to back into the yard.

It was neat. If someone was breaking in further along, they might be reassured. And if they were watching, out there in the dark, they might not notice that some of us had slipped through this door at the back of the garage.

They might not know, with any luck, that such a door existed. Or that it led, as I saw. directly to the network of storehouses.

Johnson picked up Amy's torch, and switched it on as the garage doors closed. Raymond shot the bolts with one hand. With the other, he was holding Porter. In Amy's code, S.A.S. tiger-wise.

Porter's face was white with fury. He was a tall, well-made boy. He had probably never been physically compelled to do something he didn't want to do in his life.

'Oh, dear,' Johnson said. 'Do run along if you're worried. If we find Mrs Sheridan, we'll send her back to the house with a message. Raymond, let him go at once.'

Raymond did, a bit slowly.

Porter said. 'That was just as well. But I'm coming. I want to see what you're up to.'

Lenny waited beside me at the door, as if he'd seen it all happen before. I wondered if he had. Amy hadn't come back, but I thought I'd heard the house front door bang, and hoped she had safely stopped Dodo from interfering.

Raymond, like a good lieutenant, was watching Johnson, whose current style was a sort of slow attentiveness, as with an angler in a boat he wasn't rowing.

Johnson said, 'All right, Porter. After the next chamber, the rooms connect without any doors, so we have to put out the torch and be quiet. Can you, as Amy would say, shut your effing mouth for five minutes?'

Porter glared, but he came. Johnson and Amy. The gerbils were lucky. I wouldn't want to be trained by Johnson.

Blundering along in the dark past the Faflicks' junk, I tried to work out myself what he was up to.

The dogs had warned of a break-in. They were trained, and I believed them.

In such a storm, no one in his senses would break into a storehouse to steal anything. Even if you had somewhere to put it, the thing might be sucked out of your hands before you got there.

In such a storm, a guy in his senses might, however, break into a safe place to stow something. To hide it for a short time. To store a priceless, portable commodity such as the load of cocaine planted on *Dolly*.

For that, the Faflicks place was ideal. Remote, with only Amy to reckon with. And possibly Joe, the rich old yob from the big yacht. Amy had told the world about Joe. But not about the presence of the rest of us.

The rest of us. Here and now, three men and Porter and me. With Johnson's wiring and Porter's ego as handicaps.

The bushes had not been full of Neurosis officials tipped off by Johnson. Narcotics.

Narcotics officials would be storm-stuck in Castries.

Equally, the cautious sounds, half-drowned by the storm, that came to us now from the occupied lock-up didn't seem to indicate a platoon of drug smugglers. Or even twelve Spanish-speaking bastards with guns.

Which might argue that drug-smugglers, as well, could be held up by blocked roads and flash-flooding. And even that Johnson had suspected it.

I ran into Johnson's hand, and realized that we had all stopped, and that Raymond had been sent on ahead, to see what that dim light could show him.

He was away only for moments. When he came back, he touched Lenny on the shoulder, and leaving him with Porter in the gloom, drew Johnson and me as far away as he could.

We were in a store full of oil cans. Raymond faced Johnson and whispered, 'I bloody owe you a tenner.'

There was almost no light, but I swear that Johnson put out his hand, and Raymond paid him. Then Johnson said, 'Many?'

'Three. The Owl, the Cockerel and the lady. They've parked her outside, but I've heard her.'

'Car?' said Johnson.

'Yes. As Amy thought, under the palms. I hope she's fixed it. The room's full of old crates, with double doors to the front, like the garage. They're loading through one of these. You'll have total surprise. The wind's deafening.'

I hardly heard that bit. I stared at them.

Our intruders, according to Raymond, were wearing the Carifesta masks. The boss-masks. The masks worn at that top-level meeting in the Brighton Beach chalet, Barbados, when this consignment of drugs was first mentioned.

No heavies. No porters. No Indians. Because of the storm, we had got ourselves into top-level management. The dope was being brought in, of necessity, by the Chiefs in this racket. The Cockerel. The lady. And Roger van Diemen.

Johnson gave us our orders before he went in to challenge them. He told Porter to do what he was told, and me to stay out of it, and we both agreed.

I hoped Lenny and Raymond meant to obey him. I thought of the severed head in the blue bag. And the men who had wrecked *Dolly* and given Johnson himself such very special attention.

I thought of Kim-Jim. I remembered the ten-pound note that had just changed hands and wondered what sort of people could keep as laid-back as that, no matter what happened.

I watched Raymond and Johnson, Lenny and Porter collect, quietly, at the throat of the passage and wait, quietly, until Raymond signalled that all three people were inside the store.

There was a moment, before he signalled, when Raymond's head turned, and his eyes met Johnson's with pure surprise in them.

Then his hand fell. I moved into the entrance. And all four men sprang forward and fanned out into the storeroom itself, surrounding the two men bent in the centre over a crate, and the woman sitting inside the half-open doorway beyond them.

Because of the noise of the wind, it was a second before they saw us. A second in which we could see quite clearly the cockerel head and the owl head of the two men bent by the storm-lantern loading the chest.

And the exquisite crêpe-de-chine dress and bare head of the woman, whose blonde hair and vivid, self-confident face were known all over the world.

'Natalie!' Porter shrieked, and she spun round, her arms flung out, before Lenny and Raymond had stopped running.

The Cockerel whirled round, but the Owl was quicker still. I saw his hand swing up. I saw the revolver in it, with Johnson in its sights. Then came the flame and the report, echoing round the low room and clashing with another report, this time from a gun in Johnson's hand.

Mixed with the smells of wood and sulphur and pulp, the smell of cordite. Mixed with the roar of the storm, the rustle of the Owl's feathers as he leaned over and slithered slowly downwards, dislodging his mask.

Beneath it was the broad, Dutch face of Roger van Diemen, with the brown kinky hair streaked over his brow, and the light eyes shut.

Johnson watched him. Watched, quite unmoved, as Kim-Jim's murder was avenged at last.

The Cockerel didn't watch. The Cockerel caught his partner's gun in one hand and turning, pulled the woman towards him and held her strongly across his body.

'Now,' he said. His voice boomed through his mask. 'Now you do what I say, or I shoot Mrs Sheridan. Many times. The eyes. The stomach. Many times, before she is dead.'

After all, there was no need to be anything other than laid-back. It was like blackjack. I said, 'Rush him.'

I counted on the Cockerel firing at me, and he did. I'd already jumped to one side. It gave Raymond, if he'd been quick enough, a chance to pounce, but he waited too long. And Johnson couldn't.

Porter said, 'You stupid little bitch. He'll kill Natalie.'

'He won't,' I said. 'She's one of them. Rush him.'

No one moved. The Cockerel laughed. Using his gun, he pushed the strap of her dress off one shoulder and then poked the muzzle playfully down and under one neat onion breast, pulling her round and up to look at him.

'Are you one of us, darling?' he said.

The gun had just been fired. I wondered if it was burning her. I wondered if this was one situation Natalie Sheridan couldn't turn to her own advantage.

I should have remembered the banana plantation. She didn't scream, or struggle, or plead. She spoke, not to the Cockerel, but to us.

She said, 'They don't know Rita as we do. They think she resents me. That she'll believe anything. But listen. Listen to me.'

Her voice, in spite of herself, got high.

'I'm not on their side. This is Roger's idea, because I broke with him. I was kidnapped from the Hurricane Hole Hotel this evening. They're smugglers. They're smuggling drugs from Colombia and Roger was one of them. *I didn't know.* Try to believe. I didn't know. You may not like me, Rita, but you know I don't harm people ...'

She was breathing quickly. She said, 'Kim-Jim was the one real, staunch friend in my life. We would have married, if he'd agreed to it. We loved each other for fifteen years. I have his letters, every one, still today.'

I stood, with my nose running and tears pouring down my face, through the sweat and the tiredness.

I said, '*He didn't write you any letters. He couldn't write letters.* He was word-blind. He was a dyslectic.'

Johnson said, 'Oh, Rita, lass.'

Raymond didn't say anything. He just took a great leap towards the Cockerel and the woman, his shadow huge on the wall.

Porter shouted. The woman screamed. But no shots, as promised, thudded into her heart, or her eyes, or her stomach.

Instead, the Cockerel threw himself out of Raymond's path, dragging the woman with him and jerking up his revolver.

Johnson spoke fast. 'Rita. I may hit her.'

'Then hit her,' I said.

I saw him do it, flinging himself sideways like a man who had practised it often before, in the days when he skied, and raced beautiful ships.

The shot from the Cockerel's gun hit the wall. The shot from Johnson's gun hit Natalie's beautiful dress, and stained it all over with blood.

The masked man hesitated, but only for seconds. Then he was out of the door, and racing hard for the palms.

Where the car was. The car that Amy, we hoped, had disabled.

Behind us, someone was screaming. 'He shot her! He shot her! You son of a bitch, what did you do that for? Natalie!'

Johnson slowed. Porter, still shrieking, ran up to him and was stopped by the force of Lenny's arm. The Cockerel dashed over the path. Johnson, ignoring Porter completely, began to stumble forward again and Raymond said, 'No, Jay,' and plunged past into the palms.

I saw the outline of the disabled car under the lashing palm trees. I saw the Cockerel reach it. I saw, from the corner of my eye, Amy run from the direction of the house, her hair barred white and black by the shutters. She was shouting something.

A moment later, I saw the Toyota rocket round from where Amy had left it and screech to a halt beside the stranded car and the masked figure trying to start it.

'Jump in!' shrieked Grampa Joe from the driving seat of Amy's Toyota. 'Jump in! The bastards won't get you!'

The Cockerel looked up. We saw him hesitate. Then the next moment he had left his own car and vaulted in beside Joe Curtis, slamming the door. The Toyota roared, got into gear, and set off like a thunderbolt for the far end of the yard.

Beside me, Johnson stood still. Porter, in Lenny's grasp, had stopped shouting. Amy, withdrawing from the engine of the intruders' car, yelled, 'Are you all effing dummies? Come on! We can catch them!'

Porter said, 'Gramps?'

Raymond and Lenny had already jumped into the car, and Amy had taken the wheel. Johnson said, 'You'd better come,' abruptly to Porter, and made for it too. I paced him but he was all right, and Raymond pulled him in.

It was a big old Mercedes: Golden Memories Day. Porter and I jumped in while it was moving. The other car with the old man and the Cockerel in it had disappeared, but there was only one way to go. The wind blew and whined in the rain forest, and flung leaves in our faces, and lumps of mud, and torn flowers, and great gouts of air filled with sulphur.

Amy said, 'Who's that with Joe Curtis? In the mask?'

'His son Clive,' said Johnson.

'Then they don't know the road,' Amy said.

Porter spoke. His voice sounded quite funny. He said, 'Doesn't it go down to Soufrière? To the coast?'

Soufrière means sulphur-mine, actually. I know that now. There are lots of them. The one in St Lucia isn't an active sulphur-mine. It's a caldera, a collapsed volcanic crater. Natalie had told us all about it when she came back from her trip to Malmaison.

The St Lucia caldera is a broken grey-white shallow basin like a quarry, set in the top of a hill. The smell of sulphur is choking. The air is full of cool and warm draughts, and you have to watch where you are walking, because of scalding water trickling over the rocks. There are also, here and there, nooks of bubbling water which vary in size and even place, but puff steam hot enough to take the skin off your hand.

The first of the big pools is full of steaming pumice-grey mud, like watery porridge. On calm days it carries a boiling rosette in the middle, capped by steam plumes.

On less calm days the liquid jumps, in handfuls of grey-black gouts. The surface is dull and not shiny.

The temperature of the first pool is somewhere about 196° F. Over a high broken ridge is another, and beyond that, one so hot that steam hides it completely. In a breeze, it is best to keep away, for the steam swaying towards you can scald.

The road which leads to the caldera is a dead end.

This was the road that Grampa Joe Curtis had taken, driving his masked son to safety.

Amy followed, her eyes straining ahead in the darkness. No one spoke. Only Raymond said, 'Clive?'

And Johnson said, 'Of course. From the beginning.'

Porter didn't say anything.

The end of the road isn't exactly easy to see, or to accept. The Toyota, when we came up to it, stood on the far brink, and the cockerel mask lay where it had been chucked, when the owner went off to look for the track that didn't exist.

I didn't care about the Cockerel, I found. I looked at the grey cauldron of steam that filled the darkness beyond the lights of the Toyota, abandoned by Old Joe, and our borrowed car, where Amy sat, gripping the wheel. The men had spread out, across the road and round the slopes that would look green in the daylight.

Lenny and Raymond. Johnson and Porter. And suddenly, others.

I turned to Amy, and she pointed behind. Unheard in the wind, other cars had driven up behind us. Cars still letting out men, who ran like clockwork, lining the road and the rim of the caldera, with rifles in their hands.

Rifles.

I didn't hear what Amy was saying. I had seen the man who was giving them directions, his dark clothes hardly picked out by the car lights. I couldn't see who he was, so I listened, to hear if he was speaking Spanish.

But it was English. And the shoulder flashes of the men he was commanding, when they came round to where our car was, showed the RSLPF of the St Lucia police.

Our Indians had arrived.

Porter had seen them too. He stood outside our car, his fingers white on the window-ledge, his hair like fire in the light of the circle of cars, and watched Johnson limp over.

Porter said, 'You son of a bitch. You drove them into this trap. What did they do? Smuggle coke, you tell me. Ship out a few snorts to make some party swing better. Cheating the Customs: who doesn't? Dodging the lawmen: who doesn't? At least it makes the party go, man. It doesn't make you sick to your stomach like wet-nosed cripples who shoot women because they can't lay them ...'

He was shaking. He said, 'That's my grandfather out there. That's my uncle. You know what? I admire them.'

Johnson was looking straight out over the caldera. In the gale, the steam acted like a sort of white fire, flickering and darting and sometimes almost hidden by gushers of black that sprayed up and shuddered and fell down again anyhow.

When that happened, the line of men nearest the edge dropped unevenly back, like a ripple, until the steam eddied and cork-screwed and finally dropped down again.

I said, 'Out there? They're not in the caldera?'

And then I saw that they were. A tall figure, and one that was short and crooked and determined in the set of its shoulders, crouching a little too late when the jets of steam came; turning a little too slowly when the tall man, without his cockerel mask, took advantage of a lull to make ground from one ridge to another.

He didn't look back. You could hear the old man calling, at times, when the wind came round. And behind the steam, at the end of the caldera, was what the tall man was making for. The steep, forested slopes of the hill, where he could blend into darkness and run.

I said, 'Could he make it?'

'It's full of banks and ridges,' Johnson said. 'If he keeps clear of the mud.'

Perhaps Clive could keep clear of the black, boiling mud being sucked up and thrown by the squalls. Perhaps he could dodge the eddying steam. Perhaps he could avoid the scalding pools, and the lakes fountaining liquid at an average heat of 196°F.

But Old Joseph couldn't.

Amy said sharply, 'Rita! Where are you going?'

'Nowhere,' said Johnson. A megaphone blared, followed by a sparkle of warning rifle fire all round the crater.

Inside the bowl of the caldera the tall man stopped, half hidden in steam, and looked round. The megaphone blared again.

Surrender. Or we shoot.

For a moment, it looked as if Clive would ignore it. He looked ahead, to the dark slopes beyond the steam. To get out of rifle range he would have to run. And between him and the slopes lay the deep pools, with the steam blowing all ways in the gale.

He was no hero, Clive. He half put his hands up and turning, began crossing the crater to where the nearest line of police was.

He had left his father behind.

Johnson swore.

In the distance the tall man dropped his loud-hailer and turning towards us, seemed to be signalling something. Johnson banged once, abruptly, on the side of the car with his fist. He said, 'Watch her, Amy,' and made his way, painfully, to meet the other man.

I stood on the edge. I said to Amy, 'You know the caldera. Tell me what's safe.'

She said, 'You'll kill yourself as well as these two. Is it worth it?'

I said, 'I don't care about Clive. I don't think the old man knew a thing about this till tonight. I don't think he's any more to blame than I am.'

'You're probably right,' Amy said. 'But he chose to save Clive.'

'Then I choose to save him,' I said. 'Porter. He's your grandfather. Are you coming?'

'*There?*' said Porter. 'For that crazy old coot?'

I thought he would come, all the same, when I stepped off, but he didn't.

I didn't bother Amy any more for instructions, because I couldn't have followed them anyway, now I thought of it. Peering from one side to the other, Old Joseph seemed to have lost his grasp of where he was, or what dangers he ought to be looking for. I guessed he had got himself scalded already.

Clive had nearly got to the edge. The police had got their criminal. If Joe's grandson wasn't going to rescue him, I doubted if anyone else was.

I walked to the edge of the volcano, and set out.

The car lights lit up the near side of the crater. It shelved down in sharp crumbling ridges and hillocks, and sometimes there were tracks, with the crystals of sulphur sparkling like hard yellow frost underfoot.

After a bit, I found one of these. Then the slope gave way beneath me, and began to crumble like shale, and steam from an unseen pool lashed my leg like a whip through the cotton, warning me to jump aside.

It was all like that for a bit, or worse. When I was far in, and thought I was safe for a second I stood, my heart thumping, my breath whining, and looked across the crater.

Old Joseph had paused as well, against a billowing black and white backdrop, like the spray of a snow-plough on peatland. Except that this peat and this snow were scalding. Were hot enough to boil the flesh from your bones, if you let it.

Old Joseph turned my way a little, and I shouted.

The megaphone suddenly took up the call. I realized that it was directing Old Joe's attention to me. And that it was telling him, very slowly and clearly, how to get out of the caldera.

Also, that all the cars had now been driven up, and their lights joined in a circle of beams that lit up the steam, and me, and Joe's short, distant figure. The megaphone spoke, clearly, in Johnson's voice.

'Rita. Stay where you are. We'll get him out this way.'

With a younger man, I expect they would. A few hours ago, even Old Joseph himself would have listened, scowling, to such instructions and would have carried them out well and defiantly.

Tonight was different. Tonight, his whole view of his family had been turned upside down. Tonight he had just seen his son giving himself up to the police. Tonight he was old, and very tired, and probably already in pain. The megaphone boomed, and he tried to follow it, but he didn't succeed.

I didn't know if I could follow it, if I were standing where he was, but I could try.

I started moving again.

I had got halfway towards him by the time the bigger pools were coming close, and I had to find them and watch every flurry. The steam itself helped, white as milk in a brook, showing the swirls and the currents.

There was no way to guess how the spray would fall. The splashes pricked and bit like the sand-flies that annoyed you at Marigot, as you ate your candlelit dinner on *Dolly*'s satiny deck.

But the sand-flies didn't leave blisters, or the breeze from the frangipani thrust your nose and throat full of dry sulphur, so strong and so choking that breathing was like inhaling a pepper-pot.

I caught a bad gush just after that: a ladleful of bubbling grey custard that draped my shoulder and sank into the skin, even though I tore the thin cotton straight down from the neck.

The booming of the megaphone was an enemy as well as an anxiety. I needed my ears, to hear the warning cluck of the mud, and the change in tone of the wind. I saw Joseph had stopped, and was neither looking about him, nor paying attention to what he was being told.

The megaphone noticed it too. After a pause, it addressed me instead.

This time, it didn't try to tell me to stand still, or how to get to Joe, or how to take myself back to the rim. It just said, in a new voice; a voice I didn't know:

Rita. There is a ridge on your right, with a hollow behind it. Get there quickly.

To my right.

The megaphone said, *Towards me.*

I turned towards the sound, and I jumped, and I rolled to the bottom of a hot, gritty dip that was not full of boiling liquid, so that it was the correct right.

As I jumped, I saw Old Joe still standing. I think I yelled at him to lie down, but of course a voice wouldn't carry, and in any case it might have been the wrong thing, otherwise they would have told him.

They hadn't told him to do anything.

It wasn't that they didn't care. I had heard them trying.

It must be that there wasn't anything that would help.

Which was right, of course.

A second later the squall hit that they'd had warning of, and churned round the big pool of boiling grey mud like a butter paddle, and lifted it into the air.

I saw it come. I saw it arch like a tongue over the spot where Old Joseph was standing, the friend of Louis B. Mayer, the confidant of the Warner Brothers, and begin to fall.

I put my head in my arms and heard it spattering, too, on the other side of the ridge where I'd been standing.

It didn't hit me.

After a while, the megaphone started again.

The new voice said, 'Rita? Stand up if you can.'

I stood up, and turned to where Joe Curtis had been standing, and there was nothing there.

After a bit, I turned the other way, and faced the necklace of car lights round the rim.

The voice said, 'He's gone, Rita. Now we want you out fast. Listen, do what I tell you, and hurry. Now. There's a hot pool three steps my way. Take three steps instead straight ahead. Now four steps away from me. Right? Now another four towards me and stop. Wait. Right.'

I waited.

To me. Away from me.

Right. And left.

Someone who knew the crater, and had a map, and binoculars, and a lot of briefing about Rita Geddes.

I didn't wait long, and then the megaphone produced another burst of directions, another pause, and even at one point some questions which I answered by waving my arms.

He made one mistake, and I got splashed, but only a little. By the end, I was mostly out of the steam and it was just a case of climbing uphill.

It was a nuisance, climbing the soft grit, and I stumbled a lot, and wasn't helped very much by the glare of the lights just above me. When there was no more use for it the megaphone stopped, and instead the speaker's ordinary voice, just above me, said, 'That's a tough slope. You're in all the rubble. It's better this way. Over to me.'

He came down and helped me the last yard or two, his binoculars banging my shoulder, but I didn't actually see who he was, because when I got to the top, I appeared to pass out.

I woke as they carried me into Amy's house.

I was no longer in my borrowed pants and ripped top, but in a man's shirt and what seemed to be someone's loose overalls.

I had, what's more, been in the hands of a party who knew his medical stuff. I was covered in ointment and bandages.

Under them, my shoulder felt pretty awful, and my skin seemed to have caught fire all over, including my face. My lips wouldn't work. The sulphur I'd been inhaling seemed to have stuffed my head to twice its normal size and my lids felt thick and swollen.

I had an impression of passing a police van already parked in the yard, and seeing lights in the storeroom where the cocaine was, and where the shootings had happened.

I also had an impression of Porter's voice in a squabble, but I couldn't make out what about.

Then Raymond laid me down on the sitting-room sofa, and Amy brought in a thing like a vet's bag which probably was a vet's bag, and prepared to check over the results of the journey.

When I opened my eyes, she seemed to be pleased, and so did Raymond and Johnson, who stopped murmuring together and came over and looked at me.

Johnson's glasses were cordial. He said, 'You look like a mock-up for an onion, but you're going to be fine. Join the club. Any club you want to join would be proud to have you.'

'Hear, hear,' said Raymond. 'They clapped as you climbed out of the crater. The whole island would be agog, poor sods, if they hadn't to deal with this bloody visitation.

'We've had a ham message through three relays from Maggie, stuck all night at the airport. She and Ferdy weathered it all out together.

'They're O.K. Total frenzy of excitement and frustration because she missed everything. Other garbled greetings to you. Wants to start up a meaningful Lesbian relationship, if I got the French patois right.'

He wasn't tight. It was just the kind of relief Ferdy gets after his P.M.T. sessions.

I was terribly glad about Ferdy, and quite glad about Maggie, but not much about anything else. Johnson said, 'Amy, what about brandy?'

'There it is,' Amy said. 'What there is of it. I'm going to take this lady off to bed.'

'But a drink first,' Johnson said.

I looked up.

He said, 'A lot has happened. We should talk about it.'

Amy said, 'Can't it wait? What's that effing banging? Where's Lenny?'

On cue, the sitting-room door opened, and Lenny's head came in.

He smiled at me, and I smiled back, painfully. He said, 'Mrs Faflick ... Mrs Sheridan's maid.'

He didn't get any further, because he was pushed aside by the person he was talking about. Dodo strode in.

We all looked at her, and I heard Porter draw in his breath.

She looked the same as she had when she had come to report that Natalie had vanished. She looked unslept and rather cross and rather worried and extremely surprised as she looked at the sofa and saw me.

She said, 'My good Lord, you bin scalded, girl?'

The hostile stare moved to Amy. 'You-all lock your guests up when you go out? But for that Porter I might still be with those animals.'

Johnson said, 'You didn't go out, Miss Dora?'

Dora. I never knew that was her name.

She stared at him. 'In that storm?' she said.

Of all the events of the night, she had heard nothing.

I wondered how they were going to tell her. I saw Porter wondering the same thing, and realized suddenly what was going to happen.

It happened. Porter said, 'You missed something, *Miss Dora*. You missed the shooting-match along near the yard there. You missed seeing Johnson shoot and kill Mrs Sheridan.'

'Miz Sheridan?' Dodo said.

'Yes?' said a charming, effectively-pitched voice from the doorway behind her.

Dodo moved to one side.

Natalie stood on the threshold. Her golden hair was a little ruffled, and the dress she wore was not her own but one I guessed Dodo had found in Amy's room.

But the well-photographed face was the same, and the smile, and the large violet eyes sweeping the room, and finally dwelling on me.

'Oh, dear. Poor girl,' she said. 'Has she pulled the kettle over?'

Johnson was watching Porter, and so was I.

Natalie was alive.

We saw Porter work out what that meant, the thoughts crossing his handsome face one by one.

The woman Johnson had shot, the woman whom Clive Curtis had tried to make us believe was his hostage, had not been Natalie Sheridan. It had been someone made up to look like her.

Someone wearing a make-up so perfect that we had all been taken in. All except Grampa Joe, the oldest hand in the trade, who had seen the face from outside and recognized it.

And who, from that, had known at once that the cockerel mask must hide Clive.

You could see Porter's thoughts reach that point and then boggle.

And you could see him begin to realize, slowly and finally, who the woman with Clive and Roger van Diemen had been.

Porter turned to Johnson. He said, '*You shot my mother.*'

He began talking in short, howling breaths. 'You turned your gun on my mother. But for you and your ridiculous tart, she would be alive. My uncle would have gone on with his career. My grandfather would have kept the *Paramount Princess*, and he would never have known. He'd never have gone to that damned volcano. He'd never have died that disgusting death ...'

His face was all spoiled with amazement and fury and venom. There was no sorrow in it.

He said, 'A famous old man. Everyone knew him. Everyone had heard of him. And now, because of your Mickey Mouse conscience, Joseph Curtis can't even be buried. I watched my grandfather boil to death in that cauldron tonight.'

'So you did,' Johnson said. I have never heard such chilly dislike in anyone's voice.

'So you did, you squalid, unmentionable brat. You stood still and watched him without lifting a finger. He would be alive now, and so would your mother, if you had kept your mouth shut when you were told to.'

Porter started to speak. Johnson's voice splintered his words like an ice-pick.

'And if you found your grandfather's end horrifying, spare a thought, won't you, for Rita? She had to stand inside the crater, inside the cauldron, inside that hellish place.

'She had to stand there and watch, as you did, your grandfather boil to death, as you so graphically put it.

'Except that he wasn't Rita's grandfather. He was her father.'

22

'Rita's father? *Joe Curtis?*' Natalie said.

Her amazement was absolutely genuine.

She stared at me, seeing me, and then not seeing me, as the rest of what we had been saying took hold in her mind.

Then the amazement faded, and in its place came the look I now knew well. The look of the clever woman. The political observer. The syndicated journalist.

Natalie sat down gracefully, as was her habit. She crossed her ankles and, smoothing the terrible dress she had on, folded her hands equally gracefully in her lap. Then she looked at us.

'Put me in the picture,' she said.

Johnson left Raymond to tell her. While he did, Amy found a half-bottle of brandy, which she handed to Johnson before seating herself, and Johnson gave me half of it immediately, in a very large tumbler. Then he took a chair at my side, rather carefully.

I drank quite a lot of it quite quickly, and didn't listen too hard to what Raymond was saying. I hadn't got used, yet, to what I'd lost. What I'd never had, anyway.

I suppose Raymond knew it. He gave only the barest bones of the story, beginning with the boarding of *Dolly* and the lining of her bilges with dope, which the Customs had discovered in Marigot.

I didn't know they had discovered it. I thought Amy had. But he went quickly on, and ended with Clive and Sharon finding a temporary home for the dope in Amy's place, thinking her in Castries, or safely indoors in the storm.

Halfway through, I realized that Natalie didn't know yet that Roger van Diemen was dead. I wondered what she would say, and what capital Porter would make of it all.

But Raymond had thought of that. He didn't go back to Natalie's affair with van Diemen. He left out Coombe's altogether, and just said that there had been another man helping Clive, and that he had been shot dead.

Later, no doubt, someone would break the news to her. She would probably be quite relieved. And then, when she thought of the publicity, she wouldn't.

All through, I could see Porter walking about, and picking up things, and putting them down with a thud, even though Natalie wasn't looking at him. The police had been quite satisfied that Porter and his grandfather didn't know of the smuggling. Raymond had told Natalie all that as well.

She wouldn't forget, either. You could see the computer brain, filing and docketing. She hadn't forgotten what Johnson had last said, either.

She looked with sympathy at me, and said helpfully, 'And Rita was part of the family? How does she come into it?'

'She doesn't,' said Porter. He walked past Dodo and Lenny and Raymond, and found a dog dish at his feet and flip-kicked it out of his way. It broke neatly, and he watched it with satisfaction.

Then he looked at me and flashed his perfect, spaced teeth.

'You spinning some tale that Old Joe was your *father*?' he said. 'Boy, the lawyers'll have some fun with that. Pity the old man isn't here to take you to pieces himself.'

He received, full front, the Owner bifocals.

'The famous old man?' Johnson said. 'Whose reputation you found so handy? Or the crazy old coot you weren't going to risk your skin for? Whichever it was, I'd like to see his lawyers try. They'll get a shock.

'Rita is Joe's legitimate daughter. Her parents were your grandparents. Your mother Sharon was her full sister. Your uncle Clive is her brother. So was your other uncle Kim-Jim, who died on Madeira.'

Natalie looked surprised. Natalie said, 'I always rather thought Kim-Jim was her father.'

Sitting there, wearing Amy's terrible dress, she still looked alert, and sociable, and intelligent. But when the coldness in Johnson's face didn't alter, moving from Porter to her, I saw her eyes narrow and open again.

'If you did, I must say you concealed it very cleverly when Kim-Jim was found dead,' Johnson said. 'He was her full brother. As I'm sure you noticed, they were both dyslectic. And their colouring was the same. Rita, may I?'

He was indicating my filthy Bird of Paradise hair.

I had nothing to lose, the way I was looking. I took my wig off myself. Underneath, my cropped hair was still white at the ends. At the roots, the natural red had begun to grow in.

I have the skin to go with it. I always try to wear hats and cover myself up in sunshine, or else I blister.

Blister. My God.

Johnson went on telling them about the Curtises and I let him, because he was really telling me. Standing outside all the emotion and telling the straight facts, as they were, to let me see them.

Since this evening, I knew that he knew. Since Sharon made her mistake, and he saw me recognize her, and asked me, in four words, for permission to shoot.

He said, 'What's the age difference, Rita? More than twenty years between you and Kim-Jim? Less between you and Sharon, who was born at the very end of the Second World War.

'Robina must have been in her mid-thirties then, and everyone thought, including herself, that she had completed her family with these three children: Clive, and Kim-Jim, and Sharon.'

'Colin, and Kenneth James, and Robina. Sharon was called Robina, after my mother,' I said. 'They all changed their names in Hollywood.'

'After your father made himself a great name in the new movie industry,' Johnson said. 'After the money began to come in, and the keeping up with the M.G.M.s, and the pretty ruthless ambition. You didn't think much of your grandfather, Porter. But all that vulgar display was just a show of pride, because he'd risen from nothing.'

'Barnum and Bailey,' said Porter. He walked across to the brandy bottle, lifted it, and emptied it into a glass for himself. His hand was shaking. 'Happens in the best families,' he said. 'What sort of bums did you have for parents? House painters?'

'Don't be childish,' said Natalie. 'Amy, is that all the brandy you keep in the house? I think we have all had a trying time. Although, of course, this is fascinating.'

Amy looked at her. 'Glad you think so,' she said. 'Always try to put on an effing cabaret. When this is over, you can have some tea, if you want it. Meantime, I think you should effing shut up.'

Down, Fido. Back to the kennels.

Natalie's expression was one of controlled patience, but her foot tapped. Johnson, rearranging his position, didn't pay any attention to either of them.

I held out my brandy glass until he noticed, and looked at me, and then borrowed it, saluting me mildly.

I had seen him do that once before, when Ferdy had made a joke I hadn't followed. It was different now, since I'd begun travelling. I took the glass back. He had left quite a lot. I said, 'Next chapter?'

'Next chapter,' Johnson agreed. He still looked rather rotten. He went on.

'The trouble was, that Joseph's family had grown up accustomed to plenty, so that when the old man's work slackened off, and there was more competition, and their tastes needed more and more money, they began to cast around for other ways of making the fast buck or bucks.

'Hence dope. Hence a number of other dubious things. Their mother, Robina, saw the way things were going and tried to stop it in the early stages, but couldn't. Her husband simply didn't care. He had lost all interest in his family. He wanted to be accepted as the big man, and recognized. He expected his children to make a splash, impress people, throw money about, get their names in the papers.

'Robina couldn't do anything about it. She hated the life. She left, and came back to Scotland, and divorced Joe, and married someone else, a schoolmaster called Gordon Geddes.

'Two of the three children she left behind in America were fully grown-up. The third, now called Sharon, was seven or eight.

'Sharon never forgave her mother for leaving her. Old Joseph never forgave her for wrecking the great public image. He never wrote to her again. He never saw her again. So when Robina arrived in Scotland and found that, in her early forties, she was pregnant again, she didn't send to tell Joe that they were to have a fourth child.

'Rita was born in Scotland, and Gordon Geddes, her step-father, became known as her father. When she was old enough, her mother told her the truth, so that she could decide for herself whether to make herself known to the rest of the family.

'Rita's reaction was to take her mother's part. Her step-father was, I think, a good man, though strict; and of course he couldn't understand Rita's word-blindness. Nor could the schools of that time. Until recently, it simply wasn't recognized. He just thought her stupid, which she most emphatically is not.

'So, academic training being out of her reach, she turned to the thing that was in her blood. Show business, or the branch of it that the family did best of all. She became what she is, a superb make-up artist.

'Her step-father hated it. It's a pity, perhaps, that he died before she got to where she is now, on the verge of making it to the very top. She would have got there long before now except that she had given herself an embargo. She would never move out of Britain. She would never go where she might meet and compete with the Curtises.'

'It's quite a case history,' Natalie said. She was listening with real attention. I could see the syndicated articles fattening up inside her clever mind

She considered further. 'So Rita stayed in Britain until she went to work on a joint-production film, and came across Kim-Jim, her brother. Of course And was Kim-Jim in the drugs business?'

So clever. So stupid.

Johnson said, 'Don't you really know what he was like, after all these years? Rita knew who he was. After hearing her mother, she probably expected a monster. After the kind of beastly childhood she'd had, she didn't trust people much anyway. All that, Kim-Jim overcame simply by being a genuine, decent, rather simple man, who had the same disability she had.

'You knew what it was, although his family didn't. He was dyslectic. It runs in families.'

'My mother, too,' I said.

All the T.V. sets. All the video tapes. We were experts on old films, in my family.

'So that was the first bond,' Johnson said. 'But you liked each other from the start. You kept in touch. You couldn't write to each other, but you exchanged tapes. And then, when he knew he was ill, and not going to get better, Kim-Jim wrote and told you that he was thinking of retiring, and suggested that he should arrange for you and Natalie to meet, and work together.'

'Bloody traitor,' said Porter. 'There's a car.'

I didn't want to know about cars.

There had been movement outside since we came in, as the police worked in the storeroom and yard. I thought of them unloading, laboriously, all those bags of cocaine. I had tried not to think of the stretchers coming out of the jeep, and my sister Sharon being carried away, and Roger van Diemen.

Clive was the only one left untouched, somewhere in a prison in Castries. Like the survivor of the Martinique earthquake. About to hit the news, a freak for the rest of his life.

Clive, and me, and Porter. A great monument to Old Joe.

Johnson flicked my hand. 'Let it be,' he said. 'Look who's come, and look what they've brought.'

And when I turned my head towards the bustle at the door, I saw it was Maggie, laden with bottles, her Vidal haircut stuck to her skull with fright and salt, and her eyes beaming.

And Ferdy behind her, his arm in a sling, and flapping a large square of cardboard. A large square which, reversed, turned out to be a ravishing photograph, in colour, of a small fat bird with this great fancy tail.

'Bird of Paradise, darling!' he said. 'Forgot to give it to you. My God, nearly never got the chance. Dear Jesus, what the hell have you done to your hair?'

Ferdy was back.

And after that, it was great, because Amy went and got all the food she and I had made while the others were resting, and Raymond opened all the new bottles and told the story all over again, and Porter, because he was forgotten, managed to give his temper a rest, and settled down to drinking himself steadily senseless.

Natalie got her drink first. She had quite a good story to tell, of how she had been stripped of her dress and left outside in the darkness, so that Clive and Sharon could create themselves the perfect non-existent hostage.

She hadn't seen who they were. Remembering Dodo and the ham radio, she had got herself taken directly to Amy's.

She didn't thank Ferdy for the drink, which wasn't surprising considering the explosion when he'd left her because of me.

From the moment he and Maggie had come in, Natalie had been restless.

She sent Dodo outside to ask the police if they had a transmitter. She inquired of Amy when the telephones usually came back into service and badgered her several times into sending messages on the ham radio. She tried, and failed, to persuade the emergency centre to put her in touch with New York via the Miami Hurricane Centre.

Hurricane centres having, naturally, other things on their minds, she continued to get the brush-off, to her annoyance.

It was, of all people, Dodo who at this point stared Johnson in the bifocals and said, 'You were going to tell us. How the girl and Mr Curtis moved in on Miz Natalie.'

Then Ferdy said, 'What?' and all eight of them, from their various positions of sloth, looked at Johnson, who had stayed rather rooted in the chair next to me, while I still reclined on my couch like Not Tonight Josephine.

Without whom none of us would have been there.

Jinx Josie. Compared with us, Napoleon was laughing.

'Are you sitting comfortably?' said Johnson. 'O.K. The rest of the tale about Rita.'

Public school people are great exclaimers. From the moment Johnson fed them the compressed story of the Curtis family and my mother, Ferdy and Maggie formed a most satisfactory audience of two, alternately whistling or yodelling and sometimes saying the same thing together.

Maggie said, 'It's *the* sensation. So Kim-Jim asks Ferdy to use Rita for this commission he's got to photograph Natalie. And as a result, Natalie offers Rita a temporary job, and then makes it permanent. And all the time poor Kim-Jim knows he's going to pop, and that Rita will be left with a nice job, and lots of contacts and no more hang-ups about going abroad. You should see *my* bloody brother.'

Amy got up from picking bits of meat off the carpet round the dog bowls. She said, 'But you hadn't told him, I thought, who you were?'

I hadn't told him who I was. He didn't know who I was, I would swear it, all the time we were working together, and later, when we exchanged all the tapes. All the tapes about work.

And then, I had begun to wonder. And after the legacy, of course, I was sure.

I said, 'He found out, I think. He never said. The thing is, he was quite keen on families, although he'd cut himself off from his own. He'd sort of placed me where I could meet the other Curtises if I wanted, and make up my own mind. He never talked about them.'

Ferdy said, 'He was a gentleman, Kenneth James. Never gossiped about anyone. Natalie thought he was your father: bloody rubbish. Brought him back from Lisbon to cope with you when she thought some funny stuff was going on. I should think he would detest his family. Probably guessed what they were up to.'

I said, 'No. Or he would never have brought me over.'

Natalie caught Dodo's eye and sat up.

She didn't look sympathetic any more. She had got her story. And she owed Johnson quite a few digs.

'Well,' she said. 'It is, I must admit, a new experience. To discover oneself the gullible centre of a neat family conspiracy to arrange soft living and a fair amount in wages — what did I pay you the other day, Rita? A thousand pounds? — between brother and sister.'

She surveyed us all coolly, ending with Johnson.

'Not to mention between sister and Ferdy. How much of the thousand pounds went into that rather tight pocket, I wonder? How lucky that the Josephine film is not to have the benefit of your joint attention.'

Ferdy stood up. He said, 'Natalie, old lady, it sounds like sour grapes.

Rita's done great things today. You don't want to appear in the gossip columns as the world's most beautiful bitch. You keep quiet, and we won't tell on you.'

Natalie lay back and looked at him. 'Oh dear,' she said. 'Of course. She's an heiress now. Having benefited hugely from her brother's death, and now, one supposes, from her father's. Doesn't Maggie object?'

They stared at one another. My head throbbed and buzzed. I wished I were somewhere else. In Glasgow. In Troon. With Napoleon.

I shut my eyes.

Johnson's voice said, 'Are we stranded, Amy? Or can we get transport back to Hurricane Hole?'

The dog at Amy's feet stirred, and she rubbed its ears.

'We're stranded,' she said. 'The police won't let anyone leave.'

'Pity,' said Johnson. 'You mentioned a cabaret?'

'I did,' said Amy drily. 'Can't tell you how to stop a fight, though. Unless you want to watch some video. There's a set.'

'I suppose,' said Natalie, 'there inevitably is. But need we see it?'

I opened my eyes.

'Vote from Rita,' said Johnson. 'And considering everything, a casting vote. Suppose we all stop talking and let her relax. Amy, what have you got?'

What she had, we discovered, was four cassettes of the Ty-Phoo Chimps, one of the Guinness Toucan, and a very old film of Tom Mix.

It was a very small T.V. set, and it took some time to connect it. Eventually, Tom Mix flickered on to the screen.

Porter was already asleep. Dodo followed. In turn, Ferdy, Raymond and Maggie slumped in their seats.

Natalie's anger and frustration kept her awake longer. Then slowly, the self-applied eyelashes dropped and her nicely drawn mouth fell slightly open.

Johnson's glasses remained vertical, though his face was much the same yellow-grey as the caldera. He said, 'Amy?'

She jumped. 'Christ!' she said. 'The effing bird'll be missing it.'

She got up, groggily, and went out.

The room wheezed with heavy breathing, and the sound of the wind outside the shutters. Johnson said, 'Are you all right?'

I had been watching Tom Mix, with concrete on my eyelids, but I looked at him, and stayed looking. I said, 'I'm all right. What about you?'

'Nearly finished,' he said. 'Trust me if you can.'

He paused, and said, 'Amy and I exchanged a few coarse words a while ago. She overruled me about letting you go after your father. I gather she classes you roughly somewhere between a chimpanzee and a jaguar. Thought you'd like to know.'

'I knew,' I said. I knew they had been anxious about me. I knew they had hoped to lead Old Joe out without risking lives. I said, 'It's O.K.'

'It's not, very,' said Johnson. 'Especially as I have something else to ask. Will you do something for me?'

I could hardly hear him. I meant to say, 'What?'

I said, 'Yes.'

'Will you remember, then,' said Johnson, 'that there is no such person as Roger van Diemen?'

I only had time for a nod. Then Amy came back, and he turned to her.

On her shoulder was a green St Lucia parrot, with a bright eye in a brilliant blue head.

It was nearly midnight. After a long and terrible day, the lines on her sunken face were like the graining on teak, and her cropped white hair was limp.

The parrot, hyped by the light and the company, was bright-eyed as a drunk, and as talkative.

Travelling across to its stand, where Amy chained it, the raucous Californian voice drowned out Tom Mix.

'*Pieces of eight! Pieces of eight! You get that damned dialogue wrong once more and you can take your ass right over to Disney,*' the parrot said.

Natalie opened her eyes.

'*Mr Christian!*' said the parrot. '*Effing bread-fruit for breakfast again!*'

Raymond, Dodo and Maggie opened their eyes.

'*Bugger the bitch!*' said the parrot slily, in Ferdy's voice.

'*Cohn!*' I said.

Ferdy opened his eyes. He sat up. He said, 'My darling Toucan. You've never traded the Ziegfeld Parrot of 1933 for hard bleeding cash. Is it Cohn?'

'Mind your own effing business,' said Amy placidly. 'What Rita chooses to do with her legacy is her own effing affair. Lay golden eggs, do these birds.'

Ferdy's eyes gleamed. 'It's too old, darling,' he said. 'Check it out, do, or you'll give the poor thing a stroke. I'll bet you it rewinds all the way back to *The Jazz Singer*. To Edison. To Bell.'

I was tired, and I was fed up, and I didn't want to think about Cohn. I said, 'Do you mind? I'm trying to watch the film.'

'Sweetheart,' said Ferdy, 'it's your day. It's your party. I am now shutting up.'

He was nice. It would have been fine, except that the telephone rang.

It rang twice, and cut off.

It was enough for Natalie.

She sat instantly, calling for Amy. 'The system's connected again! You don't mind if I make a few calls?'

The telephone system might have come back to life, but Tom Mix had disappeared into a haze.

It didn't come back. I lay there like the dogs and the parrots and the snakes and Natalie and said, 'Amy!'

Amy was swearing into the telephone, and drumming her hand on the rest. She said, 'Nope. There's no sound on the wire. No effing dice, Mrs Sheridan. O.K., Rita, what's your worry?'

I explained dopily, wishing I hadn't mentioned it.

Amy was undisturbed.

'*Cohn!*' she yelled.

Everyone who had been asleep woke up.

The parrot fixed her with an uneasy eye, looked away, and then gurgled under its breath, scraping a claw on its perch.

Tom Mix suddenly returned.

'It's a miracle,' said Johnson, with interest.

'Bloody parrot,' said Amy.

I felt suddenly cold, which in that heat was practically frightening. I said, 'What's the parrot to do with it?'

Natalie said, 'If it's Cohn, Kim-Jim taught it to watch all these films. You remember. It talks all the time.'

'Sure effing does,' Amy said. 'Switches the programmes all the time, too. Every time the effing phone rings.'

'What?' I said.

Maggie was listening too, and Raymond, and Dodo and Natalie, turning round with the telephone still stuck vainly in her ear.

'*And* calls the effing dogs,' Amy continued. 'Ultrasonic sound. Parrots have it. Imitate the sounds you can't hear on the T.V. control pad. Change the effing programme.'

'When the telephone rings twice,' I said.

I had the full attention of Johnson's bifocals.

'Explain,' he said.

I said, 'It doesn't matter. It reminded me of something.'

Raymond said, 'Rita. It does matter. You look terrible. What?'

They were all looking at me. This couldn't be what Johnson meant.

This could be what Johnson meant.

I said, 'It reminded me of the night Kim-Jim died in Madeira. He was watching video in his study. I passed his door, and heard the telephone ring twice. Then he turned the video off while he answered it. That's how we knew he was still alive long after everyone had gone. That's how the police were sure it was suicide.'

Maggie said, 'But we know it was suicide. The gun, the wound and everything. He had cancer. The only person around was you, and my God, you're his sister.'

Ferdy said, 'Wait a minute. What you're saying, Rita, is that it was the *parrot* that switched off the video?'

'We've just seen him do it,' I said.

Ferdy stared at me, thinking, and nursing his bad shoulder absently. 'Consider, then, children,' he said.

'Bird responds to telephone ring, and puts the video off. Poor old K-J doesn't put it on again, so is presumed done for. Call unimportant: could be a ring-through of the one I made to what's-his-name ... Aurelio, to tell him we were getting a free ride home. But still doesn't help very much. Guy was alive when I left him, and dead by the time the phone rang.'

'It doesn't help at all really,' Johnson said. 'Except, of course, that if Kim-Jim were murdered, it shows us what time the murderer wanted his alibi for.'

Maggie said, 'Look. We've had enough killings tonight. Kim-Jim wasn't murdered. The police said so.'

Johnson said, 'But look what we've found out since then about the Curtis family. The police might think it well worth while now to have another look. Think of all the new possible motives. Revenge by someone who thought Kim-Jim was in the drugs business. Execution by someone who thought he knew too much and might give away his own family. A murder of passion, over Natalie. A murder for gain, by someone with designs on Rita.

'It's only an idle thought, but so many of the principals are dead now, that it might be quite easy to find someone who is willing to talk, now that he knows there's no one around to make him pay for it.'

Maggie said, 'But it doesn't alter the facts. Rita's brother was alive when we all left. The house was locked. The kitchen people were in each other's company all the time. And the only person roaming about after was Rita.'

'That is true,' Dodo said. 'The girl came home early. The play was still on. The Queen Elizabeth play in the study.'

'*My name is Bond. James Bond,*' said the parrot. It let off a lot of gunfire and added, in a strong American accent, '*I guess there's just you and me left.*'

It was beastly. I said, 'It said that as we were leaving. As we left Kim-Jim to come to your party.'

'Did it?' said Johnson. 'With the gunfire?'

Maggie said, 'Well, what's that to do with it? That's rifle fire your star-struck little green friend has just come out with. The thing that killed Kim-Jim would produce one single bang, I suppose. Or pop. Or whatever.'

'I think,' said Natalie, 'the point Johnson is making is that the parrot may have produced its gunfire sounds after being triggered off, so to speak, by a real one. Is it possible?'

'I don't know,' said Ferdy. 'No gunfire in Queen Elizabeth's day, unless they'd got to Plymouth Hoe. Talking of Spaniards, did anyone ever track down the filthy dozen who did down *Dolly*? My shoulder and I would like to meet them.'

'Not yet,' Raymond said. 'Being smugglers by trade, they're a bit elusive. They're maybe even a bit dead, if the Curtis family wanted it that way. But they've found the first step in the chain. The place where the dope was loaded into the Dozen's boat by Clive Curtis's other partner.'

Natalie said, 'Other partner? Who? Where was this?'

'Oh, let's leave it,' said Johnson. 'They only got half the story before the wires went. Once the storm's fully over, we'll hear it all. And the police say that now his sister is dead, Clive seems quite keen to talk.'

Natalie said, 'So they don't know who the man is in Colombia?'

'Not in Colombia,' Johnson said. 'Or maybe originally. But the boat that attacked *Dolly* had loaded the dope in Tobago. You didn't see them, Ferdy?'

Raymond grinned. 'I bet he's glad he didn't,' he said. 'Or it might have been Good night Ferdy, like it was Good night Kim-Jim.'

'*Good night,*' said Kim-Jim's voice.

It was fairly horrible. It was such a good imitation that we turned round.

The parrot liked that. He clucked and bobbed, and then gave a repeat performance.

'*Good night,*' said Kim-Jim's voice again. '*Have yourself a good time. Don't do anything I wouldn't do.*'

Everyone avoided looking at me. Ferdy got up and stretched. I looked at Johnson.

I said, 'Those are Kim-Jim's last words. I told you at the time. Those are the exact words Kim-Jim said to Ferdy as we left for your party. And Ferdy said, "I have news for you. Tonight, old boy, you are enlarging your scope. See you tomorrow."'

Natalie said, 'But how could the parrot ...?'

'From the tape,' said Johnson. 'The tape Ferdy faked up, to make you think Kim-Jim was alive, when he'd just killed him. They'll produce it in court. They'll also produce Carl Thomassen. The fourth man at the Brighton Beach Hotel. He's just been arrested at the airport, Ferdy. Give up. Give up.'

'Would you?' said Ferdy. 'That's a bloody insult, old boy. Braithwaites never give up. Ask the family. Graveyard's full of them.'

Because he hadn't been running about volcanoes, he was the freshest of us all, in spite of his wounded shoulder and his sling.

His bald head always made you think he was old, but he walked and ran and everything like a dancer. And was good at kissing. And would take No for an answer, after a struggle.

He had a revolver, and his back to the door.

'What a shame,' he said. 'It was such a nice, *well-paying* business. I mean, sexy flowers are all very well, but it palls.

'Natalie, hang on to that girl. She's got your nose licked.

'Maggie, you've got a technique worth millions. Stop showing it to millions.

'Rita, my Scotch Bird of Paradise, don't trust anybody. Especially not that low-geared, witty, implacable bastard, my friend over there ...

'Good-bye, J.J. It's been nice knowing you, but expensive. If Frances Emerson hadn't offered me your studio, I suppose I'd be a millionaire and you'd be wining and dining, a drunken self-pitying ruin, in some expensive harbour on *Dolly* ...

'Actually,' Ferdy said, 'I'm sorry about *Dolly*. I hope that collection of wogs has duly been crucified. They weren't meant to wreck your little ship. Or lose their tempers with you. Or bloody lose the place and drill me instead of one of the others ... You knew, I suppose, from the way that they kicked you, that someone close to you was behind it.'

'Yes,' said Johnson. He had pulled himself upright. He was full in the sights of Ferdy's revolver.

Ferdy said, 'Once you would have paid me to do this.'

I didn't know what he meant, but I saw Raymond's face, and the fear on it.

Johnson said, 'Actually, no. But as you say, we both go back a long time. So it's your choice. Gold watch for long service.'

There was a silence. No one moved. No one spoke.

Then Ferdy said, 'You're a bloody unfair bastard. I ought to take you at your word. Tell your little bottom-wipers there not to trust you. That this is what you do. That this is why you live while everyone else round about you gets theirs ...

'Have yourself a good time, my dear friend Johnson Johnson,' said Ferdy, with a sudden, terrible smile. 'For tonight, sure as death, I am enlarging your scope for you.'

He waved with his gun, and went; and Raymond, starting to his feet, dropped into his chair again after one brittle glance from the Owner.

A moment later, we heard the gun fire.

Natalie said, 'You knew he would do that? How did you know?'

'Sexual strategy of bloody human beings,' Maggie said. She was crying. 'And it bloody stinks.'

An hour or two after that, a car came to take Natalie and Dodo to a hotel, from which they were to fly to Miami as soon as the airport opened in the morning.

Fred Gluttenmacher, comfortably asleep all night on board the *Paramount Princess* and, apart from three hookers, the sole object of attention of its entire crew since the storm began, was to join her there and fly with her, discussing on the way what to do about replacing the co-producer of *Josephine*.

Before that, both Natalie and Dodo had been subjected to a short pep-talk by a senior police representative, in which I gathered it was made clear that, there being some sensitive areas on both sides of the case, if she didn't publicize theirs, they wouldn't publicize hers.

Or so Johnson said. He was there while Natalie said good-bye to me.

She still didn't care for me, but her computer-brain, which had hardly registered me except, as Ferdy had dog-nosed, as a show-piccaninny, was full of relevant information now.

She had seen both my cropped hair and my wig. No doubt she drew her own conclusions. She knew about my link with the Curtises, but also that the authorities, for their own reasons, would rather it didn't get about.

She had promised to keep it quiet, and I thought she would. Natalie never gossiped. She had enough power. She didn't need to.

She had style, as well. She would have offered me that post again, if I had wanted it. The post Kim-Jim wanted me to have, that she thought was above me. The work on the film that she'd passed to Clive Curtis.

She didn't, for the opposite reason. I didn't like her, but I appreciated that. And I wished her well for her film, although I wouldn't go to see it.

At the last moment, Amy found Porter on the floor, and loaded him into the car as well, with the consent of the police. Tomorrow, the hangover and the funeral arrangements. The next day, not even Porter knew what.

Everything hurt. Thinking hurt. Raymond, Maggie and Johnson, deep in their chairs, didn't talk even to each other and neither did Amy, treading heavy-footed among us, preparing to send us to bed.

When she took the parrot out, I said, 'Will you keep Cohn?'

She looked at Johnson.

He looked weary to death. He said, 'It isn't Cohn.'

I should have known, if I'd thought. I said, 'Amy trained it?'

It would have been easy. All they needed to do was tape the real Cohn, and play it over and over for one of Amy's St Lucians.

They could even have put together, from Kim-Jim's tapes, a duplicate of those last words he was supposed to have spoken to Ferdy. And hearing them, Ferdy would assume he was trapped.

Raymond had been at Faflick's in England, as I had been. Maybe spying on me. Maybe because Johnson had spotted, as I had spotted, that the parrot had something to do with the time Kim-Jim died.

Because two rings of the telephone must have been a signal, not a call which Kim-Jim answered. The telephone was not beside his chair. With the telly on, it would have taken him the length of at least one ring to hear it.

And by the time he switched the telly off and got to the phone, there would have been several rings more.

But I hadn't known that it was Ferdy the alibi was for.

Ferdy, who had been a victim, as I had, of the sledge-run, and who had barely escaped with his life on board *Dolly*.

But who had killed Kim-Jim, it seemed. Who was the man I had sworn to follow and find. Whose death, by his own hand, was in the end worse than the death of my own father and sister, because still, in my mind, he was my joyous friend, of whom I was proud.

How can you know whom to trust?

I fell asleep, and got covered up somehow. Much later, a voice I had heard somewhere before said, 'Don't wake her. Ah, she's stirring. Let's have a look, then.'

It was daylight. 'Well, young lady,' said a man I had certainly seen somewhere before. 'You seem to be making very good progress. Just let me look at this shoulder once more.'

Henry. Henry, the well-mannered doctor who had dropped into the Owner's flat, and discussed Bessie. Whose depth-charges had been mentioned only yesterday.

He had on an open-necked holiday shirt, showing a lot of new suntan, and was peering at my various dressings. I said, 'You patched me up yesterday?'

'Oh yes,' he said. 'Not much rumoured abroad, you know. I'm on holiday round the coast.'

'What a coincidence,' I said.

He grinned. 'Why not? And if there's some valuable property around that people want an eye kept on, then why not, again?'

He replaced the bandages. 'That won't even leave a scar. I'll write you a prescription. I expect you'd like to get home pretty soon, anyway.'

I said, 'You strapped up Mr Johnson, then? How is he?'

'Remarkable,' Henry said. 'Remarkable, considering. Nothing that a little embroidery here and there won't put to rights. He's flying back as soon as possible, I'm glad to say. A week in hospital, or two, and he'll be walking around. A limit to what drugs can do. Ah, there you are.'

'Yes,' said Johnson. 'Fully paid-up member of the Friendly Burial Society. Good-bye, Henry, and thank you.

'Rita, I am sending you to the airport in half an hour, and in twelve hours you will be in London. A grateful government will provide you with any accommodation you want, or Maggie would be happy to share with you, or you may have friends of your own whom you would prefer to stay with anyway. Or go to Troon or Glasgow. Which?'

Henry had gone out of the room. I looked at Johnson the way he was without his drugs and said, 'I'd rather stay with friends. Thank you. My luggage is in . . . is in Ferdy's house.'

'It's being collected,' Johnson said. 'Amy and the others are sleeping. I'll say good-bye for you. Also, I wouldn't presume to fix you up with a job, but the American film project you were interested in is still open, and you could always ring them.'

The information ran to a stop. He said, 'I'm sorry. I'm trying to sort out your life in what feels like the middle of a quadruple bypass. If Connie rings you in a couple of weeks, will you come and let me talk to you?'

'Yes,' I said. 'Look, forget about me. You don't owe me anything.'

'It's been the Fun Bus for Under-Fives. I know,' said Johnson. 'See you in London. Why hang about? The St Lucia Rotary Club rang this morning to bloody cancel my lecture.'

23

Three weeks later, I lifted the phone in London and heard the voice of Connie Margate, Johnson's housekeeper, asking me to go to Flat 17B again.

In between, I hadn't been idle. I had a lot of business to see to. Accountants. Stockbrokers. Bills.

I went up to see my aunt in Troon, and arranged for her to take over proper ownership of Robina's house, with a sum of money to pay the rates and give her a living.

She was horrified at my hair and my blisters and the speed with which I was taking big decisions without a man to advise me, and I got out of it as fast as I could.

In Glasgow, I saw my friends and had my white and red hair made all the same colour as the natural red, and went to sit beside Robina, who didn't know me, but liked the nurse that brought her the bedpan.

I sat, and inside my head I told her that her daughter Robina had been shot, and her son Colin was in prison on a drugs charge, and that her son Kenneth James was in his grave, killed by this great photographer pal I liked working with so much.

And that her first husband, Old Joseph, was a heap of clean, small, yellowed bones, with not a shred of flesh on them, at the bottom of a hot grey pool in the West Indies.

I thought, inside my head, that, it would have been Gordon Geddes's final triumph, to see what had become of his wife's bummer of a first husband with the cheap set of values.

Then I thought that, in fact, he rated a bit higher than that. He would have been sad, for Robina's sake.

I bought an apartment in Glasgow, for a lot of money. I answered a bunch of calls from people who had rung Troon while I was away. I thought I ought maybe to get a secretary. I rang back the man who wanted to talk about the make-up for the film of the American book, and flew to London to see him, and got the job.

I went to see a lot of old films, and a lot of new ones.

I bought a new Abu fishing case, and re-stocked it.

I went to see Johnson, but this time I left my fishing case behind me.

There were new security men on duty, who bowed me in between the two little round trees, and through the plate-glass door and past the desk to the lift, where they pressed the button for me.

Changed days. I was no different really. Except that my hair was one colour instead of two, under this opera hat I had on, and I'd put on my new check knicker suit for visiting invalids.

No one had written Ta Love on the door of the lift.

I thought about it, and decided that I didn't want to go to 17B after all. I waited until the lift stopped, and then I pressed the button for ground again.

I made to get out on the ground floor, but Lady Emerson was standing there.

We looked at one another. I said cheerily, 'He's much better, isn't he?' and tried to get past, but she didn't budge.

She looked much the same, if maybe a little less tweedy, it being the end of August.

She made a speech. She said, 'I expect this is the last place in the world you really want to be. If he was rotten to you, I don't think you should go up. If he wasn't, then it would be a kindness to let him see you and explain. And to me, too. I was the one who originally brought you here.'

I didn't see how she made that out. I found we were both in the lift. I nearly didn't bother to dictacount her, but finally I did.

I said, 'As I remember, I came here in the first place to make up Mrs Sheridan, because Kim-Jim and Ferdy fixed it between them.'

I didn't want to talk about either of them. But after all, I had eavesdropped on her sniffy telephone call to the Owner. When she'd asked about this girl Ferdy had brought in.

Frances Emerson said, 'They arranged your job. I arranged for Ferdy to borrow the studio. Jay guessed. That's why he was so bloody-minded about you all tramping about ... We'd better go up.'

I let her press the button. I said, 'Why? Why did you want us all to work in his apartment? Had it to do with his job?'

'Yes, it had,' she said. 'In a way. He'd been involved with the Madeira business, you see, before his ... illness. We thought he ought to take an interest in it again.'

'We?' I said.

'Really ... Bernard, my husband,' she said. 'It's his business.'

I gazed at her. Poor bloody Johnson.

291

'So you knew all about me,' I said.

She had very direct eyes. She didn't dodge anything. She said, 'Yes. Most things.'

'About the dyslexia? Before he explained it?'

She still didn't look away, but this time she flushed a little.

She said, 'Yes. I knew before he did. Actually, we were taking a risk. We weren't at all sure that you and your brother weren't involved in what was going on. We did take precautions, but Jay's own team didn't like it. Raymond was furious with us. That's why he kept hovering round, and why he was given such a bad time when Jay finally came across him.'

Mary-had-a-little-lamb country . . .

And of course –

I said, 'The security men? That's why they searched me?'

She looked half guilty, half tickled. 'You won that one,' she said. 'You should have seen the fuss in Establishment over dry-cleaning their uniforms.'

I said, 'Wait till they get the bill for dry-cleaning a set of bloody bloomers with ostrich feathers.' I only half listened to myself, I was thinking so hard.

'We weren't very popular with Boy Johnson,' said Lady Emerson ruefully.

The lift had come to a halt. I said, 'You don't seem to have given much thought to his point of view. He was hardly over whatever had happened to him. Which wasn't a plane crash. Was it?'

She opened the doors and we walked out of the lift and both stopped.

'Of course it was,' said Lady Emerson. 'There is no other explanation that could possibly be put about without doing a lot of harm, and most of it to Jay himself.'

'How?' I said. 'By the people who did it? Are they still about?'

She had her hand on Johnson's door.

'He doesn't think so,' she said, and pressed the doorbell.

Neatly overalled, Mrs Margate came to the door, and showed us where to put our things. She had a nice smile, and the look of anxiety had left her face, along with the weariness.

There was no dog, of course. Raymond's famous visit to Pets Inc. had been to do with parrots. And watching me, furiously, in case I harmed his precious Boy Johnson.

I went the wrong way, and found myself in Natalie's bedroom. Before I came out, I noticed how different it was. So was the hall. All the gilt and flock paper and contract plants had gone, which was a deadly waste, as it was all new that spring.

Instead, everything was a lot quieter andd shabbier, and I wondered even if the Owner had had a bit of bad luck, such as having to rebuild two hundred thousand quids' worth of shattered yacht; until I had another look.

The stuff was really nice, if a bit worn, and a lot of it was antique. It looked as if it had come from another house, maybe with bigger rooms, but it fitted in all right.

The biggest change was in the studio, which had lost all its plants and half its furniture too, and was partly occupied by a wooden platform with an armchair on it, and an ancient easel and painting table, both clearly in use.

There was no sign of Johnson. The canvas on the easel showed the head and shoulders of some man, blocked in lightly. The smells of oil and paint were thick and ripe, like they used to be in art college, and Lady Emerson sneezed.

The sliding glass windows moved, and someone came in from the balcony.

'Bless you, Frances,' said the Hon. Maggie; and caught sight of me.

'Rita! You came!'

'Nearly not,' commented Lady Emerson. 'She was sneaking away as I came in.'

Maggie looked nice but covered-up, in a striped seersucker suit with a wisp of silk at her neck. She had kept up her tan, but changed the straight cut for a crimp-perm.

Fair enough. Win them, lose them. With Ferdy gone, Johnson was the natural successor.

Lady Emerson said, 'Raymond and Maggie work for Jay, as I expect you'll have gathered.'

'No, she hasn't,' said Maggie. 'We were all kept apart from one another on this job as if we had hepatitis. Raymond and I nearly went crazy.'

'And Lenny?' I asked.

'He's Bernard's sailing man really. My husband's,' Lady Emerson said. 'But we loan him out to fashionable watering-holes now and then with his judo pyjamas and a book of sauce recipes. He really is a very good cook. And, of course, the best possible man on a boat like ... on a boat.'

There were no potted plants on the piano, or tantalized fruits. There were still a lot of books lying about, but with markers in them. The piano was shut.

I said, 'It was awful, what happened to *Dolly*.' I was angry.

Lady Emerson looked at me quickly. She said, 'Among all the other horrible things that went on? Why that especially?'

'If you weren't there, you couldn't understand,' said Maggie with surprising bluntness. She added, 'He's rebuilding her, God bless his dividends. I hope I get a shot when she's done. He's decided to stay on the job, Frances? What's going on in his head now?'

'If you're not there, you can't understand,' said Lady Emerson with resignation. 'Look, is Raymond coming? My instructions are to remove you both and leave Rita.'

I was surprised. I thought I was going to get Johnson filtered through all his protectors. I had found the idea quite comforting.

Raymond appeared, inside the room this time instead of out on the fire escape, strode across and kissed my cheek and said, 'Hullo. You look fine. Are you all right? You're getting lunch: Connie's making it. We've been chucked out. Small sitting-room. Have you got your rights and lefts on, or will I take you?'

It was like a sort of briefing for hockey: all quite matter-of-fact, including the brush on the cheek.

I said, 'You'd better show me which door again. Or Mrs Margate.'

'Connie,' he corrected, and stopped. 'Hey, the St Lucia Rotary Club!'

I looked about. I said, 'What?'

'Hurricane Disaster Fund. List of subscribers came in yesterday, Raymond said. '*J. Johnson, Esquire*, as you might expect. And forsooth, *Miss M. Geddes, one thousand pounds*? Rita?'

What Natalie had said had hurt. I didn't want her money. I said, 'What do you think? It's for the rebuilding and upkeep of the Narc ...'

I paused.

Raymond was watching me anxiously. 'Don't spoil it,' he urged.

I knew what the word was. It was the one bloody word I had learned in the whole awful disaster.

I opened my mouth, and murdering the whole of my childhood, I threw it away.

'... the Nemesis Department,' I said.

Raymond put his hands under my arms and, lifting my feet off the ground, spun like a top, crowing, 'She qualifies! She qualifies! You get the Johnson sorority pin and join us in daily singing of the company song ... Christ, you're going to be late, and he'll kill me.'

He set me down. I felt great. I remembered why I was there, and didn't feel quite so great.

Raymond said, 'Look, he won't make you feel bad. If you want to belt out something, then go ahead. He likes it that way.'

It sounded as if the embroidery had worked. I therefore said, 'How is he?'

'Making great strides, considering,' said Johnson's voice irritably from the doorway. 'It really is very nice to see you, and a different colour too, but you are supposed to be cheering me up, not the Bowling Club here. The vodka's getting warm.'

He waited for me. I thought he'd be in pyjamas, but he was wearing a nice easy sweater, and had both hands in the pockets of a pair of comfortable and expensive light trousers.

Behind the bifocals, he still had some suntan on top of hospital white, which produced a tone quite close to Beige, and certainly less than Weird Effect, which is how I'd last seen him. He'd had his hair cut.

As I came up, he said, 'May I?' And withdrawing a hand, dropped a kiss on one cheek as Raymond had done.

'Graduation Day,' he said. 'The rest of the time, as you know, we hit you. Come along in.'

He took me into the small study with his hand on my arm, and shutting the door, pointed me in the direction of a seat.

This room, too, had lost all the shiny, new look of the spring apartment. There were a lot of bookcases I didn't remember, and a long oak table.

I looked at the window to see what sort of curtains he'd chosen, and for the first time noticed the man standing there.

A tall man, with brown hair that curled a bit over his ears, and a fresh complexion glazed by constant sun into a golden tan, and very light, steady eyes.

The twin of Roger van Diemen, the Financial Director of Coombe's, left for dead with his owl mask among the cocaine on St Lucia.

He stood harmlessly before me. And Johnson, when I looked round, just gazed placidly back.

'Let me introduce you *formally*,' said Johnson, 'to Mr Roger van Diemen. He is alive. He is one of us. And he is standing there very, very frightened because he doesn't want a bag of peanuts in his vodka ...

'Roger, sit down. The worst is over. Rita, only a week in hospital could have brought me to the point of hysteria where this seemed the sensible thing to do. Take up your vodka and listen.

'Now, Roger. Explain.'

Among all the other things Johnson was, he could be a bastard. Lady

295

Emerson was quite right, and I'd seen quite a lot of it. As I've said, I wouldn't want to be trained by him.

He hadn't told me, allowing me to blunder off after Roger van Diemen, that Roger van Diemen was in the same intelligence department as himself. He had known perfectly well that he was high on drugs and unhinged with jealousy and anxiety over Natalie. It was van Diemen's increasing unreliability that had attracted the attention of his colleagues in the first place.

But nothing could be done about it, because he had been picked by Clive Curtis to be the lynchpin of his new smuggling scheme, using Coombe International. And whatever he did, from bashing me in the Mercedes to trying to smash Kim-Jim and me out of his way on the sledge-run, Johnson wasn't going to expose him, or warn me about it.

Not until the drug business was safely over, and the leaders identified and caught. Not while van Diemen might get himself caught and exposed as a member of the precious Department.

And Johnson was a bastard, because he forced Roger van Diemen to sit there and tell me about it. Tell me that he was, in a way, to blame even for Kim-Jim's death. The Curtises didn't want their prize contact removed by the police because he'd made some wild attack on his rival. So they forestalled him.

Van Diemen didn't know then who they were. He didn't know if they knew Kim-Jim was ill. He thought they were afraid Kim-Jim knew something about them. So Kim-Jim had been killed, and through a faceless go-between, whom he now knew had been Ferdy Braithwaite, he had been warned and rushed out of Madeira.

He spoke in a flat, dry voice, his hands locked together between his knees, accepting a very bitter medicine, and making the best of it. Johnson was absolutely silent. I sat holding my drink, and then put it down because the ice kept making a noise.

I listened, and thought my own thoughts. When Ferdy had driven me selflessly up that rotten hill to Eduardo's, he had already warned van Diemen to leave.

It didn't really matter to Ferdy if Kim-Jim was dead. I remembered how, more than once, he had tried to pump me about all I knew about Natalie. They must have hoped I would be a good source of blackmail material. It must have been disappointing to find I wasn't.

And, of course, in time van Diemen had come to his senses, and had begun to give Johnson the help he needed to open up the smuggling racket and expose the leaders.

I wondered when that had happened. After the row with Natalie in the Barbados house, maybe. That was when Johnson suddenly had all the information he required about the Brighton Beach meeting and the rest.

Or perhaps, as soon as Kim-Jim was removed and I came into his money. Then he could afford to turn back to his job again.

Van Diemen was talking about the Carifesta meeting as the turning point in the chase. It had narrowed down the number of suspects. Because of the scare about intruders, it had resulted in the change of plan.

The premature load of cocaine had been scheduled for Miami. Instead, much more handily, it was going to St Lucia, and to Amy Faflick's underground caverns. Braithwaite already knew of them from Natalie. The Curtises had been told. Van Diemen had encouraged the idea.

It let the Department go into action, with some prospect of keeping van Diemen's part in the business private.

At that point, I said, 'Wait a minute.'

Johnson moved, and lifted his glass. Van Diemen raised his pale eyes and waited.

I said, 'The Brighton Beach meeting. We didn't need to listen in to that, or try and bug it. You were there, reporting on everything that happened.'

'That is correct,' van Diemen said.

'So that all we were there for was to be discovered?' I said.

I glared at Johnson. 'That was why you wanted the disguises? You knew we'd be seen. We had to be seen, to make the scheme work.'

Another thought struck me. 'What would you have done if my bloody watch hadn't conked?'

'I'm sure,' said Johnson peacefully, 'we should have thought of something. Anyway, it didn't matter. The storm diverted the plan for us anyway. Everyone had to go to St Lucia for safety.'

'And you *expected Dolly* to be boarded?' I said.

Johnson said, 'After what we turned up in Tobago, it seemed very likely. The unsolicited violence was a bit of a facer. As ... Braithwaite told us himself, it wasn't his fault. Clive's, perhaps. Or just that the men got out of hand. The storm was a bit unfortunate too. But it let us take Clive himself, and end it there. And we were able to whip Roger away unseen, after the fake shooting at Amy's.

'Natalie won't mention him. He returns to being a perfectly respectable Financial Director of Coombe's without any stain on his character.

'That, O my prosthetic soul,' said Johnson, 'was why it was so important that you shouldn't give vent to your perfectly just and understandable anger and denounce Roger all over the countryside.

'And if you were determined to pursue him as the murderer of Kim-Jim, all we could do was give you your head, within limits, and see that you were protected, as far as possible. And hope that you did uncover the right man, and didn't catch up with Roger and make things awkward for him. You may now slap me down.'

They had no need to go through this. In sitting there and letting me fire at them, they were doing the right thing, and it was up to me not to take advantage of it. But all the same, there was one item that needed airing.

I've tried most things, but I'd never get into the heavy drug scene. That's a killer, to yourself and everyone you know.

I said, 'I see why you had to go on using Mr van Diemen until the Coombe business was out in the open. I don't see how the Department can go on using and protecting someone who injects, mainlines drugs.'

Roger van Diemen said, 'I am stupid, but not so stupid. I don't inject, Miss Geddes.'

'I saw the tracks,' I said.

Johnson said, 'Then you know how they are done. Collodion, liner and nail polish. It was done by make-up, Rita. He had to appear vulnerable. He was, but not to that extent.'

Make-up is my business, as Johnson said. And I had seen van Diemen's arm only twice, in the dimness of the Mercedes, and through a window in Barbados when he was speaking to Natalie.

But these tracks, when they are real, stay and can't be disguised. If I was being lied to, I wanted to know it.

I said, 'Show me your arm.'

Today, no one was going to refuse me anything. Without speaking, van Diemen took off his jacket. Under, he had a formal shirt with long sleeves and fine cuffs. He prepared to unbutton them. 'Which?' he said.

I couldn't have told. Johnson said, 'Show her both arms.'

Head bent, my one-time attacker undid both sets of buttons and began to roll the sleeves up.

I watched him. Because he had been stupid, as he said, it was right that he should pay for it, but only as much as was due.

I had thought of him over many months as the killer of Kim-Jim, and hounded him. He was not, and I shouldn't forget it.

I hoped that he hadn't been lying. For if he had, it would be Johnson's lie too.

The arms were bare, and he held them palm upwards and looked at me.

There were no tracks. Instead there were the pale pink, wrinkled blotches of recent burns. I had them myself, all over my body.

I looked at Johnson, and he in his turn looked, smiling a little at van Diemen, who drew his arms back.

This time, neither of them helped me, and I had to ask. 'The man with the megaphone?'

The man who, long familiar with every inch of the banana islands, had stood still at the lip of the caldera, ignoring the flurries of steam. The man who, with his hands upraised to his hailer, had steered me, patiently and clearly, out of that boiling mud in St Lucia.

To me and *Away from me*.

'It was the least I could do,' said Roger van Diemen.

Revenge and jealousy. It isn't often that they unravel so easily, or that the punishment is so light.

We had lunch, the three of us, and talked about nothing serious, at which Johnson was very good; and Roger van Diemen did his best. I was rather glad when it ended.

After the coffee, van Diemen left. I have never seen him since. He owed me a debt, and Johnson let him pay it.

Half an hour after that, I left myself, to let him rest.

Alone, he had talked to me of a lot of things. About my work, and my mother.

I didn't think Robina would live long.

When I said so, he said, 'Another cat. Do you know, Rita, that that's how I traced you? Marguerite Geddes, born to Robina Curtis, or Souter, of Kirkcaldy. Your nice yellow cats with their flowery coats are Kirkcaldy cats. Not from Ayrshire at all.'

'I shall have two more,' I said. 'Three, when Robina dies. You wouldn't like one?'

We were still sitting at table. He took off and put down his glasses, and then looked up.

He said, 'I should be honoured. A woman with the courage and determination of Genghis Khan. Look it up, and don't be annoyed: it's a compliment.

'You don't need any help from us now. You're on your way. But if you would like it, Raymond could add a little seamanship to your accomplishments, once *Dolly* is herself again. Racing is a game for you.'

He broke off and was quiet for a bit, fingering his spectacles. I didn't interrupt.

Then he said, 'Rita? What do you really feel about it all? It was your decision, to come out of your safe hole and look for your family.

'It wasn't your fault what hit them after that. It would have happened anyway. It was our fault, though, that you had such a rotten time. You were in a lot of danger. We might well have killed you amongst us all ...

'You've got such a bloody heart that it mayn't have occurred to you to hate us for it, but you may very well wish you had never left home. Do you?'

'And that's a silly question,' I said.

He laughed.

'I hoped it was,' he said. 'And I'm really very glad. And so is Roger, whom you were kind to as well.'

He put his hand on the table and got up, to come with me to the door of the room. He was wearing the bifocals again.

Standing there, saying good-bye, he said, 'Tell me. Will you change your hair? Maggie has.'

I smiled. 'I saw,' I said. 'I don't know. Should I?'

He said, 'I liked it when it was orange. If you want a life of battle, go ahead. You're in the illusions business. You know the dangers to keep clear of. And I'm all for reminding people that there's a lot of illusion about, and that it's quite a good idea now and then to have a look under the paint.

'You don't need to keep in touch with us. Raymond will keep in touch with you,' he said. 'More often than you want, I shouldn't wonder.'

Which was as nice a way of parting as I had ever heard of.

Connie took me to get my coat.

That was where I saw the photograph. In fact a lot of photographs, that had never been there before, but one that struck me particularly, because I'd first seen it in Lady Emerson's house.

The picture of this pretty, open-faced girl. Smiling, and good-looking enough to be in pictures.

Connie saw me looking at it. She said, 'It's nice that he's got it out. And the things from the house. It was a great worry, for a while.'

I said, 'Who is she?'

She didn't answer, just looked taken aback. Then she said, 'He hasn't told you?'

I felt cold. I said, 'What?'

Connie Margate said, 'But that's his wife. Judith. Judith Ballantyne, daughter of the judge.

'She's dead. She died when ... he was the only survivor.'

'Of the plane crash,' I said.

She didn't answer. Then, 'Of the plane crash,' she agreed.

I don't remember leaving 17B, or taking the lift, or walking out into the bright streets of Mayfair, and looking for a taxi to take me the few paces I had to go.

I was thinking of Johnson, and of 17B, and of all those terrible letters.

'You've been a great help,' Lady Emerson had said.

She'd taken a bloody great risk in sending me to 17B. I understood Raymond's fury.

It nearly hadn't worked, either. Johnson had resented Natalie and Ferdy and being forced to think of Roger van Diemen. What had made him change his mind, you couldn't tell.

But I could see that, in a way, I had been of use, and not just because of the quiche, and the dog. Even the jazz and the phone calls and things must have dragged him out of himself a bit, anyhow.

I was glad I had helped him.

I gave Cohn to Celia, though. I'm told he's now breeding in Jersey.

That's fine.

I don't mind bifocals a bit. But I find parrots are asthma.